THE RESISTANCE GIRL

Mandy Robotham saw herself as an aspiring author since the age of nine, but was waylaid by journalism and later enticed by birth. She's now a former midwife, who writes about birth, death, love and anything else in between. She graduated with an MA in Creative Writing from Oxford Brookes University. This is her fifth novel – her first four have been *Globe and Mail, USA Today* and Kindle Top 100 bestsellers.

By the same author:

A Woman of War (published as *The German Midwife* in
North America, Australia and New Zealand)
The Secret Messenger
The Berlin Girl
The Girl Behind the Wall

The Resistance Girl

Mandy Robotham

avon.

Published by AVON
A division of HarperCollins*Publishers* Ltd
1 London Bridge Street
London SE1 9GF

www.harpercollins.co.uk

This first format edition 2022
1
First published in Great Britain by HarperCollins*Publishers* 2022

A catalogue copy of this book is available from the British Library.

ISBN: 978-0-00-852375-6
ISBN: 978-0-00-851606-2

Typeset in Bembo by Palimpsest Book Production Limited, Falkirk, Stirlingshire
Printed and Bound in the UK using 100% Renewable Electricity at CPI Group (UK) Ltd

MIX
Paper from
responsible sources
FSC **FSC™ C007454**
www.fsc.org

This book is produced from independently certified FSC™ paper
to ensure responsible forest management.

For more information visit: www.harpercollins.co.uk/green

To all those who selflessly manned and supported the Shetland Bus, and the unknown masses who worked for freedom in the shadows of World War Two.

Author's note

Immediate thoughts of World War Two often go to the big theatres of conflict, those focused in Europe and the Pacific: the D-Day landings and the combat in South-East Asia. But the tentacles of this enormous battle stretched far and wide, all the way up to the Arctic Circle, where a more shadowy struggle was taking place. As a country swiftly overrun by the Nazi scourge, Norway saw little open fighting by comparison, and yet the suffering was felt acutely by its people. Their liberty was snatched away by an enemy that arrived in numbers; they endured the biggest German troop concentration of any occupied nation. It proved to be an enemy intent on controlling, but also on befriending. In his vision of a thousand-year Reich, Hitler had a plan in mind – a far-reaching strategy intent on a new master race of blond and blue-eyed citizens. And for that he needed the numbers.

Long before the brilliant Margaret Atwood created her dystopian world of breeders in *The Handmaid's Tale*, Hitler and his right-hand man, Himmler, were turning their vision into reality. The Lebensborn programme was conceived in

Germany, with centres dotted across Europe; Norway had the largest number of maternity homes outside of Germany, and the difficulties of those children born to Norwegian mothers and German fathers is well documented. Lesser known are the chilling lengths the Nazis would go to – the pamphlets detailing Hitler's perfect 'kinder' are, sadly, all too real, as are the cases of children snatched from their biological families and placed in German families, with long-standing repercussions into adulthood.

In writing *The Resistance Girl*, I wanted to highlight yet again how the indiscriminate wave of war sweeps up individuals in its path, with widespread effects on families and their futures. The bravery, too, of ordinary individuals who stepped up in a time of need to help not only friends, but strangers in peril. The Shetland Bus – manned by British and Norwegian sailors – was one such example of out-and-out bravery in wartime, where men would venture into unforgiving waters, knowing all too well that they may not return. And yet they did it all the same. Their courage defies description.

Rumi and her 'crew' are, I hope, a fictional representation of the bravery, the hurt and the humour that surrounded families in wartime, in the way they fought back against their occupiers. Many of the events detailed in the book are based on fact – the horrors of Televåg included – but we writers get to weave and embellish, and I have necessarily played with dates and events. Despite my best endeavours (and two cancelled trips), I did not manage to visit Bergen in the midst of lockdown, and so I hope that with my endless reading of first-hand accounts, plus staring at old maps, pictures and newsreels, I have represented Bergen as the bright, beautiful city it appears to be. My boundless thanks goes to the many Norwegians who gave time and answers to my pernickety questions about wool, food, fish and general life in wartime Bergen. Without their patience, Rumi and Jens would have had no stage on which to play, and I can only apologise if I have made any glaring errors.

This book marks a return for me to the subject of birth; while I'm loath to be labelled as 'that ex-midwife who writes', I felt this was one story that warranted a good birth scene and I enjoyed myself immensely, delving into my memory of homebirths to open Rumi's eyes to the wonder: without any spoilers, fiction and my experience as a midwife merge nicely here.

I hope, too, that I've highlighted a little corner of this gargantuan conflict and brought it to life, to show that it really was a global battlefield, and that while everyone lost to some degree, there will always be positives to emerge from the sadness and chaos.

PROLOGUE
The Kraken

Bergen, South-West Norway, 14th November 1941

Rumi

The horizon, normally so present and correct – her grounding in life – is absent. Its flat, reassuring focus has been scrubbed out by the sheer height of the boiling, furious waves, the sea fist-fighting itself in what little distance she can see into. There it meets a bruised, near navy sky of equal ferocity, like a brawl of sailors going at each other hammer and tongs after weeks ashore and far too much liquor.

A sudden gust of gale punches at Rumi's body as she stands on the limb of the jetty, the force bending her sideways at the waist. She almost topples, but rights herself in time. She, the sea and its associate winds have known each other her entire life, and they'll need more ammunition than this to break her stance – or her vigil. The fierce squall changes tack and whips about her head, flipping her single, heavy plait of hair to and fro like an angry snake until she catches the end and pulls it down against her

1

breast, for comfort. It's what she used to do when she missed her mother. Now she misses someone else.

Magnus is out there, somewhere in this terrifying tempest, the worst they've seen for some time; even the weathered old men on the quay are saying it, shaking their heads with despair at the inevitable losses to come. She wonders what Magnus will have felt, on the exposed deck of that tiny trawler, facing up to towering waves that spill like landslides in seconds, the vessel lurching on the crest of a swell, a tiny speck in that vast, angry cauldron. In his last, dying moment, will he have been gripped by fear and dread, or a strange inner calm that the sea can be merciful; either spare him or else take him quickly?

Magnus often said he wasn't afraid of the sea; that he felt sure it would take him one day, but not before he was an old seadog, and they'd had at least five children and he'd paid for his own vessel in full, nets and all.

'Then it can bury me in its depths,' he'd joked often enough. 'When I'm ready to go.'

'You mean I'm going to have to put up with you in a grey, old beard, wearing a disgusting hat that reeks of brine but refuse to give up?' Rumi teased him.

'Yes, definitely. Does that mean you won't marry me? Because I'll shave off my beard, but I won't lose the hat.'

'You!' She made to punch at his heft of torso, the muscles embedded since childhood summers on his grandfather's boat, but smoothed her strong hand over it instead, lay her head in the thick wool of his sweater, pungent with the odour of work and salt sea.

What had she to complain about then? Magnus was no film star but, equally, Rumi saw herself as no oil painting. And not exactly delicate either, with a strength equal to any hand on her father's boats, hence her skin on his chest as rough, fingers coarse and her nails chipped by toil. Not a lady's hand, for sure. Rumi is everything but a sweet, demure catch. But she is Magnus's girl, and would-be wife.

Or she was. Until the sea took him. Too soon.

Peering into the volatile chaos of the broil beyond the harbour, there is little doubt. This storm has been raging for four whole days; he is gone. Swallowed. The entire trawler and its crew disappeared under the black swirl. If she were a woman of the 1600s, centuries ago, Rumi would believe fixedly that it was the wrath of a dispossessed whale causing the sea's rage, or that a monstrous, multi-limbed Kraken had risen and pulled all ships to its lair in the depths. Doubtless, such myths helped the lonely, widowed women couch their grief. But Rumi knows that a fisherman's watery fate of today rests on nature, bad luck and the modern-day Kraken of Adolf Hitler.

Rumi will never lay the blame with her family's lifeline, so it's not due to the fury of the ocean. It's the war – this bloody, suffocating insurgence into their lives as Norwegians. Without the war, without his need to help in the fight, Magnus would never have set foot on that trawler and self-lessly sailed into the North Sea to save others. He'd be standing by her side at this very moment, marvelling at the ocean's tantrum and thanking his luck he wasn't out there in it.

So, he is a victim of the war, as are so many, killed by the marauding, parasitic Germans who simply marched in and took their city and their country away, as if they had the right. And if she hadn't already hated them for such a theft, she does now, her swell of revulsion as high and mighty as the scaling waves out there.

Rumi Orlstad is grieving and incensed. Livid.

'They will pay!' she howls into the twisting gusts. 'BE

SURE, MAGNUS – I WILL MAKE THEM PAY!' Her words are swept up and pocketed in some secret cloud space, dragged into the funereal sky for safekeeping, where the Germans can't prove her treason.

And all Rumi can do is stand alone on the jetty and weep solidly, battered by the unending fury of a sea that she loves and hates in unison.

PART ONE

1

A Frosty Welcome

Outskirts of Bergen, 2nd January 1942

Jens

It's not the vista he'd imagined, though the unending blanket of white is perhaps what he expected this far north of the equator. The fir branches are reaching skywards, rather than sloping into the smooth white carpet, and for several minutes the view only aids his confusion, long after he's recovered from the painful jolt of descent, his brain shaken like an underset jelly in the process. He must have been out cold for some time; the light is coming up and threatens to leave him more exposed, save for the clump of trees where he landed, if you can call it that. Baffled though he is, Jensen Parkes recognises he has technically yet to land on firm ground. Hanging unceremoniously from a Norwegian pine like a bauble on a Christmas tree does not count as being on terra firma. And upside down, too. None of this happened in training.

He tugs at the straps of his parachute, rammed in tight

against his body by the weight of his hanging torso and heavy backpack. Under thick gloves, his already frozen fingers can barely push in under the straps, let alone feel enough to release the catch.

'Shit!' he berates himself, too late to stop his voice from echoing off the trees, though it falls dead on the sound-proofing snow. He writhes furiously, a madman in a strait jacket, hoping to dislodge himself, bracing his body and head for the final thud more than six feet below. But the straps only pull tighter, the tree creaking its distaste and shedding a branch's worth of snow on top of him. Ice cold. As if he wasn't already freezing enough.

Realising his efforts are futile, Jens stops and listens. Thinks. It's what they were taught: to work it through, systematically. His options are few, and not altogether welcoming. He could wait for death by exposure, or for discovery by a friendly search party, though that might take days. Alternatively, he could be found by a German patrol and face the inevitable punishment; here, there's often no arrest, tribunal or imprisonment in the raw, frozen wastes, as per the Geneva Convention. Interrogation, judge and jury happens out on the snowy hills within minutes, German Lugers primed and ready for any stray dissidents and the blood staining easily swept over by a fresh blanket of snow. He's painfully aware of the consequences of capture. And a shuddering, shivering tree is a giveaway for any passer-by, friend or foe.

Slowly, Jens begins to move every part of his body, first to push the near frozen blood around his limbs and regain some feeling, then to slowly wriggle from his tethers, like some oversized bug worming his way from a soft-spun cocoon. He has to stop himself from laughing out loud at the image he presents.

Ten minutes of consistent movement only leaves him breathless and without much progress, causing his body to swing like a pendulum and giving rise to a growing nausea. Upturned as he is, excess blood is settling like sediment in his head, and his eyes see double. He shakes his head frantically to expel the feeling, struggling to remain conscious.

Don't pass out again, I can't pass out again.

Despite his efforts, the white begins to blur and merge, the branches no longer distinguishable. There's a rushing in his ears, a roaring wave that he knows is not real, but can't push away. He can't push anything away, physically or otherwise, not even the feeling of falli—

The crack of a branch leaps out of the muffled, white haze, whipping his lolling head to attention, eyes snapping open with alarm. His ears strain to hear above the inner turbulence for voices, the guttural edge of an accent, orders and the 'yes, Sir', 'no, Sir' of military speak. Only silence beats back at him – save for his own laboured breathing inside the confines of his parachute prison.

There it is again, a definite crack, the shush of snow moving. Jens struggles violently to free himself, since there's nothing to lose in making noise now. Where the hell is his gun? It's buried deep in his jacket, cut off by a strangulating strap. *Damn! This bloody parachute was supposed to save me from dying, not push me towards the end.* Better that they had used the longer route of the trawler from Shetland, except for the losses suffered recently, too many vessels, sailors and agents succumbing to the weather rather than the Reich.

The shush turns to a trudge, footsteps distinct now, two at the most. It's no animal – a reindeer would be too skittish to approach an alien human smell. He has no option but to stiffen, hang stock still like some butchered carcass at a hunting lodge, and hope that the German patrols are blind, lazy or stupid. Or all three.

Seems not. The click of a gun barrel echoes just beyond the clump of trees. Jens Parkes sucks in what little icy breath he has, and does the only thing he's able to: wait for luck or fate, and pray they come combined.

2

A Welcoming Party

Bergen, 2nd January 1942

Rumi

'Rumi! Rumi! Where are you?'

'I'm right here, Pappa. You don't need to shout.'

'What are you doing under the table, girl?' Her father's urgent tone mixes with surprise and irritation.

'Re-laying the mousetraps,' Rumi huffs, her deep red crown of hair emerging from beneath the wide, wooden desk. 'They're hungry little buggers, and I won't have any lunch left if I don't do it.'

Peder Orlstad shrugs away the mice issue, as if his daughter's working conditions in the cluttered boathouse are nothing, looks squarely at her and lowers his voice to a whisper. 'You need to get up on the plateau, quickly. We've had word there was a drop last night and so far no sight or word – it'll be getting dark early and anyone up there will freeze.'

'Don't they have maps and skis?' Rumi's irritation matches

her father's urgency. She's just too busy right now to play nursemaid to ill-equipped resistance fighters, whoever they are, despite her previous commitment to the cause; there's the accounts to finish, the oilskins to clean, stock to audit. And besides which, she doesn't do that anymore.

'Isn't Rubio able to go? He's a competent skier,' she bristles.

Rumi's father looks at her, already contrite, no doubt knowing he shouldn't ask it of his daughter, not after what she's been through. 'He's had to go on another run – won't be back until tomorrow at the earliest.'

Now Rumi is cross. 'You didn't tell me, Pappa! How am I supposed to keep this yard running, with all the coming and goings, if you don't let me know when the boats go out?' What she really means is: *Why is Rubio out there risking a lengthy trip, when he promised he wouldn't?*

But Pappa brushes it off in his customary phlegmatic way. 'You know that when the herring runs, a fisherman has no choice but to give chase.' He shrugs, though they both understand Rubio is hauling something far more incendiary than herring. 'So, will you do it, Rumi? Please? Hilde's packing up soup and food for you to take up there.'

She knows he wouldn't ask unless it was life and death. But then, what else is there in this existence now?

'Just this once, all right? Maybe Hilde will make me some soup if I get stuck in the snow,' she grumbles. 'A dry sandwich is about all she usually manages for me.'

'Come *on*.' Peder herds her out of the boathouse, following in her wake.

Despite her reluctance, she can't deny a break from the day's routine comes as a welcome relief, a chance to breathe, for a while at least. When she's working alone in the boathouse,

Rumi finds her mind can wander into places it daren't go, but climbing into the frozen expanse clears the ugly clutter of her thoughts.

The lone journey up into the hills behind Bergen is steep and arduous, more so with a fresh flurry of light flakes, but each time she needs to catch her breath, she turns and looks back down at the beloved sight of the city – *her* city – and takes pleasure in its distinct U-shape couched in the nook of the land, jigsaw pieces of the hundreds of tiny islands butting up against the winding crags of the coastline. This high up, there's only the faint parp-parp of returning boats making its way up into the silent snow lands.

She's already been going an hour and her pack is heavy, so too her skis and the spare pair she carries – her legs are beginning to ache and her lungs smart with the freezing air. Although she's been making this journey since she was a girl and Norwegians, she likes to boast, arc a hardy nation, the past two years – and the last month especially – have begun to sow doubts in Rumi's mind.

Pappa's information has given her a rough area of around five kilometres to search, and once on the plateau, she attaches her skis and moves fast to skirt the area, stopping every few minutes to peer into the white expanse and scan meticulously. If her quarry is on the move, it will be hard to spot them in this snowy swathe, dressed as they will be in bleached windproof ski jackets, any baggage also camou-flaged. Better for them, but harder for their hunters – or, in this case, saviours.

Rumi blows into her thick woollen mittens to push some life into her fingers, turning in a slow, full circle. If the drop hasn't made it down the mountain, either they've been caught by a German patrol or they're still up here. There

13

are no caves or rocks to hide within – she knows every inch of this terrain – but there are four or five large clumps of firs. They'd be unlucky to come down on one, but it's not impossible they've used it as a refuge, to wait out the snowfall. She winds her circle inwards, searches the first cluster of thick stumps and foliage. It's eerily silent, cut only by the shudder of the branches bending to the wind.

The second thicket is the same, but on approaching the third, Rumi senses something – a disturbance, perhaps, and a heaviness to the freezing air. She scouts for footprints, bound to be deep here and not easily covered over. Nothing the size of Nazi jackboots for sure. An animal in the midst? She reaches inside her pack for Peder's hunting gun, holds it to her body one-handed and punts slowly forward with one ski pole. She loathes the idea of killing an innocent, but she will use a bullet for protection. Or survival, if it comes to it.

Rumi says nothing, breathing at a minimum as she moves with silent stealth under the canopy of trees. Here, there are fewer flakes falling, and she spots the lumpen cargo caught in the branches within seconds. Still, she doesn't rush towards it, listens instead for any other movement: the tiny squeak of a coiled spring in a trap, or the heavy, combined breath of military stalkers in waiting. Only when she's satisfied that they are alone does she approach the hanging man. His head is just above hers and she stretches up to see a face frosted with snow, lips blue, and eyelashes fringed with ice. He looks already dead.

Rumi sighs. It is a sad waste of life and courage, but it's not the first dead agent she's seen and it doesn't shock. What's most concerning, she thinks fleetingly, is how much it *doesn't* move her. She knows death intimately: in war, and before. In life and in love. She only wonders how to cut the body down and haul it far enough that some others

14

from the town can access and bury him. She can't leave him up here – her own humanity and the rules of the resistance tell her that. Pulling off her pack, she rummages inside for her knife, turns and makes to try and leap, to grab for a branch and pull it down. Instead, she staggers backwards from the shocking sight – two eyes snapping open in an instant, fronds of white spray falling.

'Christ!' She can't stifle her cry.

There's a strangled noise coming from inside his throat, full words prevented by lips almost frozen together. He begins to squirm, causing more snow and ice to shower on top of them both.

'Keep still!' she orders sharply. 'I'll cut you down.'

This time his eyes widen, doubtless with alarm at the large gutting knife Rumi pulls from her pack, brandishing it near to his face as she jumps again for a branch to grasp. On the third attempt, she clutches at a sizeable bough and yanks it down.

'Where?' She gestures with the knife, and his solid digits just manage to point to the main parachute straps of constraint. Rumi edges the knife in underneath and slices. As one is severed, half his body judders and drops partway, and she sees him squeeze his eyes shut in preparation for an eventual thud on the snowy carpet. On the second, he drops like a stone, with a concerted groan from inside his many layers.

'All right?' she says, looming over his curled torso that's landed in a heap. 'Are you hurt?'

He's silent, just looking at her, and she wonders if he understands much Norwegian at all.

His lips prise apart. 'I'm not sure,' he says, in some odd dialect of her own language. 'I'll let you know once I can feel any part of my body again.'

She huffs. *Oh Lord. A joker as well as an invalid.*

There's nowhere else to shelter, so she pulls and he shunts himself to the base of the tree. Steam from her open flask billows into the air, and this man – who begins to look less like a cadaver with each passing minute – swallows the hot liquid with utter relief.

'I never thought soup would quite literally save my life,' he breathes.

'You're very welcome.' She grunts, one ear on the expanse beyond the trees. 'I could string you back up, if you want?'

'Oh, no, I didn't mean to sound ungrateful . . .'

'Well, you did.' She packs up her bag again, feeling cross with herself for snapping. *He's not the target for your anger, Rumi. Only the world and everything in it.*

'What's your name?' he says after a heavy pause.

'Rumi. Yours?'

'Better not say – security. And we'll probably never see each other after today.'

Her resolve to be tolerant vanishes as quickly as it came; she can't hide her irritation. *Let's hope so*, she thinks. 'Are you worried I'm not your contact? That I make a habit of roaming the plateau in my spare time, looking for waifs and strays with a flask of soup for all eventualities?'

'No, but . . .'

'Suit yourself,' she says. 'Listen, we should get going downhill. Can you feel your legs yet? Better still, your toes?'

'I think so, at least some of them. But we can't leave yet.'

'Why not?' Rumi's patience is fast running out. She's used to this cold, but to be out for too long risks danger. She's tired, irritable, and wants to be on her own, war or no war.

'We need to look for the other one,' he says.

16

'What other one?' she snaps, wrong-footed by this response. Pappa either doesn't know or didn't impart the whole story.

'My partner. He was right behind me on the drop. He has all our vital equipment.'

'Oh, wonderful.' Her sarcasm is deliberately undisguised.

He seems to ignore it, gets up and shakes his body into being, strapping on the spare skis. To Rumi's relief, it looks as if he knows one end from the other.

He glides closer and holds out a frozen hand like an olive branch. 'Jens. Thanks for rescuing me, Rumi.'

'Hmm.' She turns away. 'Come on, we've got about an hour or so of light, if that.'

3

Blinded

Jens

She's angry, he thinks, watching her work hard to punt through what has quickly become a blizzard. That dismissive tone, the clipped irritation of having to be around others when all you want is to curl up into a ball and turn the fury in on yourself. Oh yes, he recognises it all too well.

Perhaps her anger is justified, Jens thinks, being forced to come out here in this weather, risking all to search for a stranger, who may or may not benefit the resistance in making life hell for the Nazis. He'll damn well try his best though, and he wants to tell her that: why he's doing it, and what for. *Who* it's for. For one person, but also for an entire country that's his, too. Partly, at least.

They find one half of the equipment cargo a few hundred metres away, fortunately intact in its white metal capsule, and almost completely coated in snow now that it's falling fast.

'This contains our food and maps, but not the hardware we need,' he shouts over the wind, watches her nod with resignation that the search must go on.

They push on for almost an hour, stopping every ten minutes or so to catch their breath, which near on freezes as it puffs from their lips. He notes that, miraculously, hers are still a ruby red in the midst of her heart-shaped face, hair fully tucked under her woollen cap, eyebrows a fiery red. *They match her mood.*

By contrast, his entire face feels nothing other than a lifeless grey. The training up in Scotland had been freezing – meant to emulate the Norwegian and Swedish climates as near as possible – but this . . . He doesn't remember ever being as cold as this, where even the glaze on his pupils feels as if it will crack on blinking, as though a sudden warmth wouldn't slowly melt but instead splinter his entire body into shards. Only the thought of Karl, out here alone, makes him go on.

She stops and turns quickly, her eyes sable pinpricks against the tableau of white. 'It's no good, the light is going rapidly. Has he food to keep him going for one night?'

Jens nods – the main bulk of their survival food is in the capsule, but each of their backpacks contains emergency rations.

'Then we'll have to come back tomorrow. If we can't find him, chances are the patrols won't either. They generally don't come up this far unless they're on a specific search.'

Chances. That's the reality now, he thinks. My life, Karl's, and everyone around us, depends on luck, fate and probabilities. A deadly gamble.

Get used to it, Jens Parkes. Again.

He nods in agreement and she turns to lead the way

19

down off the plateau, moving with the grace of all those brought up in such harsh climates, as if skis are merely extensions of her feet. Even with the capsule tethered by a rope to her waist, she seems to slide effortlessly over her home terrain. His skiing isn't bad, but practice has been patchy over the last few years. Now he'd better get a whole lot better to keep up with this Rumi woman and her countrymen.

As they reach a halfway point of descent, the solid sight of Bergen's sprawl comes into view through the white haze and the blizzard subsides to a few flakes. Instantly, he feels a pang of nostalgia and a sudden yearning to be down below, in the city centre – to glimpse the cathedral's bronze-green tower again and smell the pungency of the fish market, like he did as a boy. In spite of what the day's already brought, it grounds him properly and he feels at peace, even with the war raging around them, and the whine of Allied and German planes that chase each other's tails across the Norwegian sky.

The snow is packed and crisp and they slide easily down at a pace. Suddenly, she swerves and comes to an abrupt halt, digs her pole into the snow and pushes up a hand to signal his stop, a finger to her mouth. She's looking intently to her left, scanning like a predator. Except he knows she's on the hunt for another predator.

'Over there. Movement,' she says into his wool-covered ear.

He peers, but the beyond is just a bleached-out world. He follows her lead in doing nothing, statuesque. Her ski jacket is purposely dark, to appear like a local if she's stopped, and not commando white like his. It does mean, though, she's all the more visible to whatever's out there. Close enough, any German will lock on to her for sure.

She unhooks the rope from her waist and lodges the capsule behind a tree stump, signalling for Jens to squat down alongside, then comes in close again.

'If I'm not back in ten minutes, carry on down,' she says. 'Have you a safe house to head to?'

'Yes.'

'If it's a patrol, I'll approach and distract them. Convince them I was out hunting.'

He nods and she moves off. Within seconds, her jacket merges to a blur and then it's gone, as if she's simply ghosted through a wall into nothingness. He sits on his haunches, ready to spring, but his thighs ache and, despite the training, he could fall asleep right then. He yearns for a cup of hot, sweet English tea, then laughs silently at his own weakness. *Come on, Parkes! Rouse yourself. This harsh world is what you've trained for, and what you want. What you need. To make amends.*

Every snap and crack amid the soundproofing snow prompts him to swing his gaze wildly into the white sheet of the world, ears straining for conversation, the approach of footsteps or skis, the cock of a pistol in his ear. But all around is an icy void, as if it's behind his eyeballs, drifting across his vision. He's virtually blind in this milky ocean.

Then, out of the mist, a darkness looms. He blinks away the haze. It's her jacket, moving at a pace towards him, one arm flailing in between punting with her pole. A warning, to turn tail and flee?

Her voice makes it through the dense air, shouting: 'Come! Come!' She's beckoning, urgently, for him to move towards her.

Or is it a trap? Despite their intelligence, she could well be a Quisling. They've been warned of Norwegian collaborators who scurry back to the Germans with information, leading to deadly betrayal. The home-grown resistance has been infiltrated by seemingly 'genuine' loyalists, with scores of Allied agents caught in the net and succumbing to the firing squad. Or worse – a lengthy torture and then death.

Jens is forced into a split decision; it's what he's been trained for, to gamble swiftly, to know how to read those he can trust. But it's not an exact science. He reasons her anger and irritation isn't fake, that she would have been nicer if she was intent on reeling him in and delivering her quarry. If anything, Rumi's irascible welcome makes her more real.

He pushes up and moves towards her, comes close and sees her heart-shaped face is different, alight.

'I found him,' she says eagerly. 'I found your partner. Alive.'

4

House and Home

Hop, 10 kilometres south of Bergen, 2nd January 1942

Her fingers feel dusty and cracked, and she surveys her once smooth skin as the last of the family's best china is packed tightly into a tea chest. Soon, Gunnar will haul it up into the large attic space for safe keeping, where pawing hands can't get at it, along with the family's furniture and a stack of oil paintings that until recently adorned the sweeping stairway and the walls of the hall. Piles of photograph albums detailing the generations through winters and summers in and around Bergen will join them, too. It's like stuffing people into storage, *she thinks.*

She sighs, a deep resonance that she identifies as the only consistent sound to emerge from her of late. It won't be the same with the family gone; the Lauritzens have been in this grand old house for almost a century, and she for a good quarter of that. Whichever way you look at it, the family are being evicted, though they'll be far from homeless – merely moving to their summer house up the coast, smaller but still twice the size of any house she ever lived in as a child. It's a wrench, nonetheless, to think of squatters invading the family home.

She, however, is staying. It's been agreed. Whoever is taking over the place now has apparently insisted on the housekeeper staying put, for a 'smooth transition', they said. It was written in the instructions as a kind of compliment, a sweetener, but she knows there's no real choice. It's either stay and minister to whatever the Nazi occupiers want or be out of a job, and a home. What else would she do at her age? Fifty-six is no time to start over again. Yes, she might get a post in one of the hotels in Bergen, but most are already filled with Nazi officials and officers living the good life and, despite her years of experience, she could end up as a maid, being lorded over by some young girl way above her station. Better to stay put. After twenty-five years, she knows every inch of this beautiful house. Loves every brick. Without the family here, she needs to protect it from the marauding scourge, so it's kept well for when the Lauritzens come back, for when Norway is returned. If it can ever be clawed back.

In the meantime, she tells herself again to be patient in keeping her countenance, make sure to say the right thing to the right man in uniform, melting into the background when required. Isn't that what she's done for twenty-five years, expertly? A ghost in her own home.

But as she wraps the last of the china in newspaper, and wipes away the dust set in the wrinkles around her eyes, she wonders what type of home it will become. And if, in time, it will seem like one at all.

5

An Angel in Waiting

Bergen, 2nd January 1942

Rumi

She can see instantly the shoulder is dislocated, and his lower arm very probably broken. How this man, Karl, had made it halfway down the mountain alone is a testament to his strength, Rumi thinks with some sympathy. He can walk, at least, as skiing isn't an option.

Rumi stands back and watches as the first one, Jens, shoulders both pairs of skis and takes his partner with the other arm, while she adopts one of the heavy packs. They're far enough down the mountain that she can pick her way along a familiar path, leading the way even as the light deserts them. They'd decided to dig in both the capsules and return tomorrow to collect them, leaving the rest up to nightfall and luck.

The trio descend towards the town, stopping to rest as Rumi sees Karl wince in pain. Perhaps the fracture is worse than she's estimated. If so, going straight to the safe house seems less of an option. He needs a doctor, she tells them, and both men need food and warmth, and even though any exposure is a clear risk, neither objects to her offer of help.

'Take off your anoraks,' she says firmly, 'and we'll walk through town together. If we get stopped or questioned, let me do the talking. You're my cousins from Oslo, come to work for my father, all right?'

Darkness is fast approaching even though it's only mid-afternoon, but the dusk helps them to blend in. Rumi weaves her way through the murky narrow streets, avoiding the busy intersection of Torget and the passing trams that throw their carriage lights onto pedestrians. It's where the grey-green of Nazi soldiers congregate, alongside the navy blue of colluding Norwegian police, the STAPO. As they walk, the three make a play of talking with animation like friends are apt to do, moving with relish towards a cosy fireplace, one body each side of Karl to prop up his faltering steps.

Just outside the city centre and towards the wharf, the climb up the cobbled streets towards Strangebakken is near deserted, but still Rumi circles casually to check each end of the narrow lane before slowing in front of a blue-painted house. When it appears safe, they slip quietly into the alleyway alongside two wooden-clad cottages, which opens out into a neat but busy vegetable garden, the two houses having combined their land. One set of windows is in darkness but a tiny sliver of artificial glow shines from the back of the next-door house, and the sight ignites Rumi's own embers deep inside: Marjit's at home. They'll be all right now.

She leads the two men into the back kitchen-parlour of the unlit house and, instantly, the stiffened sinews of her body relax. Despite the gloom, the comfort of Rumi's own home begins to melt the cold inside, the air thick

26

with the smell of stew and the stove still warm. Hilde, their young, slightly wayward and often lazy help, will have gone for the day, but she leaves supper on the range each evening for Rumi and her father. Despite her indolence, Hilde is a dab hand at creating something edible out of the dwindling rationing all Norwegians now face.

'Pappa? Pappa?' Rumi calls, to no response. He's likely still at the boatyard, or gone to play cards with others who work on the wharf. 'Okay, in here.' She ushers the two men into the cosy parlour, urges them to strip off their wet clothing and, like children too cold to even think, they obey. She gives each a blanket and hot bramble tea within minutes, stokes the fire and watches them begin to shiver back into their bodies, making contact with fingertips and toes again.

'I'll be back in a minute,' Rumi says, and then to a look of clear alarm from Jens: 'I'm just going to get help, for his arm.'

He thinks it's a trap, she realises. *That's what he'll suspect always now, of everyone, until he gets home: betrayal.*

She's surprised to find her previous ire has dissipated a little with the task at hand, reminding herself that she can't be angry with these two, shuddering souls – not directly, anyway. They just happen to be in her line of fire as she targets her resentment towards the war and the Nazis, and if she's entirely honest, at the resistance, which enticed her future husband to his death. Worse yet, her anger has extended in recent weeks to the entire world. But these men, huddling together and drawing every ounce of warmth from the fire, are in need right now, and the very sight outstrips her widespread fury.

Is she mellowing, perhaps, just a little? No, no one can accuse Rumi Orlstad of being mellow. Not since Magnus.

Rumi steps outside and crosses the few yards to the next door, rapping on the wood in a practised rhythm. The curtain twitches in the glass pane, followed by the face of an angel in the door's gap. The skin is far from cherubic, slightly plump and lined, topped with short, wayward hair that's white-grey with age. But to Rumi, Marjit Sabo represents everything that has kept her whole as a person for more than a decade and, in the last two months, alive. She *is* an angel.

'Come in, come in,' the older woman urges with a quizzical look. 'It's a bit of a mess in here – I thought you were coming a bit later?'

From anyone else, her tone might have seemed a little sharp, but Rumi knows Marjit and her demeanour inside out, like a daughter. It's just her way. In the past, Marjit has both guided and chided Rumi – motherless since she was fifteen – and she has baulked and sulked in response. But they always, always forgive and forget and, despite an age difference of twenty-seven years, remain the best of friends.

'Yes, we did arrange for eight o'clock,' Rumi tells her, 'but something's come up. I need your help. Right now.'

With a scant run down of the task at hand, Marjit rifles in a wooden chest and pulls out a heavy cotton pouch, collecting the lengths of fabric off-cuts strewn around her parlour. 'Come on, then,' she says, her high cheeks flushed from the wood burning grate.

They step next door and into the hallway of Rumi's childhood home, seeing Jens startle noticeably at Marjit's entrance, his eyes white and wide like a surprised fox.

'It's all right,' Rumi reassures him again. 'She's here to help. You can trust her.'

Karl has fallen into a doze, but wakes and groans as Marjit

manipulates his right arm to assess the damage. She's no doctor, but having spent three years of the Great War driving ambulances across the battlefields of France, Marjit knows her way around a damaged body. And somehow, she always has the supplies to deal with those that can't access a doctor openly, usually Jewish families and agents on the run.

'The shoulder I can put back with some help,' she says. 'But there are two breaks that need to be set, and we won't get him to Dr Torgersen until tomorrow. The best I can do is brace it and dose him up. Rumi, have you got any brandy or Aquavit?'

'Maybe,' she says, searching the small sideboard in one corner of the room. 'Yes, here, but there's only a little of each.'

'Then we'll have it all. I'm sure your father won't mind,' Marjit directs.

Karl is conscious enough to understand his fate, and the pain he's likely to feel before any relief; he drinks down the alcohol like a dutiful infant swallowing his medicine. Marjit lies him on the woven floor mat, directs Jens to hold his feet and Rumi to bracket Karl's good shoulder with one hand and grip his fingers with the other for solace.

He's wide eyed, but fast sinking into another world as Marjit's voice shushes him and counts under her breath in unison: 'one, two, three!' In one deft move, she cracks the shoulder down and back into its socket. They all hear the crunch, Karl bucks violently and Rumi's palm flies to his mouth to muffle his cry of agony. In the next second he flops back into a faint, limp and silent.

'Poor soul,' Marjit sympathises, but Karl's inertia makes it easier for her to position his arm and strap it close into his body with lengths of fabric.

Jens pushes himself back on the sofa, and Rumi sees a

glow from the fire highlighting the mask of white drawn across his face; hunger, nausea and exhaustion combined.

'How far is your safe house?' she asks him. It's within their power and their ethos to help the resistance, but to be caught with not one but two in the house is tantamount to suicide, with Germans everywhere.

'Across town, beyond the harbour,' he reveals. 'It's all right, I'll get us there somehow.'

Marjit, though, is uncompromising about her patient. 'He can't be moved until the morning. Rumi, is the attic room free?'

'Yes, but it's freezing.' She calculates swiftly. 'Karl can have my room, and I'll sleep down here tonight.'

'Perfect,' Marjit agrees. 'This one' – she gestures to Jens – 'can go to my house and I'll sleep down here with you, Rumi, in case Karl wakes. I take it you've got weapons?' she asks Jens. He nods and pulls a pistol from his jacket.

'You keep yours, and I'll borrow his.' She eyes her patient, sleeping like a baby on the floor.

'But . . .' Jens goes to protest.

'I didn't get through one world war without firing a weapon,' Marjit says defiantly. 'And aiming at the right enemy too. You'll get it back, I promise.'

Rumi's pride rises above her own exhaustion at her friend's unbridled fortitude; the courage harboured inside her small, squat torso. Who needs an army of thousands when you have the likes of Marjit Sabo as a brick barrier against Adolf Hitler?

Peder Orlstad comes through the door as Rumi is dishing out fish stew to Jens.

Typical for him, her father is unfazed. 'You found them then?'

'Yes, but no thanks to your directions – or your prowess for counting numbers, Pappa,' Rumi swipes, though she fails to conjure any real irritation. The last eighteen months has taught them that intelligence is often like Chinese whispers, where one slip of the tongue could be deadly.

Peder treats Jens like the long-lost cousin he's pretending to be, and together they manoeuvre Karl up the narrow stairs to bed, then share the last dregs of brandy before Jens says goodnight and heads next door to Marjit's.

He falters, hand on the door knob. 'Thank you, Rumi,' he says quietly. 'I am grateful for your help, truly. We both are.'

'I do it for my country, for Norway,' she replies, not intending for it to sound petulant, though when she hears herself speak, that's exactly how it comes out.

'As do I,' he says, and disappears through the door.

She stands in front of the steaming kettle, musing over his departure. He's blond and tall, well-built, with the palest blue eyes; certainly the look of a Norwegian. And yet he speaks their language oddly, as if his mouth is feeling its way around the sounds. The injured Karl is undoubtedly Norwegian-born, that's obvious from his accent, but the Allies might have selected Jens solely for his Nordic looks, to blend in for this operation. Something about him bothers her, but she can't decide what. In any case, it doesn't matter; he'll be gone in the morning, and although she might spot him in the town centre, or the fish market, it will be at a distance. And before long, he's likely to be off on some mission up into the north where the resistance is most active. *Let's just get tonight over with,* she tells herself, and not be caught harbouring enemy agents, hauled to German HQ and then the grim fate of Grini camp. *One step at a time.*

6

Reunion

Bergen, 3rd January 1942

Jens

'Ah, there you are.' Jens is energised by more hours of uninterrupted sleep than he's had in months, and is up early, breaking eggs into a pan in Marjit's kitchen. He starts on hearing the click of the door latch, but breathes again at a familiar face coming through the door. 'Coffee? You look like you could do with some of the real stuff.'

'Glad you're making yourself at home,' Marjit quips and sidles up beside him, depositing fresh eggs from the chicken house outside.

He turns and bends to envelop the small woman in his long arms, drawing her body in tight for a lengthy embrace and kissing her hair firmly. 'Oh, it's so good to see you, Aunt Marjit.' He pulls away. 'Though you did give me a bit of a fright when you walked in last night – I wasn't expecting to see you so soon.'

'You and me both. Something of a coincidence.'

'I didn't know whether to let on, or how safe it was,' Jens goes on. 'In the end, I thought it best to keep quiet until we talked alone.'

Marjit nods. 'Ordinarily, it would be a good call, but I can vouch for Rumi and Peder – they're solid, loyal resistance. Rubio, too. You won't find better in Bergen. You can trust them.'

They eat as they talk, catching up with life, the war and the impact on their scattered family across Norway and back in England.

'So, how is my sister? Enjoying the London life?' Marjit asks between sips of the best coffee that she's tasted in months, real grounds pulled from Jens's knapsack.

'My mother is fine,' Jens says, though his attempt at loyalty can't hold up against his aunt's knowing stare. He blows out his cheeks slowly. 'Well, if you really want to know . . . she's furious with me for volunteering, and thinks I've already "done my bit". She can't understand why anyone would want to place themselves in danger again.'

'Does she know you're SOE?'

'What do you think?' Jens barely dared to confess an intention to return to active service to his parents, let alone his being part of the Special Operations Executive, a specialist undercover group bent on creating mayhem for the Germans – one that involves explosives, armoury and a good deal of fallen agents.

'And your father?' Marjit wipes up the yellowy yolk with a slice of potato flatbread and licks her fingers with relish.

'Oh, you know him – more interested in his business and his newspaper, despite bombs falling all around them,' Jens says with a disdain he can't hide. 'But then, he's British. I don't expect him to feel any allegiance to Norway. But my mother . . .'

'Don't be too hard on her, Jens.' Marjit clears away the plates and reaches into the cold cupboard for the small block of cheese she's been hoarding. 'She left Norway a long time ago, and her trips back since have been like holidays. Unless you're actually here, it's hard for anyone to imagine what it's like seeing those German bastards strutting around Bergen as if they own the place.'

'But you went away, Marjit,' Jens bemoans. 'You came back here.'

'I didn't, however, marry and follow the man I loved to another country,' she says pointedly. 'Only up into the hills, in my case.' He sees her pause, deep in thought, then watches her turquoise eyes – stunning against her pale pink complexion – begin to swim. Instantly, she caps it off with a sharp: 'Besides which, Kirsten always hated the winters, from when we were girls, and I love them! So, it's a good thing really.'

He feels her playful eyes turn serious, settling on his face, until he says: 'What?'

'How are you really, Jens? After Dunkirk?'

Jens puts a hand to his left thigh automatically and rubs the skin under his trousers. 'It's fine. The doctors say it's mended well, just aches every so often.'

Marjit brings her bottom lip under her teeth, in the way that signals she's not fooled. 'That's not what I meant and you know it.'

'I'm getting there,' he says, eyes focused on his empty cup.

'It's going to take time.'

'I killed someone, Marjit. A good person. Do you think there's a real recovery for that? I'm not even sure I should.' Before his aunt can offer any well-meant sympathy, Jens pulls himself up and scoops in a concerted breath. 'Time is what we don't have, not if the bloody Germans are to be stopped from annihilating Norway and the rest of Europe. I'm here, and I have a job to do. Everyone has to face up to hard truths – I'm no different. The best I can do is limit the damage from now on.'

It's clear that neither of them is convinced by his bravado, knowing that there are more than bones still to be mended, but Marjit smiles weakly and ruffles his hair. For a second he feels eight years old again. And he doesn't mind, because Jens has always adored Marjit; the memories of childhood summers spent with her on the farm just north of Bergen are among his most precious. Whenever he's with her, he's somehow convinced of being wholly Norwegian, and not the half-blood imposter he often feels – or is made to feel. His thoughts go immediately to the girl next door: courageous but cross.

Now he's in Marjit's house once again, and by some fluke she is neighbour to his first contact. Seeing his aunt scrounging in her kitchen for morsels of cheese, and her little moue of delight as she savours the rare taste of true coffee, makes him all the more intent on his true mission: to be an infuriating, irksome, prickly thorn in the side of their German foe. To weave lines of communication among the home-spun resistance, of course, but mainly to make bloody, ugly mischief and gouge large holes in the Reich's infrastructure. To help steal back what's already theirs, and make it impossible for Hitler to bleed Norway dry. That's the plan, and now he just has to carry it out.

Agreeing to ignore austerity for one morning, they indulge in a second pot of coffee while Jens is filled in on Bergen's day-to-day life under German occupation. The wider picture he knows all too well, having been forced to watch from the sidelines while the country he's always viewed as a second home was first invaded in early April 1940, alongside Denmark. From newspaper reports and gossip among the troops, Jens pieced together German movements as they orchestrated Operation Weserübung with pincer-like precision at various points along the coast. The Nazis concentrated first in the north, protecting heavy industry and the passage of precious iron ore from neighbouring Sweden, but the relief he felt from Marjit being out of harm's way didn't last; the Germans soon turned their sights south, assaulting the population, infesting towns and cities in varying shades of grey, green and black – Army, SS and Gestapo. The Norwegian military was unprepared, and the resistance barely formed, with little armour or hope of deflecting the might and will of the Reich. The Allies, too, were equally taken by surprise; British and French troops arrived in Norway four days after the invasion, and although they fought bitterly alongside Norwegian resistance, their numbers were needed to fight the rapid German advancement in Europe. Already in France, Jens would have happily swapped places to prevent the withdrawal of Allied troops at the end of April, to feel like he was at least doing something for Norway, and for Marjit, instead of being forced to imagine their isolation.

Little over a month later, King Haakon VII fled to London, compelled to set up his government in exile, almost 2,000 kilometres to the south. New rulers were foisted upon Norwegians then – the Reich-controlled *Kommissariat*, backed up by the Wehrmacht German Army, and *Nasjonal Samling*, the small Norwegian Nazi party led by Vidkun Quisling.

Worse still was Hitler's intent. Again, Jens had to glean the details from intelligence and his mother's fears laid out in her letters, but it became clear that Hitler wanted

36

Norway for a reason. Not to conquer or overrun. It was worse than that, and still is. Yes, Germany's dictator is intent on usurping the country's valuable natural sources, but what the Führer covets is more precious: he wants their blood. The rich, Nordic genes are seen by Hitler and the architect of his master race, Heinrich Himmler, as a bedrock of true Aryanism: blond and blue-eyed. And pure.

So Hitler doesn't want to alienate Norwegians. He wants to befriend them, colonise them. He wants to *use* them, and to blend their cultures. To be as one. For Jens Parkes, the only solace is that the likes of Marjit Sabo – and thousands of resistance fighters still active – are having none of it.

With her experience of war and recent subterfuge, Jens is confident that his aunt won't ask anything of his mission, his contacts or his plans. And the less she knows, the safer she is. Instead, he fires a volley of questions as they pore over a map of the town and the outlying areas: the fjords, tiny islands and possible landing spots for boats that Marjit knows. He nods, cramming his memory with her detailed descriptions – the boathouse with the fading red door, or the fisherman's cottage with a sculpted, wooden seagull on its roof – tiny particulars that might one day save his life. Asking shelter of the wrong house could spell disaster if the occupants are Quislings ready to run straight to the Germans with their betrayal.

Every few minutes, Jens stares at a portion of the map and closes his eyes in a bid to commit Marjit's minutiae to memory. As a trained mapmaker before the war, it's how he sees the world, a curious combination of two- and three-dimensional shapes – for him, it's like embroidering a flat piece of fabric with heavy thread, layering the hills and contours instinctively. It's his own strange way of fixing the landscape deep into his being, a skill he can't ever remember not having, even as a child: the ability to close his eyes and 'see' a map of the terrain instantly.

They scrabble to fold and hide the map at a sudden rapping on the window, followed by the lifting of the latch.

'Marjit? Marjit, it's just me,' comes a woman's voice, followed by the shape of Rumi entering the kitchen. She stops dead. 'Oh.'

Jens stands, awkward; he detects an instant frost in her stance as she senses the familiarity with his aunt, and he shuffles his chair backwards a little. In the daytime, and without her snow gear, he can observe her in a true light: the vibrant russet hair that's pulled back in a single loose plait from a wide jawline, and lips even more rosy in the warm. The amber of her eyes is soft, though hardened by her expression. Oddly, he wonders how they would be lifted by a smile.

'Rumi, how are you? Did you sleep all right?' Marjit says lightly, cutting into the tense atmosphere.

'Fine. I slept fine. I came to tell you that Karl's awake. And I've sent a note to Dr Torgersen.' Her voice is clipped. Suspicious. *And annoyed,* Jens thinks. *Again.*

'Oh good. I'll just freshen up and come by in a minute,' Marjit sings.

'Hmm.' But Rumi doesn't move, just stands and stares. Jens sees her nostril flicker, as if she's sniffing out the situation like a wolf. Her solid shoulders are pulled back, squaring up, perhaps?

'Jens, will you come along to see Karl?' Marjit pushes the conversation along.

'Yes. Yes, of course.'

Rumi spins on one foot to go, but stops halfway and points her attention to Jens. 'We'll have to go up and retrieve your equipment today, before a fresh layer of snow settles,' she says. 'But we'll need three of us, and Karl obviously can't go.'

'It's heavy stuff—' he starts.

'I can manage,' she snaps. 'But I have got someone else to come with us.'

Marjit cocks her head with curiosity.

'Rubio's back off the trawler,' Rumi explains. 'The engine was faulty and they docked early.' She faces Jens. 'He's trustworthy, and a good skier.'

Jens can't be sure, but she might have shot him a look of real disdain then, loaded with accusation: you're not a natural skier. Not a Norwegian. Or is he being too harsh, and more than a little paranoid?

'That's good.' Marjit fills in the awkward second of silence. 'We'll both be over in a minute.'

Rumi takes the hint and leaves, shutting the door on the icy air both inside and out.

Jens's shoulders sag with relief. 'Is she always so friendly?' he says sardonically.

'Don't judge her right now,' Marjit replies, clattering dishes in the sink. 'She's been through a lot.'

'So have we all. It doesn't mean—'

'Not like her.' Marjit's voice is sharp, almost remonstrating. 'For a woman of only twenty-five, it's too much.'

Jens can tell by the sudden tension in the back of his aunt's shoulders that she means it, that her heart goes out to the serious girl next door.

Marjit turns with wet hands and rubs them on her old trousers, sighs deeply. 'She lost her mother at fifteen, and her fiancé less than two months ago at sea,' she says plainly.

'Oh, that's awful.' He's sympathetic, though Jens also knows it's a common enough tragedy in these parts; the area's population largely thrives, and sometimes falls, by the whims of the ocean. It's not a rarity to hear of a drowning.

'He was on the Shetland Bus,' Marjit goes on. 'In that almighty storm we had.'

Now it's Jens's turn to sigh. It is both sad and unfair. Those Norwegian sailors who work the treacherous North Sea route between the coastline and the Shetland Islands, sometimes way up into the Arctic Circle, are heroes to SOE agents like himself, at times their only transport to escape determined German search parties. Using fishing trawlers to cross the unforgiving waters under the cloak of winter skies, the sailors sneak into the skerries and coves, where agents are waiting to be plucked off the coast, hauling them back to Shetland and safety, a perilous 300 kilometres to the west. Hence its nickname of the 'Shetland Bus'. And not only people – tons of arms and munitions are transported in the hold, plus currency to keep the resistance afloat. Few of the sailors are army or navy trained, simply boatmen with a wealth of experience and gutfuls of courage. They man this vital route because they want to, because they care deeply for their country. And they die for their country, too: drowned, bombed or strafed by German planes if they're spotted too far out to sea.

'Was he a regular on the Bus?' Jens asks.

'No, and that makes it even worse for Rumi, I think,' Marjit says. 'He was a patriot, of course, and he wanted to be on the crews, was waiting his turn for a place, even though Rumi dreaded his going. He'd done one other trip, in early November, and she was a bag of nerves the entire six days he was away, so relieved to see him back in one piece. Then, a boat came in soon after – one of the crewmen had broken his leg on the journey over, tossed about by the swell. He had to stay in Bergen and, of course, Magnus jumped at the chance to replace him.'

She goes back to chinking dishes in the sink. 'And now Rumi is a widow without even being married. So, yes, she's grieving, and angry. Wouldn't you be?'

Yes, I would, he thinks. Bloody furious. As he was less than a week ago, when news arrived at the base in Scotland of an operation gone awry in Maloy, north of Bergen; their company commander – and everyone's hero – Martin Linge killed amid an act of sabotage. The anger in Jens quickly gave way to a deep sadness and loss; he'd known Linge little more than six months, but in that time the Norwegian-born soldier had become a respected mentor and more; almost like a father to Jens, with his own parent distant in so many ways. So yes, he knows grief – the raw, stinging type that makes you wonder if it's worth going on. That lives with him now, though in his darkest moments it's also what spurs him on. That and the ever-present spectre of . . . He pockets the guilt and the memory swiftly, before it can take hold and cripple his day before it's begun. He will deal with it – later, and in his own way.

Marjit dries her hands. 'Come on then, let's go and see Karl.'

'Should we tell them about you and me? Come clean?'

'Do you mean that I used to bathe you as a boy and read you bedtime stories?' An irreverent smile lights up her pale face.

Jens nudges at her arm playfully. 'Don't you dare.'

'In which case, not yet,' Marjit adds. 'I'll tell Rumi tonight, in private.'

'Minus the bath stories?'

'Maybe.' She laughs. 'Even so, you were a very cute baby.'

41

7

Spinning Truths

Bergen, 3rd January 1942

Rumi

'Your nephew!' Rumi cries with real astonishment. 'But how is he here? And why didn't you say anything last night?'

'I was genuinely shocked to see him there,' Marjit says in her own defence. 'I mean, not that he would become an agent – that doesn't surprise me – but to turn up at your house, just next door. And when he didn't acknowledge me, I felt it best to follow his lead. I didn't know what his objective might be.'

Rumi looks at her with mock suspicion. 'And I still don't,' Marjit insists. 'And I won't ask either. You know how it is.'

Rumi does. She knows it's survival. Sometimes, ignorance is far more than bliss. It's life and death.

The two women go back to their knitting, their needles clacking alongside the crack of the wood in the burner, both hunkering close enough to get warmth and light from the blaze in Marjit's small, lived-in room.

'But he's English,' Rumi states, as if lobbing an accusation.

'*Half* English,' Marjit corrects. 'Yes, he was brought up there, though I'll wager a bigger portion of his heart is in Norway than England.' She looks up over her needles. 'And since when have we Norwegians been in a position to refuse help from any quarter against the Germans, particularly SOE?'

Rumi is silently contrite. What Marjit says is right: there are pockets of resistance across Norway, groups working tirelessly to thwart the Nazi occupiers in every way they can since April 1940, but communication is poor – more so since all Norwegians were forced to give up their radios in the summer of '41, by Nazi decree. Now, every radio set owned and secretly stashed is an instant route, at best, to the concentration camp at Grini. It's the SOE and the fellow British SIS – Secret Intelligence Service – who help to keep the network of messages running with their undercover stations and hidden transmitters. Rumi looks at the mesh of home-spun wool in her lap, knotted and needing to be re-wound; for a second it reminds her of all the virtual waves and wires criss-crossing her country, above the heads of the German intelligence, making plans and causing military mischief, and then she knows she should be grateful, even if the very word 'resistance' now sticks in her throat. A word that once meant freedom, but for her now conjures only loss and death. Alongside the name of 'Magnus'. What Marjit says is true, and she has no right to be hard on Jens, even if his accent needs knocking into shape.

Marjit seems to read her mind. 'And he did bring us real coffee,' she says, holding up the pot. 'Another cup?'

'Why not?' Rumi readily recalls the liquid taste on her

tongue. The beans were bitter, but in the most delicious way, a welcome relief from the sharp, coarse taint of cereals or burnt dandelion root – ersatz coffee at its very worst. Jens is to be applauded, if only for bringing them coffee.

'So, did you find both the equipment capsules today?' Marjit asks as the coffee is poured. 'Up on the mountain?'

'Yes, they took a bit of digging out, but we emptied them and dug each one back in. By the time the snow melts in the spring they won't give up any secrets.' Rumi knows that even if the capsules are discovered, the presence of Allied agents will be no surprise to the Germans, with their nearby construction of submarine pens as prime targets, alongside the crucial shipping lines up and down Norway's coast. The mere presence of any resistance causes thousands of Gestapo and Wehrmacht troops to be tied up tracking the underground network of patriots. In turn, it means fewer German soldiers are sent into the battlefields of Europe; if Hitler is intent on befriending the Nords, then they'll make sure he has to pay for it.

'And did Jens come back down with you?'

'Only to the edge of town,' says Rumi. 'He had a small suitcase, which I presume is his radio, and he left us to go and lodge it somewhere. Rubio and I stowed the rest of the contents in the boathouse and it was all gone when I checked a few hours later. We also got Karl over to Dr Torgersen, and I doubt he'll be back either.'

Marjit nods, though Rumi detects some regret in her silence and puckered lips. A slight feeling of loss at her nephew's absence perhaps, so soon after his arrival?

'Do you think you'll see much of him?' Rumi wonders.

'Probably not. He has a job to do, and I'd rather he keeps as safe as possible. Too much contact will get us all noticed.'

Even through her hardened heart – the flesh made solid by a granite injection of grief – Rumi can sense Marjit's affection for Jens, warm as the embers pulsating in the fire. It's no wonder, really, since she's a widow who lost her husband, Lars, six years before war broke out, and they were childless, though not by choice. Rumi can easily picture Marjit showering devotion on a nephew, in the same way she receives love from her daily. As a mother might. As her own mother always did.

Marjit stifles a yawn and Rumi takes it as her cue. 'I'm off to bed,' she says, getting up. 'I've an early start at the yard and that trip up the mountain tired me out.'

She looks conspiratorially at Marjit, notes the older woman reading it perfectly. *But don't tell anyone*, it says. *Don't let anyone see a weakness in Rumi Orlstad.*

'Goodnight, my love,' Marjit says at the door, pulling her in close and kissing her cheek. Just as any mother might.

8

House of Mystery

Hop, 21st January 1942

They've moved in all right: military lorries full of furniture and office equipment spitting out their dirty diesel onto the drive, crushing the flower borders so beautifully tended by the family's team of gardeners, all of whom left swiftly, leaving poor, aged Gunnar to be the all-round dogsbody. She wonders how the old boy will cope.

It's odd, though. Alongside thirty or so beds delivered – which she imagines to be for officer billets – there are six cots. Tiny ones. Plain and functional but they are no bigger than a large pillow. Only a newborn would fit comfortably in one. Babies. Why on earth would the forging, marauding, thieving Reich want babies in their midst?

Instantly, all thoughts of having to cater for twenty burly German soldiers and their appetites had disappeared, but even now she's none the wiser. She looks at her housekeeping ledger, a new one for each year, this one still pristine since the family's departure almost a month before. How can the Germans expect her to run a house efficiently when she doesn't know who it's for? Will she have to contend with the frankly pathetic rationing, or will there be luxuries for workers of the Reich? There's one officer, Captain Kleiner, who seems to be directing operations but he just waves her away each time she tries to question him about how many people will be under her roof. Doesn't he know how difficult it is to feed and house large numbers of people? She's done it for years, at Christmas gatherings and in summertime, when the family threw lavish parties with guests staying over, but that's temporary and this is bound to be different; the beds alone suggest they're expecting the house to be some sort of hostel. Why won't they tell her? I mean, how bad can it be, *she thinks,* when our country has already been invaded and our freedom usurped.

It still strikes her as strange, though. She pictures the tiny cots now sitting in a line in one of the rooms and – she doesn't know why – a brief chill ripples through her. Tiny infants.

What on earth can the Reich want with babies?

9

The Mission Man

Bergen, 29th January 1942

Rumi

It's little under a month before Rumi sets eyes on Jens again, and by then he's almost disappeared from her thoughts. Almost. She sees Marjit nearly every day and Rumi's noticed that – for someone who earns a living by sewing from home – her friend has been out more than usual, the house silent on several occasions when she's called in. She wonders if Jens is claiming some of her time and if, despite good intentions, Marjit can't quite stay away from her nephew.

Rumi is idly chatting to one of the fish stall owners she supplies, eyes roaming the market, when she sees him in the near distance, buying *skrei* cod from a rival trader. He looks less frazzled than their first meeting, his pink cheeks signal he's healthier and definitely warmer, and yes – she hates to admit it – more Norwegian. In a casual knitted sweater and jacket, with tweed trousers and leather lace-ups, he blends in with the usual market crowd. He's clearly not holed up in one of the radio listening stations eating salted cod and tinned food or hiding out on a tiny island off the coast, as so many SOE agents are forced to do. Her curiosity overrides her previous irritation then: so what *is* his cover, to be out and about so openly in Bergen?

The market packs up in the early afternoon, and after stowing her leftover stock in the boathouse, she's at a loose end. Really she ought to sit at her desk and start the week's books, or organise the chaos in Pappa's wake when he left with Rubio at five a.m. that morning on the trawler. But she doesn't want to. In all honesty, she can't be bothered. She's weary, too, having woken when her father so-say tiptoed through the house on getting up, all with the delicacy of an elephant tottering over a carpet of broken glass. After he left, she spent an age staring at her bedroom ceiling and fretting, irritation rising and threatening to leave her submerged. Like the waves stalking her dreams, her angst is always around Magnus, washing over her and seeping into her waking hours.

Endlessly, the scene of his leaving drowns out the good times: their first dance, that kiss, him proposing marriage on a clifftop overlooking the whispering sea. She's haunted by her harsh words when he last sailed, berating Magnus in a roundabout way for choosing the resistance over her. 'Why do you have to go now?' she'd pleaded. 'Surely you can wait your turn for a chance on the Bus. It'll come soon enough.'

'But I'm needed now, Rumi!' he shot back, fired with loyalty for the Norwegian flag. Eager to do something other than wave it; to actually fight for it.

And Rumi didn't mean to seem disloyal – she'd wholeheartedly believed in the resistance since the outset of the war, worked for it, allied with it – but a nagging sensation inside told Rumi that he shouldn't go this time. Magnus could ably sail a bath tub across an entire ocean, but something about 'this mission' – as he called it – didn't feel good. And, in the end, she was right. And being right had never felt so wrong. So escaping her nagging thoughts is what's needed now.

At the boathouse, she endures the icy water of the outside tap, trying to wash off the worst of the fish smell, though acutely aware it will take more than a trickle and tiny tablet of soap to peel away a lifetime of living, working and breathing the salt sea. Will I ever *not* reek of fish, she wonders.

In her desk drawer, she scrabbles for a small bottle of cologne kept for such 'emergencies', dots a little on her wrists and neck, and then immediately feels the wrench to her insides. It was her mother's, taken from her dresser on the morning of her funeral, without Pappa's knowledge or permission, though Rumi feels sure he wouldn't begrudge it. Still, she keeps it hidden, fears that the odour of lavender and spring might catch in his nostrils, causing his weathered face to flatten with the pain of such memories.

Striding ten minutes into Bergen's city centre, Rumi slows to a wander. She has only a vague idea of meandering through the lofty Sundt building, the town's most upmarket department store. The shelves are increasingly empty, having been stripped months ago by a plague of locusts in the guise of German soldiers eager to send goods back home, and the best she can hope for is some material that Marjit will use to make up a new pair of work trousers. Mostly, she likes to look and finger the beautiful knitting yarn she can ill-afford, left on the shelf because few people will pay such prices. Then, she will treat herself to coffee in a café where the ersatz is better than most, and where the Germans rarely go. They're out in force on the streets as she heads down the open, rectangular space of Torgallmenningen, the Wehrmacht troops with stark, uniform expressions, and SS chatting in that more relaxed, superior way, their heads making no effort to mask a wide turn as well-dressed Norwegian women walk by. Their accompanying desire the SS wear with pride, though it causes a queasy revulsion in Rumi. Luckily, she's too plain to attract their attention. And sometimes, she thinks with humour, that stink of fish can be a blessing.

It's then that she spots Jens for the second time in one day, hauling in boxes down a small side street. She would have sailed past, but her attention is caught by the sound of his efforts, cursing to himself at the load he's lifting. She hesitates. He could do with some help, clearly. Should she? Does she want to? And is she in the right mood?

While Jens represents the resistance that she sees as the cause of her misery, Rumi has always harboured a natural empathy for any underdog, and it's that which propels her towards him. She swears her weakness comes from those childhood years on her father's boat, landing a sizeable catch on the trawler and watching the fish flapping and floundering before the inevitable end. Pappa had shouted at her with exasperation when she tried to scoop up each and every one and return them to 'their families' amid the waves. Though she's long since become hardened to necessity and life within a fishing family, Rumi's penchant remains. Watching people suffer needlessly, as she's become accustomed to in the past year, and standing idly by are entirely different things.

'Can I help?' She strides forward as Jens is struggling to

his feet with a large box. His eyes land on her, and she's amused to see his brain juggling for recognition.

'Oh, yes, hello,' he says at last. 'Rumi. Sorry, I didn't recognise you without your . . .'

'Skis?' she jokes, then tries to recall the last time she attempted to make one.

'Hat,' he says. 'Your ski hat.'

She nods, followed by a pause heavy with their joint embarrassment. *Start again, Rumi.*

'Can I help, with the boxes?' she says. 'You look swamped.'

He doesn't try to tell her they are heavy or bulky, just says 'yes, thank you', and they make several trips up a small set of stairs to the second floor of an office, doubling as a dumping ground for the cargo. It's the same sort of chaos as when she once left the boathouse for a week's trip to Trondheim, leaving Pappa in charge of keeping order. Disarray in every corner.

'What's in these?' Rumi gestures at the cartons, sure they aren't heavy enough to be resistance equipment, supplies that Jens wouldn't be stupid enough to transport in broad daylight.

'Clothes,' he says, panting, as he drops the last box. 'Children's clothes. For the mission.'

Rumi looks around. Yes, it's convincing enough as a front – the office of a charitable mission intent on distributing clothes to refugees from the north that are sailing into Bergen on a weekly basis. In the early days of the invasion and occupation, the fighting was fierce – whole villages and towns torched by the Germans – and the human cost inevitably high. The mission workers have trickled in from Oslo and Stockholm, and as such it's the perfect, legitimate cover for an outsider to be in Bergen. And a perfect excuse not to speak with a local accent, though in the few words Jens has spoken now, Rumi notes a distinct improvement in the flow of his Norwegian.

Marjit. That's where she's been.

'But shouldn't they really go out to those in need?' she asks. 'I mean, however good they look for a cover, they could be useful to *someone.*' She can feel her irritation rising, heat prickling behind her ears.

Jens looks squarely at her, and she watches his understanding catch up. 'But they are,' he says. 'I mean, I'm not intent on hoarding everything. I will be distributing it soon, but it all needs sorting first, and there's only me . . .'

'Well, come on then,' she says crisply, taking off her coat and pulling open the first lid. 'Four hands will be quicker than two.'

'Oh. Of course. Thank you.'

Rumi trips down the stairs two hours later with a sense that she hasn't experienced in some time. Satisfaction, she thinks; a warm sensation against the freezing afternoon air as the darkness descends on Bergen. Yet she hasn't set eyes on any yarn this afternoon, or tasted even a half decent coffee (supposedly, Marjit has all of Jens's good stock), let alone a good piece of almond cake. Instead, she was galvanised into helping others, and for a short time was pulled from her swamp of grief by those in a far worse position than herself. And it felt good, to rise above the quagmire of self-pity for a change, for the first time since Magnus di— Well, since Magnus.

She and Jens had worked solidly, emptying and sorting boxes of donated clothes into different sizes for girls and boys, and setting aside those only useful for rags.

He wouldn't be able to devote a large amount of time to the distribution, he said, but he was determined the office would function partly as a mission should, in doing some good. 'Otherwise, why else am I here?'

She'd nodded, still wondering why he wasn't out there doing what was considered solid resistance work; most SOE agents lived out on the islands – gathering intelligence and plotting ways to sabotage German installations – in safe houses well beyond the reach of the German HQ. Hiding in plain sight meant taking more of a risk, surely?

She'd ventured to ask how Karl was doing, and Jens offered that he was 'well hidden' while his arm mended, which likely meant he was the one holed up in a safe house, eating the tinned herring and salted fish that Jens didn't have to.

Something, however, made her stop short of expressing her thoughts. She doesn't have the energy to make small talk, or invest too much in the lives of others; while moments of light are beginning to seep through her grief, Rumi still feels essentially dead inside, fighting against a tide and swimming endlessly towards a surface she can't reach. And the way she pictures it – that analogy with the ocean – is no accident. It's Magnus, ever present as a deep watery hole inside her.

In the late afternoon, the streets are moderately busy, and Rumi feels she still has time to squeeze in her reward of coffee and cake, heading along to the Café Boulevard. She's unusually preoccupied, eyes to the ground, when she looks up from the pavement to a distinctly unwelcome sight. It's too late to swerve into a side street, or feign ignorance. He's seen her. His smiles says so. Her scowl signals more.

'Rumi! How lovely to see you.' He strides forward and seems to remember just in time to lower his arms, avoiding an embrace that wouldn't do on the street, in public.

Why can't he see? she thinks. Why can't he know that his heavy, studded, dark blue uniform of the STAPO marks him out as no longer her friend or confidant? As anything but the enemy he's become.

'I haven't seen you in ages,' Bjarne Hansen starts. 'Where have you been?'

Avoiding you, Bjarne. 'Busy,' she says, her words clipped. 'It's herring season, lots to do, you know. I don't get much spare time.'

He bobs his large, blond head repeatedly. 'Yes, I suppose life goes on, despite the . . . And how is your father?'

She answers his questions in staccato sentences, coupled with an irritation that comes all too easily. But Bjarne seems immune to her barely concealed scorn, ploughing on despite Rumi stamping her feet against the cold seeping up through her soles. This blindness must come of wearing the police uniform as some kind of heavy armour, she thinks. Everyone in Bergen saw the young Bjarne as an engaging, delightful child, in the same school year as Rubio. His closest friend, in fact. With Rumi tagging along, they were a constant threesome, inseparable during the long hot summers and cold winter snows. Until, out of the blue, just days after the invasion, Bjarne joined the Norwegian police force, now taking its orders directly from the German Security Police. He became the enemy overnight, or as good as. Rumi remembers with bitterness the first time she saw him strutting through the streets in the distinctive button-down navy tunic, his broad chest puffed out, a look of actual pride on his face.

'Bjarne! What the . . . what have you . . .?' she'd cried with reproach.

He capped her off, defensively. 'We all have our part to play, Rumi,' he'd snapped. 'If we want to get on, to avoid bloodshed for our country, we have to accommodate.'

His cool, ethereal grey eyes were strangely ablaze.

It was a common argument among Quislings in the face of invasion; accommodate the Germans to survive – 'it's not our war', 'we can be neutral', they bleated at the beginning. But since when did being neutral involve occupation? In Rumi's eyes, and those of her fellow resistance, accommodation sat next to collaboration all too snuggly.

And Bjarne had gone a step further – he'd joined the pro-Nazi *Nasjonal Samling*, the Norwegian National Socialist Party and the equivalent of Hitler's bully boys, fronted by that puffed-up Nazi puppet Quisling. It made Bjarne instantly 'one of them'. She couldn't fathom how he'd come to that point; as a boy, Bjarne had lost both parents to a fishing accident and was brought up by his grandmother, who died just before war broke out. He might have been searching for some kind of belonging, and Rumi's own losses should make her more sympathetic, especially now, but . . . to come to *this*? The countless hours that Rumi, Rubio and Bjarne spent down at the boathouse as children have simply disappeared from her memory stock like salt spray in a breeze.

'I'm sorry, I have to go,' Rumi cuts off his rambling questions. 'My father will wonder where I am.' He won't – Pappa isn't due back into harbour until the morning, but Bjarne heeds her lie.

'See you around, Rumi,' he says as she turns, and she detects a slight longing in his voice, loneliness perhaps. She skips the idea of coffee then, already tasting too much bitterness without the acrid ersatz taint to add to it.

10

Trust

Jens

He locks the door of the mission house minutes after she leaves, soon enough to watch her dark coat round the corner of the street. Rumi. *She's a strange one,* he thinks. Crisp and cold as the mountain snow a month ago, and yet today he's seen a different side of her. Not warm, exactly, but certainly less frosty. And it was nice to be working with someone for a time, to be able to talk freely and not in code. Back to normal now, though. To being a nameless ghost who speaks in riddles, whose messages sometimes bring smiles, but more often than not a grimace at the demands from the Allied high command, at more intelligence to glean, or a perilous mission to plan.

Instinctively, Jens follows her path into Bankgaten and watches with interest when he spies Rumi talking with a STAPO officer, the back of his head nodding. Is she simply pretending to be engaged? He thinks so, judging by her stance and the way she's almost dancing on her soles. He hopes so. Besides, Marjit trusts her, and that has to be good enough, when there are so many other elements that are less certain.

He peels away from the sight of them and walks in the opposite direction, hauling the rucksack packed with mission clothes, just feeling the edge of the metal radio parts digging into his back at the bottom of the canvas bag. Hat pulled low and head down into the still, crisp air, Jens forges down Kong Oscars Gate and begins to climb upwards, away from the city centre. The effort makes him pull in freezing breaths, but he's grateful; it's the fuel he needs to keep moving.

The knock on the cottage door he does in a practised rhythm: three taps, pause, another three, pause and a single rap. Measured and calm, nothing like the frenzied hammering of a Nazi or STAPO raid. The wait for a response makes him feel exposed, but it's necessary.

The man who opens the door is smiling, and it's relief on both sides. There are no names, but a distinct hand signal, at which the man grabs his coat, and they both climb further up the cobbled lane.

'How far?' Jens questions.

'Ten minutes, maybe less.'

Jens isn't slighted by the curt response, because everything is on a need to know basis. Details are a luxury they can't afford. They reach the end of a narrow lane, and the man turns into an alleyway, and then through a side gate to a shabby workshop. It's always at this moment that Jens wonders if he's being led to his death, having to make an instant decision towards that leap of faith on which his life depends. And strangely, it doesn't always fill him with dread, sometimes mere curiosity. Tonight, he senses that the man leading is an honest believer in the cause, and it's that faith which pushes him forward.

Both men keep winter scarves wrapped around their faces as another rhythmic rap on the door admits them into a small shed with a young man and woman inside. These are unknown people to Jens, and clearly only acquaintances to his resistance colleague. The couple don't shake hands, but ask swiftly if their two visitors 'have the goods'.

Jens doesn't shift his pack. Something isn't right. Through the wool against his nose even the air smells of betrayal. He watches the woman shuffle uncomfortably, push the fringe of her hair back twice. The bow of her lip ripples.

Jens's colleague mutters something irrelevant, then says that they have no goods, and what is the going rate for fish? It's a signal, a crucial one, and Jens heads for the door, haste in his steps. He and the other man are down the alleyway and running at full stretch by time they hear shouts of the STAPO behind, sprouting from around the workshop like weeds. Bullets glance off the flint underfoot as the two men skate at speed across the cobbles, sprinting for an age until they land breathless in the garden of a large house, a curious goat coming to sniff at them.

'Close shave,' Jens pants.

'And good instincts,' the man says, his smile of relief just visible in the moonlight.

Back at the man's house, Jens is glad to be invited in to the stove side, accepting the coffee on offer.

'And what is it you do?' he asks. The man is resistance, clearly, but everyone has a cover, and it's giving nothing away to talk of past lives that can't be reclaimed.

He stokes the fire and sighs. 'I was in the clergy. Now, I just pick up whatever work I can.'

Jens nods again. It's unlikely this man has lost his faith, not with the crucifix fixed so prominently on the wall. More that he sacrificed his formal place in the church; brave and principled clergy stood up to the Nazis from the outset, refusing to be bullied by Quisling, and many were displaced as a result. He'll be grateful to still have a home, plus a renewed purpose with the resistance. Ever thankful, too, that he's not in the clutches of Grini detention camp, as so many clergy already are. Or else dead.

With no names exchanged, the two men shake hands at the door and Jens slips into the night again. In a short time, it's become colder and he wraps his scarf tighter, wants to run again to keep warm, but the cobbles remain icy and any haste would only invite suspicious glances from any passing patrols. One flight for survival is enough for tonight. Instead, he trudges back into the city centre, his load still heavy but feeling as if he might well have shed a life. He's little more than a courier, a simple go-between, though the task carries its own dangers. Is it enough? As a payback? In France, there was real combat, a sense that they as a unit were working together, making a difference. At least until they were pushed back by the advancing Nazi scourge, Panzer tanks nipping at their backsides. But would he rather be back there, in the line of deadly fire, day after day?

When Jens pictures the bloodshed of his dreams, then it's a defiant no.

11

Weaving a Life

Bergen, 29th January 1942

Rumi

The house is empty, though the parlour is warm. A pot of thin soup sits on the stove, left by Hilde, alongside some salted cod, and the singed, blackened roots of dandelion, ready to be ground into a sad excuse for coffee. Rumi sniffs at the fish and puts it back in the cold larder. She eats the soup, hardly tasting it, but the liquid fills her stomach just enough, and she cuts off a good slice of the cake Hilde has made; potato based, but the young girl's skill at baking means it's more than edible. She wraps it in a cloth, pulls out her knitting bag from beside the parlour chair and steps next door.

'Come in,' a voice calls out as Rumi raps on the glass, greeted then by the sight of Marjit's backside as she opens the door, the older woman's body bent over a robust easy chair and tugging at something. 'Come on, you so and so,' she huffs into the upholstery. 'Just *move!*'

'What are you doing?'

'The damn catch has stuck,' Marjit mumbles, her head halfway into the seat of the chair.

'Here, let me try,' Rumi says. Marjit's top half appears, hair ruffled, and Rumi sidles by. She reaches her long arm down between the arm and the seat, fingers scrabbling and landing on the metal catch. It takes a good tug, but she feels it give, and the seat springs up slightly, Rumi pulling at the cloth so the stuffed seat folds out completely like the top of a box. Underneath is more than mere stuffing; it's the workings of Marjit's old radio, neatly compacted. Another ingenious lever causes the set to rise, enough to pull it upright and turn it on. Rumi twirls the dial to find some music, but is careful to leave the volume low. It's one thing having a banned radio, but another for anyone else to hear it. Already there have been executions for merely listening to the BBC broadcasts aimed at Norwegians, although Rumi likes to imagine that in any given moment a good half of Bergen's residents are sitting with their ears held close to an illicit wireless in a subtle act of defiance, humming to some light music that balances the oppressive air of the outside world.

'Perfect,' says Marjit, smoothing down her hair. 'Coffee? I've been saving the good stuff Jens brought.'

There's no need to answer, and Rumi doesn't stand on ceremony or wait for Marjit to settle with her. Instead, she pulls out a box next to the sideboard and lays out the necessary equipment – one wooden spindle each – and divides up the material from a linen sack, handfuls of puffy white wool alongside an equal amount of jet black. Marjit's clearly been shopping up in the hills of her cousin's farm, the cousin who shears and dyes the sheep fibres for her customers to spin.

By the time Marjit comes in with a tray of coffee and cake, Rumi is already in a half-trance, humming to the music as she instinctively spins the stick and ekes out the wool into a thin strand, pulling it to her nose to draw in the pungency of the lanolin, forever embedded in the wool.

She opens her eyes to catch Marjit staring at her intently. 'What's wrong? Have I got some dirt on my nose?'

'No.' Marjit sets down the cups. 'It's just, you look so peaceful when you're doing that. It's nice to see.'

Rumi winces inside, though she's not offended because it's Marjit, and she's right: Rumi is never so relaxed as when she's spinning or knitting, feeling the problems of her life, Bergen, the world even, fall away as the soft but sturdy wool runs through her fingers. Magnus is ever present, floating along with her, but he's not tugging or reeling then, as in her nightmares.

The two women are soon in an industrious rhythm, sitting opposite each other and spinning the quickly depleted sack into skeins. There are blocks of silence, or humming along to the music, only speaking when it seems prudent.

'I saw Jens today,' Rumi says, reminded as she swallows down the last of her coffee.

Marjit's eyes flash in the firelight. 'Oh yes, where was that?'

'Skostredet. Outside his office. The mission.'

'Did you speak to him?' Marjit is clearly holding on tight to her curiosity, and Rumi finds it faintly amusing.

'Yes, and before you even think it, I wasn't rude to him. In fact, I went in and helped him.'

'You did?'

Rumi laughs; the first of the day, if she remembers rightly. 'I can do it, you know. I'm not angry *all* the time.'

Marjit's smile disappears, her voice softens. 'I know, my love. And I don't mean it that way. I just thought you didn't like him.'

Rumi pulls at the last of the wool and breaks it off. 'Hmm, it's not unfair to say I don't like many people right now. But he's growing on me. His Norwegian is certainly better.' She flicks her eyes upwards. 'I wonder why that is?'

Marjit looks sheepish under her grey mop. 'Just being here, I suppose,' she says lightly. 'We could use the last of the coffee, but do you want tea instead?'

12

An Invitation

Bergen, 9th February 1942

Jens

'Me? You want me to come to a reception, as your escort?'

Rumi seems faintly amused by his invitation, rather than angry, and immediately looks down at her rough woollen working trousers and scuffed lace-up shoes, as if she might have to hold court and waltz around in the same clothes.

'Yes, if you could face it. Marjit said . . .' Jens strains his neck towards the kitchen where his aunt is clanking about with pans and making herself scarce with real skill '. . . she said you might consider it. For the cause, I mean. As head of the mission I've been invited, and it's a good way of me getting close to the city's dignitaries, feeding back those who are close to Norwegian Nazis and any potential Quislings. And it's right here in Bergen.'

This, he thinks, is bound to garner her attention. Not his request, so much, but the needs of the resistance. He knows from Marjit how she feels, how Rumi has withdrawn from

65

overt activity since losing her fiancé, in fear of losing another of her close circle so soon. Equally, he senses something in her – that she wants to be involved, and her holding back is a solid barrier against any more pain waiting to leap out and ensnare her. Equally, he's aware of mercilessly exploiting her loyalty, and inside Jens feels distinctly uncomfortable about doing it. When dealing with friends, or family especially, he's quick to remind himself that he's SOE. This is business.

'All right, I'll do it,' she says. 'How much trouble can we get into at a dance? But heaven knows what I'll wear.' She shoots him a look, brow furrowed, *all* business. 'Don't expect me to float in with some off the shoulder evening dress. I don't think I've got any make-up left, and there's no hope of finding any now.'

'I have some.' Marjit sweeps into the parlour on cue. 'I'll help you.'

Jens and Rumi join forces in flashing their astonishment, since Marjit has never been seen wearing so much as a smidge of rouge.

'You have? Where from?' says Rumi at last.

'It's your mother's,' Marjit says plainly. 'You were too young when she died, so I kept it for you. I don't think it's turned to dust – yet.'

'I'm twenty-five, Marjit! Don't you think I might have had it before now?'

'Yes, I suppose.' Though Marjit doesn't sound too sorry. 'But it's probably a good thing I hung on to it, with the shortages now.'

Rumi and Jens swap looks of frustration, coupled with a sentiment that says they would both put up with a whole lot more, because it's Marjit. He thinks he detects the hint of a smile on Rumi's blush lips. Fleeting, but present. In her eyes alone, there's a good deal of love for his aunt.

66

'It seems I really don't have any reason to refuse now,' she mutters as Marjit sweeps out again. 'For the cause.'

'Well, I would be grateful, and it will make my posting appear more convincing.' Jens looks at her directly. 'Two sets of eyes are much better than one at these things. You'll see things that I don't. Important things.'

'Why? Because I'm a woman?'

He reads it as an accusation – wrongly aimed. 'Because you're Norwegian,' he comes back smartly. *And I'm not. Not fully. Not yet.*

And then she does smile, properly and with purpose. Not smugly, but with a flicker of humour; it does suit her, just as he's imagined. Sweeping away the anger suits Rumi Orlstad very well.

13

Too Close for Comfort

Bergen, 14th February 1942

Jens

Jens is late, or he soon will be if he doesn't get a move on, not helped by the slightly too tight shoes borrowed from his landlord, which pinch his toes as he skates over the leftover ice towards the Hotel Norge. Even so, they're better than anything he has in his very sparse wardrobe; SOE agents don't tend to be issued with an evening suit for their kitbags.

His route takes him near to Skostredet and although he was only at the mission yesterday, he can't help making a slight detour to the end of the street and checking the STAPO or Wehrmacht patrols are staying well clear. Like peeking at a sleeping child, it's just something he needs to do for peace of mind.

But that's not what Jens gets. His soles clip noisily on the pavement where slush and new snow has been cleared away, although he hears the others over his own approach;

three soldiers, all Wehrmacht, pulling at the mission door and rattling at it noisily, shouting 'Hallo, hallo' up at the windows. Jens freezes at the end of the street, rapidly considering his options. He could simply turn and walk away, hoping they do the same; the building is in total darkness, and at almost seven p.m. on a Saturday they shouldn't expect any traders to be working. But perhaps that's their intention? Without an open door, the Reich can easily fabricate suspicions and force entry. And Jens really doesn't want them rifling through piles of seemingly innocent clothing, even if his precious hardware is buried deep within the office fibres. That would spoil more than one evening of his life.

'*Hei, Hei,*' he says in greeting as he walks forward, in Norwegian first, and then in broken German. 'What can I do for you?'

'Are you the occupier of this property?' one of the soldiers barks. He seems annoyed at Jens's sudden appearance, as if crashing through the door would be a much better return for having to work the worst duty of the week.

'Yes, middle floor – I run the mission office.'

'We need to search it,' a second one says, in Norwegian this time. His voice is softer, but the look in his eyes against the weak light is equally threatening.

'For what?' Jens asks, trying to sound jaunty. 'I'm just on my way to the Hotel Norge, for the trade alliance dance, and I don't want to be late. I'll happily come back tomorrow morning, early as you like . . .'

'Now,' the second one barks. 'We have strict orders.'

Jens acquiesces at the soldier's tone of voice; it's obvious that too much protesting will do more harm than good. He unlocks the outer door and climbs up two flights of stairs, mentally calculating with each step how he can steer the search party right instead of left once they get into the office – away from the transmitter hidden in the cupboard behind bundles of clothing stacked high. It was well concealed, he'd thought at the time, but equally hadn't banked on irritated Wehrmacht wanting results for their pains.

'You can see it's a bit of a mess, but that's the way with all this stock,' Jens says as he leads them into the room's chaos. He watches eyes under their hats turn from irritation to disappointment – there's a *lot* to search.

'Don't you ever tidy up in here?' he hears one of them mutter as the three go to work, fanning out across the office and picking at the clothes with disdain, wrinkling their noses at the stale odour of old, often filthy, fabric.

Jens stands back, adopting a nonchalant look. Inside, he's anything but relaxed, sweating under the collar of his suit despite the freezing temperature of the room. With one eye on the poking and prodding into cupboards and drawers, he walks towards his desk that's spread with his parapher-nalia, pocketing a tiny metal washer used for repairing the transmitters and rebuking himself for leaving it in full view. *Lesson learnt, Jens Parkes. Too sloppy.*

The third officer, the one who hasn't yet spoken, is getting dangerously close to the transmitter cupboard. He's throwing aside boxes and sacks of clothing with abandon, like someone determined to make this inconvenient search bear fruit.

'Is there something you're looking for in particular?' Jens tries to strike the right note with his tone; not too irritable, or challenging. More of an innocent enquiry, as in 'I'd really like to help you boys, if only I knew what you wanted'. He works hard to avoid the words becoming strangled in his throat.

It doesn't matter – all three go on ploughing through the piles of clothes and sacks, poking their gun butts into the rag mountains with force. The third man is now one box away from reaching the transmitter cupboard and Jens's shirt collar is uncomfortably sticky. He needs a distraction. A big one.

He fiddles in the desk drawer for the Swiss army knife he knows is there, flicks open the blade and takes a breath.

'Oh Christ! Shit!' Jens's forceful shout draws the glances of all three soldiers immediately, then garners their full attention at the sight of dripping blood, great globules splashing on the worn wooden floor. Jens grabs a nearby rag and tries to stem the flow, wondering if he's made the cut far too convincing and might really need medical help. But then, a superficial scratch wouldn't have done the job – and so far it's had the required result, all three crowding around him with a genuine, human concern. The third one quickly peels away, looking quite green, as the second one mutters: 'Idiot – a soldier who can't stand the sight of blood.'

Jens holds up his hand, gaining more effect as a river of red runs down his arm, staining into his shirt and nicely embellishing the drama. All thoughts of the search have faded into the background, and he guesses these three young guns haven't seen much war action yet.

'You need a doctor,' the first one – the mean-eyed leader – says gruffly.

'I'll be fine, honestly,' Jens comes back. 'I just need to stop the bleeding. My aunt is a doctor – she lives nearby. I'll go there, but perhaps I need to go soon?'

'Yes, I suppose,' mean eyes says, surveying the room and clearly assessing if they've done enough; the increased chaos certainly looks like a concerted effort. Jens holds himself

71

for the decision. Is he satisfied? Finally, mean eyes shrugs towards number two and they shuffle out, making sure Jens follows them, locking the door with one hand while holding his comically swaddled other aloft.

'Sure you're all right?' number two says as they go to traipse down the street to where number three is recovering himself in a doorway.

For a second Jens feels warmed, as if they are all just soldiers in a stupid, stupid war, and why don't they all just go for a drink and agree to disagree and stop this ridiculous farce? Then he thinks of what's gone before, the life-blood of those he loved draining away, and such a thought is crushed instantly. 'Yes, thanks. I'll go and get it sorted.'

Jens rounds the corner of the next building and slips into an alleyway, head peeking out to watch the soldiers trudge out of sight. He strains to look at his watch – he'll be very late if he doesn't move it now. Certain the street is clear of any more Wehrmacht, he slips back into the building and up to the office, stripping off his jacket and red-stained shirt, running his sliced hand under the cold water, freezing away the stinging pain. He did a good job; it's deep, and will likely need Marjit's needlework, but not yet. At least it's stopped bleeding; there's still work to do.

Jens dresses the wound with his basic first aid kit and rifles quickly through the piles of clothes for a white shirt that's big enough and looks vaguely clean, making a mental note to keep his jacket on through the evening. He sponges the worst of the blood off his black jacket and checks himself in the tiny toilet mirror for blood specks on his face. He'll do. Most importantly, the transmitter is undis-covered. Still, he hooks it out and squeezes the machine's bulk into a tiny space under the floorboards, the most inaccessible of his mission hidey holes.

'Jeez!' he says again, and wonders how he'll run on the slippery pavements to the Hotel Norge in these shoes, in time not to make Rumi even more irritable.

14

All for Norway

Bergen, 14th February 1942

Rumi

Marjit stands back and places her hands on Rumi's shoulders, both looking at the reflection in the dressing table mirror.

'There, what do you think?' Marjit pronounces.

The slight twist of Rumi's mouth does not signal resounding approval. 'I look like something out of *Heidi*,' she whines. 'As if I should have a stick and several goats around my ankles.'

'You look *Norwegian*,' Marjit presses with exasperation, fingering the sleek lines of plaits that she's painstakingly weaved and pinned to Rumi's head in a neat swirl. 'And German officers love that.'

'But I'm not out to attract German soldiers of any kind.' She squirms under Marjit's hands. 'I'm just there as your nephew's foil.'

'And to gain any information you can,' Marjit adds. 'Don't underestimate yourself, or your role.'

Rumi huffs at her own reflection. 'My face is too fat,' she bemoans.

Marjit comes from behind and cups her jawline, her fingers surprisingly soft for a former farmer's wife. 'It's beautifully heart-shaped,' she argues. 'I think there's many a woman who would give a lot for your bone structure. You should treasure it – it's your mother's face staring back at us.'

Rumi is drawn to the framed photograph on the dressing table. Marjit's right; if she replaces her own burnished red hair for her mother's vibrant blonde, it could easily be her smiling out of the picture. It's the image of Mamma she wants to remember, her healthy glow, and not the sallow, chalky complexion of Rumi's last sighting, despite the undertaker's best efforts.

Either way, she welcomes the reminders of her mother around the house, despite what sadness Pappa might suffer when he looks at his own daughter and feels the early loss of his wife. Rumi shakes away the disdain for her own reflection and pulls back her shoulders with determination. Even with the events of the last months and her reluctance to commit fully to the resistance now, she's certain her mother would want her to do this. *In a heartbeat*, she says to herself.

'Come on, then,' she announces to Marjit. 'Let's get this dress on. At least that doesn't make me look like a goatherd.'

She's set to meet Jens a few metres from the entrance to the grand edifice of the Hotel Norge, Pappa having dropped her two streets away in his ancient, grumbling truck. Not a limousine, but it has saved her shoes from the remnants of snow, and her from freezing to death. She and Marjit have rustled up a dress, but there's no elegant winter coat to accompany it – Rumi simply doesn't have one. Nor any jacket that doesn't smell of fish.

He's not there to meet her, and her angst – manifesting as irritation – is rising when she sees him half-running in her direction, something white on his hand standing out like a beacon. Oddly, he almost sails by her as she's stamping her feet on the ground to ward off the cold, looking into the darkness of the blackout. Behind her, the dim hotel entrance is barely lit.

'*Hei*,' she says, stepping into what little light there is.

He looks up from checking his watch, startled. 'Rumi! Is that you?'

It's only the animation on his face that stops her being annoyed. Somewhere deep inside, in a place she dare not admit to herself, she's pleased. Not to have delighted Jens as such, but that Rumi Orlstad does have a surprise in her somewhere; that the drudgery of war, the boatyard and the cycle of her routine life can be broken.

'Will I do?' She steps back. 'For the task, I mean?'

'Yes.' Jens nods repeatedly. 'If I were my commanding officer, I'd say you definitely pass muster.'

She cocks her head at the unfamiliar phrase. 'You look beautiful,' he qualifies. 'And very convincing.'

Rumi gestures towards his hand. 'What's happened?' She sees a smidge of blood seeping into the palm of the bandage.

'It's nothing – had to make a quick detour, that's all.' But the wince as he goes to make a fist says it's far from the truth.

'So, are you ready to go to work? For Norway?' he says instead.

Rumi takes in a breath, thankful the air is cold enough to centre her. 'Yes, I think so. Lead on, Jensen Parkes.'

'Teigen,' he corrects. 'In Bergen, I'm Teigen. I can't afford to seem British in any way.'

She hesitates to let go of the unashamed tease in her voice, but it's far too inviting. 'And we wouldn't want that, would we?'

The lofty, ornate meeting room on the hotel's ground floor is guarded by a STAPO officer who checks Jens's invite, and Rumi feels her goosebumps quickly recede, the temperature bolstered by clusters of people with drinks in their hand. Chairs, largely empty, have been arranged around the perimeter of the room, a quartet playing in one corner and a large fire blazing alongside. Though physically warmed, she remains stiff with caution at the sight of so many grey-green and navy uniforms, and it's only Jens's guidance that draws her into the room; his uncovered hand around the sinewy muscles of her arms makes her feel comfortable and edgy all at once.

'All right, I will have to do some hand shaking and introductions, awkward as they might be,' he says in a low voice. 'If you see anyone important that I should approach, let me know. Otherwise, just follow my lead, as we discussed before, and jump in when you want to.'

Jump in. What will she say? How will she act? People here might not identify her at first glance in this . . . disguise, but they will recognise her eventually as the girl always in a pair of working boots and an oilskin jacket, hefting boxes and packages from her father's boat, cheeks ruddy with heat or cold. They'll be wondering what the hell Peder Orlstad's daughter is doing here, dressed like a woman, in a midnight blue dress that skims her generous hips and shows too much cleavage for her liking. Thankfully, they won't know enough of her true self to question her politics; she and Pappa have been careful to conceal their outward opinions under the guise of a hardworking family, just getting through troubled times. Rumi's eyes skim the room nervously as Jens moves to pluck drinks from a roaming waiter.

'There's champagne, if nothing else,' he says. 'And at least we can dance if we're not talking.'

She is regretting her attendance now, her love of Norway notwithstanding. When was the last time she'd danced properly? Before the war, certainly, and never so formally. Besides, public dancing among Norwegians is now banned, though clearly it's permitted if you have a Nazi presence to oversee any potential dissent. And God forbid the musicians playing classics in the corner would dare to break into some lively jazz or swing.

Her eyes settle on a familiar face, and suddenly it's a focus. 'Over there,' she says to Jens. 'Don't look now, but at your four o'clock is the local Lensman, Einer Melhus. He's unashamedly in bed with the Germans, but if you want permits or the ear of the German command, he's your man to befriend.' She's feigning a smile but her voice is thick with disgust.

'All right, let's wander over,' Jens says.

On her arm, she feels something change in him – his confidence gathering, perhaps – and he strides with purpose towards the Lensman and his group.

'Good evening, might I introduce myself? Jensen Teigen . . .'

They are swallowed into the group and the conversation, moving from cluster to cluster, the dialogue focused on the week's news, which is dominated by a national – and legal – move to force all teachers to join a Nazi organisation, and to found a Hitler Youth. Of course, this crowd is generally in favour, and where there is opposition, it's only in silence, by omission. Rumi looks at the committed collaborators and hates them all the more, careful to re-arrange her face so as not to show it. She's furious at their weakness, but finds herself not angry at everyone or thing in the world; instead she has a focus for her disdain tonight, and it feels strangely liberating.

Jens leads her away after almost an hour of exhaustive hand-shaking and obsequious celebration of their 'German visitors'. *They are marauders, not visitors,* she wants to spit. *Nothing more than raiders, thieves and plunderers.*

'Let's dance,' Jens says, eyebrows raised, and she reads his suggestion: safety from more conversation and a chance to re-group.

'I'm sorry, I didn't imagine it would be so intense,' he says as they move across the dancefloor. 'They can really talk, this lot.'

'At least they don't seem opposed to your mission being in Bergen,' she says. 'Which means you won't be hounded. Or suspected.'

He purses his lips, eyes dipping in unison towards his hand, and she wonders if there's a link. 'The Germans only tolerate the missions because it makes them look good – more humane,' Jens says. 'In truth, they'd rather not have any outsiders.'

'It is working?' she says. 'Being here, tonight – are you gathering information?'

'Let's talk about that later,' he replies. 'Or we might just give ourselves away. For now, we need to . . .' he struggles to find the word in Norwegian and resorts to English '. . . *chit-chat.*'

'To what?' Her face is riddled with confusion.

'All right, put it this way: tell me about yourself. Your name, for instance. It's not traditional, is it?'

'No, it's Persian, I think,' she says, 'and Japanese, too. My mother's idea. She apparently said that, given the family business, any Orlstad girl would be instantly robbed of her femininity and so she had to stamp it from the very beginning. Something to carry me through.'

'And what does it mean?'

Rumi hesitates, considers lying and then decides against it; he looks genuinely interested, and she won't decry her mother's memory. 'Beauty,' she says pointedly.

He narrows his eyes and nods.

'What's that look for?' she asks, then wonders if she should have dared to enquire.

'I think it most appropriate,' he says, breaking his gaze and leading her to the other side of the floor.

It's what Magnus used to say, too. Only he never glimpsed her in a midnight blue satin dress, rarely out of her work trousers, in fact. But still he told her, snuggled up in the hold of the boat whenever they could find a private moment. Would Jens, or any man, afford her the same compliment if she wasn't using her place as a woman to outwit or spy on the Nazi scourge? She doubts it.

'May I cut in?'

They both stop for a beat at the voice pricking at their conversation – a distinctly German edge to his competent Norwegian. He's in uniform, though not the cold grey of the SS, his hand already held out to Rumi. She's learnt questions such as these from officers are almost always rhetorical. Jens tenses under her, though it's limited to his middle finger on her upper arm, but she's grateful all the same for his concern. This dance, she decides, will be for Norway.

'I'd be delighted,' she says.

The officer leads her away without a second glance for Jens, who hovers and then sits at the outskirts of the room, pretending to appreciate the scene, though she can feel his scrutiny boring into her back; the eyes of the room, too. Some locals stare with admiration, others a look of accusation; any Norwegian woman seen enjoying the company of a German officer is in a precarious position and needs to be wary. Every female has one phrase memorised and ready to recite as a clear deterrent to predatory Germans: *'Ich bin eine Norwegerin'*.

I am a Norwegian woman.

Rumi has to ensure that her consent to dance is viewed by all as a courtesy rather than pleasure, and she's careful to fix a contrived expression.

'Lothar Selig,' the officer says, by way of introduction.

'Rumi Orlstad, pleased to meet you.' The spread of her lips covers the lie. 'Have I seen you in Bergen before?'

Normally, Rumi avoids the gaze of Germans in uniform whenever she can, but there is no mistaking this face: broad, with a long, straight nose, sandy hair cropped neat and short. It's the scar that marks him out from the general blond, blue-eyed swathe on the streets; a deep maroon groove etched in the left side of his face, sweeping down to his chin. Close up as she is, Rumi can guess at its origins – it's clean, sliced, sutured and newly scarred. Its cause is no childhood accident, she wagers, or shrapnel from battle. Someone took a knife to Lothar Selig's pink, Aryan skin. Someone who didn't like him.

'I only arrived last week,' he says, 'and I must say I find your city lovely. Stunning, in fact.'

'Bergen always looks beautiful in the snow,' she counters. 'Do you ski?' It's a moot question. No officer, German especially, would be sent to this far north without the ability to move at a pace in the snow. 'There are some lovely paths up in the mountains.'

'Yes, when I have the time, I'm hoping to explore a little more,' he says. 'And what is it you do in Bergen, Frøken Orlstad?'

The music ends and the dancers come to a halt all around them. *Lucky escape.*

'Oh, I think that's my cue,' Rumi says. 'At the risk of sounding like Cinderella, it's my time to go. It's been a pleasure.'

'Goodnight, then,' he says. 'I hope we meet again. Soon.'

She peels away, walking steadily towards Jens but with effort. Inside, she feels poisoned by her duplicity, disgusted at herself for being so . . . so nice. She's never had to do it before, to be so false or flattering. Up until the war, life's inconstancies for Rumi had merely been unpredictable tides and cantankerous sailors. But then, her country has never been invaded in her lifetime before. And needs must.

Jens stands when he sees her face. 'Everything all right?'

'Can we go now?' she says.

15

A Predator Comes Sniffing

Bergen, 14th February 1942

Jens

Jens is too preoccupied by the throb of his hand to feel the cold as they walk towards the Orlstad house, the jacket of his suit draped around Rumi's shoulder. The evening has been worthwhile in terms of intelligence gathering, if unsettling. He re-runs the faces, married with uniforms or civilian clothes, determined to keep them alive in his mind until they reach the Orlstad home and he can put names to descriptions with Rumi's help. He has to concentrate, though – finds it more difficult mapping one person than an entire landscape. Why, he wonders, are people far more complex than nature?

'Penny for them?' Rumi says, and it's Jens's turn to be visibly startled at her colloquialism. A British one especially.

'Marjit taught me that,' she says. 'Am I using it in the right way?'

'Yes, perfectly. And I'm sorry – my head's crammed full, and there's no room for any words in my brain.'

She seems strangely amused and leans in to whisper in his ear: 'That's the life of an agent. Perhaps a cup of berry tea will help oil your memory.' He thinks the slight tincture of champagne on her breath has oiled her good humour.

They're close enough for him to absorb the scent of her hair and her skin, a light and spring-like aroma, and it settles him somehow. He grasps swiftly at a sensation and pulls it close; a bright day in Marjit's meadow with the lambs, the farm where he spent so many happy holidays as a child. The same farm swiftly commandeered by Hitler at the war's outset, though Marjit – pragmatic as always – says the Führer might well take their land, 'but he's damn well not having our memories'.

He and Rumi come across several patrols, only one of whom asks for their identity papers, and Jens is able to show the party invitation as proof of where they've been and a good reason for roaming the city centre at such an hour. Rumi is virtually mute beside him, but he can feel the sizzle of her anger when her arm touches his.

'Bastards,' she mutters, as they move away.

'Bastards who didn't ask too many questions,' Jens comes back.

The Orlstad house is echoey, and Rumi finds her father's bed vacant. 'He'll be next door,' she says. 'He can't bear an empty house.'

Marjit welcomes them into her warm parlour and offers up tea automatically. 'Though I've only a few berry leaves left, and it'll be quite weak,' she adds. Jens only has to look at his aunt for her to pluck out her first aid box and begin laying out bandages, steeping a needle in boiling water.

Peder sits in front of the fire with a weary, glassy film on his eyes. 'Have a good evening?' he asks.

They both nod. 'The music was a bit tame, but yes,' Rumi says.

'And it was useful,' Jens agrees.

Marjit turns up the radio slightly and begins teasing away Jens's makeshift bandage, shooting him a stern look on seeing how deep the cut is. But as she begins her work, no one prods him for details. He's SOE – best left unsaid. With the wound freshly dressed, Rumi makes more tea and they get down to the debriefing: Jens offering his descriptions and Rumi confirming the names of those she knows, Marjit and Peder pitching in with identities of the older dignitaries.

'That sounds like Nils Marken buttering up the Germans,' Peder grumbles in disgust. 'He and I grew up together, always called himself a patriot. Bloody Quisling!' He almost spits his repugnance into the fire.

Jens scribbles furiously in his small notebook, though it's in code – his own – and he'll burn the pages once he's etched everything into his memory.

Rumi fails to mask a yawn, looking suddenly drained. 'There's just one more name I need,' Jens says. 'The officer you danced with.'

'Lothar Selig,' she reports casually.

Jens's pencil skitters across the page. Not for the first time that evening a river of ice runs through him, despite the fire's glow. 'Selig. Are you sure?'

'Yes, I won't forget that face in a hurry. Why? Do you know him?'

'Of him. By reputation, unfortunately.' He wonders if Selig's appearance in Bergen and this evening's mission raid are merely a coincidence.

Jens senses his disquiet spread across the room, watches Marjit's face take on his concern. 'He's Abwehr – German

Military Intelligence,' he explains. 'Which means he must be here to seek out SOE operatives, radio bases and anything else he can find and destroy. Selig has a fearsome reputation for doggedness. He brought down a whole network in the Netherlands. Seems his eye might be turning towards Norway.'

'Do you think he recognised you?' His aunt's face is openly worried now.

Jens shakes his head. 'I doubt it. We're pretty faceless, and Selig won't care about that anyway. It's the code-names and signals that he'll want to root out, catching agents in the act – the chase is his pleasure, I've heard. Along with the punishment.'

Somewhere amid the crackle of the wood, there's a slight moan from Marjit.

'And he has the latest equipment,' Jens goes on. 'The terrain and the mountains will hamper him, but with enough men and time, he can feasibly comb over this coastline and pinpoint exactly where we're broadcasting from.' He sighs. 'So it looks like I've got my work cut out for me.'

'And all the more reason to keep everything in this room absolutely confidential,' Marjit commands with a dark frown. 'No loose talk on the boats or in the bars.' She looks accusingly at Peder, who shrugs in receipt of her order. 'We have to keep everyone safe. *Everyone*. Agreed?' Her face is ablaze; this is Marjit at her most determined.

They nod in silence, the radio's tinny sound tempering the solemn atmosphere.

It's broken by another yawn from Rumi. 'I'm so sorry, but I've got to go to bed. Early start for me.'

'But it's Sunday tomorrow,' Jens points out.

'And?' She half laughs. 'Do you think the herring know

that? There's a boat to get out, and lots more to do.' She turns towards Peder. 'Pappa, are you coming? You're captain of that boat, remember?'

'I'll be a few minutes behind you, my love,' he says dutifully.

Jens watches from the corner of his eye as Marjit sees her to the door, absorbing their intimacy. 'Make sure Pappa comes soon,' Rumi pleads. 'He gets tired now, and Rubio will be in a foul mood if he's the one left to organise the rest of the crew, with me as a referee between them.'

'I'll turn him out in a minute,' Marjit assures her. She pulls back and sweeps her eyes over Rumi from head to foot, takes in a satisfied breath.

'What?'

'You look lovely, that's all,' the older woman says. 'Beautiful. I wanted to appreciate it fully before you climb back into your oilskins.'

Rumi scoffs. 'I'm the same person, Marjit – in or out of a dress. And my oilskins are a damn sight more comfortable than this outfit, I can tell you.'

16

Stepping on Eggshells

Bergen, 15th February 1942

Rumi

Pappa is gone from the house by the time Rumi wakes at seven, with a nagging headache and a dry mouth. She's not used to that much champagne – or any champagne, for that matter. She must have been tired, she reasons, having slept through Pappa's noise upon getting up. He's left his usual trail of destruction in the boathouse, and she wakes herself by doing the heavy manual work first – tidying, mending several nets and stacking the fish pallets – her body soon warm with exertion and her breath clouding the freezing air.

They call it the boathouse, but in reality, it's more of a storage shed for the assorted supplies carried around the islands on her father's boats. Pappa likes to think of himself as a fisherman first and foremost, but there are few commercial anglers living in Bergen anymore – it's mostly seasonal whalers, as the real fishing families live out on the islands. Which is why Pappa likes to go chasing herring when he can, to stroke at his nostalgia, to think of himself as a man living from the sea. And why Rumi may never escape its smell.

Jobs done, she places a pot of weak barley coffee to heat on the small stove and pulls out the thin ledger wedged behind the hot metal, the edges of its pages singed and a little crisp. With one ear listening out for any approaching footsteps, Rumi goes through her own neatly written code – details of the week's boat traffic in and out of Bergen's harbour and the surrounding landing points. The sister ledger that's open alongside is thicker and busier, containing the balance of Pappa's legitimate stocks in and out of the boatyard; the ledger that the Reich's ruling *Kommissariat* are welcome to scrutinise at any time. Aside from the odd times when Peder and Rubio might venture a little far out beyond the Reich's fishing cordon, it's all above board.

But the thinner journal with its singed edges, that's for her eyes only, its coded lines for the numbers of arms and explosives, and sometimes a nameless person – an agent probably – brought in from Shetland. She has the perfect cover, being justifiably on the jetty at all hours of the day and night, helping to unload supplies whenever the boats dock. The information about undercover drops she receives only a day or so in advance, messages left by resistance ghosts at various points around the boatyard, often hidden among the most repellent of odours. She's watched the Wehrmacht officers wrinkle their noses in disgust at having to search the fish barrels for contraband; they pick at the surface and are loath to delve a hand into the ripe contents. So far their deep disgust has worked in her favour. This is the job she can do with her eyes shut, the one she's good at – the organisation – and the one she is still willing to undertake as it doesn't call for her to step off the quay and into the sea and its swell of the unknown. Last night, however, in a hotel she rarely has cause to enter, Rumi felt herself being drawn in again, little by little. She wonders now: Did I – *do* I – really mind?

Her tiny office is quiet, save for the gulls whining and wheeling overhead, yet Rumi can't shake off her fatigue; her mind just won't concentrate on the figures and her eyelids are heavy. She pulls out the already opened letter on her desk and re-reads it: it's from Anya, her best friend while at school. Though they became physically distanced when Anya's family moved to Oslo in 1936, they've remained close and write to one another often, albeit a little less often since the invasion. With what turned out to be incredible foresight, the Lindvigs emigrated to England the year before war broke out. Anya, however, opted to stay in Norway, forcing separation from her family by sea *and* a war. Though according to this latest letter, Anya is inching further west with a job as a hotel receptionist in Stavanger, south of Bergen.

The place is full of German officers, she writes, though the tone says that's not a welcome state of affairs. *I don't know what it's like in Bergen, but they walk around the place—* The remains of her sentence have been scratched out with black pen, the censors having been through the text with a fine toothcomb, though her true sentiments shout from between the lines. What Rumi wouldn't give right now to head out on the town with Anya, dressed up just a little, to have a drink or two and dance together with real abandon, laugh like they did as young and innocent schoolgirls. But there's little chance of that with almost no alcohol available to Bergen's real residents, and dancing banned. And no Anya, too. Stavanger is two hundred kilometres away and feels like it might as well be the moon right now.

Rumi stows the letter in her desk, twitchy and unsettled. It'll be hours before she hears the distinctive tonk-tonk of Pappa's trawler engine drawing into the docks; she thinks of walking across Bergen to see Magnus's mother, but the idea of dealing with their conjoined grief that sits like a grey mist between them makes Rumi decide against it. The guilt of not being an attentive almost-daughter-in-law she'll have to tussle with later.

Instead, she walks the ten or so minutes towards home, for lunch, and perhaps half an hour's knitting, something to focus her mind. Being Sunday, it's quiet on the streets, and Rumi's mind wanders, counting the cobbles climbing up the narrow lane like she used to as a child, her mother's voice chiming in her head as they counted together ' . . . ninety-eight, ninety-nine, one hundred. Mamma, I made it to a hundred!'

The back door to the cottage gives too easily as Rumi slots in her key. Immediately, she's on alert, checks in Marjit's window for any signal there's something amiss. But nothing. The air surrounding their row of cottages is unchanged, her and Marjit's chicken brood pecking and clucking as usual in the back gardens.

'Hello? *Hello*?' She wonders why she would be so polite to any marauding Germans invading her house, but her approach seems second nature. She edges down the hall towards a clanking from the kitchen, heart in her boots or her mouth – anywhere but behind her ribcage. Are they searching the house? Should she turn tail and run next door to warn Marjit?

The door to the kitchen sweeps open, a man in shadow holding something aloft, giving off a metallic glint. It's several seconds before her eyes adjust to see Jens brandishing a fish slice.

'Ah, good, you're here,' he says. 'I was thinking about coming to get you.'

'Get me? What for?' Relief dulls her irritation at the angst he's caused.

'Lunch,' he says. 'Well, sort of late breakfast, really. Your father said you sometimes come home to eat at weekends.'

She follows him back into the kitchen, feels the blanket warmth of the stove and smells something undeniably pleasant above the strong frying odour of cod liver oil. 'Er, I normally just have some bread and salt fish.' Rumi is unsure of what she's feeling with Jens here in her house, a hot pan on her stove.

He must sense her unease. 'I hope you don't mind,' he says. 'Peder said to help myself when I got up. And that using the eggs was all right, since the chickens are laying well.'

'You stayed last night?' she asks. Her understanding remains cloudy, making her words economical.

'In the attic room, yes,' he explains. 'By the time we'd sat up talking, it was late and your father offered me a bed. Better than walking home and having to dodge any curious troops. Especially with this.' He holds up his bandaged hand.

'I see.' On reflection, it was a sensible suggestion. 'And how is it?'

'Much better, thanks. So, would you like some eggs?' He smiles, though now he appears uneasy, as if he's treading on the eggshells that now sit in the swill bucket to one side.

'Yes, thanks.'

She isn't used to this. If she's lucky, Hilde leaves a plate out for her, but it's never hot or enticing. And on Sundays, Hilde's day off, there's nothing. She washes her hands, pulls them to her nose to detect any residue of fish (*why do I even care?*) and sits as Jens goes back to the pan. He's still in the clothes he wore at the reception, minus his suit jacket, the braces of his trousers loose around his back, and his shirt not quite tucked in. His hair looks uncombed and merely flattened by a hand. He looks relaxed, she thinks. *More than I am.*

Rumi surveys the kitchen; it's unusually ordered, the laundry stacked and the sideboard clear of debris, piled neatly to one end. This isn't Hilde's doing, since her idea of clearing is to push everything into one corner, books, pens and sewing teetering precariously until it topples into a fresh mess. And it's certainly not Pappa's work.

'Did you tidy up?' she says, failing to stop the accusation in her voice.

'Yes.' He spins on one foot to face her, lips pursed at her prickly question, scanning the tidied room. 'Sorry, I can see now it looks presumptuous. I was just trying to make myself useful, to repay the hospitality.'

'And are you some sort of homemaker back in England?' Now she's trying desperately to inject some humour into her voice, to defuse the moment.

'Me?' He looks faintly confused. 'Oh, I see. No, it's the consequence of army training, I'm afraid. "Clean house, clean mind", or so they say. Though they might actually be right.'

'And so what must you think of our slovenly house then?'

'I think,' he says, placing a plate of eggs and bread in front of her, 'that it's the house of a hard working family. And a home.'

Rumi surveys the fried eggs, their yellow centres slightly soft, glowing, reminding her of a sun that hasn't shone so brightly in a long time. In every way. And this room hasn't felt like a real home for much, much longer, without Mamma, or Magnus's big frame almost skimming the ceiling when he came for dinner. Even Pappa works so hard that now he rarely sits in the parlour chair by the stove and falls asleep with his pipe tipping from his lips. Looking at her plate, though, Rumi feels a pinch of that comforting sensation – taste, smell and aura combined – and she hauls it to her chest until each delicacy is absorbed or melts away. The home of old, in two heartbeats. And then it's gone.

'Are they all right?' Jens punctures the daydream. 'My mother thinks I don't cook the yolks enough, but I like them soft.'

She cuts into the eggs and the yellow-orange curd flows out. It's just how she likes them, too. And they taste good, salted just right. 'Perfect.' She swallows down a mouthful. 'So, you two were up until the early hours?' she adds, conscious of their awkward small talk.

Jens looks apologetic. 'Your father seemed very keen to talk, but in all honesty, I do find his stories of sea life fascinating, and intriguing.'

Rumi sighs internally. It's funny how those on dry land revere the life of a man on the sea as romantic and in some ways mystical, when the reality is long hours, back breaking work and the enduring taint of fish. Not forgetting the inherent dangers of putting your life in the hands of the ocean and its powers, mythical or not, each time you go to work. Outsiders only see that her father owns a total of three trawlers and has carved out a steady living, not that he faced bankruptcy or barely saw his family as he built his business over many years. But she's too weary to object or explain now.

'It's clear that he loves fishing,' Jens says. 'I just wonder why he's been drawn into doing other things – the transport and such.'

'It was my mother,' Rumi explains. 'Pappa grew up on Sotra, in a fishing family, and he'd still be there if he hadn't fallen in love with her. She didn't mind being a fisherman's wife, but she did object to living so far out on the island. She was Bergen born and bred, and so he followed her back here, and he had to adapt, I suppose. The fishing in Bergen is piecemeal, but Pappa still thinks of himself like that, and it is quite useful – there are plenty of things you can hide well in a stinking barrel of herring.'

Jens clears away the plates. 'Talking of which, I thought I'd come down to the boatyard sometime today, perhaps when Peder gets in,' he says casually. 'He said he'd take me over the routine, for when we go out.'

'Go out?' Rumi's interest is piqued.

'Er, yes. I'll need some transport soon' – she notes straightaway that he's being deliberately vague – 'and your father is willing.'

The scrape of Rumi's chair is unequivocal; pushed back in anger across the wooden floor. 'Willing? Or persuaded?' she aims at him, noting the flame in her own voice already. Let him hear it. She *is* angry.

'I-I don't understand . . .' Jens stutters. 'He said—'

'Clearly, you *don't* understand,' she seethes in a dull whisper. 'We are in sympathy with the resistance, and we will do a lot to help. We already run messages, receive supplies and rescue agents from the mountain. We help organise what we can to save our country from these bastard invaders. But what we don't do is go out there and put our lives at risk on the sea to ferry agents or arms. Not anymore.'

She stops, nostrils flared like some fiery dragon, her stance and the sudden silence posing the challenge: *explain yourself, Englishman.*

He takes up the mantle, his voice equally determined. She detects some regret in his tone, but he's not about to back down. 'I promise you, Rumi, I did not ask your father.

He offered, and then insisted when he knew I'd have need of a boat soon. He *wants* to help.' He pauses and takes a breath, calmer. 'Do you think I'd dream of asking him now, after knowing about your fiancé—'

'You know nothing!' she blazes, feeling her features crumple, from anger to abject sorrow in one half second, whipping her face away. 'Nothing.' Her voice tails off in the hallway as she turns and heads back out of her own kitchen, seeing her knitting bag tidied into one corner and grabbing it instinctively, hearing him sigh deeply as she goes. So much for a quiet lunchtime escape.

In the boathouse, Rumi hunkers in front of the stove, curled into one of the chairs that the lovely Rubio nailed together out of pallets, with Marjit's handmade cushions for defence against splinters. Despite the fading light, she knits quickly, weaving the wool from memory and touch. It's taken half an hour of frantic stitching for her fury to abate, to re-run the exchange between her and Jens and think of it differently. She flew off the handle, she knows it now, too quick to blaze with blame. But it doesn't excuse Jens, does it? If he knows about Magnus – and clearly Marjit has told him – then he should be prepared to refuse Pappa's offer categorically: lie, tell him another boat owner is already engaged, but don't let her father risk the sea or capture. Please. Not after Magnus. It's entirely selfish to own such thoughts, but who else would she have left? Marjit, yes, and Rubio as the nearest she'll get to a brother, but not her blood family, to share life, and the future with, whatever it might be. It's bad enough that Pappa goes out to sea at all, but experienced fishermen watch the weather; they are wary of it and honour its warnings. They stay on dry land when the Kraken threatens to rise. The war doesn't allow that respect; when agents need picking up, it's often at a specified time or place, narrowed to one day, or else they're running over snow and mountains from determined Nazi patrols, sometimes for days or weeks. More than one has perished in the cold from being hounded. And so the sailors feel duty bound to set forth in any weather, to pluck the agents to relative safety at the appointed time. And that's what Pappa would do, what he *will* do now. Rubio, too, out of loyalty. It's what terrifies her the most.

The knitting is in her lap and the fire down to the embers when the tell-tale chug of the approaching trawler rouses Rumi from her doze. She gets up and moves outside to the jetty, watches Rubio's face light up as she grabs the ropes and helps tie up the boat, relief that there's another hand to help unload the day's herring catch, though it's fairly meagre for this time of year.

Pappa shuts down the engine, secures the wheelhouse and climbs onto the quay. Despite his late night and early start, plus a full day's fishing, he doesn't seem weary now, though Rumi knows he'll be asleep at the table this evening by the time she's cleared his plate of stew. But they have things to discuss, before she allows him the luxury of deep slumber.

'I want to talk to you later,' she mutters to her father, out of Rubio's earshot. Her look is unambiguous and his return glance says he knows exactly what's in store.

17

The Scales

Hop, 20th February 1942

The cots are still empty, along with the beds set side by side, three to a room in places, but she suspects they won't stay vacant for long. One downstairs room has been earmarked for a 'special purpose', though the bed that's been moved in looks to her like a doctor's examination couch, and she's been instructed to make sure the cupboards are scrubbed clean, the carpets pulled up and the tiles scoured with carbolic. Elsewhere, though, it doesn't look as if they will be set up as some kind of hospital, and so their true purpose has yet to emerge.

Despite her mild protestations, Kleiner remains tight-lipped, though he's commandeered Herr Lauritzen's study as his office, spacious enough that they could have used it as a second sitting room, or another bedroom. Her heart sank when he announced his intentions, as it clearly means he's planning to spend plenty of time here, checking up on them. Already, she's wary of him, not just his uniform and his rank, but the swagger of his demeanour and the arrogance in how he carries himself. His smell, too, is off-putting, a dense combination of raw meat and cigars that oozes from the flesh sitting on his collar, his sweat obvious even in this cold weather. Perhaps a silver lining in that it's easy for her to detect the odour when he's prowling, leaving vapour trails in the corridor.

There's plenty to do, but she's not run off her feet, not like in the old days when all the family were here, when guests would come and go and the bedrooms had to be cleaned and turned around with regularity. The heavy snow has kept many of the servants in the house, but weather has never tethered her before, always out at least once a week for good coffee and cake, or into Bergen to watch a film. Now, though, it's the gossip she's keen to avoid – the talk in the village, and the whispers as she's waiting in a shop for some small luxury. As if people believe that everyone in the old house is suddenly a Quisling. 'We're not collaborators!' she wants to shout in the queue that hums with gossip. 'We've been commandeered. What would you do, eh? Leave everything behind – your whole life?'

But there's no point complaining, is there? People in this war have their own problems just surviving day to day, with their own principles sitting on a labile set of scales. And until she discovers more – who will sleep in the beds, and occupy those cots – she doesn't honestly know if she is merely a coward or a collaborator.

And if there is a difference between the two . . .

18

Into the Unknown

Bergen, 28th February 1942

Jens

He watches his breath billowing white against the early chill; nature has been kind and offered up its calmest welcome, the water beyond the jetty almost like glass under the still dark sky and only a ripple seen if you stare long and hard enough. Not being much of a sailor, Jens is relieved to be avoiding a rough sea and an upended stomach, but it also means they have legitimate reason to be out on the water today – not setting forth into a storm while other sailors choose to stay safe on land.

Calm doesn't equate to warm, though, and he blows on his numbed fingers, cursing himself for leaving his gloves back in his tiny room as he left in haste to make the six a.m. start. He imagines the tips of his fingers will be strangers to him for some hours to come.

'Here.' Rumi steps up behind him and holds up a pair of thick woollen mittens, hand-knitted in the complex

100

black and white pattern so common across Norway. 'You can use these.'

Her weak smile is the most he can expect, though he's glad her manner towards him has softened in recent weeks, since the day he cooked up eggs and then whipped up her anger, too. Peder has told him since that father and daughter succeeded in clearing the air; Orlstad senior explaining his desire – his *need* – to do more for the resistance. He told Jens that it took some convincing for Rumi to appreciate his reasoning, but that now she understands her father's fear isn't so much dying in this war, as not helping others to *live* beyond it.

'Thanks – very much,' Jens says to her, pushing his hands into the wool made crisp with dried sea salt as they throw up a tang of the ocean.

'Come on,' she says. 'We have to get you looking like a fisherman if we're to pull off this ruse.'

The tall, dark-haired and olive-skinned Rubio – the Spanish portion of his genes trouncing the blond, blue-eyed Norwegian – is already rolling barrels towards the foredeck and lashing them down. To the pilots, with their bird's-eye view from the cockpit of German fighters patrolling the skies, they are innocent herring tubs. Today though, these are packed tight with guns and grenades, a far more valuable catch for the resistance groups in receipt.

Jens climbs into his oilskins, sees Rumi do the same and – to his utter surprise – she hops on deck as they cast off and cause the first ripples in the harbour's glossy surface. His startled expression is poorly concealed.

'I couldn't let you all get into trouble without me,' she says in answer, though there's no acrimony in her voice.

'More the merrier,' is his weak response.

'You might think so, but don't let the other fishermen

hear you say that,' she counters, hefting a rope coil from one side of the deck to the other.

Jens is perplexed – at her comment, but also her tone; today it's humoured and light. Again, his brow speaks for him.

'I'm a bad luck charm, being female,' she explains. 'Myth says women on boats are supposed to make the sea angry.' The edges of her mouth tip up, perhaps with irony.

'And don't forget the one about that cursed red hair of yours making it extra perilous,' Rubio shouts above the throb of the engine. 'All in all, you're a real liability, Rumi Orlstad.' She picks up a remnant of seaweed from the deck and throws it at him, forcing Rubio to dodge and they both end up laughing like children in a snowball fight.

For one silly minute, Jens imagines the mythical hex of her red hair is the reason she's pulled her hat down low to cover every wisp, but then realises it's simply survival; any German patrol coming alongside will be immediately suspicious of a woman on board, whatever the colour of her hair. Yet from afar, in the way she moves across the deck in her heavy oilskins, already rolling with the speed as Peder pushes the engine, Rumi looks like any experienced trawler man folding and pulling the nets. In fact, she looks completely at home, despite her former fury at Peder's decision and her fresh distrust of the sea. Jens is perplexed all over again by this fearsome, and now seemingly fearless, woman: Is she really coming around so soon to her loss? Or is her good humour all for Peder's benefit?

As they move northwards out of the harbour, Jens joins her at the bow, where she's staring intently at the water and the boat's prow slicing through its calm surface.

'I wasn't expecting to see you today. On board, especially,' he says, watching her nod and bite down on her bottom lip.

'I can't pretend I'm happy about it,' she says quietly, 'but I have to respect my father's wishes, and I suppose I do understand why. Because of everyone out there fighting, and Magn— Well, Pappa has his reasons.'

Her voice is clipped, short, and she looks up at him, giving a brief smile that he thinks lights up her pale features. Her amber eyes are speckled with golden shards, and they remind him of tawny owl feathers, though he doesn't think he should tell her that. It's too personal, and this is Rumi.

'I owe you an apology,' she adds, 'for raining my fury on you like some raging old fishwife before talking to Pappa.'

'More a fire-breathing dragon, I thought,' he says. 'But equally, I'll take an apology from a fishwife. My first, as it happens.'

'And your last, if you know what's good for you,' she jokes. 'You haven't seen some of the old women down at the market arguing over prices. Even the Gestapo run for cover.' Her shell might be testy at times, but he's relieved at her mood today. And despite the slight churn in his stomach as they lurch over an increasing swell, it makes Jens feels strangely untroubled.

Peder has set a course north-west, but in the wheelhouse he's singing tunelessly, clearly navigating by sight of the craggy coastline and the coloured wooden houses that look as if they are about to topple from the cliffs into the foaming waves below. Jens follows the lead set by Rubio and Rumi in looking busy on deck, pretending to ready the nets and waving casually to a couple of boats heading back into Bergen. After weaving through the narrow fjord, they head north and alongside the island of Sotra, eyes scanning constantly for signs of Nazi vessels; resistance look-out posts have detected an increase in German naval units, prompting more sea patrols to offset any sabotage attempts on the Reich's precious fleet. With the arms hiding in plain sight on deck, and the transmitter from the mission house stuffed under blankets in the galley, Jens doesn't relish being boarded and searched.

The long, stretched coastline of Sotra becomes a thin peninsula as they chug on, the weak winter sun rising higher, though it's colder than Jens imagined with only a calm breeze. Every human breath pushes out puffs of steam, white enough to match the snow caps on the surrounding hills. Instinctively, he starts to shiver, cursing himself again for not wearing enough layers and knows that once he sheds his oilskins on arrival, he'll be very, very cold. After his unceremonious landing in Bergen, it's another mistake to learn from. Training in Scotland had taught them plenty: how to hide currency in sealed tobacco tins, to write notes and maps on silk, and the art of blowing up a battleship with limpet mines fastened to the hull, but not the bone-aching temperatures of a Norwegian winter. Those boyhood memories of holidays with Marjit must have adopted a sugar coating, blocking out the reality.

He hears Rumi's voice over the chattering of his own teeth. 'Come on, let's go below. It'll be a little while before we get there.'

Gladly, he follows her to the tiny galley with a small stove, and she lays a flame under a metal pot. 'It's your life-saving soup again,' she says on turning. 'Though probably just cabbage at this time of year. Rationing, you know.'

'I don't care, as long as it's hot,' he says, arms wrapped around himself.

Rumi rummages under one of the wooden seats and pulls out a large, knitted sweater, black with a white speckled pattern at its yoke. 'Here, you'd better put this on,' she says.

He puts out a hand to accept her offering and catches

her expression as she goes to let go, though the tension in her grip lingers. There's a second's lull where the wool is held aloft in a gentle tug-of-war, until she releases and her eyes drop.

Jens's understanding catches up. *It's his, isn't it? He wore this, maybe only days before he sank to the bottom of the sea.*

'I'm sure I'll be fine once I've warmed up,' he says. *It's too much to sacrifice,* he's trying to relay in his refusal. *It's too soon for you.*

But his pity is poorly disguised.

'It is his,' she nods, 'in case you're wondering. It was. And if you are worried about that old mariner's myth that says it's unlucky to wear the clothes of a dead sailor, then you're obviously not as cold as you look.'

'I am as cold as I look.'

'Then put it on,' she urges. 'I don't mind, honestly.' Smiles warmly. 'And I promise it's only unlucky if you wear it on the same voyage.'

Jens fingers the thick weave, knitted in the same intricate monochrome pattern as the mitts he's already so grateful for, the sort of sweater so many around Bergen wear, men especially, marking them out as locals.

'Did you make it for him? For Magnus?' he asks, then instantly regrets it. Except that she seems pleased to hear her fiancé's name, as if the dead man becomes suddenly present in the tiny galley kitchen tipping to and fro, a live participant in their conversation.

She swallows. 'Yes, it was one of the first I ever made. To be honest, there are a few holes in the sleeve, and the pattern's gone wrong in places, but he didn't seem to mind. He loved it all the same.'

'It's beautiful,' he says. 'I don't know how you manage to work it so consistently, to remember how.'

'It's in the culture, handed down through the family,' Rumi says casually, ladling out cups of soup, then laughs aloud at Jens's exalted expression. 'And we do work from patterns, too! We're not just old ladies in rocking chairs, whiling away life with knitting needles.'

The soup is interrupted by Rubio's sudden appearance at the galley entrance.

'*Hei,* we're approaching the landing point,' he says. 'Up top, you two.'

'Aye, captain,' she says with a mock salute.

As they climb onto the deck, the trawler draws alongside a wooden jetty at the south end of Rongoy Island, nuzzling the upper end of Sotra. It's almost deserted, a few houses visible from the boat; Rumi reports there's only a handful on the isle's main village of Rong, directly in front of them. But it's only one house he needs to find.

Rubio ties up the boat and Peder jumps down from the wheelhouse, pipe in situ.

He turns to his daughter. 'Are you prepared to go ashore with Jens? I'm probably too slow, and although Rubio is happy to, I think it looks better if you're stopped. It's only for a short while.'

Jens catches the flash in Rumi's eyes – irritation, surprise or scornful mirth, he can't tell – but she nods without hesitation.

'Sure?' Jens checks.

'Yes, fine,' she confirms. Underneath her woollen layers and well-contrived armour, he can't tell what she's really thinking.

He's deliberately not released any details of his task until now – resistance rules, and it's safer for all. It's a simple assignment: he and Rumi will take the suitcase transmitter to the safe house acting as a radio substation, while Peder and Rubio motor into a small crevice that is the drop point for heavy equipment and unload the arms, before returning to pick them up. The word from his SOE colleagues is that all on the island are patriots, if not actively in league with the resistance. Other partisan groups will then collect the cache and distribute the munitions as needed.

It's late morning and the sun sits in purdah behind a wide seam of cloud, but the temperature is well below freezing and smoke spirals out of the chimneys of several houses dotted about.

'How does anyone live out here?' he mutters, more to himself than Rumi. 'It's so remote.' He thinks of all the luxuries he was brought up with and those he misses now – plentiful food, good coffee and special birthday teas at The Ritz. Here, nothing in his eyeline is soft or warm. Not a hint of respite from this cold, hard land.

'They're used to it, I suppose,' she replies. 'Born with pretty thick skin, and keep themselves to themselves. I do love the quiet but I think like my mother – it's just too remote for me.'

The two hop off onto a jetty barely three planks wide.

'Two hours?' Jens turns back to Peder.

'Two,' the old man confirms. 'Or the same time tomorrow.' It's a common plan, not to risk the boat hovering and arousing suspicion, instead heading back to Bergen with purpose and returning the next day. Even so, Jens hopes it won't come to that.

He and Rumi hoist a large rucksack each, one with the transmitter padded out with blankets, and the other full of tinned food and a few luxuries, including precious bags of real tea and coffee. They climb several steps worked into the rock, and the wind hits as they reach the top; Jens is grateful for his woollen insulation, his cheeks smarting with the salty gusts flurrying about.

'A fairly mild day on Rongoy,' Rumi quips, and scans with her eyes narrowed against the wind. 'Did you say it's a blue house we're looking for?'

'Yes, blue clapperboard with a small porch.'

Fifty or so metres ahead they find it — alongside an identical blue building, each with a porch.

'Which one is it?' Rumi asks. 'Any other features to look out for?'

'No,' Jens says, feeling a tight gathering of nerves in his stomach. Choices like this are not comfortable to make. Rong village has a tiny population, and there aren't many places to run, but the German patrols are frequent visitors to the islands, to pick up information, or 'chat' to the locals in their subtle but threatening manner. 'Have you a gut feeling?' he asks Rumi.

She shakes her head slowly. 'No, I suppose we have to pick one and hope for the best.'

They approach the first, Rumi leading them up what passes for a dirt path. There's a tiny glow of firelight from inside as she raps on the wood. They hear a faint scrabbling inside and it's a good half a minute before the door opens a few inches. A woman stands stiffly in the gap, her face pale and her eyes wide with surprise.

Rumi speaks quickly, apologises and says she must have got the wrong house, while Jens observes the woman's face twitch. Nervously and stiff with fear. She replies 'all right', but doesn't go to close the door, instead gesturing with a flick of her lashes towards the blue house next to hers. It's not the actions of a woman simply giving directions, and it's then that Jens's concerns spike; there is something wrong. Something very, very wrong.

Is she signalling there are German troops in her house, lying in wait behind the door? Or is this woman fearful of anyone invading her peaceful existence, a potential risk to her family and the baby they can hear crying in the background?

He nods at her slowly, one, two, three times, indicating with his eyes that they will go and leave her, presenting no threat to those inside. She smiles weakly, as if to say 'thank you' and disappears behind the door, like a mouse in a hole.

Jens and Rumi move the few metres to the next house and knock in a rhythm on the door, and the seconds they wait feels like forever, ears straining for any noise inside. A single, dead seagull is hung from the porch and sways in the wind. Jens's attention is shifted to its lifeless black eye and, try as he might, he can't stop staring.

'Good meat when there's nothing else,' Rumi offers, but Jens can't help seeing it as an omen. A bad one.

There's no point telling Rumi to go back to the boat, he thinks, because Peder has already chugged off into the distance and she'll be far more exposed on the jetty. Tentatively, he turns the handle and notes the door is unlocked. The rush invading their nostrils is immediate as they step inside: metallic and pungent, and they follow it upstairs, looking over shoulders with sharp movements and checking in every corner, stopping to listen for any breath disturbing the still but foul air.

They find the source of the stench in the small bedroom. It's Karl. Though they can only tell by the cast on his right arm and the shape of the body that's splayed in a dirty pool of red; his face has been taken away by a bullet, or a volley aimed directly at him. Jens hears Rumi gasp and then swallow it back, wholly relieved that he can rely on her not to scream, to keep herself together in the face of such vivid horror laid out before them.

'Poor bastard,' Jens whispers, as he spins to Rumi. 'There's one other agent – Olav. He might have been taken, or he could have got away. How well do you know the island? Where could he have run to?'

'Let me think,' she says, turning from the sight of Karl and his contorted body. 'I haven't been here for years, but there is a cave about a kilometre away that we used to play pirates in – it's dry except in a very high tide. That's the only place I can think. Did they have a boat?'

'Not unless they borrowed or stole one. And he wouldn't have got far up against a German motor boat.' Jens works to employ the age-old advice not to panic, but to calculate a strategy. It was easier being under fire in Dunkirk, he thinks – there was simply no time to analyse, only to run for cover. Would he rather be back in France, among the troops whose names he didn't know? Looking at Karl, a friend for only a few months, but a friend nonetheless, someone he'd been drunk with, who loved his fiancée and couldn't wait to get married after the war, then yes, he would. Death *is* harder to accept when you know the man who's lying dead next to you. He knows that all too well.

But there's no saving Karl now and all those weeks of training come to the fore. Reluctantly, Jens bends and touches the blood pooling near Karl's shoulder, feels that it's cool but hasn't quite congealed yet. His instinct is to hold his breath and repel the sharp scent of death, but he forces himself to draw in the smell that denotes it's neither fresh nor rancid. Not days, but hours old maybe. Rumi is silent behind him, as Jens nods to himself. Finally, he stands.

'It will mean missing the rendezvous with Peder, and staying in Rong all night,' he says, 'but I think we – *I* – need

110

to search for Olav. If the radio they had is gone, it could still mean he had time to grab it and run.' In reality, he fears poor Olav is already dead, or worse, in the Gestapo's hands – to be tortured and then killed. But there's Rumi's safety too. 'Do you want to meet your father at the planned rendezvous?'

'No.' She seems resolute. 'I'll need to show you where to go. But what about Karl? We can't just leave him here.'

'Let's search first, and come back once we're sure the Germans have gone. If they thought Karl was alone, they're not likely to return.'

She nods, but he catches her hesitation. Rumi steps towards the bed and pulls off the sheet that was once a home comfort to Karl, now acting as a shroud as she drapes it over his distorted features. He's thankful again that it's Rumi, with her obvious strength, to witness this horror; someone who knows death. Still, there is a deep sadness in her act, in cloaking the lifeless hand she once held to offset his pain. No comforting palm will help Karl now.

They check first in the shed outside for the transmitter. The hole dug beneath the floor has been covered over neatly, and to Jens it tells less of a frantic raid than someone plucking it out and masking their tracks. Olav. It affords some hope that the secret messages they can ill-afford the Germans to possess just might be safe. Something to be salvaged. Now they just have to find the messenger.

Rumi leads as they head for the cove, the wind picking up and noticeably colder, a stippling of sleet piercing their cheeks like pins. Jens's body is soon warm with the pace Rumi moves at, and his heart racing in anticipation of what they might find. She stops on a rocky crag before an obvious descent downwards, appearing to listen between each noisy gust.

She looks back at Jens and shakes her head. 'If the Germans were here, they look to have left already,' her voice rises above the howl.

Given the strength of the wind, they descend carefully and drop onto the sand of the small bay; Jens follows Rumi as she climbs again to the opening of a cave, the air inside thick with the pungency of old seaweed – it is a child's perfect pirate hideaway. At the mouth of the hollow, they both stop to gauge the feeling within for any presence.

When there's nothing obvious, Jens dares to call out: 'Olav? OLAV!'

They stop and Rumi closes her eyes, as if to concentrate the sound. 'Did you hear that?'

'What?'

'A groan? I think. Maybe,' she says guardedly.

They venture in, slipping on flotsam left by the highest of tides. 'Olav, are you here?' Jens calls.

They find him virtually unconscious, but still gripping the smaller transmitter he must have fled with, the pockets of his jacket stuffed with coded papers. It's not clear at first if he's been shot, but Rumi feels around his neck and palms her ungloved hands over his scalp, finding the gash responsible deep in the back of his head.

'It doesn't feel like a bullet wound and I'm sure he'd be dead if it was,' she says. 'It's possible he slipped on these rocks, carrying his load.'

Olav is semi-conscious, a stream of nonsense slurring from his cracked lips. Only the word 'Karl' and 'run' is identifiable.

Jens's decision is quick and direct. 'We'll all freeze if we stay here tonight,' he says. 'I think we get him to the house, and take our chances of the Germans returning.'

Rumi nods, her eyes bright in the gloom. 'Absolutely.

I'd rather die warm, if we have to,' she says, and Jens feels grateful a second time at her forbearance. And for the humour, rather than any anger, that's pushing forth from her right now.

19

Brandy for Comfort

Rong, 28th February 1942

Rumi

Rumi takes the radio set and scans the cave for any other evidence of their presence while Jens hauls Olav – who is tall but not heavily set – into sitting and then, in one stealthy move, pushes him over his shoulder in a fireman's lift. She senses the effort needed as Jens's face skews with determination, can almost feel the burn in the core of his long limbs as his muscles fight with the dead weight. Getting down from the mouth of the cave and then back up the crags is slow-going for Jens, but they agree it will be no quicker in sharing the load, only more unwieldy.

It's at least an hour before they approach the house again, and Rumi scouts a hundred metres ahead, again sniffing out any dangers before Jens moves forward with Olav's dead weight taking its toll. He's beginning to limp notice-ably and discomfort is etched across his face.

She hears a sound from the house next door, and guesses

it's the woman again, peeking out from her mousehole. Against the ripping wind, Rumi hears a faint click as her door shuts firmly closed.

Inside, they re-ignite the fire only when the blackout blinds have been fixed on the windows, then boil hot water and brew tea, pushing it to Olav's lips. He is still drifting in and out of consciousness, though his breathing is normal and he doesn't seem fevered. Rumi washes the crimson crust away from his head and confirms his wound is a gash rather than a bullet-graze, but it's oozing blood and needs closing up. Jens is up, searching the house to find the emergency aid kit and the supplies they need.

'I'm really glad you're good with a needle,' he says, as he holds Olav's head towards the firelight while Rumi does her best to join the rough edges of the wound with sewing thread. 'I know you're pretty adept with wool, but who taught you this?'

'Who do you think?' she says, her brow knitted with concentration. 'Marjit, of course. She's amazing.'

'She certainly is.'

With her eyes focused on Olav, Rumi can hear his wistful tone loud and clear, their thoughts aligned. If only they were both back there right now, in Marjit's orbit – her sanctuary – instead of nudging up against shades of death.

Olav is sleeping finally, and Rumi unpacks the supplies the safe house no longer needs, setting about making something warm to eat. While she's no expert in the kitchen, she would much rather tackle this job, her eyes rising to the ceiling where she can hear Jens moving about upstairs, breathing heavily with his attempts to roll Karl into the tarpaulin they discovered in the shed. She's grown up gutting fish and can expertly take the head off any variety, but seeing the poor man like that made even Rumi Orlstad recoil. She'd tried not to show it when they first found Karl, but the shock sent her reeling inside, her stomach contents rising rapidly at the sight of his maimed features. She recalled the brief conversation they'd had the night after Marjit set his shoulder, before he left for Dr Torgersen. He was in pain, but didn't allow it to dampen his humour.

'Put me in a sweater and I look exactly like a Norwegian fisherman – I think that's why they picked me for this mission,' Karl had joked.

'Can you fish?' Rumi asked.

'I know they've got a head and tail, and they taste good, but beyond that I'm lost. I grew up in the centre of Oslo.' He glanced down at his stocky form and then his swaddled arm. 'But I won't be much use as anything now.'

Strangely, Rumi's only saving grace now is that Karl's body has not been dredged from the sea, bloated and mutilated by the hunger of the ocean. Her tightly clad grief would not be contained at such a sight, sure to spill openly and vocally. Wherever death is, Magnus hovers still.

Rumi is relieved when Jens comes back down, leaving the body in situ but at least dignified now, and announces darkly: 'It's done.' She's certain neither of them will opt to sleep upstairs, preferring the tiny, cramped room on the ground floor.

They eat wordlessly, except for when he tells her the food is good, and suggests they finish off the precious brandy used to sterilise Olav's wound. 'After all, it's far too much to carry back.' He shrugs and gives a weary smile.

'Should we? Don't we need to stay alert?'

'I think we deserve it, don't you?' Jens says. 'Besides, I brought a bag of coffee we can use to keep ourselves awake.'

'Do you need brandy for something else, perhaps?' she

probes, gesturing at his leg, the top of which he rubs intermittently, wincing as he does.

He looks down, like a child that's been found out. 'Oh. It niggles, that's all.'

'Looks more than a niggle to me.'

'Shrapnel,' he explains. 'Dunkirk. I was too slow dodging a barrage from the Germans. Though it did get me off the beach via a hospital ship, so, you know, it had some uses.'

'And now?' she says, too curious for her own good. 'How do your SOE bosses view it?'

For a second, he looks truly contrite. 'It sort of never came up in training,' he admits. 'At worst, it's only an ache. With the climbing and carrying Olav's weight, it's just having a grumble.' He looks at her intently. 'I promise, Rumi, I would never endanger anyone − I can and will run through the pain, however bad it gets. I wouldn't do that to you. Your family especially.'

'I know,' she says. Truthfully.

Use of the brandy is not in doubt then, and in minutes it has the desired effect: she's warm and the shock of finding Karl is waning slightly, while the physical effort of finding Olav catches up. Rumi would be hard pushed to take flight and run herself, even with Germans hot on their heels. Her nerves are on edge, but her body is achy, complaining, and her cheeks are caked with a layer of salt and grime. For a change, she can detect the faint tinge of seaweed coming off her rather than fish, but she's too drained to get up from her chair and wash in tepid water.

They sip the brandy, one ear out for any untoward noise, but hear only the wind tearing around the house and the seagull carcass swinging against the porch.

'Thank you − for today,' Jens says lazily.

'What do you mean? It was hardly a good day.'

'For coming, first of all, and for what you did. I don't think Olav would have had much of a chance if it wasn't for your skills.' He pushes his head off the back of the old, battered chair to look at her squarely. 'You made a difference.'

'Not to Karl,' she says stiffly, but it's fuelled by a lingering sadness instead of anger.

'Perhaps not. But to the cause, yes. We can't use this safe house again, but we will get another up and running. Olav has a good chance of survival.' He pauses. 'To his mother that means the world. And it made a difference to me, how you were. No matter how much death you see, it's never easy. But it is *easier* when you don't feel alone.'

She doesn't voice it, but Rumi knows exactly what he means about loneliness and being alone. In those endless days after Magnus sailed for the last time, it was only Pappa, Marjit and Rubio that got her through, in their different ways; Marjit as a mother, Rubio holding her like a surrogate sibling, Peder sharing in her deep grief for his would-be son-in-law.

'We all do all this for one thing,' she says, looking at the dying fire and wishing it would spark into life spontaneously. 'For Norway.'

He nods, fighting his fatigue. 'For people. Everywhere.'

She looks at his lids drooping, at his body wrapped in the wool that she had painstakingly weaved for Magnus, loose on Jens's much leaner frame, and she thinks that, possibly, not everything she did today had been for her country; a little something might have been for him. And is that good or bad? Or even allowed, so soon after Magnus?

'*Hei,* wake up sleepyhead,' she says sharply. 'I think we need a large pot of coffee.'

20

Private Hall

Rong, 1st March 1942

Jens

They emerge from hiding the next day crusted with remnants of the sea and a night of fitful sleep. Jens knows he must have slept at some point, because there were dreams involving that blasted seagull coming at him with its beady eyes, pecking incessantly as if it were Gestapo trained. And, of course, his victim stayed close beside him. Always there to colour his nightmares.

He'd woken with a start in the darkness to find Rumi asleep, her long plait of hair tucked under her chin like a scarf, arms wrapped tightly around her body, but looking so peaceful. It was then that another wave of guilt hit him squarely – the first had been at the initial sight of Karl's maimed face, and the second on seeing Rumi sleeping so serenely, blissfully unaware of his own subterfuge. He shouldn't have brought her here. He knew the dangers all too well; at the very least he ought to have warned her.

Peder and Rubio, too. Did they know about the crew of the Shetland Bus infiltrated by Abwehr agents in that first year of occupation, luring an entire SOE cell into the lion's pit? That it was possible for Germans to be everywhere and anywhere, if they were astute enough? The men – British and Norwegian – had all been captured, facing months under Gestapo interrogation before a cruel execution. Amid his stirrings of self-reproach, Jens thought carefully: Would it have changed Peder's decision to transport Jens and SOE munitions? Given the old man's enthusiasm, probably not, but Rumi . . . yes, she might regret becoming embroiled. With Karl lying above them, murdered, she would have every reason to be furious. What right had he, a half-Norwegian, to keep intelligence from them – to offer up *their* lives for Norway, especially with this newest hunter, Selig, on the loose?

This fresh wave of remorse positioned itself neatly on top of existing layers stacked inside him, the biggest seam being Charlie Hall. So deep is his hurt over Charlie that he hasn't even been able to tell Marjit the true story. Not fully. Of how his best friend in arms for all those months in France, pushing forward and then retreating with the entire Allied force northwards, had succumbed so close to home.

For three days, he and Charlie had wandered with the remnants of their unit on the overcrowded beaches of Dunkirk, settling at last amid one of the endless, snaking queues of bodies across the sands, waiting. Just waiting. For rescue or death. Jens's mind had warped with lack of food and dehydration, imagining himself back home in London, on the no.14 bus to Piccadilly and sitting happily beside his mother. It was Charlie who chivvied, kept him sane, who gave up the last of his own water. Charlie who scrambled them both to standing when the gulls squawking overhead were drowned out by the ungodly roar of approaching Luftwaffe searing across the sky, intent on picking off prey that were sitting ducks on the sand. But it was Jens who said 'no', whose leaden limbs refused to move, lying heavy on the beige, grainy ground. Was he driven mad, stubborn or simply bad in that moment? Even now, he doesn't remember. All he knows is that Charlie, his constant shadow, wouldn't leave without him. They'd been a twosome since the first day at training camp in England, like twins, the company always joked. Together or nothing.

It was Charlie who stretched for Jens's hand to yank him to safety, turning to shout; instead of words, however, the perfect 'O' of his mouth brought forth a bubbling purge of red. It was his best friend who crumpled and fell on the Dunkirk beach, a strand of wheat under a scythe. When the sharp sting hit Jens's thigh a second later, like an angry wasp delivering its load, he thought logically: *that's only right. I should die too.* Amid bewilderment and hot, white pain, he looked down at the crimson stain spread across his thick, woollen trousers, lying with sand and chaos in his ear, and waiting for the second bullet, the one to pick him off properly. Motionless, he forced himself to watch Charlie's last laboured, bloody breath, to properly live the pain with him, until the blackness descended and the gulls went quiet, ending the nightmare that, nowadays, is never so silent. He believed it then, as he does now; he was the one who put the fatal bullet into the best, most loyal friend a man could ever have.

Churning with unease, Jens felt sick and hungry when he woke once more in the early hours to hear the wind whipping through Rong and battering the wooden slats of the safe house. Somehow, though, the immediate danger seemed to have passed; no one in their right mind would have been out in that, not even the most zealous of Nazi officers. The layers of his guilt sat heavy, and he wondered before drifting off again: *when would they stop multiplying?*

When he stirs finally, at seven, it's no longer pitch-black and Rumi is coming through the door, windswept and shaking her head.

'There's no chance of us digging a grave,' she says with certainty. 'The ground is far too hard. We'll have to take Karl with us.'

He doesn't need to answer, because there's no question of leaving Karl behind without a decent burial. The dead man's family will need that, and Jens knows Rumi understands it more than most.

They spend the morning clearing the house of any remnants, set a fire outside and burn everything that might leave any evidence. It's Sunday, and the few families venturing out in this weather have gone to church on nearby Sotra, so there's nobody about. Everyone nearby will have heard the raid and the shots, and they are shielding from any repercussions. The door to the house alongside remains firmly shut.

They are both on the jetty at the appointed time to watch Peder and Rubio glide towards the shore through a mist, and Jens notes the utter relief on Peder's face, seeing his daughter is both alive and standing. 'Aren't you supposed to be worried about me, my girl?' he says, pulling her in tight with both arms, showering the crown of her red hair with kisses. 'Not the other way around.'

'I'm fine, Pappa,' she replies. 'I need a bath badly, but I'm all right.'

If Jens isn't mistaken, she steals a glance back at him, as if to say: *We looked after each other.*

He nods, but inside his guilt fidgets uncomfortably.

With their innate pragmatism as fishermen, neither Peder nor Rubio baulk at the task of moving one dead and one injured man. Olav has roused a little through the morning to drink more tea, but his words remain jumbled in his concussion and groans of discomfort. They settle him among blankets in the hold, and Jens goes up on deck to help if he can, taking one last look at Rong as they sail away. It's hard to make out anything in the mist, but he imagines the mouse-like woman at her door, relieved at their leaving. He hopes her obvious fear, and the needs of her family, will fuel her silence if the Nazis come knocking again.

The journey back is unremarkable, though Jens stands at the prow despite the intense cold, eyes skimming the horizon and tensing with each sighting of a fellow fishing boat, suspicion buried in the friendly greetings across the water to each other. It's not difficult to fetch help for Olav in broad daylight when they reach Bergen; any fisherman could have slipped on deck during a voyage and need attention. Rubio runs for the doctor, who professes the wound 'well sutured', and then helps move the injured man to his own surgery rather than the larger clinic: who knows what Olav might say as he climbs out of his disorientated state? Karl is a different matter, and they all agree to keep him in the chilliest part of the boathouse until they're able to move him after dark.

'Are you sure you're all right with that?' Jens says to Rumi. The space is big enough that she won't be side by side with the body of a man she knew so briefly, but it is her workplace and − he thinks − her respite, too.

'Needs must,' she says, though it isn't clipped or irritated, just practical.

'I'll arrange something as soon as I can.' He smiles. 'I hope you get some sleep.'

'You, too.'

He thinks then of falling into bed himself, in his tiny, cold room across Bergen, little more than a cabin in the garden of a resistance sympathiser – stark, but well hidden – and then of the Orlstads' cosy parlour, with their stove fuelled by seasoned wood and aromatic heather, next to Marjit's equally warm house, and the tendering she would give him. But he can't risk too much contact, especially as the Gestapo and the Abwehr will be on alert after Karl's shooting. It's the perfect scent for someone like Selig to start sniffing out the network he's hunting. And after yesterday, Jens already feels too much like quarry.

Wearily, he makes his way across Bergen, through the city coming alive and people hopping on and off trams near Torget, as a weak sun arcs in the late morning sky. He passes a *kafe* on Kong Oscars Gate and is desperate to step in and satisfy his growling stomach, thinking that sailors must spend their entire lives being ravenous, but he's equally wary of the coded papers tucked firmly in the waistband of his trousers and under the bulk of Magnus's jumper, which Rumi didn't ask to be returned. Not yet, anyway. He trudges on, beyond the collection of wooden houses and upwards to a small churchyard overlooking the centre of Bergen. On the way, Jens has bought a small flower posy from a market seller, and looks casually left and right as he lays them on a flat grave, pretending to tidy the surrounding dirt and tiny tufts of grass, but feeling under-neath for a void under the false headstone and sliding out the small suitcase. Checking again that the space around him is clear, he moves quickly into the tiny church, sees it's also emptied of people, then slips behind the altar and into a small ante-room, through another door that sits behind a heavy curtain and into a windowless cupboard barely three feet wide, with a small table, a chair and a lantern. The clasp on the case clicks open to reveal his own transmitter, a conduit for the dispatches he needs to send, whatever the hour. Jens palms the exhaustion away and sets to work.

21

Fury and Fulfilment

Bergen, 1st March 1942

Rumi

Marjit is angry. Rumi is more acquainted with rage than most, and this is it. Since her mother's death and Marjit's adoption of the maternal role, she's never witnessed a side like this to her good friend, though she recognises the red hot hue of fury all too well.

'You could have told me!' she glowers at Rumi, who is drying her curtain of hair, bent low against the open door of the stove. Marjit checks herself and her voice becomes a hiss: 'I mean, not what you were doing, but that you might be away. I was worried sick!' Her normally pink cheeks are crimson, and not from any heat. 'A whole night with an empty house next door. You could have been anywhere, and my mind . . . well, it went to the darkest places.'

'Sorry, Marjit,' Rumi mutters.

'It was my doing,' Pappa says as he walks in, lighting his

pipe. 'It was my decision to go, and if anything, I'm the reason Rumi came along. She was looking out for me.'

Rumi shoots him a curious look: where was Pappa last night while she and Jens were in Rong? Didn't he come home?

'Rubio and I slept in the boathouse,' he explains. 'Better than being in sight, attracting too much attention.'

Marjit spins and re-directs her anger, but Rumi watches it dissipate into the evening gloom. She knows Marjit finds it difficult to be angry with Pappa. Frustrated, yes, with his laidback take on life. But rarely furious.

'Well, next time, just warn me, eh? I realise you can't give details – God knows, I don't want the ins and outs, but be kind to my nerves. Please.'

'Yes, Marjit,' Rumi says.

'Understood,' Peder echoes.

Her father stares pointedly at Rumi, with a subtle shake of his head. She understands: Marjit doesn't need to know about Karl, about the danger they were directly behind, that arriving an hour or so earlier in Rong might have meant one or all of them facing a messy or tortuous fate. It's over and they can't think about that, or they would never go on fighting. And Rumi is certain, without asking or confronting her father, that he means to go on. She saw it in his eyes as they chugged out of Bergen, and again on the return, despite the heavy weight of cargo in the hold. Perhaps it's *because* of Karl that Pappa wants to continue, to step up their efforts for the resistance.

As Rumi climbs wearily to bed, she surveys her own thinking. Since Magnus, the thought of Pappa and Rubio sailing off into Lord knows what had filled her with horror, certain to face peril from the sea, the German patrols or

127

the strafing by Reich bombers flying low in the fjords. The fear created by Allied bombers frequently whining over Bergen's streets and industrial areas is different somehow; their bullets are intent on destroying German industry and it's more like bad luck to be caught in it. The hole that her father's loss would create remains unfathomable to Rumi, but now the prospect holds a different light – not a cavernous black void, but something brighter, because of what he might achieve in the face of death. Should it happen, Pappa's pride would set the whole of Bergen aglow.

And how does *she* feel about the previous twenty-four hours – that creeping quiver of fear on Rongoy, the gruesome discovery of Karl's body, and the sharp spike of adrenalin in searching for Olav? She's exhausted, mostly, but there's something else she's struggling to recognise in herself, a little thing making her smile as she flops onto the blissful comfort of her own mattress. As she's sinking fast into sleep, it comes to her with rapid realisation: Rumi Orlstad feels almost whole.

22

House Under a Cloud

Hop, 8th March 1942

Up in the linen cupboard, she's doling out sheets again. It's all she ever seems to do these days, since the 'guests' finally arrived. All female, one or two to begin with, and then a steady trickle until the house is almost at capacity. When she was finally told by the reticent Kleiner to expect women, she'd imagined them to be German support staff, typists and clerks and the like, and she'd sagged even more at the prospect. She's always found men easier to deal with, especially with her advancing age; they treat her almost like a mother or a much-loved nanny, the hand that feeds them, and she feels that young officers – German or not – would be no different. Women have more guile, she thinks, and they are much harder to hide from, even though she's become very adept at concealing herself, having melted into the fabric of the house for so many years. These days, she hides from Kleiner especially, always extremely busy when he comes looking for her like a fox down a hole. He has the stench of officialdom in him, and perhaps a tincture of evil in his black eyes, too.

'These women must be treated with respect,' he'd instructed

her the night before the first arrival. In his tone, and the sneer poorly hidden behind his ridiculous moustache, she could see he had no such regard. His look was of pure disgust, but he has orders, clearly. She simply wonders what they are.

So the first that came were German, three midwives in all, followed by a trickle of strictly Norwegian women, some from Bergen, a couple from further up the coast. The German women are middle-aged on the whole, squat and square, austere but generally civil towards her. The Norwegian 'residents', however, all arrive with the same startled expression, pinched cheeks and eyes way too old for their young bodies, a waxen worry replacing the previous bloom of their cheeks. Without exception, they look baseless and afraid. There's one other crucial similarity: they're all pregnant. Some are sporting an obvious roundedness, others trying to mask it for as long as they can manage. More markedly, each one has no wedding ring, and there's no point pretending anymore, especially here. There are no babies yet to occupy the tiny cots; so far no woman is bumptious enough for that. But she learns quickly that from now on the purpose of the house – once a busy pillar of the community in Hop – is to be shrouded. No neighbourhood guests will be permitted to visit, no loose talk or chattering when she goes to the post office or out to run errands. Its tenants are tainted by virtue of their 'folly', as Kleiner terms it, and they must 'make the best of it for the good of the Reich'.

Is that how he thinks of this, *she wonders. Is occupying a country and stealing a nation making the 'best' of a bloody, filthy war? With everything they glean from the radio Gunnar has stowed in his potting shed, the Germans are ploughing across Europe like locusts. She knows little of military matters, but it's plain to see the war is eating up resources, and yet their invaders are spending money on pregnant women. Not the wives of Reich officers, but young Norwegian women. To what purpose?*

Her ruminating, however, won't get the beds changed or the kitchen in order, and there's so much more to be done now that one of the young maids had promptly left, probably as a protest to being lorded over by Germans both at work and in life. Whatever the reason, the girl needs replacing. Doesn't her cousin in Bergen have a daughter who works as a family help, and who's apparently good at cooking too? She wonders if this girl – Hilde, she suddenly remembers the name – wants a job? 'A fresh start' is how she could phrase it, to make the post appear more attractive.

Another question keeps coming back, though, the one she asks herself as a welcome flowery scent wafts about the linen cupboard: will I ever have the courage to take such a stand like that young kitchen maid? Am I too old, and too set in my ways now?

Soon to be set in the German way?

23

Hiding in Plain Sight

Bergen, 16th March 1942

Rumi

Life beyond the Tyskebryggen bench where she sits is industrious, and Rumi drinks it in; her beloved city is climbing out of its winter shroud, Bergen's bones finally emerging to reveal a little of the colour underneath. The glorious radiance of spring that seems so unique to her city is picking its way through the fading winter haze, the breeze replacing a fierce wind. It makes her feel lighter. Alongside the lingering patches of snow, there are still too many grey- and green-clad bodies for her liking, and she wouldn't normally hover so close to the German headquarters by choice, but she'd needed to access the northern-most wharf for supplies.

After an encounter with Hilde's mother in the nearby rope store, Rumi craves ten minutes' peace to quell her temper. From behind the counter, Fru Viken has never been shy about airing her views on the Nazis as Norway's saviours, and the resistance as 'troublemakers who'll get us all killed'. What would the old hag think about her own daughter unwittingly working for a family of diehard resistance, being infected by their wayward politics just by being in the Orlstad house? Rumi and Pappa are careful never to discuss anything while Hilde is there, and – lazy as she is – her presence does help avert suspicion from them.

'Hilde says you've been away, on and off?' Fru Viken had probed as Rumi paid for her supplies. 'Visitors coming and going, too.'

'Yes.' She'd smiled sweetly, intent on quashing the inquisition.

But Fru Viken wasn't to be thrown off so easily. 'Go anywhere nice, did you?'

'Just up the coast to see some cousins,' Rumi lied casually.

'Would that we could all take a few days off,' Hilde's mother replied tartly. 'I'm here six days a week, and Hilde works all hours. I do think, Frøken Orlstad, that you might consider giving her a raise, what with all this rationing. She's had other offers for her services, you know – the Germans would be only too grateful.'

Rumi thought it time to paste on her own sour expression. 'There is a war on, Fru Viken. Perhaps Hilde *would* be better off tending to our visitors and their needs. We'd give her a decent reference, of course.'

'Well, there's no need to be hasty, I don't think . . .' Fru Viken blustered as Rumi turned to leave.

It was bluff on Rumi's part, of course. Despite Hilde's tendency to be late, and to slope off to the dockside to flirt with some of the younger lads, she and Pappa couldn't do without the help. Not with so much legitimate and resistance work to be done. Besides, running a house has never been Rumi's idea of fun and her cooking is basic at best, despite her mother's natural skill.

So, the respite she finds on the empty bench is all the more welcome after the morning's encounter, the light focused on one corner of it looking out on the quay, as if tendering a special invite. Rumi sits and spends several minutes with her eyes closed, face into the sun, before she remembers an unopened letter from the morning's post and reaches into her bag, pulling out a single sheet of paper and staring at the familiar handwriting.

Dear Rumi . . . It's from Anya again. *It's very dull here,* she writes, *and the hotel is full of German officers coming and going, flitting about as if they're still on some sort of holiday. Those of us that live-in are stuck in our rooms when we're not working, and the food for us is fairly atrocious (though not so for the German guests). I long to come back to Bergen and see some familiar faces. How are you and your Pappa? Rubio, too?*

Astonishingly, this letter seems to have escaped the censor and the irritation in Anya's words leaps off the page. As much as she adores her home city, Rumi thinks wistfully of escaping for a day or so to Stavanger to act as a timely reminder of Bergen to her friend, but it's more than two hundred kilometres, and any journey would mean risking the scrutiny of roadblocks – if Pappa's truck could even make it – or else the watchful eyes of the guards on the steamer. For now, a reassuring letter in return will have to be enough.

Her eyes are pulled from the print by something blocking her portion of the sun's rays, and she looks up, a little irked.

'Oh, hello,' she says, surprised to find she's not too displeased after all.

'I wasn't sure if it was you,' Jens says. 'May I?'

'Of course.'

He sits, and she watches him quickly survey the area, rapidly totting up the numbers of Wehrmacht and Gestapo within sight. While she's always wary, she realises for Jens it must be akin to breathing in scanning every scenario for potentially fatal risk. And yet he looks relaxed, as if he belongs in Bergen. *All down to the training,* she thinks.

She hasn't set eyes on him in almost three weeks, since Rongoy, although once or twice she's imagined hearing his voice through the wall at home, but equally it could have been Marjit laughing heartily at the radio. She'd hoped it was the wireless, felt an unexpected pinch of jealousy at the thought of beloved Marjit − *her* friend − sharing intimacy with someone else. Jens especially.

Or perhaps it was more the fact that she wasn't included?

'How have you been?' he says, facing her. He looks to have eased into the Nordic way of life, his blond hair cut sharp into his neck and wearing the type of clothes Rubio would like to buy, if he didn't fritter his earnings away.

'Fine,' she says. 'I've been busy.' She gives him a look which he seems to understand. Pappa has been out on the boats almost continually since the thrill of Rongoy, though only locally, thank goodness, mixing his own business with resistance runs, sometimes with the thin pamphlets of underground newspapers tucked into boxes of supplies. It's kept him happy, and more importantly for Rumi, well away from a lengthy, perilous operation. She still dreads the day that − despite his age − he'll announce his intention to work the Bus.

'Have you?' she adds. 'Been busy, I mean?'

'Yes, very.' He nods. 'Always a lot to do at the mission.'

He's talking in code, surely? She wonders whether he's travelled out of Bergen, been involved in the sabotages she'd heard of, detonating explosives in warehouses with crucial German supplies. None of it is likely to halt Hitler in his tracks, but it does serve as an irritant to the smooth running of the Reich's occupation. 'A fly in the ointment,' she'd heard Marjit say once, and knew instantly it was an English maxim that she'd adopted from Jens.

There's an awkward pause and they both look to the water for inspiration; Rumi can't quite marry herself sitting on a bench in her grubby work clothes with the woman dancing at the Hotel Norge, Jens leading her confidently in her satin dress and coiffured hair. It seems a lifetime ago.

'Oh, have you heard how Olav's getting on?' she says at last.

Jens effects a false sneeze, which helps him to check left and right before he speaks. 'Yes, he's doing well, away from here,' he says. 'But very glad to be alive, and thankful to have a very neat scar.'

'Did you discover what happened?' Rumi finds she's suddenly enjoying the charade of them appearing to chat about the weather or rationing, and yet be talking subterfuge with a cluster of Wehrmacht only metres away. Inside, it thrills her.

'Once he recovered from the concussion, he remembered everything,' Jens tells her. 'Seems he was in the shed transmitting when the Germans arrived. He heard the raid, and then the shots that killed Karl. Olav followed protocol to get out of there fast and take everything he could. He remembers getting to the cave entrance, but after that, nothing. It must be when he slipped and fell.'

'So . . .?'

'As far as we can tell, nothing got into German hands. All the coded messages were hidden outside, away from the house. He took them all.'

'That's good,' she says. 'And Karl?'

'Decent burial,' he says quickly. 'I made sure his parents knew.'

'Knew?' The bloody image comes rushing back – Karl's face. Or the absence of it.

'That he was a hero. That he died for Norway.'

Died for Norway. Rumi knows it might be some comfort for his family. When will she feel the same about Magnus, that he died gallantly for his country? How long before she stops feeling that the man she loved was lost so needlessly?

'Listen, there's another favour I need,' Jens says, as he shifts on the bench, making ready to go. 'It is asking a lot, and you can say no, of course.'

It's clear to her then that he didn't simply chance upon her, sitting casually on a bench on Tyskebryggen as he strolled by. And yet she can't help but invite his request. She's running with curiosity – in danger of adopting the desire that Pappa already has. To do more. 'Go on, then.'

'Not here,' he says.

'You can come to the house this evening.'

'No. The boatyard, perhaps? When Peder's not there.'

'Tomorrow afternoon.' Rumi looks towards the bright rays, eyes closed. 'But I may say no.'

'I'm anticipating you will,' he comes back. 'But I'll ask anyway.'

She rises a few minutes after Jens's departure and heads towards the boatyard, spying Bjarne Hansen in the distance, strutting about in his STAPO uniform and dipping his head reverentially to any passing Wehrmacht. The sight of him disgusts her, and she's almost certain she will say yes to whatever Jens asks. In defiance. To be that bloody fly in the Nazi ointment.

★   ★   ★

137

It's colder and the sun has retreated when he arrives at the warehouse the next day. Rumi is poking the tiny stove in her office and grumbling into the embers, which refuse to take.

'Having trouble?' he says.

'The wood's damp,' she huffs. 'And I haven't any dry heather.'

He holds out a small package. 'It's not combustible, but will this help?'

Her nose deep into the bag, Rumi fills her nostrils with the heady aroma of a bona-fide elixir – ground from real coffee beans – and wonders how much of an addiction it can be.

'Oh, where do you get *this*?' She breathes deeply again. It's only coffee, but it's also so much more – normality, a life without war, of happiness, friends around a table with a warm pot at its centre, sharing food and fun and laughter. Memories they can only nudge at for comfort. Rumi looks up sharply. 'You won't buy me off with this, you know,' she warns Jens. 'I still may refuse.'

'I know that. But I do love the way it makes you and Marjit so happy. It reminds me of a child getting an ice-cream.'

'I'm delighted we're so amusing to you.' But her mood can't be dampened. 'Don't you want to keep some for yourself?'

He grimaces. 'I'm very bad at making good coffee,' he says. 'You'll do it far more justice.'

'Well, the least I can do is make a pot now and share it with you.'

Jens fiddles with the stove while Rumi fills the pot, succeeding in coaxing a flame from the embers. Closing the partition doors to her small office, they sit on the pallet chairs and hug small thermals of heat coming from the stove.

'So?' she says. 'Ask away.'

Jens takes in a large breath. 'I've a confession to make first.'

'Oh yes?'

'I probably wasn't entirely honest with you all before we went to Rongoy,' he starts.

Her red, expressive eyebrows lift in a perfect arch. 'Hmm?'

'You should have been aware of what could have gone wrong.' He pauses. 'What *had* already gone awry in the past.'

She considers, watches the discomfort move across his face, and decides that his remorse – his honesty – stems from something true. That he cares.

'Yes, you probably should have told us,' she says bluntly, and then watches his face fall. 'But if you're talking about the debacle with the Abwehr and the Shetland Bus, we already knew – me, Pappa and Rubio.'

'You did?'

'The underground press, and the grapevine, works very well in Bergen, you know – with or without SIS or SOE.'

'Sorry – on both counts.' He sighs. 'Lord knows I should never underestimate Norwegian resistance, but I should have given you the full picture.'

'Even if we hadn't known, it wouldn't have made the slightest difference to Pappa or Rubio,' she says plainly.

'How about you?' His blond eyebrows rise now.

'I told you already – I go where my father's mischief takes me,' Rumi says plainly. 'Who else is going to look after him?'

'Does that mean you're up for another trip?' He looks suddenly confident of grabbing her attention. 'For Norway, of course.'

She takes a long sip of coffee, using it to consider. Will

she? Rongoy was both scary and stimulating, and she wouldn't go as far to invite a close shave with death again, but yes, she does crave that sense of usefulness, of directly obstructing the invaders. 'What have you in mind?'

'It's a trip out of town, by steamer,' he says. Then quickly, perhaps sensing her disquiet: 'A stay in a hotel, just to absorb the mood, be a bit nosy and report back.'

'Is that all?' Rumi says. Only yesterday, she was thinking about the joy of a trip away, and now this seems a strange but nice coincidence.

'There is one other thing,' he says.

'What's that?' She's guarded, suddenly suspicious.

'We'd be going together. As husband and wife.'

When Rumi reveals the proposal at home, Marjit throws back her head and pushes out a noise, direct from her belly, giving off a hoot of delight no one has heard in months.

'It's no laughing matter, Marjit!' Rumi cries. 'How on earth am I going to pull this one off – being a wife, of all things?'

Marjit couches her humour, her eyes still dancing with amusement. 'Very well, I should think,' she says. 'Besides, it's in name only. And I can vouch that my nephew is a gentleman.'

'How do you know that for sure?'

'Because if he's not, he'll have me to answer to.'

'We'll have to share a room,' Rumi moans. 'How am I going to get a wink of sleep?'

'I dare say Jens is thinking exactly the same, though mainly because he'll be on a hard floor or the sofa. But that's the least of your concerns.'

Rumi lays her palms open: what else could pose more of a problem right now?

'Your wardrobe!' Marjit says. 'No matter how much you love them, you cannot wear oilskins in any hotel.'

Throwing up her hands dramatically, Rumi feels defeated already. She has one week to turn herself into the well-bred wife of a businessman. One that would wear a dress. 'It's hopeless then,' she says flatly. 'I can't go.'

Marjit looks at her with a rare expression of disappointment wrinkling her brow. 'Good God, woman, you're a Norwegian – never beaten. And when has any one of this earth's elements ever defeated Rumi Orlstad?'

All of them, since Magnus.

'So what do we do?' Rumi says.

Marjit adopts that look, the one which reminds Rumi of her own mother when she couldn't wait to throw herself into a project. Determined. Impish and roguish too. 'We beg, borrow or steal,' Marjit says. 'And we make you into a wife.'

24

Sailing Away

Stavanger, South-West Norway, 24th March 1942

Jens

The mood is good as he strides towards the wharf, his overnight bag in hand, and the spring sunshine winning out against puffy clouds overhead. It's unusual to feel this relaxed when setting out on a 'mission', but this is hardly a normal day at the office for an SOE agent; a decent hotel, good food and observation work that's become second nature of late. All those months ago, back at their training hub in the Scottish Highlands, Jens had questioned his own suitability for the job. Sitting there, in front of a roaring fire opposite his mentor Martin Linge, he'd been flattered at his appointment as a liaison for the scattered resistance groups around Bergen, but wondered aloud if he was 'Norwegian enough'.

Linge had laughed heartily, and then adopted a dark look. 'Would you contemplate dying for your country?' he'd asked. For Jens, the answer was simple; he almost had for one country – some small piece of him perished along with Charlie, and again as the Luftwaffe's bullet on that Dunkirk beach struck his femur, piercing his artery and causing a near fatal haemorrhage, a tiny piece of shrapnel still embedded as an unwelcome souvenir. This time, Linge's plea had been for Norway, and the reply was the same; Jens was English-born, but if he was truly honest, his heart had been fixed in Norway since childhood, whizzing down the slopes near Marjit's farm, devouring her hot, salty *plukkfisk* and her showers of love. So, yes, he feels at home here. Whether Norwegians consider him a countryman – and Rumi comes to mind especially – is another matter. And the guilt he feels at bagging such a comfortable operation as this? That he can shoulder more easily. He's had plenty of practice.

The twin funnels cough out a plume of white smoke as the steamer prepares to leave for the long journey south. Jens and Rumi bury themselves in the throng of passengers on deck, some jostling with excitement, mixed with trepidation at the peppering of German guards amid local travellers and refugees. Strangely, the minute he'd told Rumi that Stavanger was their intended destination, any misgivings on her part had seemed to melt away. If he wasn't much mistaken, she seemed actually keen. Now, her face is one of anticipation amid the crowd, no irritation apparent. His eyes scan the deck – it's only natural for him to constantly assess any characters out of place – and then onto the dock, where a few family members are waving away relatives. Much like the SS, the austere Abwehr uniform stands out as distinct, particularly under the sun's rays and alongside that stern expression: Abwehr are to be reckoned with. That scar, too, the image of it etched in

Jens's memory, to marry with the name he's come to know and be wary of. The only comfort is that, today, the solemn face of Lothar Selig is looking intently to the left of the crowd and not staring directly at him, or Rumi. Further reassurance comes when the steamer drifts from the dock and Selig's form remains firmly in Bergen; Jens considers that a few hours sailing to Stavanger seems a good distance to keep between them. Maybe now he and Rumi are permitted to enjoy themselves just a little?

In his travelling case is the best suit he can afford, looked over and tweaked by Marjit, and his false identification card for one Leif Kristiansen, which Rumi had openly laughed at a few days before. 'What is so funny?' he'd said.

'It's only that you don't look anything like a Leif.'

'Perhaps you'd like to tell my forger – I'm sure he'd be very willing to change it. Besides, you are Fru Elise Kristiansen, don't forget.'

'I wish I could,' she says. 'I had a Kristiansen for a teacher once – and I hated her.'

Looking at her on deck, wisps of her red mane so vibrant under the day's brightness, he thinks she looks perfect, down to her blue tweed suit and hair coiled in a neat twist, along with small but understated earrings that he suspects are Marjit's and may well have been a present from his own mother. This transformation – much like his suit – is largely his aunt's doing, but still Rumi has adopted it beautifully, despite her minor grumbles. *She wears it well.*

'You look . . .' he starts, just as a long blast on the horn signals their departure.

Rumi whips her head to face him. 'What?' she says with suspicion.

'Lovely,' he adds with a slight reticence. 'I mean, like a businessman's wife.'

144

'All borrowed,' she counters dismissively. 'Marjit the marvel up to her tricks again.'

'Well, she's done a great job. And you look the part.'

It's cold on deck and they go below to while away some part of the journey. After an hour or so, he leaves Rumi dozing in the lounge and climbs back up on deck to placate his stomach, which is more unsettled than the waves beneath them. She emerges eventually into the chill air, blinking away sleep and the brisk breeze.

'Oh, there you are – *husband*,' she says with a wry smile, leaning alongside him on the railing that looks out towards the fjord landscape.

'Have a good nap? I didn't like to disturb you.'

'Hmm, yes.' She pushes away stray wisps of hair fighting the wind. 'I think it's a consequence of growing up with a father as a fisherman – the minute I sit still in a boat, it rocks me to sleep.'

'I wish I had your knack,' Jens says. 'I'm not the best sailor.'

'Have you been up here all this time?' Rumi says. 'You must be freezing.'

'Better cold than sick.'

They both stare out towards a white landscape, patches of green trying hard to push through thinning snow in places, the tiny bright houses perched on crags grasping tightly to the coastline. Jens narrows his eyes, closes and opens them again like the shutter on a camera, then feels her attention fixed on his scrutiny.

'What are you doing?' Rumi says inquisitively.

'Me? Oh, I'm just, well, drawing it. Logging the scene in my memory. I can't help it.'

'How?' She looks genuinely curious. 'I've seen my father do it with shipping routes, but he learnt that from years

on the boat, from boyhood. It seems different with you
– instinctive.'

Jens pulls up his lip as he considers. 'I've honestly no
idea – the curse of a mapmaker, I suppose. I just "see"
everything as a series of lines and contours, and they knit
and sit inside me like a vast model.'

The word 'knit' sparks a smile from her. 'And colours?'
she asks.

'Yes, lots of colour – shades of green especially. Lately,
reds and yellows for warning.'

She nods and makes a little moue – of understanding,
he imagines.

'What about you, how do you see the world?' he says.
'I notice you seem to knit in black and white.' He laughs
away his own silly analogy.

She doesn't, though, and her amber eyes wander towards
the view. 'Mostly, that's Norwegian tradition,' she says
eventually. 'Oddly, it's also how I wish life could be.'

Her voice is quiet, but her sorrowful tone booms louder
than the steamer's horn. He turns his body purposefully,
drawing her attention towards him, for her to explain more.

'No shades of grey,' she qualifies, expression fixed on the
water. 'I want a world where I know whom I can trust
again. That's what I wish for in all of this, Herr Leif
Kristiansen. No grey ghosts.'

A few hours on they dock in Stavanger's busy port, and it
feels fresh and yet familiar, too, meandering lines of white-
washed cottages climbing up and out of the town. Good
to be somewhere different, and yet not so alien to the
Bergen he's only just come to know well again. Jens takes
both cases and leads Rumi a short distance towards a large
square building facing the wharf, handing their luggage to

a bellboy as they enter the plush interior of the grand Victoria Hotel.

Inside, he checks in confidently as Herr and Fru Kristiansen, addressing her as 'darling' on one occasion and watching carefully for any surprised or irritated reaction in her. But she only smiles dutifully, as if being in a nice hotel with her husband is merely second nature.

Rumi Orlstad, you are perfect – and full of surprises.

25

Taking Tea with the Enemy

Stavanger, 25th March 1942

Rumi

'What is my mission today, oh dear husband?' Rumi peers over the coverings of her ridiculously large and sumptuous bed at Jens, who lays wrapped in several blankets on the sofa opposite. Her voice is unusually flighty; inside, she's still running with disbelief at the luxury of their room, which Jens insists is necessary and worthy of the information they might glean. From the crags and chaos of Rongoy to this. Unbelievable.

'Loose words and good intelligence come when people are relaxed and well fed,' Jens told her as they opened the door to what seemed like an entire suite, checking the room carefully for any listening devices secreted under the bed, in the sideboard or the drinks tray.

As any businessman might, he headed for the bar soon after and positioned himself within a short distance to several high-ranking Wehrmacht enjoying the company of

148

Stavanger's most prominent traders, later labelled as 'bloody traitors' by a seething Rumi. She'd been instructed by Jens to take afternoon tea, and had sat in the busy lounge with a magazine perched on her lap, though tempted to stare open-mouthed at the opulence and apparent lack of rationing. Fortunately, she remembered to stay calm and appear to live the lucky and relatively untouched existence of the demure Elise Kristiansen.

'May I join you, dear?' An older woman, swathed in expensive furs, offered herself as a convenient tea companion. As it happened, she was also a great source of information, boasting to Rumi in hushed whispers of her husband's 'vital' business in moving coal for the Germans. Rumi smiled and looked suitably awestruck when appropriate, frantically memorising every detail and then relaying it quickly to Jens on return to their bedroom. It was valuable intelligence, he told her. How was she so good at this, and so quickly?

In the hotel restaurant that first evening, they ate good food and maintained a constant appearance of conversation.

'So what are we actually doing now?' she'd said. 'I mean, for the cause?' The thrill of sustaining a persona and eliciting something valuable for the Allies was mixed with guilt at the expense, when she knew so many in Bergen were scratching for basics.

'We're bedding-in,' Jens told her. 'Being seen as part of the fabric. Tomorrow, at the hotel dance, it should pay off even more.'

'So what are we doing today, after our *bedding-in*?' she repeats now from under her luxurious eiderdown, suddenly hungry for breakfast.

Jens yawns, ruffles his hair and palms his face; the sofa clearly isn't as sumptuous and comfortable as her bed. 'I've

149

several people to catch up with this morning,' he says, and Rumi notes a brief disappointment that she's not invited. Nevertheless, it's convenient, since she has her own undertaking. 'But I would like you to take tea again,' he goes on, 'as it proved so worthwhile yesterday. And then we have the dance in the evening – that's our prime hunting ground. It'll be a mixture of Wehrmacht and Norwegian dignitaries.'

'A full day's spying then,' she says matter-of-factly, and catches him looking at her, his mouth slightly twisted. Evidently, he can't make her out. And that's good. It makes her better at this – the pretence – if no one can tell what's going on inside her head: that, guiltily, she's actually enjoying it. Being independent of Pappa and the boatyard means Rumi has loosened the tethers to home and thinking of Magnus a little bit less. And it's that realisation which causes a fresh swell of remorse. *But you're always there, really. Floating with me.*

The hotel that Anya Lindvig works at is much smaller and decidedly less opulent than the Victoria, the sort of place where middle-range traders and minor Reich officers might stay.

The woman on reception calls for Anya, who emerges from a back room behind the desk. 'Rumi! Where have you come from?' Her face is all surprise, delight mixed with some slight embarrassment; it's obvious that Anya's letters have been slightly embellished to give the hotel an upgrade. She whispers something to her stiff and heavily made-up colleague, who scowls but nods all the same.

'I can take my break early,' Anya says as she links her arm with Rumi's. 'There's a café around the corner we can go to.'

Anya stares in wonder as they sit opposite each other in a vibrant *kafe* two streets away. As the well-adorned Elise

Kristiansen, Rumi feels slightly out place, but in her Bergen guise it would be the perfect venue, with a buzz of conversation that's distinctly Norwegian. And the coffee is passable.

'So, why are you here – in Stavanger?' Anya begins.

'My neighbour, Marjit, had a sister here,' Rumi lies. 'She died and Marjit wanted company at the funeral.' Rumi looks down at her suit. 'Hence the dressing up. And why I didn't have time to write that I was coming.'

It seems a plausible excuse for Anya, who only wants to catch up on the news from Bergen, and is full of her own woes about occupied life.

'It was bad enough in Oslo after the invasion, but now these bastards seem to be everywhere,' she moans is a hushed voice. 'Our hotel is half taken up with Wehrmacht lieutenants and captains who think they own the bloody place.'

'Why don't you come back to Bergen?' Rumi asks. 'At least you'd be among friends.'

'Is there any work?'

In all honesty, Rumi can't think of much that doesn't involve servicing the Nazis' twin desire for domination and good living, though with Anya's striking blonde looks and blue eyes, she would be snapped up. 'I could find you something at the boathouse,' she suggests. 'There's always plenty that needs doing. And you could stay with us – we've a spare room.'

Anya clutches at Rumi's fingers. 'That's really kind of you, but my parents were teachers – I don't know one end of a boat from another. I'll keep scouring the papers for an opening in Bergen, and come as soon as I do. I can bear it here for the time being, and I am working my way up in the hotel.' She tries hard to paste over the pretence; her laugh, at least, is familiar, and to Rumi there are shades of the fun Anya from their school days. 'Either

151

that or I'll meet a nice Swedish businessman who will marry me and whisk me back to their properly neutral nation. I can but hope.'

Rumi flinches inside at the flighty suggestion of marriage; Anya knew Magnus briefly, and that they were an item, but not too many details. Or that it's all gone. And Rumi is weary of bringing it up, tired of the grief dragging her down and the sympathy that she doesn't know how to accept. And which won't bring Magnus back.

The time flies by in swapping news of old friends, some already lost forever, and some to Quisling's false promises, including their mutual friend.

'Bjarne Hansen! In the STAPO!' Anya is aghast. 'He, of all people? I can hardly believe it. It's a good job his grandmother is no longer alive, or she'd give him a piece of her mind.'

They hug tightly in parting at the hotel entrance. 'I'll write,' Rumi promises. 'And I'll keep my eye out for anything that will tempt you back to Bergen.'

'Me, too,' Anya pledges. 'Let's not leave it too long until we meet again.' She throws a look of disdain at the German officer striding through the hotel doors. 'We need to stick together, don't we?'

Back at her post, the Victoria's tea lounge proves rich pickings again. Rumi spies Fru fur-woman, hovers long enough to catch her eye and wanders over to say a casual hello.

'Do join us, Fru Kristiansen,' the woman insists, drawing her into the little circle of three other well-to-do's, one with a tiny puff of a dog perched on her lap, the animal nibbling at a cake that would be a human luxury in Bergen. Rumi smiles with gratitude, hoping her sycophancy is adequate and her disgust well-disguised.

It's a good trade; the other women are equally immodest and ridiculously proud of their husbands being in bed with the Nazis, and between information about receptions and parties they had attended, she gleans some intelligence about coal and iron movements, with enough detail for Jens to make further enquiries. Warmed by good tea and duplicity, it still feels satisfyingly like real work, and she sits back, allowing her eyes to take in the splendour of the Victoria's parlour. And then, as her gaze drifts through the doors and towards the lobby for a mere second, the temperature plummets, causing her cup to rattle against the saucer, almost falling.

Rumi is chilled. To the bone.

'Careful, dear!' one of the women warns. 'You'll spoil your lovely dress.'

It's the least of her worries. Rumi can't be sure with only one look, but then he turns and quashes any doubt – the deep gash carved into his pink cheek is apparent, wrinkling as he laughs and shakes hands with another in uniform.

Selig. The Abwehr hound.

'It's been a pleasure, but I have to go.' As Fru Kristiansen she rises and backs away in one movement. 'No doubt I'll see you all this evening.'

Rumi takes the stairs instead of waiting for the lift, cursing as she finds the bedroom empty, then hears a tuneless singing coming from behind the bathroom door.

'Jens! Jens!' She raps hard to grab his attention.

There's a splash of water in response. 'Yes, hang on.'

He emerges with a towel around his waist, hair wet and spiky, face flushed. She takes a step back, though why she can't comprehend in that moment.

'Jens, I've seen something.'

★　★　★

153

'We need to leave – now.' His reaction to the news of Selig switches his mood instantly and spurs Jens into immediate action, pulling open his case.

'Do you mean right this minute?' As Rumi speaks, all of her good work downstairs supping tea with traitorous old women drains away. Surely, there has to be more benefit, a true pay-off for their trip? 'But if Selig is here, there'll be more Abwehr at the dance tonight, plenty of brandy and loose tongues.' She dares to pull at his naked shoulder as he's throwing clothes into his case. 'Jens, we could take pains to avoid him, but if I get to dance with other officers, it'll be gold dust for the cause.'

He stops to look at her, pale eyes suddenly darker. 'Or dynamite,' he says. 'Have you thought about that?' He breathes out through thinned lips, his voice direct. 'Please pack, Rumi, we need to go.'

'You said yourself that you're faceless,' Rumi pushes, perhaps too eagerly. 'That Selig won't know you by sight.'

The anger on the face that whips towards her isn't hard to read. 'And that's how I want it to stay.' Amid furious packing, he mutters: 'I'd rather not be lifeless if it's all the same to you.'

She steps back, the air between them thick with mutual recognition; an image of Karl hovers in the space, the loss still raw and recent.

She hears Jens tell the reception desk they've been 'called home urgently', and they exit through the hotel's doors openly, emerging from the Victoria's main entrance and skirting the building at a relaxed pace. Having missed the last sailing of the day, they walk away from the steamer quay. Clear of the hotel, Jens noticeably picks up speed. In her work clothes, at home, Rumi would easily keep pace, but after ten minutes walking – suddenly hot in a woollen suit and heels that she never wears – she has to ask him to slow.

'If you want me to be your wife, you have to treat me as one and not some marathon runner,' she grumbles. 'Especially in these ridiculous shoes.'

'Sorry,' he replies. 'Force of habit – haste without seeming to run.'

It's another ten minutes before he steers her to a white-washed doorway bearing the sign of a small guesthouse. The Victoria Hotel it is not, though the woman who greets them appears to know Jens and asks no questions. Rumi wonders: *How often has he been here? And was he alone, or did he have another pretend wife in tow?*

In a tiny attic room with one bed and no sofa, the owner brings them a flask of hot raspberry tea and slices of her own potato cake that tastes even better than Hilde's back home. Rumi lays back on the bed, noting that Jens looks weary folded into the tiny chair in the corner. She invites him to join her on the small but comfortable mattress and he doesn't hesitate, sighing with relief as he props himself up with pillows, prompting Rumi to laugh into her cup.

He turns, eyes full of surprise. 'Now what's so funny?'

'Look at us – we're like an old married couple, drinking tea in the late afternoon in some parochial guesthouse. If we're not careful, we'll be finishing each other's sentences soon.' For the second time that day, something nips sharply inside her at the allusion to marriage – of Magnus, of them perhaps on their honeymoon making the same joke – and again she's shocked to find how fleeting it is.

Jens takes a sip of his tea. 'I quite like it, actually. It reminds me of wintry Sunday afternoons at home. And at least we're hidden until the morning.'

155

There's a tinge of regret in Rumi at missing the evening's dance, having moulded into Elise Kristiansen more easily than she'd imagined. It falls away when she thinks of having to waltz with unctuous, boastful Quislings and German officers, their hands roaming up and down the blue satin dress she'd planned to wear and pushing their foul cigar-tainted breath at her. Perhaps she should be relieved.

'So, no more hiding in plain sight,' Rumi muses, picking at the cake crumbs. 'Why do you do that? I thought SOE were ghosts by nature, tucked away in substations, out on the coast. Certainly not roaming around Bergen for all to see.'

'I've been sent as a sort of liaison,' Jens says, 'between the resistance groups. They – we – have had a lot of setbacks. You'll know there were lots of arrests in autumn last year, and whole groups have been wiped out.'

She nods. The underground pamphlets and papers reported as such, each capture and inevitable death brewing a heavy feeling in the Orlstad household.

'It seems we're all very good at opposing the Nazis,' Jens goes on. 'Just not so great as a combined force. That's my job.' He turns and pulls up his bottom lip. 'I'm nothing more than a glorified runner, really, passing messages, trying to get groups to talk to each other. In England, I'm what we call a "jack of all trades, and master of none".'

Her eyebrows arch with suspicion. 'So, no real action for Jens Parkes – sorry, *Teigen*? Not even a few satisfying acts of sabotage? I mean, while I've seen with my own eyes how accomplished you are at parachuting, I still find that hard to believe.'

She watches a wry smile creep across his face, that perhaps he's trying to bury memories of the satisfaction it's already brought him, the heady danger of being a large fly in the ointment as he lays a limpet mine under darkness or sets a charge to de-rail a transport train packed with German supplies. His silence says everything, while he rubs instinctively at the top of his leg.

'And how is your resident shrapnel?' Rumi prods.

He laughs, perhaps at her mockery, and in being entirely caught out by gentle interrogation. 'Fine,' he says. 'It sends its regards.'

'That's nice. I wish it well,' she counters.

The journey home is on calm waters the next morning, though Rumi watches Stavanger merge into the distance with some sadness – Anya remains alone and at arm's length, and she mourns the intelligence she and Jens might have gathered, if it hadn't been for the scar-faced Selig.

'All right?' Jens asks, handing her coffee on the deck. 'It's ersatz, I'm afraid.'

'Back to real life then,' she says with the weakest of smiles.

She stares at the white foam washed up by the steamer's prow. What will she tell Pappa of the trip, since he's bound to ask? Will she be inclined to embellish it, to pretend that Rumi Orlstad has risen from warehouse manager and fisherman's daughter, to being a vital cog in the resistance wheel, a spy in a satin dress? And what of Marjit? Will Rumi confess that she and Jens shared the same bed that final night, when she insisted he could not contort himself on the tiny chair or suffer the cold, wooden floorboards? And that while they didn't purposely touch, or caress, or any of the things she seemed suddenly to dream about, that once or twice he or she turned and their bodies made brief contact. And that it felt good.

Will she admit those secrets to anyone, least of all herself?

26

Televåg

Bergen, 26th April 1942

Jens

Jens sits nursing an unenticing sandwich, picking at the dense, dry bread as he stares out of the café window. Beyond the glass, spring has finally come to Bergen; it's not like an English awakening of colour, but the days are getting longer, with spectacular light arcing over the city and the snowy slush finally melting underfoot. He thinks he should finish his dull lunch and head back to the mission office to begin sorting the piles of paperwork and bundles of clothes that need distributing, to keep his cover afloat. In truth, he feels little motivation to do either.

His mood should be better; in the past weeks he's travelled north to Trondheim and inland to link up with several of his old troop from Scotland, now known as the 'Linge Company', in memory of their lost leader. In the moment, Jens had been galvanised by a successful mission preventing vital fuel supplies from reaching the ports and sailing on to Germany. Success, too, in that no resistance lost their lives. He felt the camaraderie as they celebrated by feasting on the reindeer one of the group had managed to hunt, and a warmth inside, despite the bitterness of a draughty hunting cabin they were forced to spend the night in. He felt as if he belonged; part of something worthwhile.

Since then, the loneliness of a liaison officer has returned, tapping endlessly on his transmitter into what often feels like an abyss – or a trap. Increasingly, the Allies and resistance are painfully aware of the German triumphs in infiltrating SOE and SIS, sometimes posing as refugees or keen helpers and then leading agents into the fire pit of Nazi interrogation. More and more, it's crucial for operators and ciphers to analyse every mark or sound in messages received: is that the true language of the sender, or the right encryption? Is the rhythm out of character, a German operator trying too hard to sound Norwegian or British in the way they form the coded words? Jens spends hours poring over each dispatch, asking the same questions and picking apart messages in tiny, dark rooms spread across Bergen, until his eyes blur and his head hurts. And for what? It's difficult to know what in-roads the resistance is making, if any. Often, it seems as if it's two steps forward and one step back, and occasionally, the other way around. There's no instruction from those above except to carry on.

Looking at the couples and groups in the café, he has to admit that he is both envious and lonely; he has acquaintances and contacts, but no friends that aren't scattered throughout Norway, except for Marjit and Peder, and – he hopes – Rumi.

He's visited only once since their return from Stavanger, though he'd like to sit in Marjit's living room more often, sprawled in her oldest but comfiest chair, the radio twittering

159

alongside, and the click-clack of her and Rumi's knitting needles offering a strange respite to his isolation. He thought at first that the noise would irritate, after so many hours spent tuning into the dot-dot-dash of endless messages, but he found the sounds of knitting and a murmuring conversation relaxing. On that one evening, he enjoyed fading into the background and watching as the two weaved, marvelling at the intricate patterns that miraculously grew as their needles danced a jig, and how much it reminded him of home. He's never seen his mother knit, but it's that familiarity he craves – probably as everyone does in wartime – alongside the balm of safety.

Once or twice in the evening, he chanced a look at Rumi as her focus flicked rapidly from her work to Marjit and back again. He noted, too, that where she might once have scowled in response to his look, she simply stared back, as if slightly perplexed. On the surface, her anger seemed much less apparent, and she didn't mention Magnus at all, though he wondered what thoughts were ticking away inside her head. How broken she might still be.

As he got up to leave, Rumi put down her work and rummaged in a large bag containing her wool. The button-down sweater she pulled out was beautiful and soft as she handed it to him.

'Here, I thought you'd need this to blend in,' she said, spreading her full red lips with pleasure. In the glint of her eye, he read a private knowing between them. 'It might help you hide in plain sight, Jens *Teigen*.'

He hadn't known what to say. Aside from Marjit's winter skiing scarves, no one had ever created something so beautiful for him, or so personal.

On saying goodbye at the door, his aunt whispered that Rumi had laboured long into the evenings to put on the finishing touches. It wasn't made for Magnus, her look alluded, or anyone else. Only for him. 'Wear it well,' she'd said, and kissed him goodnight.

'I will.' But her intent expression refused to let him go. 'What is it, Marjit?'

'Don't get the wrong idea, that's all. Just be glad she likes you as a friend.'

He'd feigned innocence, but with Marjit it was useless.

'She's still grieving and − despite how she seems − too fragile,' the older woman had gone on. 'The resistance work, well . . .'

'And that's all it is,' he protested. Maybe wrongly. And almost certainly very badly. 'She's a loyal Norwegian who's doing valuable work. I'm not getting any ideas.'

He'd kissed Marjit before she could lecture him any further, shut the door and began the walk towards his lonely, single room.

No ideas, Jens Parkes. It's too cruel. Life might be short. Your life. Remember that.

Now, Jens fingers the soft weave and top-to-bottom buttons of a garment that would almost certainly get him laughed out of any pub in London, but undoubtedly makes him one of the crowd in Bergen. Around half of the men in the café sport the same sweater in various forms, and they wear it with pride − by tradition, but also as a visible slight to the troops who seem desperate to engage Norwegians as their friends, and to absorb the Nordic way. Thanks to Rumi's handiwork, Jens is fast becoming one of them.

His attention is diverted by the appearance of a lanky teenage boy in the doorway, rapidly scanning the bar first and then the tables and chairs. He heads a little too eagerly towards Jens, slides into a seat next to him, as if it's a planned date and he's already late.

There are no niceties. 'Televåg,' the boy mutters breath-lessly into the table. 'A raid this morning, two Gestapo shot dead, one SOE, too.'

'Shit.' Jens's tone is low but full of dread. The workings of his mind are instantly at full stretch about what this bloodshed might mean. 'And the other one?' He knows there are two SOE agents camped out in the village on the exposed, west side of Sotra, until now a perfect look-out for naval traffic in the North Sea and a regular dropping off point for the Shetland Bus.

The boy shakes his head. 'That's all I know, apart from . . .' He hangs his head.

'What?' Jens urges.

'My contact says the Germans are furious. Raging. There will be a price to pay for the dead Gestapo.'

Jens's mind is racing with a cocktail of dread and appre-hension as he forces himself to wait a few minutes before leaving – fear not for himself, but for his fellow SOE out there, dotted around the craggy islands, hidden among the skerries and coves, yet still utterly exposed. He has to get word to them, and quickly. To either pack up and move to another safe house, or to be on full alert for any suspi-cious word or unwanted attention. Despite the strong, patriotic, anti-Nazi feeling among many Norwegians, there are still those who will bow to pressure from their own fear, or money, or blackmail. Not out and out Quislings, but those too terrified to stand firm. It's a fear that the Germans nurture day in and day out, and what inevitably sustains the occupation of an entire country.

As he hits the pavement along Neumanns gate, Jens longs to run towards his transmitter, to speed towards the messages he needs to fire out, carefully and rapidly encrypted. Instead, he only walks with haste, because – as ever – he's hiding in plain sight. Face to the pavement, the image of what might be happening in Televåg is already painfully vivid, and although the word says it's Gestapo-driven, there's one beacon flashing above all others in his mind. One element which almost certainly had a hand in wheedling out the intelligence.

Selig.

27

Flames of Revenge

Bergen, 3rd May 1942

Rumi

Staring out from the wharf, Rumi narrows her eyes at the dense black cloud hanging in the sky like a barrage balloon, the type Jens described to her as hovering over the streets of London, bobbing above the red-tile rooftops. Those sky-hawks are meant to protect the English capital, while the leaden, toxic shadow she sees in front of her now is the result of blatant destruction; oppression and pure revenge, in the way the Nazis do so efficiently. Despite the Reich's overtures to join the German and Nordic bloodlines, there's nothing friendly about what's happening in Televåg.

Bergen's streets have been running with rumour and fear for a week, since news of the shootings. Amid the propaganda thrown out by the Nazi command, they know for sure that a senior Gestapo officer was killed instantly in the crossfire, alongside another; it's been enough to draw in the German's principal man in Norway, *Reichskommisar*

Josef Terboven, to personally oversee the Nazis' calculated revenge. As Terboven sailed away from the island village on 30th April, all resident men between sixteen and sixty had already been arrested and were on their way to unknown camps and a formidable fate. Days later, women, children and the elderly were forcibly plucked from their homes and bundled off the island. The vast majority of villagers had not been harbouring agents, or helping movements of arms or people, but in the Reich's version of justice, they are guilty by virtue of living among the 'traitors' of Televåg. And all must pay.

The *Reichskommisar*'s sentence is the vision that's painful for Rumi and all of Hordaland county to look upon, the ripples of retribution in taking a flame to an entire village: houses, school, churches and livelihoods going up in the thick, black smoke against a clear, pure sky.

She thinks back to that brief conversation with Jens, prompting a sudden, guilty twist in her chest. She craved a world in black and white, with 'no grey ghosts', she'd said to him only a month before. And here it is, the deathly shroud of destruction held aloft for all to see – the Nazi way of warning those who aid the resistance. It might frighten some into submission, but from what she can glean of the talk around the fish market and across the city in past days, this heartless Nazi tit-for-tat will only strengthen the Norwegian resolve *not* to lie in bed with their invaders. Once, it was enough for some to pin a paperclip on their lapel in solidarity, or to sport a red hat with pride – until the Nazis realised the significance and banned red headwear. Now she thinks Norwegians want to do more. To be active.

Rumi still has plenty to do in the yard, but the sad image in the distance lays a heavy cloak of torpor over mind and body. She's been busy the entire week, hiding and hauling supplies, sending Pappa and Rubio and some of the other hands they employ into the fjords with deliveries, the façade of simply working the business as normal. But in among the barrels of fish, blankets and meagre food supplies, contraband is stowed carefully in the boats, distributed among the islands already combed over by Nazi patrols, and so deemed a safe enough haven for a time. Each time Pappa sets sail, Rumi holds her hand aloft on the quay – alongside her breath, faith and hope – often for long, lonely hours until she's able to detect the throb of his engine returning. It seems farcical that once she opposed her father's desire to be part of the fight. Since Televåg, there's no choice or argument; personal grief and fear has given way to necessity. It *is* black and white: they have to fight.

'Awful, isn't it?'

Rumi starts violently at the voice – any voice – since for days now her ears have been on constant alert for anyone approaching the yard. She spins and sets her body defensively, then sags with relief at the monochrome image of his sweater, the twist and weave she was once so intimate with.

'Jens. What are you doing here?'

Months ago, such a greeting might have been rude; now it's just sensible.

'I came to see how you were,' he says. 'I've just left Marjit's and she said you were here. That you've been here a lot.'

'Plenty to do, especially now.' She nods towards the black balloon spreading into a clammy grey smog and turns to go into the boathouse.

He follows her in, and proffers a hand clutching a bag. She's grateful, though not with any cry of delight this time. But coffee – in good times or bad – is always welcome.

166

'Where on earth do you get it?' she says earnestly.

'Good supply lines, I suppose. And a grateful market.' He smiles as if he's had to practise it over the last week. 'Oh, and Marjit has her own bag, so you can keep this as your private stash.'

'Even better. Join me now?'

He looks over his shoulder, scouts around the room for dangers. She's not offended; it's second nature to him, and survival. He lets out a huge breath, and seems to deflate before her very eyes, looking as weary as she feels. Rumi hates herself for even thinking it, but in that moment she can't summon a single ounce of zeal for anything, even Norway.

'I don't think I've been this tired since we were in Rong,' Jens says as they sit in her office, the strong, dark coffee stabbing at their taste buds. He looks to be inviting her into the memory; the peril, but also the nostalgia of their shared survival.

'Hmm, I know what you mean,' Rumi echoes. She returns his stare, her lips poised. 'Have you been all right?'

It's her code-speak this time, but will he be able to decipher it? *I know you're not in a Nazi jail,* she's hinting, *but is your being intact?* What's so surprising is that she wants to know, can recall how much over the past week she's thought of him, wondering what he was doing. Busy, no doubt, but had he also been fearful, and in danger? Near to capture with the hound Selig on his tail? The hours alone had sent her mind into dark corners, not just for Pappa and Rubio, but for Jens, too.

'Weary, but yes, I am all right,' he says, seeming to choose his words carefully. 'Thanks for asking.'

'And Selig – have you heard any more?'

Jens sits forward, elbows on his knees and clutching at his cup. 'Well, he's half the reason I'm here,' he begins.

'Oh yes?'

'As you can imagine, I've had to spend time pushing out messages, helping others stay safe,' he goes on. 'So much radio traffic has left us exposed, and it's clear that he's been only a few steps behind me, sometimes less. Uncomfortably close.'

'A bit of cat and mouse?' Rumi suggests.

'Yes, exactly that.' He smiles at her take on the chase, returning to a serious look. 'Anyway, those up top have decided that this particular mouse needs to retreat into his hole for a bit. In fact, they've ordered it.'

She manages to mask an instant disappointment, though only just; a seed of sadness threatening to take root inside her. A contrived smile is her disguise. 'Well, I envy you if your little hidey-hole involves a large slab of cheese. And plenty of good living.'

'If it does, I'll be sure to save you a bit.' He gets up to leave as the distinctive tonk-tonk of Peder's boat signals its imminent arrival.

'Will you be going far?' He won't tell her where and, in truth, she doesn't want to know, exactly, but she does wonder if he'll go up north, into a different danger, or east to Sweden or even Shetland. Safe but entirely out of reach.

'Far enough,' is all he'll commit to. 'Listen, I have to go. Say my goodbyes to Peder and Rubio, will you, though perhaps not for a day or so?'

'I will.' She stands and follows him to the door and, with one ear towards the quayside for her father, Rumi reaches out a hand towards his shoulder. She feels the soft knit of what she produced, remembers suddenly all the hours spent, her fingers aching in taming the wool, the echoes of creating something so intricate and wanting to make it right. Then asks herself yet again: why did she feel that motivation for Jens? Just why was she so driven to do it for him?

He fills the lengthy pause: 'Look after yourself, Rumi.'

She watches him walk away, and wonders how many more times, and how many more people, will disappear out of her life before this war ends?

PART TWO

28

A New Purpose

Hop, 29th May 1942

Sipping her morning tea, she casts her eyes over a list of the day's chores ahead. It's an ever-growing list, and where once she might have sighed at its length, now she savours the idea of working her way through it. Determined. She hates to admit it, even to herself, but at times it's enjoyable, being among so many women, and being useful again. She'd even venture to describe it as caring. Her mother encouraged her many years ago to go into nursing, but she'd never relished the uniformity of the clothes or the life. As a maid, and then a housekeeper, she could quite easily follow orders, but she'd never felt servile in any way. And it was caring of a sort, for the family, but it's more so now; there's plenty to do and they seem to need her. These poor young women – some already orphans, others cast out of families by virtue of their 'condition' – arrive confused and anxious. It's her job to see that they're fed and well nourished, but she's become a support too, listening to their stories, sympathising to a degree. Calling herself a friend is perhaps going too far; in service, you're taught to keep a certain distance. Even the German midwives are civil, and not

173

quite as stern as they first appeared. They all laugh sometimes at translations leading to crossed wires, and her German is definitely improving. Those midwives are under orders but they seem genuinely concerned about keeping the mothers-to-be healthy. Again, she's questioned the expense in the middle of a war, but over the weeks it's become clear as to why the Reich is happy to extend its purse. The women are unmarried, but through their confessions and tears, she gleans that all the unborn babies are half-German, most of the women inevitably guarded about the circumstances leading to their 'predicament'. With or without a wedding ring, it's evident that, as a nation, the Germans value those they consider to be their own. 'Kinder are all,' one of the midwives told her. Only Kleiner maintains his air of true detachment, and everyone is thankful he visits only twice a week now. She's heard him say the rest is 'women's work' and she scoffs as she clears away the tea things: perhaps he should try carrying a baby one day and giving birth. Or catering for a house of thirty.

The babies have begun to arrive, too. So far, there's been a single birth in the house itself, when one woman got caught out before the midwives could move her to the main maternity home – 'Lebensborn', she heard them call it. And although these midwives don't carry out many births now, mainly doing the pre-birth and aftercare, they're perfectly capable. As one said: 'an unexpected birth keeps you on your toes'.

She'd hovered outside the door in those last minutes, insisting to the maid that she be the one to take up more towels, hearing the labouring woman – Inge, she was called – pleading for them to 'end it' and 'make it go away'. The pain, she supposed. Through the door, the midwives were stern in their language then, though not unkind – they simply knew it had to reach a natural end, she supposed. And when the baby's first cries rang out through the house, loud and very clear, everything else was still, sparking memories of when the Lauritzens' first grandchild was born – in

174

the same room, in fact. Somehow, this seemed better. Something good in the midst of this strange and horrible situation, like a flower pushing through the rubble of a bombed-out building.

She'd helped tend Inge afterwards, changing her soiled sheets and bringing the extra rations new mothers are allowed, flowers on her tray that Gunnar snips from the best borders. But after two weeks, Inge was gone suddenly — to make a new life in Germany, the midwives said, with the baby's father when the war is over. One of the fortunate ones, they added. If you can call that lucky.

Now there are two more babies, brought in at five days old from the other maternity home, and she's even tended the boiler for the nappies and begs a cuddle when she's got a minute between chores. The other women glide around the beautiful grounds, waiting to become rounder and closer to motherhood, and yet she sees they are dreading the change, too. She recognises this limbo, wondering if she should feel more remorse in effectively working for the Germans. She's no Quisling, for sure, and yet it's odd that she's not entirely unhappy, when the gossip from the village says a major portion of Norway is. Picking up her lengthy to-do list, she's conscious that this strange equilibrium within herself cannot possibly last. Her nose twitches with it, like a dense, almost smoky odour that's so familiar when storm clouds roll in across a tranquil sea. Your eyes capture only the calm of the water, but the inside of your nostrils is thick with unease. Something's brewing. And the maelstrom is coming for sure. She just doesn't know what it is.

175

29

In the Mousehole

Northern Norway, 6th June 1942

Jens

With lightning instinct, Jens grabs the butt of his gun at the mere crackle of noise outside, no more than the tiny snap of a twig underfoot. Around him, three other fingers click back the safety catch of their weapons as the air in and around the tiny cabin suspends. From under his blanket, Jens tracks movement through the cracks in the thin wooden planks; it's a living being for sure, though too tall for any curious animal. But no voices. In general, Nazi search units are not known for their silent stealth up here in the hills, descending with vigour on any hunting hut they come across.

He's already upright and swinging his legs from the bunk, as are the three others. They share glances which speak volumes, the whites of their eyes flashing in the gloom. There's nowhere to go except through the flimsy, ill-fitting door, which catches and then pushes open, accompanied by a familiar humming.

'Torstein! I wish you'd bloody announce yourself a bit sooner!' Gregers pushes out his exasperation as Jens sucks in relief.

'Uh, sorry,' Torstein comes back. 'I thought you were all awake and could see me coming.'

They hadn't, all half-awake or semi-asleep, as they only ever are, leaving them all endlessly exhausted.

Torstein flops a small carcass on the makeshift table, already skinned and unrecognisable as a species. 'Thin pickings today, I'm afraid,' he says, loading whatever they have into a cooking pot. 'Might make just enough for a stew.'

Jens lays back down and pulls the blanket over him for a few extra minutes of rest. He works to shut off his senses to the sweat and filth in its fibres, the shared desperation of others who've hidden in the same hut, miles from anywhere, shivering with the night wind thrusting through the slats in the rotting wood. He has company, at least – the camaraderie of men he's known only briefly but who would work to save him in an instant, who frequently share their last morsel of rations so nobody goes hungry.

Closing his eyes, Jens fights the wave of exhaustion, but in reality he's utterly spent. He's reminded of the last time he felt quite so drained, that day sitting in Rumi's office, sharing his last cup of coffee in Bergen, wishing then he could have just melted into the chair by her fire and stayed forever.

It's the constant moving that's so wearing; from village to village, sometimes plucked from the coast by trawler and deposited at an almost identical cove, and then endless miles on foot as the weather improves. It's only down to his innate geography that he's able to tell that they're north of Trondheim or south of Narvik. A long way from Bergen, either way.

177

One factory or railway target has begun to look much like another after several weeks on the move, crouching to avoid detection from the patrolling Nazis, or hotfooting along a dicey escarpment at speed to avoid capture, narrowly dodging a volley of ammunition as the pack run for their lives. Once or twice he's felt that brief rush of air as a bullet wings past, uncomfortably close, and the sliver of metal in his leg smarts, almost in sympathy.

His mind goes to an old black cat that Marjit had on the farm once, increasingly battered and maimed though it seemed happy enough. It succumbed eventually when its nine lives ran out and Jens can empathise with that rough old moggy now. The question is: how many lives has he got left?

Oddly, it's not that element he finds so wearing – the work is necessary for Norway and he's proud to be part of it – it's chiefly that there's no respite, even briefly, from the stark necessity of survival. The tinned rations are taste-less, and in the last few days, having been holed up for almost a week, they've been forced to scavenge for the lichen that reindeer relish, creating a meagre moss soup that even a good amount of salt could not have improved. That's if they'd had any salt.

There have been one or two better nights along the way, when they've been able to bunk in farmhouse barns of Norwegian patriots, insulated by thick bales of hay and fed by those willing to run the risk of harbouring the resistance. Always, though, the company has one ear out for the throaty growl of the Nazi *Kübelwagens*, the little military jeeps which bumble over the rugged Nordic land-scape, carrying Wehrmacht who make a habit of visiting outlying farms without warning, for spot-checks and 'enquiries'. Jens thinks he's become an expert on holding his breath, as he and the men beside him forcibly paralyse their lungs while waiting for the sounds of the engine retreating, the strands of hay itching and scratching at exactly the wrong moment.

Under an assortment of rough blankets and in the minutes before Jens drifts off, his thoughts always go to where he felt he belonged. He wonders how Bergen looks in the late spring sunshine, the white of the birch stems sprouting their pale green leaves and the long daylight hours of summer to come: colourful, he imagines, unlike his current view. It's no longer the nostalgia of home or a warm hearth in London that keeps him constantly pushing on, but the thought of Bergen and its solace. More than he'd like to admit, it's *who* is there, too. Marjit, of course, but also . . .

More than once he's been sorely tempted to tap out a message to the stations still secure in or around Bergen, to get word delivered to the houses side by side in Strangebakken that he is still alive, that his mind has not deserted them. So many times he's had to stop himself, because of the dangers it would incur and the fatal repercussions of a stray, unnecessary dispatch.

Is it a weakness? As a highly trained agent, he thinks he shouldn't be harbouring such yearnings, that he's been hardened to keep a distance emotionally, look only to the job at hand. And then he reasons: what is it all for, if not for people? They are waging an intensely human war, for mankind to fend off those bent on destroying it. Yet he feels equally crippled by their task, buried somewhere in no-man's land and with only his mind free to travel unhindered. *Thank goodness for imagination.*

For now, waiting and working is all he can do, jabbing at and irritating the Nazis' rigid determination to dominate.

He and his comrades are the irritant flies fast morphing into wasps, each with a bigger and more painful sting in their tails.

'*Hei,* you lazy urchins, get up!' Torstein's voice cuts into the daydreams, and Jens opens his eyes to see the big, unshaven man laying a grubby cloth over his arm like the waiters from the opulent Victoria Hotel in Stavanger, a mock bow to accompany. 'Your breakfast is served, sir. Come and sample our sumptuous fayre.'

Suddenly, the exhaustion is cut through and they're all laughing again, the humour sweeping away any darker moments and firing Jens towards a new day.

30

The Return

Rumi

Rumi bowls through Marjit's back door, fully open to the stifling summer heat. *'Hei,* it's just me. Anyone home?'

It's cooler inside and there's a shuffling from the room above the parlour; Rumi flops down on the sofa to await Marjit's appearance on the stairs. The day has been long and hot in the yard, with barely a breeze coming off the water for hours. The smell never improves in summer, either. Rumi hopes her friend has a pot of fruit tea to offer her, in trying to dodge the grumbles of Hilde next door who is sounding off about the latest rationing and having to craft yet more meals from 'fish and fresh air'. In among her ranting, she'd hinted again of a job offer elsewhere, but Rumi knows it's a bluff; compared to a formal posting in some opulent house, the Orlstads are undemanding employers, and Hilde is workshy at the best of times.

Marjit appears within several minutes, a swathe of fabric draped over her shoulder like some Roman general from the pages of a history book.

'*Hei,*' Rumi says, squinting at the material. 'Aren't they your bedroom curtains?'

'Yes,' Marjit says matter-of-factly, as if everyone routinely wears their own drapery.

'And?'

'Oh! Oh, I see.' Marjit laughs. 'I'm making a dress, for the Ostrems' oldest girl.'

'From your curtains?' Rumi is beginning to wonder where the conversation is going, as she heads towards the stove and fills the kettle.

'Nothing in the shops,' Marjit explains through the open doorway. 'Well, certainly not enough for . . .' she tails off.

'For what?' Rumi hands Marjit the weak blackberry tea and dips her head towards the material, now spread out across the table. 'Marjit, are you making a wedding dress?'

Silence, save for the mumble behind a mouthful of pins.

'You can say it, you know,' Rumi goes on. 'I won't get upset or maudlin. Promise.'

Marjit unburdens herself of pins and joins Rumi on the worn sofa, resting her short grey strands on Rumi's broad, muscled shoulder and kissing a freckled arm. 'I know, my love. It's just that now is the time I should have been making your dress. The one I've always wanted to.'

'Not out of those curtains, if you don't mind. I might have waited until the war's over, or else knitted my own dress.' This is the light relief she plucks out for Marjit, who digs Rumi in the ribs playfully and goes back to her sewing.

'So what will you do for curtains now?' Rumi asks out

of real curiosity. In summer, the daylight hours are long and the strong sun pouring through the window can jab mercilessly at your sleep.

'Oh, I'll go to the mission house and take a few things from the piles – just the rags – and patch them together to make a new pair. Jens won't mind, and he's given me the key.'

Jens. His presence comes storming into the room and Rumi fingers the rim of her cup, judging whether she should ask. 'I don't suppose you've heard . . . know anything?' she ventures, then worries she's given herself away, exposed herself – and her heart – a little too much.

'He'll be fine,' Marjit says matter-of-factly, her voice a little clipped. Perhaps it hides her own hurt at his absence. 'Anyway, what did you come to show me?' Marjit says, nodding at the envelope Rumi clutches in her hand.

'Oh, this. It came this morning – it's from my friend, Anya.'

'Isn't she the one in Stavanger – the hotel receptionist?'

'Yes, but she's back in Bergen, or not far away,' Rumi says. 'Only, her letter is quite odd, and I can't work it out.'

She pulls out a single page letter and pushes it towards Marjit, who scrabbles to find her glasses, and then murmurs the words aloud:

Dear Rumi

I hope this finds you and your family well, despite everything we talked about in Stavanger.

I did say that I would get back to Bergen eventually, didn't I? I'm inching closer – in Hop, a few kilometres south. Do you remember we travelled to the coast there one day after school, in that long summer of '33? It's still beautiful, and very peaceful.

I wonder, would you be able to visit me here? It's diffi-cult for me to get away, but at least it's not as far as

Stavanger. I can be free any day that suits you, if you can write and let me know.

I would really appreciate seeing you.
Best regards,
Anya.

'What do you think?' Rumi asks, combing Marjit's face for clues.

The older woman peers again at the neat, handwritten script. 'It doesn't sound suspicious in what she says, but . . .'

'Yes?'

'It's more about what she doesn't say,' Marjit concludes.

'I thought so, too!' Rumi cries. 'Anya was so keen in her first letter to tell me about her job, and the troops coming in or out. This doesn't look to have been censored at all, and yet she doesn't even say where she's working, or if she is. What on earth is in Hop?'

'Lots of well-to-do houses,' Marjit says with slight disdain, getting up to fill the pot again. 'Though plenty of them have been requisitioned by the Nazis, the owners thrown out on their ear.'

'So what could she be doing that makes it so difficult for her to get away?'

Marjit considers. 'It's possible she has a job caring for someone elderly, which ties her to the house.'

'Yes, I suppose.' But Rumi is not convinced. She's consumed instead with curiosity, alongside a level of concern. 'I'll just have to go and see her, won't I?'

'Yes, I suppose you will,' Marjit says through a fresh mouthful of pins. 'Meantime, close the window and we'll have the radio on for a bit, shall we?'

31

Confession

Rumi

Getting out of Bergen reminds Rumi how constrained she feels on some days by the constant sight of Wehrmacht patrolling the city streets, crowding the shops and cafés that she feels have been hijacked by uniforms. She adores Bergen, and will fight to her last breath for it, but for now it feels as if it doesn't belong to Norwegians, though she'd never admit to it openly. Even saying the words would feel like a betrayal.

The drive south in Pappa's old flatbed truck gives her a sense of freedom as she bumps along, and a chance to appreciate how beautiful the countryside is, despite the intense heat that has transformed the truck's cab into a sauna. The greenery beyond the windscreen never ceases to amaze her, and gives Rumi a much-needed injection of pride; they will take *their* country back, whatever the cost.

She's stopped twice by patrols, and with a combination

of smiles and Peder's licence as a tradesman, convinces them she's on her way to pick up essential supplies. She flushes at the image of today's choice of clothes; her smartest tweed trousers and a pale blue shirt, neat enough to meet Anya but not so good that she can't be delivering goods in a rusty old vehicle. One soldier winks at her – perhaps in reaction to her blush – and she feels suddenly grubby with collusion, having to remind herself it's all part of the game. Then her mind goes back to having tea in Stavanger and sucking out information from gullible and gossipy old women, and the satisfaction it brought.

She finds Anya's address after having to ask directions several times, a little confused at the look her request garnered from one woman. Disgust, if she's read it right. Is Anya working for a family of Quislings and wealthy collaborators? She hopes not; if Anya is the person she knows of old, it won't be true.

Rumi parks the truck a little way from the entrance to a large house hidden behind a high fir hedge, smooths down her clothes and wipes a line of sweat from her brow. Instantly, she catches the smell of salt in her nostrils, trained by blood and a lifetime to detect when she's within near sight of the sea. Just being close to something so familiar gives her the will to step forward. The building ahead is truly grand as she walks up the gravel driveway, a sizeable, rectangular white house with a receding red roof; its shape reminds Rumi of the upturned hull of a ship. There are several people, women mostly, milling about in the sprawling garden, and with relief she sees Anya forge forward to meet her.

'Oh Rumi, I'm so glad you could come,' she says, with a tight hug that's infused with more need than Rumi can ever recall. Anya's smiling, but she looks different. Not drastically so, but there are faint lines around her eyes replacing her beautiful smooth skin, and her complexion – always so bright – is slightly sallow. She's lost weight, too, though that's not uncommon as rationing gets ever tougher.

Anya takes Rumi by the arm. 'I know it's hot and we'll go inside after for a cool drink, but can we walk first?'

'Of course.'

Anya leads them away from the house and down towards the coastline, where Rumi sees that the vast, well-tended garden stretches all the way to the water and a spectacular view across a calm stretch of sea. Whoever lives – or lived – here is certainly wealthy.

Anya fills the space by asking about Peder and the boat-house, and what life is like in Bergen. 'I can't wait to see it again,' she says, with a tinge of detectable regret. And Rumi wonders: why can't she? It's only ten kilometres away, and there is a train into Bergen. Are people contained here? She looks around: it doesn't seem like a prison; there are no guards on the entrance. So why can't – or won't – Anya leave?

They stop finally at a small, open-fronted summer house looking out to sea and sit on the wooden benches, shaded and with the respite of a slight breeze. Rumi notes with interest that Anya scans left and right before she sits, presum-ably to check they are alone.

Being Rumi, she decides on a direct approach. 'Anya, what's going on?'

Her friend startles at first, but looks almost relieved at not having to skirt the issue any longer. 'It's hard for me to explain,' she says, a tremor to her voice.

'What is this place? Do you work here?' Rumi is all too aware she sounds impatient – because she is.

'Sort of,' Anya ventures.

'What does that mean?' Rumi poses a stark expression in her need to expose this mystery. Anya clearly is harbouring a secret, dark enough for her to be scared of letting it go.

'I'm pregnant,' she says at last, switching her gaze to the open water, and letting the heavy words sink into the suddenly clammy air.

'And . . . and . . .' Rumi is stalling to process Anya's revelation and the subsequent workings of her mind. 'This place?'

'It's a . . . a . . . maternity home. For unmarried mothers.' Pause. 'Those that probably will never be married. For Norwegian women and . . . and . . .' The stuttering revelations are squeezed out, but the last Anya can't seem to let go.

Rumi waits until Anya almost spits into the pause: '. . . for babies with German fathers.'

While Anya weeps, Rumi feels the heat of her friend's distress on her own flesh, remembering how badly she needed to physically grip on to someone familiar after losing Magnus. She looks at the flat horizon over Anya's shoulder and wonders how it can be so level, so unlike the swell inside them both.

Calmer, and looking to be someway freed from her weighty secret, Anya tells Rumi the baby's father is not a boyfriend, nor a potential husband. 'I promise you, I would never contemplate that,' she says. He was boarding at the hotel in Stavanger, flirted with her and the other hotel workers, as so many did. 'And we were told by the manager to put up with it — or look elsewhere for work.'

'And so?' Rumi questions.

'Gerhard asked me for a drink one evening,' Anya goes

on. 'I admit it was stupid, but he was very insistent, and all of us girls were under instruction to accommodate the guests. I was at a low ebb, and I said yes. But it was just a drink.'

'And then?'

'I don't remember much after that,' she says, her words heavy with regret. 'I had one glass of wine in the hotel bar, and the next I knew I woke up in my own room. I must have been carried there.' She looks hard into Rumi's face, bleeding sorrow and shame from every pore. 'We must have . . . Something happened, because there was blood between my legs.'

'Did he force himself on you?' Rumi asks. She is appalled and aghast, though sadly, it's a common enough story under occupation. The thought of it happening to a friend makes her feel instantly sick.

'I can't be sure,' Anya admits, shaking her head slowly. 'But I *know* I wasn't drunk – I promise you that, Rumi – so . . .' She scoops a breath, as if voicing it magnifies the horror all over again. 'I suppose he must have.'

'And how did you end up here?' The pieces aren't quite fitting together for Rumi yet.

Anya smiles weakly. 'This is the Reich's version of "doing the right thing", since marriage was never on the cards, thanks to Gerhard's fiancée back in Germany.' She flashes a loaded look at Rumi. 'And I would never do that anyway. I could never have loved him.'

'Never?' It's beyond the bounds for Rumi, but not for some women, she knows.

'No,' Anya says resolutely. 'He's SS.'

Rumi has to stop twice on the journey home, down to the truck's ancient engine stalling, and needing a gentle coaxing to cough back into life. On the side of the road, she lays a heavy, hot head on the steering wheel, her pulse throbbing as she tries to take it all in.

As a Norwegian, it's been made clear how keen the Reich is set on courting the Nordic bloodline, for the future Reich that's intent on ruling for a thousand years or more. Tall, blond and blue-eyed, Norwegians are coveted as Aryans, set to be conjoined and absorbed into the so-called 'master race'. But she's never imagined it to be so organised, or immediate. *So controlled.*

The 'Hop House' is a hostel for women like Anya, who have – by default or design – been intimate with a German officer. *And let's not forget,* she mutters inside her head, *the other element in this shadowy scenario: rape.* Though it's never to be spoken of, or admitted, forever shrouded by a woman's guilt. Anya had told her that, far from viewing the unmarried women as shamed or unfortunate, the Reich considers them blessed, speaking openly of their 'value' in nurturing German offspring, though the very word caused Rumi to almost choke.

The subsequent reward for this exalted state is being tended and cared for in that beautiful house; she and Anya had gone inside and walked through the airy, well-furnished rooms, where women with rounded stomachs mingled with white-uniformed nurses and midwives – 'all German,' Anya had whispered – and it looked nothing like a prison, or a camp. It was spotlessly clean but not sterile, and the staff said 'good morning' in heavy-accented Norwegian, while the housekeeper greeted her politely and offered them both a drink. One obviously pregnant woman lumbered past and attempted a smile, though Rumi noted how strained her expression seemed, and it had taken her the journey home so far to perceive the real meaning, in the way her lips parted weakly and pinprick pupils fixed on

Rumi's. It was not, as far as she could tell, embarrassment or shame. It was fear.

'Come on, dammit!' Rumi hits the steering wheel in frustration as the engine wheezes with effort. 'Please. Not now!' All she wants is to reach home and talk to the one person who she can rail at and reason with, who might help her elicit some sense out of everything. If only this blasted truck would get her to Marjit.

'At last!' She bangs the wheel again, this time with relief, grinding the engine into gear and moving forward, bracing herself for the family dinner and full house Marjit is planning today, though hoping they can find a private moment and a chance for Rumi to share the fresh misery of this war.

32

Home Again

Jens

The tram rumbles by with a rattle of wheels and Jens judges his moment, slicing between the tracks on Torget as another comes hurtling towards him; a woman in the tram window winces at his close call, and he smiles inside at how much worse he's had to evade in the previous weeks and months amid Norway's unforgiving landscape.

Although today's game of dodgems isn't purely habit, since he's intent on losing the man in a black waistcoat who seems to have been close by for several blocks across the city. Mission accomplished, Jens sidles into the narrower Bankgaten, drops down on the cobbles to tie his shoelace and notes that waistcoat is nowhere in sight. Whether he was a true threat or not, it's good practice, playing ghosts between buildings and their concrete cover instead of the heather and brush of open country. One day back in Bergen and he feels at home all over again. Better still, he's ended up near the market stalls with a few decent pieces of fruit, something Marjit will appreciate far more than flowers.

'How many places shall I set?' Jens calls through to his aunt, who's immersed in a cloud of steam from pots and pans bubbling on her stove. She's already mentioned Peder and Rubio coming, there's Marjit, and he hopes . . . though Rumi can't possibly know he's returned to Bergen. Perhaps she's far too busy elsewhere?

'Set one for Rumi, too,' Marjit says. 'She said she'd try to get back in time.'

'Back?' Jens's interest is piqued, for where she's gone and whether it's resistance work – something perilous, perhaps? Then wonders why he is uneasy; out of anyone, Rumi Orlstad can look after herself.

Peder and Rubio arrive together like a father and son double-act, jibing each other as they wash up, and teasing Marjit by pretending to peek in the oven and spoil her surprise.

'Get out of it!' She flaps her cloth at them. 'Patience, you two.'

Out of sight, Jens watches through the doorway as Rubio comes from behind and spreads his long arms around Marjit, squeezing her tightly as they share a joke. He's hit again by how much intimacy he's missed by being away, and – although he's come to like Rubio and his easy personality – how envious he suddenly feels.

It's not often they gather like this around the table, for security and safety mainly, but also because there's rarely enough food to disperse, or celebrate with. This, however, is Marjit's big surprise.

'I've been on a little trip myself,' is all she would reveal to Jens when he turned up at her door, almost his first port of call since returning. She tapped her nose with a finger. 'The mystery will be revealed soon enough.'

There's still no sign of Rumi when the promised feast emerges from the oven. Marjit tells everyone to take their place, setting the heavy pot in the middle of the table and pulling off the lid like a magician.

Peder's nose is in first, drawing in the steam's aroma. 'Oh! Marjit! You're a genius. Or the best cook in Bergen, I can't decide which.'

'You haven't tasted it yet,' she says swiftly.

When large spoons of the stew are dished out to each, there are moans of pleasure. It's every vegetable from the garden, mixed with meat – *real* meat – not some hashed up fakery, though with the piquant spices it doesn't seem to matter which animal, because Marjit has cooked it long and slow, enough that it falls off the bone and doesn't need concerted, endless chewing to make it digestible. Everyone is savouring the smell before tipping the juices towards their tongues, as if reacquainting their taste buds with something genuine. Marjit is beaming – Jens looks up over his spoon as she sits at the table's head and holds court over what she wants most in the world: a family. He spies only one half-blink of disappointment as her eyes fix on the sole, empty chair set for Rumi.

But it's short-lived. Despite the heat, the door is closed to prevent their peals of pleasure drifting into the neighbourhood, along with the smell of the pot, and all eyes naturally switch to the handle being turned, combined smiles when they see who it is.

'Rumi! You made it,' Marjit sings. 'I'm so glad. Here, sit yourself down.'

The table is complete, and Jens finds himself replete with satisfaction at being part of it; good food, and easy, familiar company to be as relaxed as they ever can be, with the Germans hovering. Though not in this corner of Strangebakken today.

He's quiet, partly because all present know they can't ask what he's been doing in his absence, or where he's been. Also, because he likes to sit back and watch the exchanges of humour: Marjit chiding Peder like they've been married for years, and Rumi with Rubio, teasing each other like true siblings. He wonders if it's the same familiarity that she reached with Magnus as her future husband. It's like a family Christmas being played out, although if Jens thinks hard enough, his own celebrations at home were never this much fun. Or quite so trouble-free, with his parents waging a constant, domestic war of their own, his father distracted and his mother trying desperately to be the peacemaker between father and son. She tried, endlessly, but her successes were always short-lived.

In contrast, Rumi and Rubio have an easy intimacy; she is playfully dismissive to his jibing, prodding and nudging at his muscled shoulders, while he pretends to be mortally wounded. He knows Peder has looked on Rubio as a son since his Spanish mother was killed in the country's bitter civil war, and his father – Peder's best friend – was lost under the sea, all while Rubio still a child. It's obvious to all that he and Rumi's love is nothing more than a sibling devotion. Yet, the more Jens watches their closeness, the more it awakens the feelings buried deep inside himself, those which – despite his best intentions to anchor them firmly – are now swimming to the surface. Attraction; desire; fascination. The sensations dig uncomfortably at his being, plus one other to add when he looks at Rumi enjoying such familiarity with another man: a painful stab of jealousy.

Months away, out of sight, have not cured him. This angry woman has landed Jens Parkes. Hook, line and sinker, as the British say.

33

Decisions

Bergen, 1st August 1942

Rumi

Rumi groans as she shifts upwards and surveys the bodies around her, laughs to herself in thinking those scattered around Marjit's parlour resemble beached seals when they belly-shuffle onto the pebbled coastline and snooze, lazy and bloated, in the sun. She watches Pappa slumped against a cushion with a satisfied look on his face, one hand on his much rounder belly full of stew. Next to Rumi on the sofa, Rubio snores gently in her ear.

Marjit is the only one still up and about, clanking in the kitchen and humming with satisfaction as she insists on washing the pots. As they feasted, she relayed the tale of her fortunate 'catch' of meat, having gone to see an old farm friend a few kilometres north. While they were sipping tea in the garden, an old ewe simply dropped dead in front of the two women. Ever resourceful, they had the animal stripped and made ready for the pot in no time. Without

Marjit's careful tending with herbs and patience, it would have tasted like shoe leather, but instead, they are all pregnant with pleasure. It's that very thought which quickly rouses Rumi.

She heaves herself off the sofa, out from under Rubio's limp, protective arm. 'I need a stroll,' she yawns, 'or I'll never get moving again.'

'Care for some company?' Jens stretches his long limbs from the torpor.

In truth, she wants to wander alone and reflect properly on Anya's revelations, but there's time enough for that later. And she is pleased to see Jens. Relieved, also, that he's in one piece, even if he seems a little subdued. Those other emotions she won't chance letting in yet.

'Yes, why not?' she says. 'I thought I'd see if there are any blueberries to collect, given our larders are probably bare by now.'

They walk up and out of Bergen, needing to haul themselves up a steep incline in tackling the range of hills that act like a semi-circle of sentries overlooking the city. The conversation is mixed, about Peder and Marjit, and the direction of the war away from Norway, news which Jens delivers, and both saddens and encourages Rumi in equal measure; two French women shot in Marseille a few weeks before when a huge crowd gathered for Bastille Day – they both daring to sing *La Marseillaise* with pride – and British soldiers moving to capture key points in the battle for El Alamein.

'It all seems so far away – France and Egypt.' Rumi flops wearily down to sit on the lush grass. 'I wonder, are we doing enough? Here? Why don't we all just gather in Torgallmenningen and bellow out our national anthem, and to hell with it?'

'Because there would be repercussions, you know that,' Jens replies calmly. 'Remember Televåg? And because there are far more Germans to oversee Norwegians than in any other occupied country. We're shackled in a different way to other nations, but shackled all the same. There are simply not enough numbers to fight fairly.'

'Since when was it ever fair?' Rumi huffs. 'I feel all we're doing is sitting here, and waiting for others to fight for us. I want to do more, Jens.'

'You already do a lot. More than many.'

'It's not enough.' Her re-ignited purpose has been spurred by seeing the distress on Anya's face, by realising that as this war goes on month after month, the German resolve is not dampened by Norwegians wearing paperclips or red hats, or the short shrift they get from old women brave enough to carp at the soldiers with disdain. It merely fuels the occupiers into thinking they can build something better. With Norwegian blood, and that thought makes Rumi Orlstad sick to her stomach. 'I want to blow those bastards out of the Bergen water.'

'I promise you, there is a lot going on that you can't see,' he says. 'Things that you only hear about in the underground press weeks later. We destroyed a crucial power converter up near Trondheim, and it's made a difference.'

'We?' *Was Jens there, fully involved? In danger?*

'The resistance,' he qualifies, drawing his eyes away as he says it, perhaps to avoid her silent interrogation. 'Though, yes, I'll admit we've been knocked recently in Bergen, when the CX intelligence group was detected and pulled apart.'

'Was that Selig, do you think?' Rumi swivels her head, a nerve yanked somewhere deep inside. While she wants to be more involved, hopefully it won't be anywhere near the man with the maimed face.

'Maybe,' Jens replies. 'Almost certainly helped by their technology – they have new Direction-Finding equipment to track our signals.' He scoffs. 'You could say it's a more sophisticated cat to our poor little mouse.'

'And why is that so funny, Jens?' she snaps back. 'Or more to the point, why are you back here, if Selig has got his nose on the scent? It's dangerous for you!'

'Because I can't run away forever, Rumi – I have a job to do, Selig or no Selig.' He pauses, looks directly out to sea. The seconds beat out with several tugs on a horn down in the harbour. 'And I wanted to come back. I missed Bergen. I missed *you*. A lot.'

A gull wheels overhead, and Rumi looks up, silently giving thanks for a timely interruption.

'Did you hear me?' he ventures. She feels his eyes directly on her burning cheek.

'Yes, I did,' she murmurs.

'And?'

She feels the broiling churn of the sea. Not on the real, still waters in the distance, but within; a simmering she has managed to keep under control all these months, by simply not admitting the truth to herself. And then Jens has to go and stir it all up, letting loose the feelings she has strived to contain since Magnus. But like a stone tossed into a millpond, the calm is gone in an instant.

'I missed you, too,' she says.

His sigh of relief is heard over and above the breeze. 'So?'

He wants an answer, clearly – a sign, something of her.

'So . . . I don't think it . . . we can . . .' She's stammering with indecision inside and out, her heart and her common sense at loggerheads.

'I have to know, Rumi.'

Up above, a lone cloud causes a dim eclipse, and Rumi grasps the moment. 'It's still too soon,' she murmurs. 'After Magnus. And what with you going away, and maybe not coming back . . .' She turns to look at him squarely. 'I just don't think I could do it again, Jens. People are dying in this war each and every day, but it doesn't mean that it's not crippling for those who knew them, loved them. I'm not strong enough to do it again.'

'I think you are resilient enough for anything in this world, Rumi,' he says, though the regret in his voice is obvious and untamed. 'But I understand, and I wouldn't want to be the cause of any more sadness in you. Far from it.'

She both loves and hates him for being so considerate, alongside the push and pull of every emotion within her. To him, she pastes on a smile to hide her own regret – *if only I were brave enough* – and stands up to leave. 'Besides, what would you want in a grumpy old fishwife like me?'

That makes him laugh, at least, enough that his face throws off the disappointment. 'So, if I become an honorary fishwife, does that mean we can be firm friends, Rumi Orlstad?'

'Consider yourself a fully-fledged sea spouse, Jens Parkes.'

She reaches out to pull him up by the hand, an act which prompts a swift recall: the white, icy mountaintop less than eight months ago, having cut him down from the fir and revived him with Hilde's soup. How testy and ill-tempered she was that day, grief-stricken, fuming at the world. She's still angry, but it's been re-directed, and no longer towards him. She's changed, too, enough to have considered the prospect for a moment – they as a couple, the intimacy. Sharing things. But that war Kraken is still present. In the depths, maybe. Hidden. But it could so easily rise and rob her again. And it's that which Rumi cannot contemplate.

34

A House of Cards

Hop, 1st August 1942

I should have known it, she thinks, eyeing the women at break-fast and sensing the low hum of their conversation; never fully open to each other, despite living in such close quarters. Unlike their burgeoning bellies, they keep much of their private thoughts deep inside. Something was always destined to emerge, this whole set-up always too good to be true. Just as she's got the place running smoothly, juggling the rations, seesawing emotions and Kleiner's demands to a workable level, her world within this war shows its true colours. But then, if she really thinks about it, her perfect construction always was just a house of cards, ready to come tumbling down at the slightest puff of wind. And from what she can see, this is more than a breeze.

Looking at the women, she wonders if they suspect something; one, in particular, who arrived full of hope for a new life, has become noticeably anxious in recent weeks. As she grows, so does her angst – her eyes betray it increasingly each day, asking the maids more than once about other places to stay. Some days, the poor woman can't be calmed and she's heard the midwives talking in whispers of having to use sedation if it gets much worse.

She muses, too, on what outsiders see when they walk through the door of the house. Only today, one of the newer residents, Anya, had a visitor – it's allowed in moderation, since most women are happy not to have guests – and she watched both women as they walked through the house. The visitor, she'd noted, was all eyes, sizing up the situation through her smiles. As an outsider, she might not have known for sure, but it's clear that she senses something isn't sitting right.

The timing is ironic, since her own suspicions are newly aroused, too. Properly this time. It was all Kleiner's doing, when he insisted that none of the maids should set foot in his office, and that she herself should take up the cleaning. He's never exhibited such trust in her before, but maybe he got tired of looking at his own filth, the ashtray overflowing with cigar butts and the wastepaper bin of discarded circulars, with no fire to burn them in in this heat.

The desk, he'd told her firmly, should not be touched. But he didn't say explicitly that she couldn't look. Only now, she wishes she hadn't. One open envelope, one cursory, snatched look inside at the words 'provision' and 'product' before a shuffling outside the door stopped her prying further. It's enough, though, to harbour a guess as to why the Reich is investing in these women, spending money on babies as well as bombs in their quest for domination. She's no mother, has never yearned for a child of her own, but she is human and it sickens her, having cared for them for months, absorbing their tears and worries. There's no direct proof, of course, only her suspicions, but they are increasing each day, every time a mother leaves to have her baby, and doesn't return. Where do they go?

The bigger question is: what can she do about it? Who can she tell, and who would believe her?

She sighs, almost silently, as she's become expert at doing of late. A thought creeps into her mind: perhaps this House of Cards needs to be brought down, knocked clean over and destroyed for good?

35

A Woman in Need

Bergen, 2nd August 1942

Rumi

Perhaps it's because this is the second war where she's witnessed cruelty and injustice, but Marjit doesn't seem too shocked at Anya's predicament. Instead, Rumi detects more of an unease in her reaction.

'So, what happens after the baby is born?' Marjit asks, eyes on her wool as they sit knitting in her parlour. The summer heat means the stove is off, but habit dictates they hug close to it, drinking in an evening breeze from the open back door, the front windows to the lane firmly shut while they talk.

'We didn't get that far,' Rumi replies. 'Anya got shuffled off for some task by one of the German women, a midwife or a nurse. She's taken on some office work there, to be of some use to the other women and to stop herself going mad with boredom.'

'And she'll have the baby there, in that house?'

'Again, I'm not sure,' Rumi says. 'I saw one woman pushing a pram in the grounds as I left, but mostly it was women obviously pregnant.' She curses under her breath at dropping a stitch, and works to pick at the weave.

'When will you see her again?' Marjit asks.

'I said I'd go again next Sunday – they're allowed one visitor at a weekend.'

'Can't she leave the house, even for an afternoon?' the older woman's concern rises a note.

'She didn't say she *couldn't* leave,' Rumi goes on, 'but I think Anya's wary of the comments from the locals. People around there seem to know the house is for unmarried mothers, and she is starting to show now.'

'How far gone?'

'Almost four months. The baby's due around the middle of January.'

'And then what?' Marjit's needles are clacking in a steady rhythm but there's a quiver of concern in her voice.

Rumi shrugs. 'She doesn't know. Poor Anya – her parents are in England, there's little chance of getting a message across, and anyway, I think she's too ashamed to tell them. Her only relative in Norway is an aunt who's so appalled she won't have her to stay.'

'It's fortunate she has you as a friend.'

Rumi puffs out her cheeks. 'Sadly, I feel I'm little more than a shoulder to cry on. I just don't know how to help her.'

'You know I'd happily take her in,' Marjit says. 'Do you think she'd want to come?'

'In all honesty, I'm not sure,' Rumi replies. 'It's not ideal there, but she has financial support and a good roof over her head. It seems odd to me that this baby was conceived in less than savoury circumstances – and that's putting it

206

mildly – and yet the Reich is willing to look after Anya and women like her.'

'But then we know how much the Germans are trying to make friends of us and act as if they care. They want our country and our blood.' Marjit scoffs into her knitting. 'Not that it will work. We'll become part of the thousand-year Reich over my dead body.'

'Please don't throw yourself under a Panzer tank yet. Haven't we got jumpers to finish?'

Marjit aims a spare skein of wool in Rumi's direction. 'Just for that, my girl, you can make the coffee.'

The weather is still fiercely hot a week later as Rumi makes her way to Hop again, taking the train this time to avoid the unreliability of Peder's truck. Being holed in the boathouse most of the week means she likes to get out and see life, to mingle with her own people and hear their talk. There's a lot of grumbling from the woman sat next to her, but she doesn't mind soaking it up; the frustration is understandable, and it's a welcome distraction from her own.

Anya is waiting for her on the driveway, except her smile is scant and forced, and she barely manages a welcome.

'What's wrong?' Rumi says. 'Is it you, or the baby?' They've made it to the bench furthest from the house, looking out on the calm, glassy sea.

'No, no, we're well,' Anya says, and puts a hand to her belly, which – to Rumi's untrained eye – appears to have bloomed in just one week. Her friend's protective palm across her girth says a lot more.

'So what is it? You don't seem yourself.'

Anya heaves out a breath and wipes the dark circles under her eyes. 'I've been asked for help by one of the women,' she says.

207

'What sort of help?'

'To get her away, from here. Before the baby is born,' Anya goes on.

Rumi blinks away her confusion. 'But you said yourself you're well cared for here. And presumably, she has no other family . . .'

'She's utterly convinced that they're going to take the baby away from her,' Anya blurts. 'Forcibly.'

Rumi stares at the horizon, hoping to pull some sense of grounding from the static line, as she always used to. Marjit's warning comes hurtling into her brain: *they want our blood.* 'Does she have any basis for thinking that? I mean, have you heard of it happening?'

Anya's already pale complexion bleaches against the direct sun. 'It's difficult to tell. When the women go into labour they're generally taken to a different home – Lebensborn, they call it – and they rarely return.'

'But they do come back sometimes?' Rumi is scrabbling for positives.

'Yes, a few have. But so far just those women who are intent on marrying the fathers – there are some men willing to shoulder the responsibility – and they're just waiting to travel to Germany for a new life.'

'And no one else returns with their baby?'

'Not that I've seen.' Anya turns away from the sun's glare, her face in shadow, and her expression darker. 'This poor woman is frantic, almost hysterical. She's convinced that if she walks out, they'll come after her.'

'And do you think that's the case?'

'I really don't know.' Anya shakes her head wearily. 'But she is making herself ill. Rumi, is there anyone you know who could help her? Anyone at all?'

★　★　★

208

She goes straight from the bus to the mission office, unsure if Jens will even be there, only hoping he is. The sight of his reddened, hot face as he lugs more boxes is, to her, like a draught of iced water in a lengthy drought.

'*Hei,* this is a welcome surprise,' he says, with the smile that she needs so much to see. 'I was just about to stop for a drink. Join me?'

They walk to the only bar open on the waterfront, stare in silence over their drinks at what feels like a never-ending sun in this ceaseless conflict. Rumi's thoughts are jumbled, but she can't force them into any order, let alone make sense of them.

'Penny for them?' Jens says.

'Sorry?' It breaks Rumi's reflection and conjures a laugh in one, though her brow is still creased with burden. 'Can I ask you something, Jens?'

In almost a single breath, she tells him of Anya's situation and her request for help. 'Do you think there could be any truth in it?' Rumi says. 'Could they − would they − effectively *steal* babies to create perfect German families?'

Jens shakes his head. 'I don't doubt they're capable of it, or that Himmler would happily sanction it, in their warped vision of the future, but whether it's happening here, in Bergen?' He shrugs with both hands. 'I can only put out the word and see what comes back over the wire.'

'Thanks,' she says. 'It's odd − I don't even know this friend of Anya's, I can't possibly imagine what she's going through, and yet I already feel her desperation. So much that I want to help her.'

'And you can't see why?' The light in his eyes says he already holds the answer.

'What do you mean?' It's unnerving when Jens seems to sense things that Rumi doesn't recognise in herself.

'You've felt loss and you don't want her to have to endure the pain of it,' he says plainly.

'But Magnus wasn't . . . What could I possibly know about having or losing a baby?'

'It doesn't matter what type of heartbreak it is. It still hurts. And you want to prevent that.' Jens pauses. 'And I think that makes you a good person.'

The air hangs sticky and heavy as they ponder into their half-empty glasses – this latest realisation of what the Nazis might be capable of; this war; the oppression; the future of the world at large. The scrape of his chair breaks the dense mood. 'Come on,' Jens says, 'let's see what I can find out.'

It's only his optimism that propels her to move.

'And I think you've made me into an honorary fishwife under false pretences, Rumi Orlstad,' he goes on as they walk. 'You're really not such a grumpy old curmudgeon after all.'

'I wouldn't bank on it, Jens Parkes. There's a dragon in me that might well breathe fire again.'

36

Retrieval

Hop, 14th August 1942

Jens

He grips at the steering wheel, eyes fixed on the turning point in the road where his quarry will emerge, hopefully soon. Unusually for Jens, it's daylight, the mid-morning sun beating down; he's been more used to coaching his night vision during an operation, watching for the glint of Nazi insignia off a sliver of moonlight as the sentries kept themselves alert in the early hours by telling stories and smoking. In all those weeks spent up north, crouching silently with explosives nudging at his body, ready to be primed, he'd become adept at reading the shards of reflection in enemy eyes, as he and his comrades lay in wait to wreak havoc on their target. That's how he's used to operating and, strangely, it seems easier than this.

Here, now, it's the heat and the complete unknown forcing sweat to snake down his back and soak into his shirt. He feels hopelessly exposed. *Where the hell is Rumi?*

He checks his watch. Ten minutes late, a good twenty since she left the truck. There was no one at the gate as they drove past, so what's the hold up? He squirms, hand hovering over the ignition lever and praying, praying that Peder's truck does not fail them now.

At last, he sees both women stepping around the corner, painfully slowly, given that one of them is heavily pregnant. He's no expert, but it looks as if she's about to give birth at any minute, her cheeks puffing out with the effort of Rumi trying to urge her along at a faster pace. He hopes it's the heat – or that so-called bloom of pregnancy – causing the flush in her rounded face. But what does he know?

The two women reach the truck and Jens hops down from the cab, helping the woman up the high step as quickly as they can, she grunting and shifting her girth into the middle of the seat, with Rumi pushing in next to her. 'Let's go,' she says.

'Did anyone see you?' Jens checks.

'No, I'm pretty sure. We met beyond the driveway and there was nobody that I could see.'

The woman smiles meekly at Jens. 'I'm Trine,' she says, holding out a hand, beads of sweat at the edges of her white blonde hair. 'Thank you for coming. Thank you so much. I don't know what . . .'

He caps her off, wordlessly, with a nod. The less said is always better. But he does smile all the same, in a 'you're welcome' kind of way, so that she knows she's not a burden. Merely someone in war, in need.

He fires up the engine and they trundle at a normal speed down the lane from the Hop hostel and into a quiet lay-by a few minutes away. Jens gets out of the cab, followed by the two women, and Rumi helps him lift Trine up and onto the flat bed of the truck; the heat and effort is making them all sweat. Rumi climbs up herself and steers the pregnant woman to a wide, shallow crate fashioned by Rubio, lined with a blanket. She hesitates for a second – with dismay or trepidation perhaps – and then manoeuvres herself and her bump in awkwardly. Jens reads Rumi's expression all too well as she closes over the lid and covers it with heavy hessian: 'Sorry', she's saying to Trine with her pitying look, 'sorry that you and your baby have to suffer this humiliation.' *But better this incarceration than something else.*

'It might look inhuman but it's the safest way,' he'd reasoned to Rumi days before. It had been two weeks since their first conversation about Lebensborn and what it might mean. In that time, he'd learnt that, literally, the word means 'well of life' in German, and he'd had to suppress his laughter, both at the Nazis' audacity, and their supreme irony. But there wasn't much more; the SOE and SIS contacts knew little about Lebensborn in Norway, since their aims were focused principally on sabotaging heavy industry and not maternity homes. Rumi had gone back to see Anya at the hostel the next Sunday, returning to Bergen with an air of urgency; this 'hysterical' woman – Trine – was getting closer to confinement, more and more convinced she would lose her baby at the hands of pawing, thieving Nazis. She was desperate to escape but with no means or anyone to help her. Anya was no midwife, she'd told Rumi, but she feared Trine's anxiety was acute enough to harm both her and the baby. 'We've managed to keep her just calm enough until now,' she'd said. 'But the staff are becoming agitated too, and the housekeeper has been hovering around Trine a lot. I don't know for how much longer she can keep it together.'

So they've become the means, he and Rumi and the boatyard crew. Jens thinks of the fierce reprimand from his commanding officer if this 'mission' becomes known, but as he watches Trine clutch at her bulbous belly and lay down in that crate like a zoo animal – with a glance of gratitude – he's already justified the risk to himself. It's helping people, isn't it? And that's his job.

Rumi joins him back in the truck's cab, puffing with the heat. 'I hate to think how hot it is in there for her,' she says. 'But she has some water and there are enough slats for some air. Let's hope we don't get held up.'

Hope isn't enough. Even when the roads are quiet, the roadblocks are fully manned, and although Jens maintains a steady speed – fearing the bumpy roads might have an overt effect on a pregnant woman – they are pulled to a stop a kilometre or so from Peder's boatyard. The German sentries seem casual enough, laughing and joking as they approach the truck's open window, but they soon become stiff and more officious as a few uniformed STAPO emerge from the small hut next to the guard post. The Wehrmacht boys are not cowed or ruled over by the Norwegian police – quite the opposite – but there's a definite air of showboating: *watch how the Reich runs things*, they are saying. *Watch and learn.*

Jens reaches into his pocket for his false papers, and senses Rumi stiffen next to him; he swears he can feel the ripple of hairs at the back of her neck.

'Dammit,' she mutters. 'That's all we need. It's Bjarne bloody Hansen.'

Jens doesn't take his eyes off the officers, and with minimal movement to his mouth, whispers: 'Then use it. Be nice.'

She flashes him a look that needs no words because it speaks volumes. Rumi the Angry Woman is awakened.

'Hei, Rumi Orlstad.' Bjarne pushes his way past the Wehrmacht officer. 'I haven't seen you in a while. What are you doing with your father's truck?' He's smiling and showing off the familiarity to his comrades, and his position of influence to Rumi. She smiles in return, lips closed, but Jens knows that behind it her teeth are gritted, restraining the venom inside.

'We're just moving a few clothes for the mission,' she fires at Bjarne. 'Helping the war effort and the refugees.'

Careful Rumi. Stow the sarcasm. Be nice.

In the wing mirror, Jens watches the Wehrmacht walk to the back of the truck and scan the packed bundles they've been careful to place around Trine's crate.

'Give it a good poke,' one of the soldiers instructs another, although it's said lightly, as if they're merely going through the motions. Even so, the words will be enough to scare poor Trine to death, blind and helpless under the thick cloth.

Jens senses the heavy weight of a body land on the flat surface of the truck, as Rumi is forced to keep up small talk with Bjarne. Several sharp jolts are felt in the cab, which can only mean the sentry is plunging a bayonet into the soft bundles with excessive force.

'No!' Rumi is suddenly thrusting open the door, pushing Bjarne aside and running to the back of the truck, her fury unleashed, and Jens watches in the mirror as she berates the young Wehrmacht man. He's poked at her anger and the fire is stoked. 'The least you can do is let us help the refugees with clothes that don't have holes in them,' she barks. 'Have you no shame? Or do you hate all Norwegians?'

Oh Christ, Rumi, now is not the time. Jens daren't join in – experience tells him the German soldiers will only become more belligerent if challenged by another man, and a Norwegian at that. This way, the troops can josh each other later at how they bravely fended off a young harridan. A fishwife in the making, they might say.

Strangely, though, Rumi's short tirade seems to work. Either embarrassed or contrite, the sentry jumps down, and the troops look backwards down the road at the oncoming traffic, led by Bjarne. 'Here's some better prey,' the STAPO man jokes to them, stepping towards a carful of young men, who become instant targets for their bullying.

Rumi climbs back in the truck, her entire face as flushed as when Jens first set eyes on Trine, and the barrier is raised, a sentry waving them on.

'Rumi!' he hisses, as they drive away, out of earshot. 'You are going to be the death of me.'

'I sincerely hope not,' she says, a smile moving across her lips. 'Damned well worked, though, didn't it?'

Trine has already been in the crate far too long under a blistering sun and Jens pushes the truck to its top speed, drawing up outside the boatyard where Marjit is waiting with food supplies for the onward journey. The plan is for Peder to transport Trine in the trawler to a drop off point north, where another set of patriots are lined up to conceal her until she can be taken by car across the border to Sweden, in time for the birth. There's no Shetland Bus in summertime as the long daylight hours pose too much risk for boats exposed in the open water, and so by road is the only way. They have no idea how soon Trine will be missed, or even if the hostel hierarchy will care – babies being an unknown currency – but they plan for the worst, that at the very least the Nazis won't take too kindly to being hoodwinked.

Rumi springs from the cab the moment the wheels stop and runs to the back of the truck, is up in seconds and pulling at the hessian to release Trine. Jens climbs down from the driver's side, and reaches the back of the truck to join Marjit, who instinctively stretches one arm around his lean frame, an affectionate squeeze to his hip. Automatically, he plants a kiss on her head. But their joint attention is fixed on Rumi as she opens the lid to the crate. They both see – rather than hear – her gasp, alongside the obvious shock on her red, rounded face.

Jens is horrified, his mind in a vortex. Surely, the poor woman can't have suffocated? She had air, didn't she? Could the heat do that so quickly? Or the stress?

'What is it, Rumi?' Marjit entreats. 'What's wrong?' Already she's urging Jens to give her a lift, a woman of fifty-plus defying her years and scrabbling quickly towards the crate to see for herself.

Jens is static. In some ways it's even worse than Karl, his friend. Trine is a stranger but also a mother. Dead. And by virtue, the baby too. Such a waste. It's all such a waste.

'Jens! JENS!' Marjit's voice is demanding. 'Help us get her down. Call Rubio, too – he's inside.'

'Is she alive?' is all he can say, and hope that his aunt's urgency means it's true.

'Alive? Yes,' Marjit shoots back. 'But more than that, I think we're going to have a baby.'

37

Renewal

Rumi

Poor Trine. As if the journey isn't enough, they are forced to manhandle her like cargo as she's gripped with fear or pain, Rumi can't tell which. What she does know, even with her very scant knowledge about birth and babies, is that when a woman's waters break, the baby arrives sooner or later. And generally sooner. The fluid soaked into the blanket in the crate appeared to be far more than just sweat, and the look on Trine's face told her the rest.

'Careful, careful boys,' Marjit instructs as they shuffle into the boathouse and towards Rumi's office.

'Shouldn't we try to get her home to Strangebakken?' Rumi asks. 'I mean, this is not the ideal place.' In truth, she's fairly horrified at a baby being born so close to where she works. Fish and their detritus she can deal with, but this is another matter.

'No,' says Marjit defiantly. 'There are watchful neighbours

218

at home and tongues are bound to wag. We're better here, out of the way.' She takes a quick glance at Trine blowing hard into the air, her eyes squeezed shut. 'Besides, any distance is too far for her now.'

Rubio absents himself rapidly as they deposit Trine gently in the pallet chair and mutters something about 'keeping watch'. Rumi is surprised but relieved to see Jens linger.

'What do we need?' she questions Marjit. 'Surely, there are . . . I don't know . . . things?'

She detects a perplexing mixture of concern and vibrancy as Marjit fires a reply, her own zeal apparent: 'A pair of hands, hot water, luck, hope and a great big prayer to Mother Nature. That's all.'

'But have you . . .?' Rumi quizzes. The question hangs as Peder's throaty trawler chugs away outside in blissful ignorance.

'Helped with a birth before?' Marjit finishes for her. 'Of course. Two in the back of an ambulance, in France. And then I had to use hand signals instead of words. At least this mother is Norwegian.'

She pushes up her sleeves and heads towards Trine, who's decided she's had enough of pallets for one day and has crawled on her knees to a spot next to Rumi's desk, her face pressed into the old wood and running with sweat.

Rumi's eyes rise towards Jens, who now seems uncharacteristically flummoxed, and unable to move. In turn, he looks at her, and they exchange what Rumi believes to be an identical notion, one that resonates: *Thank God Marjit is here.*

To spare Trine's dwindling dignity, Jens is encouraged to fetch the all-important hot water. Rumi goes to leave, too, the heat creeping rapidly up inside her, but Marjit foils her with one look. 'I need you,' she mouths, her bright blue eyes telling Rumi there is no escape.

★   ★   ★

219

Jens hands her a cup of the brew, its tart aroma under her nose having the arousing effect of smelling salts. Marjit has decreed that the new mother needs only herbal tea and as much good food as they can muster, but Rumi craves something stronger. In the absence of champagne, Aquavit, or even a good pre-war beer, it's down to the real coffee grains hidden in her desk.

'Thanks,' she says absent-mindedly.

As the sun loses its strength and the day wanes, Jens sits beside her on the deck outside, their legs dangling above the water slapping against the poles of the jetty. 'So?'

She turns to look at him, still in a daze. 'So, what?'

'How do you feel?' His face is eager, and he seems fired up. 'You've just seen a baby born, a new life. In your office, of all places. How was it?'

Rumi ponders. Of course the memory will remain, not least because the actual event occurred right next to her desk, Trine being unwilling to move and Marjit happy to stay put, considering she had much more space than in the confines of an ambulance.

'It was amazing,' she murmurs. There are scores of words crowding her head, flurrying about like the maelstrom she's often witnessed out at sea: scary, messy, testing, arduous and impossible (until it wasn't). And then beautiful, incredible, astonishing and miraculous overriding all of those. Astounding in that one minute there were three of them in that hot, sweaty office amid the stink of fish, all crouched on their knees, suspended in a human animation. Then, with the next tumultuous effort from Trine, there were four, the baby slipping into Marjit's awaiting hands and squealing its distaste in the next heartbeat, squirming and wet and perfect.

Before today, Rumi has always thought of herself as

practical and – until Magnus knocked her faith sideways – stoic and strong. It was the make-up she inherited from her mother, and a reputation she was proud of. Never blown away, or shocked beyond words.

'It was bloody amazing,' she repeats over the steam of her cup, turning to see Jens look at her in a way he never has before. He's boring right inside her again, but with an air of wonder. Is he thinking what she is right now: Would she ever do that? Could she put herself in that vulnerable position, where you would cry out for help, as Trine did, because in that moment it's the biggest thing you have ever experienced? Would she grip on to a near stranger's hand for dear life, because at the point of no return you just need to feel humanity has not deserted you?

With Magnus, it had been an unspoken agreement between them to have a family, a rite of passage for most married women in Norway. By then, she felt time and marriage would have made her welcome it, perhaps. She would have duly knitted tiny baby clothes to put on her own child and dressed it with love. She likes to think she would have enjoyed it, making new life – an imprint – with someone she adored.

Then Magnus, the loss and the war had robbed her of that pleasurable future and the feelings that went with it.

And now what? After the day's events she feels hot and agitated, unnerved and restless. Not because it seems to be the most objectionable state for a woman to relish, or the most unwelcome.

But because, suddenly, it isn't.

38

Eyes and Ears

Hop, 15th August 1942

The house — her house — is in disarray, and it leaves her more than unsettled. Kleiner, when he heard, was seething at what he termed 'the escape' and ordered the midwives to spin a story that the missing woman, Trine, had gone into labour and been taken to the maternity home. But neither the Norwegian staff nor the pregnant women were fooled when she wasn't at dinner that evening, or breakfast this morning. Trine had confided in some of them, Anya especially, about her fears for the baby and she can hear clusters of them whispering behind bedroom doors, clutching tightly at their bumps when they emerge for meals. Uncertainty clings to the expensive wallpaper like musty damp in a hovel.

It's meant more than upset for her, too. Despite his general absence, Kleiner had already cottoned on to her being a constant presence about the place and summoned her to his office this lunchtime. He sat behind his wide desk, with an accusing stare focused on her. It didn't reflect well on either of them, he said with quiet menace, to lose a 'client' like that. 'Or on your family,' he followed on swiftly. She has only one sister still alive, but two nieces and a nephew, and Kleiner knew all about them and where they lived. In detail. There would be extra security in the hostel and grounds, he'd said, but she needs to be more than a house-keeper from now on. His eyes and ears, especially among the women. Though he put an abrupt halt to their conversation, they both knew exactly what he meant — his hanging thread of threat. As the Nazis do so well. And now it's been suspended directly above her.

She's loved her sister always; more of a strength and support than her parents ever were, and she thinks of her sister's children almost as her own. Knowing that her nephew is likely in the resistance a little way to the north, and the repercussions from Televåg still fresh, she is caught between being human and a continued support to the women, or a spy for that contemptible man and his loathsome Führer.

In private, sighing has been replaced by the wringing of her hands, which she does increasingly, but out of sight of the other staff. This place used to be a home full of happiness. Now, it's a house full of potential life, along with too many secrets and a well of sadness.

39

A Valuable Currency

Bergen, 18th August 1942

Jens

The Reich does care – about their lost mother, but also the brazen mettle of Norwegians to help their own and defy the occupiers. The search was evident only a day after Trine's baby arrived, the Wehrmacht sent to raid houses in Hop and some in Bergen with new babies, poor mothers having to prove, in the crudest manner possible, that their own children came from their womb.

The word spread across the wire after that, German messages intercepted alerting Lebensborn in other districts to be aware of 'escapees'. It soon becomes clear that the currency of new and impressionable humans to mould into Hitler's perfect way of thinking represents something of great value; Lebensborn is an industry in the Reich's grand plan, a 'natural resource' to be harvested, much like iron ore or fish oil. As they've suspected all along, Norwegians are a commodity.

Jens presses the crude, metal headphones close into his ear with one hand, scribbling down pencil marks with the other. Minutes later, he winces as he deciphers the symbols, those describing the 'asset' as being a priority for protection – even the most amateur of codebreakers would guess at what they mean. Having seen Trine's baby at only a few hours old, cooing into his mother's breast, and then feeling the softness of those tiny fingers as they linked into his, Jens struggles to think how any baby can be thought of as a mere product. But the Reich, as he's beginning to realise, are full of surprises.

Rumi had chanced a visit to the hostel two days after Trine's breakout, noting a guard already posted at the hostel entrance and one in the grounds, their presence causing Anya's anxiety to multiply, along with many of the other women.

'I've told her we can't risk another attempt yet,' Rumi reported after the visit. 'Luckily, she's nowhere near the birth, but I don't know how she'll stay calm in there.'

'Can they leave the hostel at all?' Jens asked.

'Only with an escort now. Apparently, it feels more and more like a camp – I sensed it too. A very comfortable one, but it's a prison all the same. What's worse, Anya is still not exactly sure why they're being confined. There are rumours, but no one knows if Trine's guess was right for sure.'

Jens adjusts the headphones and rests his chin in his hands at the thought. He's been told unofficially by SOE that one mother and baby doesn't equate to scores of Norwegians potentially saved, or justify the potential loss of agents. In effect, they have to weigh up the human cost over the gains; someone's life swinging on a set of scales.

His heart twinges uncomfortably. Doesn't that make the

Allies almost as pitiless as the Germans, in assigning a value to people? What is one human life worth? And does *he* have the right to determine those numbers, to govern someone's fate in a calculation?

He claws a hand through his hair in sweeping away the burden. It's not easy, but there are more pressing matters to face.

Something sparks in his ear, and for some reason it resonates straightaway: 'asset' is tapped out in German, followed by their own code for 'search'. Worse still, the word 'wharf' is just identifiable in the same message. Jens is up and out of his chair in seconds, and his brain doesn't allow time for any kind of calculation. All he can think is: *Trine is at the wharf. Trine and her baby.*

The journey across town he does automatically and at speed, ignoring the passing glances of Wehrmacht, who are hovering around the edges of Torgallmenningen. He hears several military vehicles accelerating across Strandgaten but has no time to worry they're pursuing him, dipping instead into side streets where alleyways between tall, imposing buildings hide his tracks. His heart beats in his ears, and it's the resounding pump, pump that he remembers from France, when his unit was under heavy attack and the Panzers nipped at their tails in the retreat towards Dunkirk. The same, frantic heartbeat he heard in the minute that Charlie's stopped dead. And as much as he hates the thought, it's his own calculation that refuses to disappear: if he saves Trine and a new young life, will it go some way to making up for his wrong over Charlie?

He reaches Peder's boathouse and slows his steps, swallows back his panting breath and scans the area. There's only the noise of the waterfront and two of Peder's static boats in view. What's more, the air feels undisturbed. Only then does he hear the cough and slow roll into life of another type of engine: a baby's cry in rhythm with the slap, slap of water against the jetty poles. Jens checks the boathouse hurriedly, praying that Peder or Rubio are there after hours, but nothing. No Rumi, either – she will have gone some time ago. Oh Christ.

Below the boat's deck, Trine is startled to see him, worried and then outwardly fearful when he rapidly explains his arrival, that they have to go – now. She eases the baby from her breast, settles him in the makeshift crib and comes up top to untie the tethers, surprisingly nimble for a woman who gave birth only four days ago. But then, she must know adrenalin all too well.

Jens scrabbles inside the wheelhouse, instantly out of his comfort zone on a boat, let alone piloting one. A jeep and a truck he can drive, had even managed to steer an Allied tank out of danger once in France. But a trawler. How does it even start? Where's the throttle, and why hasn't he paid more attention before?

Trine's impish face, shrunken since giving birth, appears in the window, silently gesturing to the approaching footsteps hitting the wooden jetty. How many? It's hard to tell. Jens scrabbles blindly to locate the engine starter, relieved to hear a grinding chug of response as the footsteps increase in volume and speed. The wheel is immovable as he yanks it down; where the hell is the lever to release it, to make this bloody thing move forward? Steps clump heavily onto the deck, but he can't spend the seconds looking and frantically surveys the boat's basic controls.

'Here, let me,' a deep voice comes into his ear and a shoulder nudges him aside, the burly, bronzed arm of a man, a ship's mate, he's never been so pleased to see. Thank God for Rubio.

227

40

Precious Times

Bergen, 18th August 1942

Rumi

'Tea or wine?' Marjit holds up the pot in front of Rumi, and in her other hand she clasps a dark and dusty unlabelled bottle.

'Where did you get that?' Rumi says in wonder.

'Found it in the cellar when I was turning out some old boxes,' Marjit replies. 'Do you know, I think it might be one of Lars's concoctions that I brought here from the farm? It looks ancient enough.'

The bottle could be nearing ten years old – eight years since Marjit's beloved husband died of sudden heart failure at just forty-six. Its age also signifies that it will be pot luck as to the liquid inside, a Russian roulette of sweet nectar or bitter poison.

'What type of wine is it?' Rumi shuffles herself forward on the floor of Marjit's parlour, where the knitting ritual is just beginning.

'If we're lucky, it's either plum or cherry,' Marjit says as she struggles to ease off the stopper.

'And if we're not?'

'Potato,' Marjit puffs. 'Lars made wine out of almost anything.' Defeated, she hands it to Rumi for a go.

The bung pops off in seconds and Rumi sniffs the neck of the bottle, nostrils braced for an onslaught. Her eyes widen. 'I think we're in luck, Marjit – and a merry old evening.'

The years in storage might well have made the brew stronger, but it's more likely the dearth of beer and wine in wartime that has dented their resilience to alcohol; Rumi is soon feeling loose-lipped and in danger of some wayward knitting.

It's the first time they've been able to talk in private since the birth of Trine's baby four days ago, a small but healthy boy that she christened Rubio, which of course has prompted his adult namesake to wander around with a large, self-satisfied grin on his face ever since. As if the women hadn't done all the hard work!

'Did you see Trine today?' Marjit coughs as she takes another sip of the dark, berry wine; it's not made of root vegetable, but it's not the smoothest either.

'No, only the day after the birth,' Rumi says. 'She looked a different woman – so alive, despite the exhaustion. Did you?'

The question is rhetorical; Marjit hasn't been able to keep away, making daily excuses to trip up and down to Peder's oldest boat on the wharf – the trawler that's been laid up and 'awaiting repairs' – until they can get word and re-organise her onward journey. Rumi knows Marjit has spent hours infusing food with nutrition for a feeding mother, delving into her best fabric supply and rustling up

229

tiny baby clothes, and even now weaving a thick blanket for winter.

Rumi herself has finished a woollen hat ready for the cold months, and a small jacket to keep him snug. She's loath to admit it even to Marjit, but she's thought of little else since the birth; playing over the noises of Trine's extreme effort, followed so swiftly by a sigh bound up in complete ecstasy as the baby made its first cry. Night and day it chimes inside her head, a melody that has weaved its way into Rumi's soul, certain that it will stay with her, no matter what. And that's what has kept her at a distance from mother and baby, wary of being drawn in too deeply and too soon. Of wanting it too much. There's no chance of that life for her. Not now – and perhaps never.

It makes Rumi feel for Marjit already, having to watch Peder finally chug out of the harbour in a few days' time with his extra cargo of Trine and the baby on board; her heart and soul in the care she gave, followed so soon by the parting, and her own lifelong void.

It's a subject that sits heavy, and the alcohol soon sweeps away any inhibitions. 'How do you do it, Marjit?' Rumi utters, face into her wool.

'Do what, my love?'

'Give so much, to Trine especially.' Her eyes flick up from the weave, and back again swiftly. 'It must be hard.'

The needles opposite are instantly still, and Rumi wonders if she's gone too far, that the wine isn't having quite the same effect on Marjit, and that her question has only pushed a sharp point into the older woman's heart. Then the tic-tac starts up again.

'I can because I know what it's like.' Marjit says it so quietly that her words almost fall unnoticed.

It's Rumi's industry that grinds to a halt then. 'But I thought . . . that you and Lars couldn't . . .'

Marjit takes in a long breath from the cloying air around them and lets it out so slowly, as if her particles of truth can only seep out by degrees. 'We never spoke about it to anyone else. We'd been married five years and I was in my mid-thirties. By then, Lars and I thought it would never happen, so when it did . . .' Her voice tails off, back into history.

A pin-prick silence across the room nudges the narration along.

'He was born too early, a good three months, and the midwife didn't get there until it was over. Lars was amazing' – Marjit breaks into a nostalgic smile – 'and I was sitting up with him in my arms when she got there. I think we were blinded by the whole thing, by this miracle, of him being there, and alive. But the midwife spotted straightaway that he was different – perhaps never meant for this world.'

Rumi has a million questions but no syllables; needles, wool and time are still.

'So we had our beautiful Nils for a whole day and a night, close into my chest,' Marjit goes on. 'And it was the best time we had, and then he slipped away. And he must have been special, because it never happened again for us.'

She looks up and wipes a tear with her sleeve. 'So you see, Rumi, I know what it feels like – that love – and despite missing him, and Lars, every single day, I wouldn't trade it for a thousand years, those hours we had. That's why you must never lose faith that you'll have it too. That one day you'll grasp it, and hold on to it.'

'Oh, Marjit.' Rumi tosses her work aside and crawls over to her best friend, her confidante and surrogate mother, and they grip each other tight, bodies shaking with a joint grief that flows and blends.

'Sodding wine,' Marjit mutters. 'I did always accuse Lars of putting something in it to make me maudlin.'

They break apart, eyes flying to the kitchen door as the wood around the jamb creaks and feet hit the doormat. Automatically, Rumi grabs her free knitting needle and holds it out as a ridiculous defence.

'Jens!' Marjit cries. 'What are you doing here so late?'

She tries hard, but even Marjit the brave can't conceal her disappointment at the news of Trine's sudden departure, of not being able to say a proper farewell and one last nuzzle of newborn flesh. The only saving grace is that mother and baby were whisked away safely. For now, at least.

'Thanks to Rubio,' Jens reports. 'Wehrmacht troops were minutes behind me – we saw them arrive on the quay as we left the harbour, searching other moored boats. It's a miracle that Rubio was already on the wharf and saw me running at a pace towards the yard.'

'So where are they now?' Rumi knows that for Jens to return within a few hours they can't have been taken far.

'About ten kilometres up the coast,' Jens says. 'Rubio and his contacts again. The family of a woman he knows, apparently. But I'll need to make arrangements for them to be taken overland to Sweden fairly soon.'

Typically, Marjit retreats to her kitchen and is soon preparing Jens something to eat from the scrapings of her larder.

'You must be exhausted,' Rumi says, having gone back to knitting.

'Frustrated, mostly,' he says, sprawled on the sofa. 'Whatever we do, the Abwehr seems to know about it.'

Rumi looks up. 'The Abwehr specifically, or the Germans in general? Surely Military Intelligence isn't interested in kidnapped babies?'

'Don't you believe it,' Jens comes back. 'The Abwehr are desperate to be equal, if not better, than the SS or the Gestapo. And the more fugitives they turn up, the better it looks for them as a force.'

'So, do you think it was . . .?'

'Selig?' He sounds resigned, his eyes boring into the ceiling. 'Oh yes, definitely. I'd bet my life on it.'

41

Hot on the Heels

Bergen, 3rd September 1942

Jens

The route to the coastal path seems clear enough as Jens dismounts and pushes his bicycle the last few feet, before unhitching a bag of supplies and steering the old machine into a convenient bush, checking to make sure it's well hidden from all angles. He hoists the bag over his shoulder and points his binoculars the half mile or so towards the ragged rocks marking the coastline, scanning for at least a minute. Satisfied, he crouches down, sniffs the air and listens intently for another thirty seconds, relieved to hear only a reassuring soughing of the sea, undisturbed by the rumble of German engineering, either in the blue sky above or motoring up the gravel road. He's pleased, too, to note the tiny stone cottage teetering on the cliff edge – little more than a fisherman's hut – looks abandoned to an untrained eye. There's no smoke curling from the small chimney, or any other sign of life. Except that he knows different.

The men inside greet his approaching footsteps with healthy suspicion, and check a second time when he mutters the password. It means Jens is left standing outside the battered wooden door a little longer, but it's sensible to be over cautious. Once inside, the two agents are fiendish for renewed supplies of tinned herring and meat, though it's anything but fresh. They can't cook anything, or risk boiling a kettle for fear of rising smoke. They look filthy, having only the option of washing in freezing spring water, and the smell inside the lone small room is pungent, to say the least. But that's the life of an intelligence agent, and for the umpteenth time, Jens thanks his good fortune; the exposure he faces in the city centre is nothing compared to this hardship.

'I think we'll give it another week, and then shut this place down,' he tells Johann and Finn. 'It's been valuable as a look-out post, but the weather is already drawing in and nobody can survive out here without a fire.'

Incredibly, both are still in good spirits and more so when Jens tells them of the month's leave due in return for their isolation, their route across the border into neutral Sweden already mapped out.

'I can't wait for a scalding bath and a hot meal,' says Finn, surveying his grubby fingers. 'Though in which order I can't decide yet.'

'So what's the news?' Johann asks. 'I'm desperate to hear anything that doesn't come by way of a dot or a dash.'

Jens gives them a brief outline of a world beyond their window, trying hard to focus on positives and not the British losses in Dieppe, or the Germans pushing into Stalingrad. 'Clark Gable went and enlisted – walked into an army recruiting office, apparently, and signed up as a private.'

'Let's hope he's a better soldier than he is an actor,' Finn counters, his mouth full of herring. 'I bet he won't end up in some godforsaken outpost eating tinned mush.'

Jens turns quickly to local business and the increase in close calls in and around Bergen; several SOE look-out stations have been abandoned at short notice as the Nazis' Direction-Finding improves in detecting the Allies' high frequency radio waves over long distances. And while the hilly terrain around Bergen often impedes the signals, the German trackers simply move their mobile detection vans to another location and set up shop again. And this, Jens has no doubt, is down to the zealous and ambitious Lothar Selig. The Abwehr hound is getting the results he needs.

To Jens, it amounts to increased worry and time-consuming leg work; he's taken to cycling around the streets of Bergen and out into the countryside most days with a trailer full of clothes to distribute. It's perfect cover for spotting the D/F trucks through his binoculars, speeding to the nearest radio when he does and sending a covert signal for other agents to cease transmissions. According to his contacts, the Germans hate radio silence more than anything. It means he's exhausted most nights, his legs ache from hauling the bike up the endless hills and the food he can muster is unappealing, to say the least. He craves Marjit's cooking, but more than that, he hankers for her company, her ability to laugh – at him, mostly, but also at the war and the world. Despite her fears, and her clear decision to avoid any complicated emotion, he craves Rumi, too.

Sometimes, Jens wonders why he didn't just listen to his mother, opt for a convenient army desk job in London and be satisfied that he'd 'done his bit' for the conflict. Then he thinks of Trine and the news that, despite a few close calls, she did make it safely to Sweden, with the brief message that the baby is thriving. In a small way, it made him feel as if they were winning at something, as well as helping to shed a few of his own demons. He looks, too, at Johann and Finn, sees their enthusiasm despite being holed up on what feels like the craggy edge of the world, and he knows exactly why he's not behind a desk.

'What's that?' Finn stops mid-forkful and puts down his plate, ear automatically cocked. Instantly, silence descends. Jens goes to the door, pushing his eye against the tiny spy hole into the distant green. Johann steps two paces to the window, which faces the sea and has a side view of the path.

'Damn!' Jens hisses under his breath. He spins on his heel and whispers into the room: 'Bloody Germans.'

'How many?' Johann's eyes are white and wide against his darkened face.

'I can see two. One vehicle, maybe. I think we've got thirty seconds.'

They grab nothing of value, but everything that could incriminate – every scrap of paper or ciphered document is plunged into rucksacks, the transmitter case snapped shut and hauled onto Jens's back, while the other two shoulder what they can.

They hear the determined trudge of footsteps closing in. Jens's German is good enough to translate the orders: 'Check left,' a voice barks.

One set of footsteps veers left and Jens hopes another soldier won't take it upon himself to break ranks and search the opposite way. All three scramble down two steps into a half-height basement painstakingly dug out of the hut's floor. Each man ducks under a low beam, crawling through a short tunnel barely big enough for an adult to squeeze through, let alone with added cargo on their backs. Jens bites his tongue as the tight confines of the ragged, chalky gap strip away skin from his knees and shoulder blades through his thin shirt. It's that split-second calculation again, knowing the contents of the suitcase on his back are capable of condemning so many if it gets into Nazi hands, that lives will be saved if he does his job right now. His skin, however scarred, will heal. That singular thought drives him through the pain as he feels blood prick and roll down his leg, hoping it doesn't form a visible trail for the soldiers who have now barged into the hut and made their discovery, yelling orders to 'Search! Find them!'

In less than a minute, they emerge to drink in the brisk sea breeze on their faces. Silently, the three men drop down towards the rocky crags, turning right onto a thin, uninviting path, the type that any sensible person would carefully pick their way along, instead of fleeing at speed for their lives. Instinctively, the trio crouches as they hear footsteps and a heaving breath on the ledge above. Jens listens intently for an added, more worrying kind of panting, then sighs with utter relief. *No dogs. Thank Christ they don't have dogs to sniff out blood.*

The presence above moves away and – without even a sign – the resistance men do what their training dictates: they split up, knowing it's now every soldier for himself. At a fork in the path, Finn peels away downwards towards the water, Johann with him, although he disappears quickly into a cave the two must have discovered over the long weeks. More importantly, Jens sees that they're both out of sight. He has no choice but to keep going on the track that winds back up to the cliff edge. He stops, squats again and closes his eyes. *Come on. Come on, Parkes, concentrate!*

In the panic, his one true skill in life has deserted him in reading the surrounding terrain, tracking where the

238

pursuers – his potential killers – are. How can it be? For years, it's happened automatically, a picture appearing inside his head, whether he summons it or not. Why won't it come now? He feels almost blind without it, like that first day up on the mountain with Rumi and stepping into a foggy oblivion.

Behind the black of his eyelids and with one ear out for any footsteps nearby, Jens counts. *One, two, three,* slowly and methodically. Agonising and sluggish, the lines finally begin to form, contours that he unconsciously noted and harboured on his short walk to the hut less than an hour before, now forming the skeleton of a map. The means of his escape.

The scoring on his knees is taking effect with consistent pain, and he stands upright with difficulty, willing away a limp in his step. Stopping and listening every few yards, he makes his way up the path until his head is level with the cliff edge. Scanning for sound, his eyes peek over the rocky verge, and he's thankful for some grassy tufts masking his blond cap of hair. The vehicle is still visible and voices are coming from inside the hut – they're clearly searching for anything of note, the dishes of food a giveaway to its very recent occupancy.

It's now or never, Jens thinks. There's more time to think than at Dunkirk, no bullets flying yet, but enough to breed doubts. Yes, no. Yes. *Go now!*

He goes, climbing as quickly as the weight and his knees will allow, and moves across open ground to a dense bushel of green nestled against a rocky mound, two hundred yards or so from the hut. His mind says sprint, but the pace feels like a snail out for a Sunday amble, the transmitter swaying left and right like a cumbersome shell as he moves. Panting, he makes it to the greenery and forces himself into the soft foliage, grounds the transmitter and pushes his back to the rock, thankful his choice of clothes today is neither bright nor black.

It feels like hours spent with a damp, brackish odour in his nostrils and something else distinctly unpleasant, ears on permanent alert. He tracks the soldiers' voices and movements – at least two he hadn't seen initially – back and forth to their vehicle, freezing as he hears one set of footsteps clomp dangerously near to his refuge, leaves rustling with a bayonet poked into the adjoining greenery. Jens shrinks back into the granite, his breathing on hold, paralysing his voice box on seeing the silver blade penetrate his shroud of leaves and land two inches from the case, then a second, concerted thrust perilously close to his leg. He hears the bearer of the blade sniff, take in the animal scent of the bush, grunt and turn away, clearly thinking no human in their right mind would consider hiding amid such a stench.

'Franz! Over here!' a voice shouts in German and the boots move away. Breath resumed, lucky stars counted and blessed, Jens lives again.

He waits for an age after the vehicle's engine is fired up, the wheels splitting the gravel and the sound of threat receding down towards Bergen. Emerging with caution, he surveys the hut's inside; the marauders have scavenged like hyenas, and Jens checks the obvious hidey-holes the agents might have used, but they're all empty.

Wearily, Jens retrieves and mounts his bike, knowing that – should they survive – Finn and Johann will convene at a safe house on the outskirts of Bergen, but not until the next afternoon. For now, he needs to stow the transmitter and begin to patch himself up after a hot bath. There's only one place he's certain will offer up both willingly.

42

The Best Embroidery

Bergen, 3rd September 1942

Rumi

'*Hei,* I'm back.' Rumi blows into Marjit's living room, and immediately bends beside her, taking up the torch to afford a better light.

'I bandaged your knees more times than I can count when you were a boy, Jens, but you've really surpassed yourself this time.' Marjit's lips are pouted in a look of deep concentration as she weaves her thinnest needle deftly over his right knee, his head laid over the back of the sofa's arm, eyes closed.

Jens's head springs up. 'Did you manage to stow the transmitter?'

Rumi nods. 'Yes. It's safe. As anything can be. We can collect it tomorrow.'

Marjit attempts another stitch to the ribbons of flesh sheared away as Jens winces, his head pushed back again. Rumi watches him bite down with the pain; they've no

241

alcohol left in either house, so it's stoicism or nothing. She finds her free hand inching towards his, dangling from the sofa, and their skin makes brief contact. His fingers stiffen, but don't quite fall into hers and he turns his head, eyes on her face. There's Karl again, hovering with the memory of more minor surgery in Marjit's living room, an enduring sorrow evident in Jens's eyes. He sets his teeth together, turns and stares at the ceiling.

'Better than another shrapnel lodger,' Rumi jokes, desperate to lighten the air.

Marjit huffs. 'Well, I'm sure if Jens could have found some other form of munition, he would have ground it into his knees just for the fun of having me pick it out. Isn't that right, my darling nephew?'

'I'm thinking of getting a tattoo that says "embroidered by Marjit". What do you think, beloved aunt?'

'Come the end of this war, it might be truer than you think,' she grunts.

Their sparring in the next best thing to an anaesthetic, with so much love bound up in its black humour. Yet, while Rumi can't help enjoying it, she's horrified at Jens's proximity to capture. It sounded far too close.

It's another hour before they've tended to his shoulders, dressing the stripped skin with lanolin and layers of muslin, enough that he can bear putting on his shirt again.

'It wasn't regular Wehrmacht that came looking,' Rumi says while Marjit clears away and raids her coffee supplies. 'When I met up with your contact at the boatyard, he told me today's raid was Abwehr. No question.'

'Selig again!' Jens blows out a sigh of defeat. 'I didn't see the uniforms clearly, so it could well have been. As I cycled back down I spotted a D/F van on the road, so yes, it's obvious they've been busy. We would have lost that post eventually, but it's sickening Selig has forced us to abandon it. Worrying, too.'

Rumi watches deep thought ripple across his brow. 'But you did make it out, the other two as well, as far as we know. Shredded but alive,' she says.

Marjit's kitchen clattering becomes a backdrop to a silent conversation played out across the table between them, Jens's finger tapping as he stares first at the woodgrain, then at her. She struggles to read his curious expression: anxiety over Selig, or perhaps regret? Alternatively, he might be thinking: *What do you care, Rumi?* But she quickly pushes that notion away, doubting that she figures in his thoughts at all. After all, she refused him, left him with little hope of a change in her solid, calcified heart.

Now, Rumi asks herself: Was she wrong? Aren't they both allowed a shard of optimism? As she listened to Jens relaying what happened out there on the coastline, she felt obvious relief at his narrow escape, but one thought insisted on bulldozing its way through: *We would have had no chance — of happiness, or at least trying for it.*

It's a feeling she knows intimately, and regrets in equal measure. The same prospects that were robbed from her in that fierce storm. Hitler scuppered her hope once with Magnus. Should she let the Führer do it to her again?

'Cheer up, Rumi.' Jens's voice breaks into her musings, seeming to throw off his current troubles. His features soften. 'We've got a saying in Britain: "It might never happen".'

She tries — and fails — to smile.

But what if it already has?

43

Surveying the Merchandise

Hop, 2nd October 1942

She feeds Kleiner titbits, details of visitors that some of the women get, but nothing of true worth, and he knows it. In reality, there isn't much to tell; the women are quiet on the whole, still wary, but she's convinced they don't suspect the full truth, or there would be more of an exodus, with or without the new security.

Partly it's because there haven't been any births of late, with most residents in the mid part of their pregnancy, and so the question of women not returning from the main maternity home hasn't come up. The rest seem only grateful to be cared for and among their own kind, protected from the disdain of the wider world. She hears that some parents have cut these women off entirely, and although she can't quite bring herself to approve of what they've done, it does seem cold-hearted, to sever ties with your own child when they are most in need. If it came to it, she wonders if she could ever be as heartless.

There is one she's keeping a special eye on, though. A friend of the escapee, Trine. Anya. She seems more aware than most, has taken on some typing for the general office, though the work isn't anywhere near Kleiner's lair. Still, it's as well to be vigilant, and she's made a point of engaging Anya in conversation a bit more, just casually, and found out her regular visitor is a cousin from Bergen. Pah – that redhead is no cousin! Quite apart from their colouring, there's no family resemblance whatsoever. Twenty-five years working for the Lauritzens tells her that, with their endless aunts, uncles, babies and cousins twice removed.

For now, though, she's biding her time in probing too far; she does like Anya and wouldn't actively wish harm on anyone, but information from this woman could be the element to stop Kleiner delving into her own family too deeply, his voice oozing with threat each time he mentions her sister. Especially after the visit they had this week, supposedly from the board of German midwives – a couple of stout, steely-eyed women who came and poked in her cupboards and deigned to rate them as 'satisfactory'. But who was the rakish man they had in tow, scratching in his notebook and wiping sweat from his high forehead? No midwife, that's for sure. He stared far more at the women than their surroundings, scribbling as he went. She can't help one phrase pushing into her head, one that a shady uncle often used when he was intent on courting girls at a dance: 'surveying the merchandise', he'd say.

Just the memory of it makes her go cold.

44

Memories

Bergen, 10th October 1942

Rumi

The wind has a hand in pushing them up the hill over-looking Bergen and they don't stop until they have a good view of the city's 'snout' – the land wharf of boathouses – reaching out into the fjord.

'When I was smaller I used to imagine it was a croco-dile pushing its nose into the water,' Jens reflects as they sit side by side, the city sprawled out beneath them in the weak sunshine. 'Marjit made up all sorts of stories about the "Croc of Bergen" coming alive at night, and I believed every word.'

Rumi lets out a long breath. 'If only we still had such innocence,' she says, stealing a glance at a child nearby, who's singing to herself as she skips through the grass, picking flowers at random with her mother. 'Children have that ability, don't they, to move on? Look at that girl, growing up amid all this uncertainty, and yet she seems happy.'

'She does — thankfully.' He picks at a blade of grass. 'Only you don't, Rumi. What's wrong?'

He clearly does want to know, the way he's looking at her, and Jens is now what she considers a friend, the trust between them proven over the last months. Still, she's reluctant to tell him the truth behind her grey, weighty thoughts. It's not just the tide of the war — though that's bad enough for the Allies — more that her heart remains locked in a vice, and today of all days. It's a trifle to others but enough to cloud her thoughts since waking: the fourth anniversary of the day when Magnus proposed, on a windy cliff atop Askoy Island, a gentle rushing of the sea below. A perfect day in every way. In previous years, she'd marked it with a sense of delight, due to the ripple of pleasure she felt at the time, and because it was the day Rumi felt herself climb out of girlhood and officially become a woman. In that very moment she said yes and he kissed her. She'd been kissed by others — innocents probing in the dark — but not like that. Not like Magnus always did, with such love and commitment.

Rumi knows her sorrow is nothing compared to the wider picture, the death and destruction across the world. And while she can command her body to fake a smile and push through, dragging her heavy, wayward heart from the depths is another matter.

'Nothing,' she says to Jens in a badly disguised lie.

'Sure?'

'Only that I've seen Anya again.' She begins fiddling with the ends of her plait. The subject is a distraction, but a genuine worry, too.

'How is she?'

'Physically, she's fine, but definitely more anxious,' Rumi goes on. 'The last time I visited they'd increased the guards to three, one on the gate, and two patrolling the grounds.

Anya types up some of the routine paperwork and says there are more women coming through where the fathers refuse to claim responsibility, where there's no prospect of marriage and a new life in Germany.'

Jens looks out towards the sea, rests his folded arms on his knees. 'What do the women think, or talk about?'

'They're understandably wary of sharing too much.' Rumi pauses. 'But there is an unspoken fear among them. That their babies will be taken away, and worse, that the whole thing – where they are, the situation they're in – is not such a coincidence or an accident.'

His face contorts, washed with undisguised horror. 'Do you mean some kind of *breeding* programme? Something that's been cultivated?'

In turn, she's surprised at his shock and bewilderment, given what he's already seen. It's a sign of the times that Rumi is disturbed, but no longer stunned. 'It's no secret Hitler wants our Nordic blood,' she says. 'We know there are some women who will enter into it willingly, but what if there aren't enough of them? The last couple of years has taught us that what the Nazis can't procure, they simply take. By force.'

Her mind goes back to that day in 1940 when the Germans arrived in Bergen, sweeping into Torgallmenningen in their large black sedans and pronouncing themselves occupiers and saviours, thieving the liberty from Norway, and from a city that has traded by its own virtues since the thirteenth century. She remembers the arrogant swagger of the area *kommandant* as he strutted about in the square, the crowd addressed like nursery children on what to expect, and the consequences if they didn't take heed. Audacious and conceited, she thought then, standing side by side with Pappa and seething in silence. *How dare they?*

Jens is quiet, but she can see from a slight twitch of his pupil that he's deliberating.

'What are you thinking?' she pushes him.

'That's if it's true, then it's another debauched example of what Hitler is prepared to do.'

'And?'

'And what, Rumi?' He surveys her, brows drawn together. 'Getting Trine out of there was urgent – and an exception. And don't forget she made it to safety by a whisker. Do you really think I can authorise a resistance rescue, ride in there on Peder's chariot and save all the women and babies?'

'Don't mock me!' she spits, pushing herself up and off the grass.

'Then don't be so naïve.' He's soon following in her furious wake. 'I don't like it any more than you, but one thing this war has taught me is that you have to pick your battles.'

'Only the ones you're sure of winning?' she seethes.

He pulls her to a stop, looks hard into her eyes. 'Yes, if you like. It's not fair, but sometimes it is the only way.'

She's rooted to the spot by her own fury. By injustice, too, and sadness, and the fact that on the day when she should be reflecting, evoking the memory of that proposal kiss with Magnus, what she really wants is for Jens to pull her close, and maybe not for him to plant his lips on hers, but to share something in their touch. Some intimacy. And guilty, too, that it feels so, so wrong to even imagine it.

'Sorry,' she says, looking over at the child humming as she gathers flowers. 'I only wish I could be more like her, lost in my own world. Content.'

'I don't,' Jens says plainly. 'I wouldn't wish you any other way. This anger, it fuels you, Rumi, to do some good. But I've learnt the hard way that it needs to be channelled.'

She looks up then, searching his face, and wondering why and where *his* anger has gone, how he's tamed it. And how long it will take her to do the same.

'We have to be patient,' he goes on. 'The resistance is being picked off very efficiently by Abwehr and Gestapo, and we need to be clever about our response. Much more than they are.'

'I know, but the wait just feels so endless and empty,' she says. 'I can't stop thinking about Anya – how alone she is. And I don't know much about babies, but I'm pretty certain they make an appearance eventually.'

He laughs at that, taking her arm as they turn back towards the sanctuary of Marjit's. 'I'll have a think about ways to help Anya, I promise,' he says. 'We will make sure she's all right.'

She doesn't doubt his intention, that he'll try. But after Trine, can they achieve it?

45

A Woman at Work

Bergen, 25th October 1942

Rumi

She's chilled from head to foot, resisting the urge to stamp her feet and help the blood flow through her toes again, but the rain wheedling its way inside Rumi's coat collar and snaking down her back isn't helping. For a woman who's grown up in freezing temperatures and always relished a good day's skiing on Bergen's slopes, Rumi hates the constant drizzle at this time of year, making the world damp and depressing.

She looks enviously at the bright lights of the café across the road spreading their glow out onto the grey of the pavement, its windows steamed with condensation of bodily heat; warm breath from the mouths of people not quivering in this incessant rain. Even the brass band stoically putting on their Sunday afternoon pomp have packed up and gone home.

Normally, Rumi would find this part of central Bergen

251

uplifting, especially as she can amble up from the wooden ramshackle nature of the wharf and, in a little over fifteen minutes, find herself surrounded by its solid architecture; buildings that seem as if they will never be felled, squat and solid in their construction, and yet beautiful in their own way. Despite that day of invasion, the expanse of Torgallmenningen plaza reminds Rumi of happier times on the family's Sunday outings, with her on Peder's shoulders as a girl, her mother walking alongside, endlessly worried she would fall off as Peder danced a ridiculous jig to the local brass band.

'Peder, be careful – she'll fall!' her mother warned nervously.

'Well if she does, I have no doubt the ground will come off worse against our daughter,' he'd laugh, and Rumi remembers being so proud at her father's faith in her strength, catching at her mother's hand to reassure her and noting how warm and soft it always seemed then.

Now it's gloomy in the late afternoon, and the departed band is German, not Norwegian. There's no Pappa, her mother, or comfort to be had. Rumi's only recompense is that she's working. Properly so.

Her task is to stand under the issuing clouds and look as if she is waiting, for a date perhaps, though the rain isn't helping the masquerade, and even locals are walking past and looking sideways in wonderment: for what unearthly reason is a young woman allowing herself to get soaked to the skin, or for what man?

Harder still is maintaining an expression of composure in the face of the drizzle, despite the black wide-brimmed hat that she's wearing, one of her mother's that she'd always coveted as a child. The rest of her very atypical Rumi outfit is cobbled together from the Stavanger trip, enabling her to look like a woman who might be heading out for drinks or dinner.

The brim does allow Rumi to squint and scan into the gloom in the direction of the Hotel Bristol opposite, a stone's throw from the other favoured German haunt of the Hotel Norge. As much as she hankers to be out of this weather, she wouldn't want to swap places with Jens in this moment, currently within the Bristol's opulent interior, though she guesses he won't be feeling in the least bit comfortable. He'll be as damp as she feels, no doubt dripping from his own sweat.

She watches a line of Abwehr uniforms emerge from the hotel doorway, putting on their caps against the rain and lighting up cigarettes as they stride quickly away. Good. Intelligence from inside the hotel has told them the daytime shift in the basement finishes in the late afternoon, after which a skeleton staff takes over for the night. It's not so good when one of the officers slows up as he's passing Rumi, his eyes crawling the entire length of her body, crown to toes, as if drinking in every detail – she's glad then to have tucked her distinct hair completely under the hat. But it's a leer more than a survey of suspicion, and while that once might have made her shiver, this time Rumi steals some succour from his motive.

'Evening, frøken,' he says in bad Norwegian, dipping his head, and she smiles back dutifully. Where are her ugly, plainly unfeminine oilskins when she really needs them?

It's been twenty minutes, and there's no obvious signal to fall back and walk away with the huff of a spurned woman. She looks at her watch every few minutes to keep up the pretence, wheeling around on her heels in a full circle and scanning as she goes.

'I'll need as much time as possible, out of sight from any Abwehr hierarchy,' Jens had said as they sat around her kitchen table the day before. He'd shown her several mugshots of German officers to look out for; judging by their succession of portly, well-fed faces, their girths won't be hard to spot. If any looked to be heading for the hotel door, or even around the side of the building to where the basement entrance is situated, she'd need to cause a distraction. Just how Rumi would warrant enough attention for enemy officers to come running, Jens hadn't specified. That was something for her to work out.

'And, of course, the main one to look out for . . .' he began.

'Selig,' she said. 'I know. Believe me, I'll recognise him.'

'We'll need half an hour to get in and out. If there's no signal after forty minutes, just walk away, but don't go home – stay out, go to a café and be seen in a crowded place, talk to people so you have witnesses.'

His manner and his face had not relaxed for a second as he'd issued the instructions; this was Jens the SOE man in front of her, intent on his work, planning to the last detail. From that point, the rest of his evening would be spent moving from place to place, in bars and backstreet meeting places, explaining the plan to all those involved, every member identified only on a need to know basis.

It's Jens who is the pivot; if it all goes wrong, if just one link in the chain is captured, his name will be the one beaten out of them. He stands to lose. *And yet,* Rumi thinks, *he goes on;* his face the night before showing nothing but resolve to make the mission succeed. There had been no intimacy in their exchange – she chosen as part of the team, and as much as she missed the familiarity, she'd been pleased, too. He was taking her need to work within the resistance seriously. Once, paper-pushing in the yard had been enough, but not now. They are both going all out for Norway. And this one, he'd told her 'will really piss them off. So we have to do it right.'

Finally, the rain is easing and Rumi takes off her hat to shake out the drips. She's placing it back on her head and checking her watch again when her eye catches someone familiar twenty or so metres away, swivelling to avoid Magnus's sister, who is heading straight for her. Not that she doesn't like Solveig, but now is not the time for casual conversation or a disastrous interruption.

Too late.

'Rumi! What are you doing here? You're wet through.' The tall, thick-set woman moves in to exchange kisses. 'Are you waiting for someone?'

'Yes, yes, a friend,' Rumi stumbles, willing her eyes to focus on Solveig's quizzical eyebrows and not roam towards the hotel door beyond.

But Solveig's curiosity is clearly roused, or she needs reassurance Rumi is not lingering for a man, it being so soon after her brother's death. 'Nina, an old school friend,' Rumi qualifies, 'but she's late as usual.'

'I'll stay with you then,' Solveig offers, just as Rumi sees a small group of men walking towards the Bristol, all in uniform.

'No, no! You mustn't . . .' she blusters '. . . get as wet as I am, I mean. I'll see you next week at your mother's, shall I? For tea, as we planned.'

Solveig hesitates, looks at the light drizzle above and touches her carefully tamed hair. 'If you're sure. Have a nice evening then.' She turns away as Rumi flicks her attention instantly to the outline of two men in particular, side by side, their uniforms well-fitting on tall bodies and the demeanour all-important, edging close to the Bristol's entrance. As the light from the opening door pushes out, it falls on one side of both men, almost a flare sent up in warning.

Pink and long and prominent, the scar shines like a beacon.

46

A Rat in the Basement

Bergen, 25th October 1942

Jens

I'd never make a bellboy, Jens thinks, pulling at the thick jacket scratching at his neck, not helped by the sweat beginning to prickle at his temple. He curses the rough, cheap fabric of his disguise and his long limbs at the same time; neither are designed to be contorted into such a small space with any level of comfort.

He half stands, rubs his thighs and squats again, careful not to dislodge the objects around him, a jumble of oddments likely dumped in every hotel basement: a pile of old cloths, a broken lamp and a stack of ashtrays. He lowers his breathing to a near silence, maximising the sounds coming from the other side of the bare brick wall; muted conversation, the occasional laugh and instructions barked out across the space that he knows from their intelligence is vast and open-plan. The soundproofing of the brick means it's hard enough piecing together a sentence, let alone in German.

257

Jens positions the torch on a box close to the masonry, scoring with his chisel at the crumbling mortar in a rhythm with the noises he hears. He's halfway to freeing up several bricks about a metre from the floor and hoping there's a thin layer of plaster on the other side so his gouging doesn't reveal itself as a clumsy peephole. Information from their hotel worker who regularly takes down drinks and food into the basement assures him the void won't be seen, and right now his life depends on the source being right – and truly loyal.

He stops scraping and freezes instantly on hearing a voice that's clearly approaching the wall; straining to listen and translate in unison.

'Hey, what's that?' the voice says, clipped and Germanic. 'Did you hear it?'

Several feet move towards the wall – and him. Jens pictures two heads leaning in to the partition, as if there's little more between them than a flimsy curtain. Common sense tells him he can't actually hear their heavy breath but it's in his head all the same. Something wet trickles down his back and his muscles scream in partial paralysis.

'I'm sure it's a kind of scratching,' the same voice says.

'I'll bet it's rats,' a second one offers. 'The night watchman told me he's seen a few.'

Jens scrapes again at the mortar to feed their imagination.

'See? I told you,' the second one says knowingly.

'Well, as long as they don't come in here,' the first one replies. 'I hate rats.'

'Coward,' the other man jibes. 'Listen, we better get ready – you know who's com—' Mercifully, their sounds muffle and recede into the distance.

With permission to act like vermin, Jens resumes his scoring of the cement, though still in line with the waves of industry he can hear across the divide. He's been in situ ten minutes or more and the air inside his cavity is becoming stale and heavy, but it takes another ten to ease out three bricks and pack the space with the explosive to blow a good size hole in the wall. It won't be enough, though, for maximum success. A greater level of peril for Jens is yet to come; he'll need to weather the explosion and crawl back towards the blast hole, near enough to toss in the crudely fashioned but effective Molotov Cocktails now lying at his feet. Then he'll sprint back through the kitchens to ground level, as rapidly as his cramped limbs will take him.

There's little choice in taking such a risk; bombs cause damage but they have to be big – much larger than this one – to cause true devastation. In its place, fire comes a close and effective second. Because when SOE commanders ordered the entire telecommunications headquarters for South-West Norway destroyed – the one conveniently situated in the basement of the Hotel Bristol – they meant it. If Jens and his team can disable the lines criss-crossing between Gestapo, Wehrmacht and Abwehr, the Allies estimate it will buy weeks for the resistance to carry out vital sabotage operations, leaving the enemy scrambling to intercept their messages.

Except there will be consequences; from the German High Command, the occupation overseer Josef Terboven, and doubtless from Selig himself. They'd be naïve to think otherwise. It's that human calculation again, the one that has made Jens writhe in his sleep for the past two weeks, ever since he received his orders, lying awake into the early hours and staring at the dawn with dread. It's the reckoning from SOE headquarters that will likely see individuals held to account. If he's caught, there won't be the degradation of a public hanging, not with the Reich's recent official edict to execute enemy agents swiftly and efficiently, no trial required. They'd already practised it fully only a couple of weeks before, with more than thirty resistance agents in the north instantly 'dispatched'.

But he can't think of that now, because here it is – the opportunity – on the other side of that wall, ready and waiting. And he has his orders.

Jens takes in a breath as he prepares to prime the fuse and take cover, and he can't help feeling a tiny portion of satisfaction seeping through as his fingers feel for the wires in the dimness. The Abwehr man will hear the noise all right, but in truth he'd give a lot to see the look on Selig's face.

47

Raining Fire

Bergen, 25th October 1942

Rumi

Rumi drops to the unforgiving concrete like a puppet suddenly devoid of strings – though not before she's made sure the hotel's doorman is looking in her direction, and so able to engage the nearest help, her targets being the two men just about to step through the Bristol's doors.

She makes a faint cry as she goes down, having judged a scream would be overplaying the role: it would certainly add to the urgency, but a cry of fright from what? Rumi is eager not to invite suspicion, only the right amount of attention for a damsel in distress.

'Frøken, frøken, what's wrong?' the doorman fusses over her, before being pushed aside by a German uniform and the face that – in this instance – she's very glad to see.

Lothar Selig helps Rumi sit up, their heads in close proximity, near enough that she's almost knocked sideways by his pungent hair oil. And is that some faint recognition she sees rippling across his eyes? The evening at Hotel

Norge was a good many months ago, and no doubt he's danced with countless women since then.

'Get some water!' he shouts into the air, and then turns back to her. 'How are you feeling now, Frøken . . .?'

'O–Orlstad,' she stammers, thinking quickly that there's no value and every danger in giving a false name that can be checked. 'Better, thank you. I must have just fainted.'

'Have you eaten today?' he asks. 'Can I . . .?'

'Yes, yes, I have, thank you.' Rumi is quick to thwart his concern; any prospect of his asking her to dinner is going too far. 'Really, I'm fine. If you could just help me up? I'm due to meet friends in town. I'll sit with them and have some coffee.'

'Let me at least show you insi—' His words are severed by a faint thud and several genuine screams coming from the direction of the hotel entrance, as people spill onto the street, followed by an acrid cloud of smoke, mixed with something else Rumi recognises: cordite.

'FIRE! FIRE!' a man bellows and – to Rumi's relief – Lothar Selig's gallantry is overtaken by the fresh emergency. He rises and runs at the hotel, while she pulls herself up off the wet, slippery ground, only to be almost spun off her feet by a real force a second later. Something grasps and yanks sharply at her arm, prompting an instant image of her own face looking out from behind the bars of a Gestapo transport wagon.

'Let's get out of here,' Jens hisses into her ear, close enough that she can smell ash on his skin, and see an incriminating black smudge on his cheek.

'I think this is probably your most extreme version of hiding in plain sight,' Rumi says, leaning across the table to wipe away a lingering patch of smut that Jens hasn't scrubbed off in the café's bathroom, the same welcoming and warm establishment that she'd been looking at with envy while loitering in the rain.

He accepts her touch without flinching, his focus set firmly on the square where chaos reigns near to the Hotel Bristol. The babble of concern amid the café's customers had diminished quickly when word spread that the target had been German military, just as Jens and Rumi sidled onto a spare table.

Now, he's emerged from the bathroom wearing the sweater she knitted for him, which she imagines he must have stashed there earlier, as part of his overall plan. She's pleased to see it helps him blend into the crowd, and gratified to think he must really like it; he does look fully Norwegian.

She scours his face for mood and meaning, noting there's not a single tremor in his finger as he lifts a cup of coffee to his mouth. Her entire body, by contrast, has only just stopped shaking, though Rumi justifies it as too long out in the drizzly cold. Still, she has to get better at this, she tells herself. If she's going to make more of a difference.

'Jens?' His stare out of the window remains fixed. 'Jens?'

'Sorry.' He snaps his attention to her. 'I think I lost a bit of hearing in the blast. It'll come back soon.'

'Do you think it succeeded?'

'From what I could see, yes,' Jens murmurs. 'I ran as soon as I lobbed in the last firebomb but the room was already ablaze. And the place was in chaos.'

'So, what's next?'

'We linger for a bit, go home and sleep, and then wait for news from our man inside the hotel as to what the damage is. Hopefully, the fire will have hit the Nazi machinery hard.' His eyes dip down. 'And then we wait for the fallout.'

'How bad do you think it will be?'

Jens shakes his head and fingers the rim of his cup. 'Hard to tell. Judging by Televåg, it will depend if anyone was killed – Germans especially.'

His hidden tremor manifests itself in one eye, a twitch in his left lid that he can't seem to control, and to Rumi it's clear that he dreads the alternate outcome of his actions more than anything. He has to both live it, and live with the consequences.

'You were great, by the way,' he says, rubbing at his eye, 'in keeping Selig at bay. I saw him as I ran through the lobby, but I might have lost my nerve if I'd heard his voice on the other side of that wall. God, he was in a rage – screaming at everyone.'

'Really?' Rumi is startled, given the courage needed for what he's just done. 'Are you genuinely *afraid* of him?'

Jens's eyes widen, his gaze set like concrete. 'Yes,' he says resolutely. 'The man is dogged and dangerous – he's already wiped out hundreds of agents in the Netherlands. And now he's been brought to Norway with exactly the same aim. So yes, Rumi, fear is probably a very healthy reaction to Selig. It might well keep us alive.'

As they sit with the sole purpose of being seen, exhaustion sets in; Rumi's limbs are suddenly dead and heavy, and her left hip aches from the heavy contact with Torgallmenningen's concrete slabs. In hindsight, she might have fallen far too realistically.

Jens drains his cup and gets up. 'Come on, I'll walk you home, after one more recce around the square.'

He links arms with hers outside, and she's glad of the support. They skirt casually around the Bristol, eyeing the fire crews still working to douse some of the embers. Smoke oozes from the ground floor windows, and around the side of the hotel they glimpse pieces of radio equipment brought out on the pavement by lines of German soldiers, in a desperate attempt to salvage what they can, some of it already scarred and reduced to molten metal.

Rumi senses a concerted pulse, a double beat, deep inside.

Job done. And that's partly for you, Magnus.

Jens steers her away as his hand squeezes down on her coat, and they swap looks of satisfaction, careful to suppress any obvious smiles.

Rumi nudges into his arm in response. '*Hei,* I'm not normally in a position to say this, but you really do stink, Jens Parkes. Like an old bonfire.'

'Noted, Agent Orlstad. I promise I will take a bath, as commanded.'

He leaves her at the bottom of Strangebakken, and rounding the back of the cottages, Rumi sees Marjit's kitchen light visible through a sliver in the blackout curtain. Despite her fatigue, she feels a need to knock on the back door and savour some normality.

'*Hei,*' Marjit says, kneeling on the parlour floor, where she's cutting out a dress from what appears to be an old tablecloth. 'Anything wrong?' Marjit flicks her eyes to the clock on the sideboard with its hands showing past ten.

Rumi flops onto the chintz chair and wonders if she'll ever be able to get up again. 'No,' she says lazily.

'Where have you been?' The words are mumbled through the thread held in her teeth, curious rather than challenging.

'Oh, just out walking with a friend, then to a hotel bar,' Rumi lies, far too easily. Jens hasn't instructed her to keep it secret, but already she senses the less people who know about her involvement tonight the better. And then: Does Marjit qualify as 'people'?

Rumi is certain of her own motives, that she's trying to keep those around her safe; she hadn't told Pappa about tonight's plans for that very reason. She heads next door to her bed with a cheerful 'goodnight' but an irrepressible ache. The day has been as undulating as the hills surrounding Bergen; anxiety and excitement, coupled with dread and running with fear, then gratitude at seeing Jens's incriminating, dirty face next to hers, neither of them within the Abwehr's grasp.

Yet there's something sharp needling at her heart: somehow it just doesn't feel enough.

48

Retribution

Bergen, 30th October 1942

Jens

His lungs are at bursting point, like overblown balloons at a birthday party about to pop, and he can feel the fibres inside his chest begin to sting, on fire despite pulling in great gulps of cold air. Running as if everything in his world depends on it. Endlessly running.

Equally it feels like a release; Jens sprints with as much speed as his legs will allow, up and above the city centre, into the lingering greenery that will soon be turned white with the inevitable snows. His energy finally peters out and he's bent double, panting loudly and scooping in air for his hungry lungs, beads of sweat finally allowed to surface onto his forehead and cheeks. Finally recovered, he walks, then ambles, looking out over the city he loves so much. Still, the gentle toot-toot of boats in and out of the harbour, the comforting base layer of Bergen that he hopes will never, ever change.

The newest seam of the city's history he hopes to scrape away, for it to be replaced with something better. More humane. Jens flops to the floor, closes his eyes and puts his head in his hands. He senses tears not far behind the sweat in fighting their way out. Alone on the hillside, he lets them come.

The visions alongside he can't push away; one part of him wants to banish them entirely, another feels he should live them again and again inside his head – for those who no longer have that luxury. Retribution for the fire at the Bristol was anticipated, but to everyone's surprise and relief – including the SOE command – it wasn't on the scale they had braced themselves for. The fire caused no loss of life, but the Reich's retaliation had nevertheless been swift and vicious; raids across Bergen on suspected resistance, scores of arrests, and one coastal station discovered, though Jens had pre-warned all agents to 'take a short respite' and abandon their hide-outs for several days. It meant no SOE or SIS were lost, and the suspected resistance held firm, being released one by one when no evidence could be found. Then, out of the blue, the Reich resorted to its 'eye for an eye' policy, plucking three civilians – all young and innocent men – at random to pay the price, hanged in full view of Bergen's horrified residents. Only hours on, Jens wonders who determines what one life equals in terms of radio equipment, and how such a formula can ever exist. That calculation again.

He'd forced himself to watch, stood in the crowd murmuring its disbelief, heard the patently false charges barked out by the Nazi *kommandant*, the faces of those on the platform trying to mask their fear with pride, their eyes betraying true panic at times; he knows he would be the same in their shoes.

Then the cruel, cruel final act. So ancient and barbaric. Inhuman.

And after, the running up and out of the crowds, Jens purging himself of the sight, to make his lungs – his whole body – scream with pain. Only he knows it won't bring them back, or nurse the agony felt by their families.

'Hold firm,' the message from SOE headquarters had said when the fatal punishments were announced. Jens imagined he would have taken a hammer to his transmitter if those on high had lectured it was all 'for the greater good'. Mercifully, they didn't, and so he followed orders and carried on. And that's what burns as much as his body and the guilt within, a new slice that nestles neatly along-side Charlie.

Descending back into Bergen, there are few places Jens wants to be. His own room is claustrophobic, and the chaos of the mission office mimics the inside of his head. He hasn't seen Marjit in over a week and doesn't want to attach any suspicion by being seen at hers, his paranoia around Selig still fresh. And although he feels the same protection over Rumi, Jens can't help but find himself walking towards the boathouse, justifying that it's late on a Friday afternoon and she probably won't be there anyway. He might well sit on the wharf and while away a few hours before forcing himself back to some element of work. Anything to stop him thinking.

She is there, though. It's her voice that can be heard as he approaches the door, along with several others. Resonant, male voices. It's neither Peder nor Rubio, and the abrupt tone is surely not from another crew member, nor the way they are addressing her as 'Fräulein' – a sharp needlepoint when the Reich wants to provoke.

'Is there . . . anything . . . you want to examine?' He strains to hear snatches of Rumi's words, delivered with no trace of that intrinsic anger he's witnessed many a time. Courteous but plain. She's learnt exactly how to court them.

'Not at . . . the . . . moment, Fräulein,' is the staccato reply, and as footsteps approach the door Jens has to hop quickly away, squatting behind several wooden barrels as three men move outside – one officer and two troops, all Abwehr, as far as he can tell. The officer stands on the step, grunts in clear frustration and strides off, the others scurrying in his wake.

Outside, Jens listens intently for several minutes to be sure the wily officer hasn't left a sentry in the boathouse. It's when he hears a melody coming from beyond the door that he knows she's alone; he's never heard Rumi either singing or humming with good humour before, and he's faintly amused. The visit hasn't ruffled her feathers to any great degree.

'*Hei.* It's just me, Jens.' He's quick to announce himself to avert any alarm, and absurdly pleased to see her features soften.

'Oh, *hei,* I was just about to come and find you, stranger.'

'Why? Because of your visitors?'

'Partly. You saw them leave?' she says.

'Yes. What did they want?'

'Fishing – if you'll excuse the bad joke.' She goes back to tidying some upended papers on her desk. 'Despite what happened in the town today' – she looks at Jens with a sorrow to equal his – 'they're still searching.'

'Anything to make you think they're getting a little too close?'

'Not really, aside from the fact my name is logged now. Selig remembered me as the woman he helped outside

270

the Bristol, and the officer insinuated I'd been a well-placed stooge.'

Jens stiffens. 'How did you react to that?'

'I laughed it off, told them I had better things to do than wait out in the rain for foolish resistance, and that it was bad enough that one man had stood me up.' She looks delighted at her creative deceit. 'I think he was so jaded by my carping that he moved on to the next question.'

'That's the well-practised fishwife in you.' He dodges the pencil she throws at him, feels his nerve begin to settle again in the comforting familiarity of the boathouse. Warmer, too, with Rumi in its midst.

'But there was one other thing he mentioned,' she goes on. 'They've got hold of a radio codename, and it's one that they're clearly intent on finding. He mentioned Selig's name in the same breath.'

'Oh yes?' Jens's nerve channels are activated again. He wonders which of the men, and which station, he's going to have to alert rapidly, perhaps to arrange a complicated escape route across the Swedish border.

'He mentioned the name "NORBOY". Do you know who that is?'

For the umpteenth time in one day, Jens's heart cranks, his stomach contracts and bile bubbles inside his throat.

'It's me,' he says flatly. 'I'm NORBOY.'

Once it was a half joke back in Scotland, his nickname from the others in his training unit. Now, it means more than that. Much more. He's in Selig's sights: a prime target.

49

The Norwegian

Bergen, 30th October 1942

Rumi

They sit out on the stoop, wordlessly peering up into the night sky, lit only by a faint cluster of stars and one lone aircraft droning over the fjord. It had taken Rumi some time to persuade Jens that he should walk her home and stay for dinner; she didn't for a second doubt his desire to eat good food at Marjit's, but he's all too wary of being seen in Strangebakken, as if he's somehow become a pariah, the guilt of the sacrificed men hovering on his shoulders like a foul smelling cloak. It was only when Rumi said she daren't return home without him and face Marjit's disappointment, that he'd relented. She noted how tightly he hugged his aunt on arrival, and the look in Marjit's eyes as she whispered in his ear, no doubt assuaging him of any blame. The intensity of their lengthy embrace made her heart seesaw with shades of envy, dark and light.

'Come on now, let's eat,' Marjit said at last, and Rumi

watched Jens swiftly brush his cheek before he helped bring dishes to the table.

After dinner, they'd played a short game of cards before Marjit said she had some work to do and, despite the cold, Jens insisted on sitting outside.

It's Rumi who breaks their silent contemplation, eyes fixed on the navy sky. 'How are you, Jens? Really?'

He turns to face her, hands folded across his drawn up knees, and manages a weak smile. 'Better for coming here tonight,' he says quietly. 'Thanks to your nagging. But what I'm feeling is nothing compared to the suffering of others.'

She watches his mind churn, conjuring an obvious picture of those three lying stone dead in their coffins, a deep red weal at their necks. Silent and cold. She wonders if seeing those boys dead is actually worse for their families; better that she was spared the ordeal with Magnus.

Jens gives off a short, derisive laugh. 'Funny how we often say *it's nothing*, when we're in the middle of this bloody great war, the biggest turbulence anyone could imagine, led by a madman that any storyteller would have trouble creating. And we just carry on. Even after today.'

The sadness seeps out of him; Rumi feels it in the tension of his shoulder touching hers, the sigh of his breath, and the tone that he's trying – and struggling – to raise. She recognises every splinter of the misery pricking at his conscience, as the same she's already experienced, the despair and desolation alongside. And it's her turn now to give something back, for him to know that the jagged spikes are smoothed eventually, made less painful, lodging inside but weaved into the fabric of your being as something that's just there. Present but benign. The process isn't complete for her, but she's getting there, slowly.

'I know my words don't mean much,' she says. 'But for what it's worth, it wasn't your fault. None of this is.'

He looks at her, head resting on his muscled forearms, and she glimpses a shade of his adolescence, as if he's been turned inside out for one moment and is laying out his soul, exposed.

'For what's it's worth, Rumi, that means the world to me,' he says.

'Well, us Norwegians have to stick together, don't we?'

Now, Jens raises his head, lips spreading slowly. 'Are my ears deceiving me, Frøken Orlstad, or did you say "we" Norwegians?'

'I might have done, Herr Parkes.'

'Surely you can't mean me? A lowly half-born?'

She aims a mock slap to his shoulder. 'Careful – I could well take it back.'

'Oh, but you can't,' he says, dragged a little from his melancholy. 'Once said, never forgotten.'

'Then I suppose it must be true,' Rumi acquiesces. 'Jens Parkes, a fully-fledged Norwegian.'

There's one other thing that she accedes to, willingly and with a renewed bump to her heart; their heads leaning together, each with an instinct to turn, and his mouth moving to hers, lips soft but with a surface chill to match the air.

It feels good: the connection, sharing again, with someone you want to. It's possible they are both a little restrained at first, steeped in a war that only ever seems to thieve. But tonight Jens has laid himself open, and it's only right she repays the compliment. Like him, no doubt, she will deal with the surplus guilt later, in private.

For now, Rumi Orlstad gives herself over to the intimacy, flushed with a sudden warmth, and is only just aware of the fluttering that reaches right down to the very tips of her toes.

50

A Mother's Plea

Hop, 8th November 1942

Rumi

The train to Hop is late and the walk to the hostel slow over rain-drenched streets, made worse by Rumi's so-called 'decent' shoes that make her more convincing as Anya's cousin, but hinder any kind of speed. She's wet by the time she reaches the hostel, and the dark afternoon shroud is already drawing in.

Anya meets her at the guard post, as always, but steers Rumi away from the house quickly and down the garden towards the coastal edge.

'Anya, can't I just dry off inside for a bit? I'm soaked,' Rumi protests.

Just a flash of Anya's face tells Rumi she'll be damp for some time yet, and the frisson from the briefest touch to her flesh confirms it. Despite Anya's general roundness in being seven months pregnant, she's moving at a pace.

'What? What is it?' Rumi asks as they reach the garden

shelter. The last time she witnessed such nervousness in anyone was Trine. And she'd had a baby within hours.

Anya is mute and her hands are shaking as she pulls a crumpled pamphlet from somewhere under her too-tight coat and passes it to Rumi, who sees immediately that all the angst is justified.

"**Your One Greater Germany**" is printed in bold Teutonic print, four words that speak volumes. One look tells Rumi it will be anything but a pleasure read.

'Look inside,' Anya urges.

There's a selection of photographs across one page: sweet newborns and older babies in the arms of women, with men in SS uniform by their sides. Without exception, all are blonde and blue-eyed, the women demure in their pose. Rumi picks her way around the German captions, recognising the words 'ideal', 'racial' and 'pure'. She doesn't need to be fluent to gauge the implication.

'Keep going,' Anya utters, a barely controlled quiver to her voice.

Overleaf, the message becomes more sinister: more pictures, this time of women whose captions read something like 'undesirable'. All are dark-haired with prominent features, a stark contrast to the images before. The rest consists of text, which Rumi could only decipher in detail with plenty of time and a good dictionary. But she needs neither, because it's obvious the pages constitute one thing: it's a catalogue. For babies. Preferences for human life.

Now her fingers are shaking in line with Anya's; it's obvious that Trine's desperation to escape was based on truth.

'I came across it in the office two days ago,' Anya manages. 'It was in an envelope that had obviously been left there by mistake. Certainly not meant for my eyes.'

'Was there anything else with it?'

'Yes. This.' She hands Rumi a typed page, which looks to be a copied circular in letter form, addressed to staff running Lebensborn programmes outside Germany.

'I picked up some German at the hotel, and I've worked out what it says,' Anya goes on, her beautiful face now white and twisted with concern. 'It basically tells them to increase their provision, that there is still a substantial "requirement" for families in the fatherland. There's an old quote from Himmler in there too.' She points to a sentence and translates it aloud: '"We only recommend genuinely racially pure men as . . ."'

'*Zeugungshelfer?*' Rumi queries.

'It means procreation helpers.'

'And this?' Rumi points to the signing off sentence, written in bold italics: "*Schenkt dem Führer Ein Kind*".'

'"Give a child to the Führer,"' Anya says. She wipes the tears now streaming down her cheeks and blows hard into the air, as if emptying her lungs of some foul element. 'It doesn't get any more obvious than that, does it?'

They sit in silence, absorbing the hard evidence that sits in their hands: Lebensborn, breeders, baby farmers, thieving. It all amounts to one, unspeakable prospect that they are forced to face. Rumi steals a look at Anya's rotund belly and tries to picture the baby inside; with Anya's looks and that of the SS father, it's bound to be a blonde and blue-eyed cherub, one of those flawless examples in the pages of a catalogue, coveted by childless German couples. The Führer's perfect *kinder*.

'I need to get away from here,' Anya murmurs. 'And soon.'

There's no room for comfort or reassurance. Instead, the two women talk practicalities for the rest of the visit, Rumi still damp inside her wet clothes, squirming with a different kind of discomfort. Anya reports there are still three guards on duty, night and day. All are armed.

'We suspect one woman was trying to leave last week,' Anya says. 'She made it past the gate but only got as far as the station in Hop before they picked her up. They took her away in a car the next day and we haven't seen her since.' Her expression is wanton. Afraid and in need. 'And there's one other thing.'

'Yes?' Rumi wonders how much worse it can get.

'I think I'm being watched.'

'By the guards?'

'No, the housekeeper. She's a strange old bird, but she's been more than friendly recently. Asking me about my family, and what I plan to do after the baby arrives.' Anya palms the dress under her coat, her fingers making circles of reassurance. 'I wouldn't ask you again, but I'm desperate, Rumi. I want to be a mother to my baby, always, however difficult that might prove. But, now . . . I'm frightened for us both.'

'We'll sort something out,' Rumi pledges, though in her heart she doesn't know how, only that she can't do it alone.

51

Cat Out of the Bag

Hop, 8th November 1942

She hovers in the vestibule, trailing with her eyes as the redhead moves down the drive and out towards the lane, head hung low. She'd watched them earlier, Anya and her so-called 'cousin' as they came back from a walk around the drizzly, sodden garden. Something about their manner signalled both had changed, their faces struggling to feign a light-hearted goodbye, their embrace long and involved. They know. Of course they do – because she's told them, in her own way.

When she found that pamphlet, not terribly well hidden in the top drawer of Kleiner's desk and left carelessly unlocked, she shouldn't have been shocked. It's what she's been suspecting for some time. But here was the proof at last, in bold black print, with helpful pictures as a guide. Suddenly, that wiry man with the high forehead and his pencil scratchings made sense; he was fine-tuning his wish list. Shopping.

She found herself dry retching with disgust into the waste bin beside Kleiner's desk, anxious the noise would bring one of the maids running, or worse, the midwives. Her fingers felt itchy and hot, as if the paper was a grenade primed and ready, and that simply returning it was like replacing the pin and making it benign once again. But it would still be a grenade.

For one long minute she wished she hadn't found it, and yet it was her who'd gone searching in the desk, wasn't it? It strikes her that there must be a reason for her discovery, something she's morally bound to do, that kept her awake all of that night. And that's why she left it in an envelope for Anya to find, to save herself and the baby. But not before she'd written to her sister, warning that the entire family should decamp out of Hordaland. And quickly.

She hates herself for not being brave enough to do more, to effect a total mutiny among the women, to warn them all. But where would they go, and who would support them? She's no hero, merely a housekeeper. But if she's right about Anya's intentions, there won't be a place here for her much longer as housekeeper, not when Kleiner points the finger. The best she can hope for is that he doesn't get the chance.

She moves upstairs and into her sparse but comfortable room, thankful that the years of living in someone else's home have taught her to keep only scant possessions. A few things she'll leave behind, but most will fit into the brown leather suitcase she pulls from the top of the wardrobe. It might be days, or weeks before Anya takes action, though not too long given how far along the pregnancy is, but she'd better be ready to move at a moment's notice. For now, it's best to be silent, to do what she's been doing for months now – to watch and wait, walk the corridors with her well-trained senses on alert.

The waiting is what she and this house are good at now.

52

Friends and Allies

Bergen, 8th November 1942

Rumi

She fidgets in her seat on the train home, partly from the enduring damp but also from the plague of creatures crawling up and down her inner vessels at great speed. Rumi is running with enough anxiety that the woman next to her huffs loudly and moves across the aisle. Even pulling knitting from her bag doesn't help; she looks at the stitches as if they are one big puzzle. Which they are, tumbling among all other thoughts in her brain.

How on earth is she to spring a second heavily pregnant woman from a guarded Nazi facility, conceal her from view and transport her out of Norway? And all before the birth of her baby in just over two months' time? One woman with a cumbrous belly has already proved hard enough, but secreting a baby with lungs that could open at any time would be almost impossible.

Rumi knows Marjit will readily help, but after their

previous acrimony over springing mothers and babies, she's loath to ask Jens again. Especially now. Their coming together – that kiss – just over a week ago was undeniably wonderful, Rumi reflecting on it time and again in her moments alone, though she hasn't seen Jens since. If prompted, she feels sure he would do anything for her. And that's the worry: putting him in the path of yet more danger. Jens has enough on his plate with Selig's game of cat and mouse turning into much more than a joke.

Predictably, Marjit is more than willing. 'We daren't leave it too long,' she whispers under the cover of the radio. 'At the very latest it has to be early December, and even then she'll be eight months gone.'

'Then let's hope this baby is destined to be late for everything in its life,' Rumi says. 'Starting with its birth.' The Trine episode still plucks at her heart in a positive way, but it's not one she would readily repeat, especially without Marjit.

They settle on bringing Rubio and Peder into the fold, knowing both will be eager to help with transport northwards along the coast, somewhere to link up with the Shetland Bus. Anya is insistent on escaping the Nazi clutches altogether, and that means being off Norwegian soil. They know from Jens that Trine had difficulties moving overland even before the snow, so the Bus is their best solution.

'And Jens?' Marjit asks.

'No – he has enough to deal with. If he has to know then we'll tell him once we've got Anya somewhere safe.'

'I suppose you're right.'

'We can do this, Marjit,' she reiterates firmly. 'Aren't you always telling me Norwegian women can do anything? Isn't this the time to prove it?'

53

A Merry Dance

Bergen, 11th November 1942

Jens

Paranoia is a double-edged sword, Jens thinks as he clips over the cobbles near Tyskebryggen at a steady pace. The training in Scotland told them it could make an agent wisely vigilant, and possibly save their life. In contrast, it can also eat away at anyone's psyche until they are convinced each and every man or woman in their orbit is Abwehr or Gestapo, intent on tailing, betraying, capturing and killing.

Right now, he's in the latter camp, more so since leaving the café on Sigurds gate. It was stupid, a momentary lapse of concentration, and he knows it's because his mind was elsewhere, thinking about Rumi and their conversation over a week before. *No, Jens, not the conversation – be honest with yourself at least!* Lingering over his coffee, he was thinking of that kiss; not the way that it felt so much – though that was lovely enough – but what it meant. That she had let him in, past her brittle grief and into the softness that he knows is there, if only she will allow it to flourish. He'd seen it in glimpses before, in her humour, and after the birth of Trine's baby, but in the few seconds of that kiss, Jens had felt himself completely immersed.

It's what his mind had lapsed to in the café, but worse still, he'd let it transfer to his lips, muttering under his breath in English. So foolish. He rarely does it these days; his internal thoughts are no longer in English. For God's sake, he even dreams in Norwegian!

But someone caught those mutterings, or that's what Jens thinks, fuelled by his agent's mistrust. He's already double-backed around the town once, stopping at a stand to buy a paper, done his proven zig-zag between opposing trams running through the bustling city interchange, and then lingered over the sparse offerings of a vegetable stall. There's a woman with a shopping basket who he's seen twice, and something about her shoes doesn't add up. Then, the man in a thick, black overcoat of the type Norwegian men rarely wear. Jens had noticed him in the corner of the café, already looking a little out of place. He couldn't have heard Jens's spoken blunder over the general hum, so it's possible he was already a target. Or is that the paranoia, now mounting like a fever?

He feels exhausted mentally, a juggler desperate to keep endless balls in the air, so that if he should drop even one, it will mean a life automatically extinguished, the harsh contact causing ripples to endanger others, too. Despite the time now lapsed, repercussions of the Hotel Bristol fire still tweak at his stash of guilt. Since then, the Abwehr's technical Direction-Finding has taken on a new life, with fresh equipment being brought in, and there are whispers they've developed a smaller, portable device that a man can wear under his overcoat to detect radio traffic nearby, bulky but much less obtrusive in the winter weather. Oh Christ, what will that do to his already stoked suspicion? Soon, he'll have to avoid every well-built man in hefty clothing. The snow will fully envelop Bergen shortly, and then how will he tour the surrounding hills to reach the coastal stations with vital warnings?

He sits on a bench close to the fish market and pulls out the day's paper, trying to sweep away the debris inside his head as words swim across the page. If he didn't need to be somewhere soon, he could casually lead his stalkers a merry dance across Bergen all day, up and down the steep lanes, in and out of the wharf warehouses, until they both become tired and fed-up. But he has an appointment to keep, and it's one that can't wait.

He has fifteen minutes. Neither the man nor woman are within sight, and Jens scouts left and right from behind his paper, spying for any convenient nooks they could hide within. With nothing apparent, he folds the paper swiftly, stands up and strides off, pretending to hail someone familiar in the distance so that he can half-swivel and scour for signs of sudden movement behind. None. Either he's lost them or they were always a figment of his overblown imagination.

The rendezvous is in another café three streets away, where he loiters at a corner table but doesn't order a drink. In minutes, a stout, older man joins him and whispers an address, and Jens is relieved to hear the new venue is only a few minutes' walk. Already, he's weary of chasing his own tail and the suspicion festering inside his own head.

The café contact insists he ring on the bell of the thin, four-storey building on Øvregaten three times in quick succession, then waits for a signal from above. He duly sees a head poke like a jack-in-the-box from the top floor window, waving him up, and he's puffing slightly on reaching the top of the stairs. 'Kolstad Textiles' it says on the lone office entrance.

There's a verbal code to mutter through the glass-topped door, and a cursory patting down by a young man with a florid red moustache. As Jens gets the all-clear, a gentle hum of industry resumes in what he could only describe as the smallest but most populated room he's ever seen. SOE agents on the coastal stations often exist in the tiniest fisherman's cottages, but usually there's only two of them. This high-ceilinged room is crammed with desks, at which several men and women are busy typing, or clasping headphones to their ears in transcribing radio dispatches onto paper, all through a fug of cigarette smoke. The walls are hung with swathes of material and bundles of yarn spill out of piled up boxes in a chaotic, multi-coloured collage. There's a gap in the haphazard wall décor, but only because a man sits snug against the wall, his chair balancing on top of a tall wardrobe, back bent over a typewriter that's resting on boxes.

Red moustache man must see Jens's mouth gape slightly. 'Helps with the soundproofing.' He gives a nod towards the wall hangings. The typist teetering on high gets no explanation, as if it's the most natural thing in the world to clatter away two metres above the floor.

Jens is led to his eventual contact in the corner, who he knows only as 'Emil', and who looks to be the chief by virtue of a pencil lodged behind each ear and black ink tattooing all of his finger pads. They exchange nods and get down to business. With Selig potentially tapping into an unknown number of SOE transmissions, Jens needs a new line of communication, and the now nameless paper Emil oversees – formerly known as the *Weekly News* – seems a perfect vehicle. Underground newspapers are slower,

286

inevitably, but with Peder and Rubio pledging to undertake more delivery rounds on the trawler, it benefits them both; the resistance gets a wider circulation and Jens is able to secrete coded messages in its pages.

Emil is willing, thankfully, and they talk politics of the war for a while, both skirting around any detail, girding any real information. They might like each other well enough, but that's still a reason to be wary of giving too much away.

Business over, Emil says goodbye and Jens watches him turn back to a tiny press in the corner, groaning as someone reports it's seized up yet again. A door to the side opens and, despite the general clamour of the room, his ears are alerted; much like the virtual maps in his head, more than a year as a radio operator has rendered Jens sensitive to the slightest nuance of identification, whether it be a dot or a dash, or the voice he hears now.

'Yes, that's no problem. Get word to me when you have an answer.' It's female, serious, loaded with concern. Not a social visit, clearly. He spins to confirm his own recognition: Rumi.

She stops mid-stride on seeing him. 'Oh.'

'*Hei,*' he says, forcing a casual tone. Neither asks the purpose of their visits; it's not something people do nowadays, those in the resistance especially. And then there's the added embarrassment of the last time they met on Marjit's stoop, Rumi feigning a yawn and taking herself off to bed. It had been too dark for Jens to see her flushed cheeks after their lips had parted, but he could have warmed his hands on the exuding heat.

'Are you just leaving?' he asks. 'I'll walk you out.'

'Yes, fine. That would be fine. Good.'

A woman to the side looks up from her task, and only

just stops short of rolling her eyes at their stuttering, pubescent awkwardness.

'I'm going back to the boathouse,' Rumi says, out on the rapidly dimming street. 'There's no need to walk me.'

She moves quickly away and Jens has to hurry to catch up. 'It's no problem. I'm glad of a stroll.' His aching feet remind him that's a lie, but he wants to talk in private for two reasons; to break the ice between them, and – if he's honest – to find out why she was in the offices of an underground newspaper, when Rumi Orlstad has never so much as mentioned a friend in the organisation before. He can't help it; this grubby, secretive under-the-counter war has made him suspicious and dubious, and he hates himself for it. Equally, it's his job.

'Really, I've got lots to do at work,' she says, too eagerly.

He catches her arm and she's forced to stop, or they might both look suspicious from afar. 'What's going on, Rumi?'

He watches excuses skitter across her forehead and swim behind her eyes. Again, he hates himself for knowing how to spot it.

'Nothing. I was just visiting friends.' He sees her annoyance surface, and it's her undoing. 'I am allowed to have them, you know. My life isn't all fish and knitting.'

'I know that. I'm just concerned—'

'You don't need to be.' She moves away again, but Jens won't be thrown.

'I could kill for a cup of decent coffee, if you have any left,' he says to her back.

She slows – with reluctance, clearly – and allows him to catch up. 'I've barely enough for one pot.'

'Then one pot is perfect,' he says.

★   ★   ★

The boathouse is dark, and she pulls down the blackout curtains before lighting two paraffin lanterns, while Jens feeds the smouldering embers in the burner. Puffs of white breath rise eerily in the dim glow as they sit wrapped in blankets with coffee to warm hands and insides.

'So, come on then, I'll spill if you do,' Jens begins.

She looks at him with irritation, as if he's an annoying younger brother who won't stop prodding. 'I told you, they are my friends. I went to school with Emil.' But she dips her eyes as she says it.

'Rubbish.'

'Sorry?'

'I said that's rubbish,' Jens punts. 'You may well know Emil, but you didn't go there to talk over childhood memories.'

'And what makes you a great mind reader all of a sudden?'

Jens detects flashes of the old Rumi, the anger pushing up inside her and threatening to breathe fire. But in the next second he sees she's become more adept at dousing her flame, leaving it sizzling rather than searing.

'What were *you* doing there anyway?' she says between thinned lips.

'I need Emil, or his paper, to be more accurate, to help send out messages. The printed word might bypass Selig.'

She nods, silent.

'So?' Jens pushes, though wondering if it might be one prod too many. Throwing paraffin on her sparks.

She stares straight at him, consideration washing across her features, then sighs with resignation. 'If you must know, I need their help for Anya.'

'Anya?'

'Yes, you remember Anya – the woman who's desperate

to escape from the Nazi bastards who might steal her baby? *That* Anya. My friend in need.'

The sparks stay aloft between them, fading eventually and dying in the silence.

'I didn't mean to sound dismissive,' Jens says.

'Well, you did.'

They both stare into their cups, noting a déjà vu moment from that first snowy encounter outside Bergen. Jens creases inside: have they really not come much further than this, after all that's happened, everything between them?

'Are you going to tell me your plans?' he asks.

She shakes her head slowly, though more in defeat. 'So far, they amount to nothing more than getting her out of that hostel, and finding somewhere to lodge her until we can make contact with the Shetland Bus through Emil. Preferably before one person becomes two. Marjit says she can stay—'

'No!' It's Jens's turn to blaze. 'She can't stay with Marjit, it's too dangerous.'

Rumi shoves her mug onto the burner, the chink echoing loudly. 'How can you say that, Jens?' she spits back. 'You take off into the wilderness, sometimes for months on end, and we're all in the dark as to whether you're dead or alive. I *know* for certain you're in the line of fire, and yet we're not supposed to worry, or risk ourselves, simply stay at home knitting mittens for worthy fighters.' She pauses, but only to breathe and re-fuel the fire. 'Well, it's not going to happen! You pledged to help Anya and so far nothing. And now it's urgent. In case you've forgotten the episode with Trine, babies tend to arrive unexpectedly, not always on time. And I personally don't want to be responsible for any baby dying out there in the freezing wastes with a mother running for their lives.'

290

She flops back onto the chair as if exhausted by her pent-up release, then jerks up to standing, agitation twitching her limbs like a cattle prod. Jens follows suit, sending coffee slopping to the floor.

'But why now? Why is it suddenly so crucial for Anya to leave?' he demands. 'Wasn't Trine's anxiety largely her own?'

'Apparently not.'

He listens intently as Rumi explains, about the Reich's pamphlet and its overt, sickening ethos, of Trine's nightmare being laid bare in print. The unashamed trafficking of babies.

'Christ.' Jens breathes deeply. 'They really are trying to sew everything up, aren't they? Birth, life and death. All in their control.' His mind goes to the tiny digits of Trine's baby curling around his own fingers, so perfect and yet so vulnerable, too.

'So you see why we have to act soon?' Rumi says quietly.

'I do. But Marjit . . . Please don't draw her in so acutely. You know she'll never say no to any helpless soul. It's not in her nature.'

'That's true, but Jens, it was also her suggestion. And we have nowhere else for Anya to stay. Not yet. Marjit wants to do this. She won't have it any other way.'

'Then how can I help?' he says. He pledged his support to her and now he needs to come through. 'I'll do whatever you need.'

Rumi shakes her head again, resolute this time. 'Nothing. If what you suspect about Selig is right, we don't want any talk of babies, or "cargo", or "packages" on the airwaves, even in code. I need to wait for a message from the Bus, that's the safest way. I can do it, Jens.' She swallows hard. 'And it's what I need to do.'

He recognises the determined glint in her eye and knows

that arguing is pointless. He has Charlie, and she Magnus: the motivation to do something right, sweeping away the loss, or the guilt, or both.

'And after that we hope,' Rumi says, draining the last of her coffee.

'For what?'

'That Marjit's house doesn't suddenly become a maternity home.'

54

Waiting

Hop, 29th November 1942

Rumi

The arrival of snow over the past days is a mixed blessing;
good for camouflage in various ways, but also slippery
underfoot, as well as bringing temperatures that Pappa's old
truck does not appreciate. Rumi and Marjit are almost late,
having had to coax the sputtering engine into life for the
journey over to Hop, and now Rumi daren't switch off
the ignition for fear it might not start again. An idling
truck in itself is grounds for suspicion to any passer-by,
though a fresh layer of snow means the lane is deserted
for now.

'See you in fifteen minutes?' Marjit checks as she lowers
herself down from the cab.

'I'll be there,' Rumi says with false confidence, gripping
the steering wheel to stop the shake in her hands.
Somehow, she felt more bravado in Trine's breakout from
the hostel; there were no guards or guns then, and

unknown retribution. It's since been made clear from Nazi command that any attempts like today's will be met with the most severe punishment.

She watches Marjit hobble towards the hostel driveway, adopting more of an elderly hunch and a half limp with each step, sliding into her role as a confused old woman with ease. Her hair is pulled tightly under a hat, while some glasses that had belonged to Lars complete the transformation. It's especially odd for Rumi to see Marjit in this guise; to everyone that knows her she's still a vibrant, energetic woman. But it's Marjit's job to look aged and lonely, and to keep the gate sentry busy with inane chatter while Anya works her way through the garden to her exit point.

Rumi's role is at the receiving end, waiting by a gap in the fence she and Anya marked out on both sides over two weeks of visits as they strolled the perimeter. She only hopes a fresh blanket of snow won't prove confusing to both of them. She and Anya have deliberately chosen a Sunday afternoon, as the guards partake of a relatively sumptuous lunch with wine, and from her careful observations Anya reasons both will be incapable of running too fast or shooting straight. Gluttony and alcohol may well be their salvation today.

Marjit disappears from view and Rumi turns the truck around, careful not to crunch the grouchy gears too loudly, and trundles fifty metres up the lane. Her watch hand nears two o'clock, the time set for Anya to appear. Any weak sun is cloaked by thick, grey clouds and the cab is freezing, but she needs to open the window and take gulps of air to abate the nausea, which refuses to shift. As each sixty seconds tick by, the heat on her cheeks rises a notch, skin beginning to itch. She thinks back to the day they rescued

Trine, and Jens having to wait it out in the truck. She feels doubly blinded by the swathe of white and the unknown, and she has to draw hard on Magnus's motivation in stepping onto the Bus – to help those in need. Still, the wait – away from the action – is definitely worse.

Where is Anya? And how is Marjit faring?

55

The Help

Hop, 29th November 1942

Dishing out the last of the sumptuous lunch to the German contingent around the table, she surveys their food-fuelled indolence while offering to top up their wine glasses. The midwives say no but the guards, predictably, don't refuse. Clever girl, that Anya, to choose a Sunday, when everyone knows that Kleiner rarely visits, preferring his luncheon at one of the hotels in Bergen, dozy with brandy and cigars by mid-afternoon with all the other Nazi dignitaries.

From the time she rose early and made her usual walk through the house, she'd sensed there was something afoot, noticed that Anya slunk away from breakfast quickly, couched in her room with the door shut ever since. And her winter coat is gone from the peg in the hall, along with a photograph that was on a desk in the general office, to look at when she was typing. Little things that no one else notices.

She'd returned to her room then, and put the last bits in her suitcase, ready for any eventuality. She's already been to the bank and drawn what money she can, keeping it in a small tin box in the wardrobe. Now, she counts it out: everything she has in the world. It's not much to show for twenty-five years — barely enough for a few weeks, a month or so if she's careful — and yet, it feels a small sacrifice in comparison.

At ten minutes to two, as the guards amble slowly back to their posts, she hears Anya's door open and trails the emerging body at a distance. The coat doesn't cover her round girth now, and she has on a white hat pulled low over her blonde hair. In her hand, the purpose is clear: a small valise, which fits even fewer possessions for her ongoing life. The redhead, however, is nowhere to be seen, so clearly there's no plan to brazen it out and simply walk out the door together.

She follows, discreetly she hopes, hoisting up one of the woven garden baskets that Gunnar keeps in the back porch, though there's nothing to harvest through the carpet of snow, but it gives her some sort of purpose if she's stopped. The same carpet of flakes does muffle her footsteps, enough that Anya doesn't look back, too busy keeping her balance on the icy pathways, cradling her still growing belly. There's no sign of the guard patrolling the grounds, as he'll be yarning with the other at the entrance for a good while yet, huddled in their tiny makeshift hut. Instead, Anya leads her to the far side of the garden, where there's no exit or even a side gate. But didn't Gunnar say that the hedge there needed shoring up against wildlife, a job he planned for the spring? She sees Anya checking her watch — dead on two p.m. And then, just as the young woman makes to cut from the path, there he is, popping out of Lord knows where. Gunnar. She sees Anya start, slip backwards a little and then the old gardener apologising, rattling on as he does; the man can talk for Norway. Anya fidgets from foot to foot, time ticking away. It's obvious from her direction, and now her shuffling, that someone is waiting beyond the hedge — the redhead maybe? And there's old Gunnar threatening to scupper everything. He's a Norwegian, a loyalist, but he's also aged and afraid; he and his wife simply want to live out their

297

days in peace, under the Germans if they have to. He may be too afraid to keep quiet, and he'd certainly crack under questioning.

'Gunnar!' she shouts, and the old man's head swivels, along with Anya's. Gunnar's expression is inquisitive, while Anya's mirrors pure terror. 'Cook needs something from the greenhouse quickly. Can you go and see what she wants?'

'Right oh.' The old man limps off, and Anya freezes like a rabbit in the snow; caught out in the open as the housekeeper strides towards her.

'Fru Nesse! I was . . . I was just getting some air,' Anya stutters, her features falling with defeat. Total dejection washes over her as her hand grips at her bump, knuckles white and the valise poorly hidden behind her.

'Quick,' she whispers gravely to Anya, stepping close. 'If you're going to go, it has to be now.' Clearly, Anya's brain struggles to work through this instruction, features seeming to morph from fear to relief to gratitude, all the time being piloted towards the hedge. 'I'll try and delay your absence being noticed for as long as possible,' she says.

'Thank you,' the young woman manages, her voice strangled. 'Thank you, Fru Nesse. For your kindness.'

It is a small sacrifice, she thinks. But there is her reward. In spite of what might happen after, it's more than enough.

56

Emergence

Hop, 29th November 1942

Rumi

At four minutes past two, clods of falling snow signal a scrabbling in the hedge separating the gardens from the lane. Rumi peers but stays put, careful not to be seen loitering in one place, her recognisable hair concealed under a dark woollen hat. The activity becomes more than any bird or creature would create, and she's desperate to get out and see if it's Anya, to help her through. But they've both been clear; if it looks hazardous in any way, they should abort.

'I'll face the consequences,' Anya had said. 'I can't believe even the Nazis would shoot a pregnant woman.' She'd looked down at her bump. 'Especially when I'm carrying what they claim as their own.'

Rumi didn't disagree, though she thinks Anya has been cushioned with the kindness of the hostel staff; she doesn't possess anything like the faith that Anya has in the Reich's humanity.

There's a sudden grunting and Rumi jumps down from the truck, forging into the bush to see poor Anya struggling to bend double in tackling a thick branch that won't yield. 'Here, here,' she hisses, pushing up the bough with one hand and hauling on Anya's coat with the other, her freezing hands clawed at by razor-sharp thorns. The urgency, the life and death nature of emergence, and the look of desperation on Anya's reddened face as she looks upwards prompt a brief and strange flashback for Rumi: the rounded head of Trine's baby trying to push his mother's flesh, coupled with the birth of piglets they once had when she was a child.

Beyond the hedge, she hears another voice – a grunting or a shout, she can't tell. Have they seen Anya pushing through? Will they both have to speed away and dodge a volley of bullets aimed at the truck? And what about Marjit?

Rumi reaches with every inch of flesh she has, grasps Anya's hand roughly and with one huge pull she's free, hauling a tiny suitcase behind her, an entire life in little more than a handbag. Wordlessly, they slip and slide to the cab – easier said than done for a woman nearly eight months pregnant – and into the carefully prepared nest that the artful Rubio has created once again. As much as she's able, Anya folds herself into the long pallet box, fitted on the floor this time, behind the seats. Covered with a blanket, it looks merely like an impromptu bed any driver might have fashioned, especially as the winter comes on and the prospect of getting stuck overnight increases.

'Are you all right?' Rumi checks. 'Who was that behind you? Do we have to go right now?'

'It was a friend, an ally,' Anya puffs. 'One I didn't know I had. I think she's given us a bit of time.' Instinctively, she sets both arms around her bump, bracing her most precious possession for the bumpy journey ahead.

'We'll be on our way as soon as we collect Marjit,' Rumi reassures, then hopes in the next beat that the 'old woman' is eyeing the clock carefully.

Marjit's reputation for always being on time is threatened as they wait an agonising five, eight, then ten minutes beyond the agreed rendezvous. The heavy pendulum inside Rumi's head swings: Marjit instructed her firmly not to wait, to leave, but how would she escape if needed, on foot and in this weather? To Rumi, Marjit is everything – she can't leave her. Behind, she hears Anya twitching, her breath heavy.

At eleven minutes, the foul, dry taste in Rumi's mouth disappears: Marjit's bent form hobbles convincingly from the driveway, with a backwards wave as the truck rolls to a halt on the lane. Out of sight of the guardpost, she straightens and scrabbles up into the cab.

'Lordy, those guards can gossip,' she huffs, pulling off Lars's glasses and looking instantly like the true Marjit. 'Everything to plan? I thought I might have spotted some delay across the garden.'

'So far all right,' Rumi answers. She refrains from 'so good'. It seems too much like tempting fate.

'Then let's go home, my partner in crime.'

It's only the spirited, satisfied look in Marjit's eye that calms Rumi's pulse and stops her from stalling the engine. She cranks the gearstick forward, mutters a swift prayer to some god of mechanics and spins the wheels on the fresh snow.

Another one in the eye, she thinks.

That's for Anya, but it's for you too, Magnus. And there's still more to pay.

57

The Fallout

Hop, 29th November 1942

She hears the rumour snake through the house around five p.m., almost as she's leaving herself. One of the midwives goes to Anya's room on a routine visit and sees her few possessions are gone. It's not so much an alarm bell, but the guards make a play of scuttling around the grounds, resigned that she's already long gone, and then retreat to their hut, no doubt fearful of Kleiner's tirade, which will hit like a tornado when he arrives.

She packs the last of her things and pockets her savings, preferring not to wait for Kleiner and her own interrogation, having borne his boorish tantrums once too often. Instead, she slips out through a door in the basement that opens out to the compost heap, an odorous but safe route onto the opposite lane that few know about. By pure chance, her evening off is always Sundays, and there's no reason for others to suspect her flight until perhaps early on Monday, as the staff know she often travels into Bergen to see a film and arrives back late. There's a train that leaves for Oslo at seven p.m., and she'll take her chances on melting into a bigger city where experienced help is always needed. Beyond that, if she can find the right route and help, maybe Stockholm, and perhaps a different life entirely. For now, the war can be her friend and the shroud under which she moves, and she doesn't look back on her departure with too much sadness.

Her memories of the place are mostly good, but it's not been a true home for some time. Strange as the prospect may be, she might actually find one of her own amid this chaos.

'Fru Nesse?'

She's stopped in her tracks, and her hope sinks into the scrubby winter ground underfoot. Kleiner. His tone is inquisitive. For now. She'd grounded her case while picking a stone from her shoe, and she wonders, quite calmly, if that simple act will prove a poignant life saver. Her foot nudges it behind the compost heap as he moves his solid frame beyond the door towards her.

'Yes, Captain Kleiner?' The words stick in her throat, but instinctively she adopts the open face of a servant once again: willing and keen to please. Hoping that it's enough to mask her guilt that is only just skin deep.

58

Safety in Strangebakken

Bergen, 8th December 1942

Rumi

Despite the extra work and another mouth to feed, Marjit is in heaven. Rumi watches her bloom in caring for Anya, who sleeps like some kind of Rapunzel in the newly warmed attic room and seems to grow larger by the day. It's clear she's wholly relieved to be away from the hostel, and Rumi sees it in her manner — some of the old Anya spark returning — and in the way her skin becomes gradually less waxen, despite the freezing temperatures outside. Oddly, Anya doesn't ask much about the onward journey, and Rumi wonders if, having spent so long worrying about the months ahead, that she's simply too jaded to think of anything other than day to day. For now, she and her baby are warm and safe, after the rumours and the searches dissipated. Initially, it was too dangerous to move her anywhere, and then the fervour seemed to die down, though Jens is keeping his ear firmly to ground for any changes.

In the daytime, Anya keeps to the rooms upstairs, out of sight of Hilde's eagle eyes, who could easily spot her when she's doing chores in the garden. In the evening, though, when the blackout curtains are drawn and Hilde has left, she joins Marjit and Rumi in the parlour. Given Anya's impending status, they are teaching her to knit, though Rumi hopes she'll be more adept at mothering than she is at weaving wool.

'I think I've dropped another stitch,' Anya moans as she fidgets on the floor, back straight against the least saggy chair, the only way she can get comfortable.

'Here, let me see.' Rumi scoots from her own position by the fire and peers at the tangle on Anya's needle. She fiddles, hooks and picks up stitches from somewhere, thinking that, at its very best, Anya's efforts will do as a blanket or a scarf. Luckily, Rumi is halfway through a tiny cardigan, after two hats and several pairs of booties; wherever mother and child end up, it's certain to be glacial. Marjit, sitting at her sewing table, is squinting at her needle and thread, working her way diligently through an entire layette for the baby like someone on a mission. How they'll transport all of this when it's time for Anya to leave is anyone's guess.

Word has been slow from Emil's contacts. The scant information so far says the Bus is willing, though struggling with its own losses and North Sea winds, which reach gale force on at least half of their crossings in the winter months, news that sends waves of dread through Rumi.

'It's going to have to be soon,' Marjit had said in Rumi's kitchen earlier. 'Officially, there's only four or five weeks to the birth, but what with everything . . .'

Marjit doesn't need to elaborate, merely purses her lips to conjure an image between them of Trine.

'I'll go again to Emil's office tomorrow,' Rumi had promised. 'See if there's another way to make contact, at least to get a date and a location we can plan for.'

Emil might well have received word, but Rumi will never know, since the entire office is empty and cleared of incriminating evidence when she visits, only the wall décor left in situ, hanging limply. She's not heard of any raid or arrests, so it's likely Emil and his crew were tipped off and have gone to ground somewhere else in Bergen, where they'll set up the presses again.

But it leaves Anya without an escape route, and forces Rumi to think creatively.

'Pappa and Rubio say they can take her a little way north on the boat, but it means I'll have to go with her, at least to that point,' she whispers to Marjit under the whistle of the kettle while, out of earshot, Anya fights with another line of stitches. 'Haven't you got a cousin living up there?'

Marjit shakes her head. 'The last I heard their farm had been commandeered. The Nazis use it as a bunkhouse for some of their officers.' She pauses. 'I don't think we have any choice but to ask—'

'No,' Rumi says firmly.

'But, my love, he might be our only chance.' Marjit looks through the doorway, at Anya stroking and singing gently to her bump. '*Their* only chance.'

Rumi frowns. She hates to admit that Marjit is probably right. 'Have you seen him recently?'

'In town a few days ago,' Marjit replies. 'I wanted to know how much talk there was over Anya's escape. Seems not as much as Trine's – the Nazis have other, more important targets.'

'That's a good thing, isn't it?'

'For Anya, yes. But not for Jens – he's one of the targets. He's been running all over the district trying to avoid detection by that Selig man. Jens thinks it's become all too personal.'

'And how is he?' Rumi ventures.

'Drained. And he looks it.' Marjit shakes her head with concern. 'I honestly don't know how long he can go on. But, of course, he won't admit it.'

'So, what do we do about . . .?' Rumi gestures in Anya's direction.

Marjit takes the kettle off the stove. 'I'm loath to ask him, too, but I don't think we have much choice. Jens is the only one we know who can get a message out urgently.'

He comes the next day, appearing at Rumi's kitchen window in the early evening darkness. She startles on seeing his face through the glass; as ghostly as the cadaver she came across in the snowy hills all those months ago. He's lost weight, and she notes a slight limp as he steps into the kitchen, no doubt his resident shrapnel giving him a timely nudge.

'*Hei,* sit down,' she says, and automatically cuts a large slice of the indistinct potato and something cake Hilde has left, rationing having become even tighter.

'Thanks.' He eyes the plate as if he wants to inhale it, but lacks the energy to chew.

'I hate to say this, Jens, but you look dreadful.'

'Always a way with the words, Rumi.' Though he seems amused rather than offended, fatigue overriding irritation.

'What's been happening?'

'I'm not sure where to begin,' Jens says wearily. 'It seems wherever we transmit from, Selig isn't too far behind. We've had to shut down two bases and three SOE have been

307

arrested. That's on top of losing the entire Theta station crew on Tyskebryggen in October.'

There's no point in asking why Jens won't pull out of Bergen; Rumi can predict his staunch reasoning – it's his duty. It makes posing her own question even harder. But she's out of options, and quickly running out of time.

His answer is swift and automatic. 'Of course I'll help.'

'Will it compromise you, and others?' she feels bound to ask. 'Because, if it does, then Anya will have to stay and . . . well, we'll just cope.'

His weary eyes are suddenly alert. 'No, she can't stay,' he says, quiet but resolute. 'I didn't tell Marjit this because I didn't want to alarm her at the time, but the Nazis are simply waiting for that.'

'What do you mean?'

'They may not be actively searching for Anya, but my contact at the Bristol says they have eyes and ears out for any "homeless" women giving birth throughout Hordaland. Word is that two other mothers felt the need to escape Lebensborn too, both from the converted hotel at Geilo. All midwives in the region are currently being visited and questioned regularly, all births screened.'

Rumi feels grateful Anya hasn't needed a midwife as yet, though the laws of nature dictate it won't stay that way.

'I'll put out a coded plea to Shetland via the BBC broadcast,' Jens says. 'But in the meantime, I would get Anya ready to move.'

He picks lazily at the cake crumbs on his plate, eyes glassy with fatigue and the grey of his sweater reflected in smudges under his eyes that are not dirt. Rumi can't help it. Despite everything that's gone between them – *because* of everything between them – she moves behind his chair and clasps her arms around his shoulders, her chin to his short, blond crown. Her lips nuzzle into the strands, which smell faintly of soap and the salt sea, but mostly of endeavour.

'Oh Jens, when will this ever end?' It's what she asked of Magnus on their last evening together as he packed his kitbag for the Bus and they huddled in the hold of Pappa's boat. Then, he had no answer, and she expects nothing more now. It's just something to breathe out into the ether.

Jens pulls up a hand, grips at her sleeve and pulls it close to his face, as if he's hungry for the gesture, the touch and the warmth. 'Only when we've given the best account of ourselves,' he says. 'And I'm certain there's something left in us yet.'

59

Time to Go

Hop, 10th December 1942

'*Fru Nesse? Please look this way.*' *His voice is measured and calm, but that's worse, she's learnt from experience. She'd rather he ranted and raved, as he did the night that Anya went missing, at the staff in general, and the sentries who were swiftly dismissed and are probably now on some godforsaken Eastern Front quaking in their boots. Those who replaced them are more disciplined, with meaner expressions. Almost no one goes in and out of the hostel now without papers to say so.* How did it ever get to this? *she wonders. A house that was once so full of hope and laughter. There's little of that left now.*

She tracks his animal scent as Captain Kleiner circles the chair she's sitting on, something he often does as a way of asserting his authority. To intimidate. There's no point in that, since she already guesses what's in store – not the detail perhaps, but that her time here is limited, to hours or even minutes. It's been almost two weeks since Anya's escape, and Kleiner's accusations have bubbled like an undercurrent, hinting slyly at her possible complicity, but nothing direct. There was the initial grilling about her whereabouts on the day, how she could have missed the signs of Anya's intent, especially as she was supposedly his eyes and ears. But there was no proof, and no one else witnessed her exchange with 'the escapee'.

But now he has the vital testimony, clearly. Poor Gunnar, he'd held firm far longer than she imagined he could, but once Kleiner threatened his wife, the old man admitted what he saw. Who could blame him?

'I'm disappointed, Fru Nesse, truly I am,' Kleiner says, lighting a cigar and blowing its foul-smelling cloud towards her. 'I thought we had an understanding. And now I'm forced to act.'

She says nothing. What can she say? 'Sorry'? Except she's not. Whatever her fate – and she can only imagine it will be Grini – it's nothing to the loss these women are sure to go through. Her only regret is that she didn't help more to avoid it.

That self-satisfied expression on his face sickens her, sitting around the folds of his jowls. He thinks he's won, but she knows her sister and family are safe and hidden, and there's nothing in this world he can possibly take from her now. Everything of value sits within her, wrapped inside. She needs no suitcase or possessions, because she's gained something precious that he will never know, a self-respect she will carry in life, and to death if it comes to that.

'Is it time to go, Captain Kleiner?' she asks.

60

Exodus

Bergen, 10th December 1942

Jens

He's running yet again. Flat out towards Strangebakken, no pretence of trying to hide his urgency this time, breath clouds snorted out with the force of a racehorse, white against the chilled black of a sky nearing midnight.

He has to get to Marjit's. Before it's too late.

Jens falters on the snowy cobbles up the lane, curses under his breath; it's like those chasing dreams that invade his sleep all too often nowadays, running furiously from an enemy that is clearly Selig, but getting nowhere, stuck in a deep pool of quicksand. Charlie is always first in line of the keening voices crying out his name while Jens flails in the paralysing mulch.

He arrives at Marjit's window, bent double and ushered in immediately. 'You need to . . .' he pants, heaving up the words '. . . to go.' Scoops in air. 'Now.'

'What? What do you mean?' Marjit's concern seems split between Jens and what he's trying to impart.

He manages to stand and look straight into her stricken features. 'The Gestapo are on their way here. Now. You have to go – all of you.'

Wordlessly, Marjit slips out the back door and is back within seconds, Rumi following behind, pushing her hair into a braid as she hurries to button her shirt.

'I intercepted a message less than an hour ago,' Jens explains. 'It was on a frequency commonly used by the Abwehr, but this was clearly aimed at the Gestapo. There were no names, only enough to know they were talking about Anya. And you, Marjit.'

The pupils in her turquoise eyes seem to shrink to a pinprick and then harden like coal. Jens has seen this look only once in his aunt; at Lars's funeral, when he'd read it as determination to fight for their ailing farm, rather than sorrow.

'Rumi, you get Anya ready to go – take her to the boat-house for now,' she says, throwing a quizzical look at Jens, as if to say: *will that be safe?*

He nods an agreement. 'There was no mention of the boathouse or Peder.' At least he thinks so. At the coded mention of Strangebakken, he'd ripped off his headphones and not looked back, running like he'd never done before. Running for *their* lives.

They can already hear Rumi clattering about upstairs, trying to hurry Anya and grabbing what supplies they've already packed. Arriving into the kitchen Anya's face is a rictus of fear; in one hand she holds a bag of her life's belongings, and in the other she clenches her bump with trembling fingers.

'Come on, Marjit, you have to get going too,' Jens urges. 'I don't know how long it will be. They could be here any minute. You have a place to go, don't you?'

'I'm staying.'

All air is sucked out of the room. Jens and Rumi look to each other and then at Marjit, who stands with her feet apart, already like some immovable sentry.

'That's madness,' Rumi tries. 'They could arrest you, whether they find Anya or not.'

Marjit shakes her head. 'If they find nothing, they'll still be back,' she reasons. 'I can at least send them off on the wrong trail and buy you some time.'

'Not from prison, you can't!' Jens cries, horrified and angry. 'Have you any idea what the camp at Grini is like, Marjit? It's cruel, and people die there. They murder people, no matter what some convention says.'

'I'm still staying,' Marjit insists. 'Rumi, you need to go with Anya right now.'

'But Marjit . . .' Jens watches Rumi looks frantically side to side, from her best friend at school, to her best friend in the world. Anya as one of nature's time bombs, and Marjit as the person who has kept Rumi whole. It's clear to Jens he's not the only one to tussle with the human calculation. He throws his arms up in disgust, feels frustration prick at his eyeballs. This can't be happening. The plans weren't properly finalised, but they always had a swift escape route ready. It was never perfect, but it aimed to get everyone away. Everyone they loved.

Yet Marjit is in no mood to argue. She bundles Rumi and Anya towards the door, only stopping when Rumi grabs her arm and refuses to let go, not until she's pulled her in tightly.

Jens hears the whispered, tense words from Rumi's mouth, teeth set. 'Don't you dare, *dare* die on me, Marjit Sabo,' she breathes. 'Or I will never forgive you, I swear.'

'Then, I won't. You be well, my girl. Stay calm. Use that

anger only when you need it.' Jens watches his aunt swallow back her emotion – needing all of her strength to prevent everything spilling forth – to shoo them into the unknown.

And then they're both gone, a waft of cold air sweeping away the hot, heavy exchange.

'Now you.' She nods at him, her expression fixed and determined.

Jens daren't hug Marjit as tightly as he wants or needs – it would splinter her physically. Instead, he calls on his own restraint, folds his long arms around her and kisses the top of her head, coercing his brain to remember every particle of scent in her, like every summer's end as a boy when he was forced back to England and life with distant father and a mother trying to maintain the peace.

'Everything that Rumi said,' he whispers, 'and more. I will never forgive you if I can't taste your *plukkfisk* again. I know it's in your nature to fight, Marjit, but not too hard. Please. Not against these bastards.'

'I promise,' she mumbles, though if he could bear to look he would know her tears are on the brink now. 'Now leave. Please, Jens. Just go.'

He does, but only as far as a few houses down, then conceals himself behind a wall looking onto the lane. Within minutes he hears the *Kübelwagens* whining up the street as their wheels slip and slide on the icy cobbles. No vehicle as large as a prison wagon can make it up the narrow lane, but Jens is certain it won't stop them in their quest.

He hears the heavy clomp of boots slightly dulled by the snow. They disappear into the alleyway, followed by the ominous, urgent rap on the door – or does he simply imagine that?

What's all too real are the shouts from inside Marjit's house; her incredulity at being targeted by the thuggish

Gestapo, then the vitriol as they clearly rip through her house in search of Anya, and the anger of the Gestapo officers when it's plain they've been duped. Made fools of. It never sits well with Abwehr, even less with Gestapo.

For a moment or so it goes quiet, and Jens has to strain his ears for sound competing with the thud of horses at full gallop in his chest. Maybe, just maybe, she's won them round? Convinced them with her charm that she's merely an ageing old lady who's sympathetic to Norway's need for strong leadership. Jens knows that might be stretching things, but to him, Marjit is capable of anything.

Suddenly, more shouts. An explosion of anger, a thud and something like a crack, with a high-pitched scream. A woman's distress.

Please no gunshot. Please. Please. No bullet. Jens screws his eyes shut in anticipating the final crack, and suddenly he's a boy on the stairs again, listening to his parents arguing and bracing himself for his father's blow across his mother's face, then a man on the Dunkirk sands looking at Charlie's bloody face and waiting for the Nazis' decisive shot to kill him stone dead.

He calculates. He could run in there now, gun cocked and pick them off, one by one. If he's lucky, he might kill all of them before the troops outside get a chance to rush in. But if he doesn't, then it's certain death for him and Marjit. One bullet apiece. All for nothing. Rumi and Anya will be left in the wilderness; they are more than capable of running and hiding, but who will contact the Bus, to keep them out of harm's way forever? There are three other lives to consider, one of whom hasn't even had a chance to breathe yet. To shine.

That fucking calculation. When will he ever have the right answer?

It's that which forces Jens to seethe in his indolence, and to have to turn away as another crack rings out – hard to tell if it's even a shot – as the heavy footsteps of a trooper come perilously close to his static body before climbing into one of the jeeps. He slides across the cobbles, forcibly tearing himself away from the house. Marjit could already be lying there dead, and he can do nothing except abandon her.

Rounding the line of jeeps and squinting into the darkness, he sees another *Kubelwagen* parked behind, the engine billowing clouds of grey fumes. Although it's the briefest of glimpses, it sends his hopes plummeting and his fear soaring into the atmosphere. Through the window, a hand rises to replace a grey-green cap, then lowers to palm at a cheek, a long finger running the length of a deep, raw scar. Even in the limited light, he sees it crease with the advent of a smile.

61

Balancing the Scales

Bergen, 11th December 1942

Rumi

It's a scraping on the rocks that startles them both out of sleep, and Rumi is immediately on alert, nose twitching like a wild animal in the hills. It's two a.m. but she's wide awake, the top half of Anya's face only just visible under her blanket, eyes staring with alarm.

Instantly, Rumi senses it's not Pappa's ungainly steps, nor Rubio's, on the mooring they've moved the boat to in a tiny, little-known cove away from the wharf. She closes her eyes to focus and detects only two feet struggling to descend, allowing herself to breathe again; a raid would certainly mean more. And besides which, what would they do? They're effectively trapped in a floating prison, with only one exit, save for the surrounding freezing water.

'*Hei,* Captain,' a voice says in a whisper at the door to the boat's hold. Jens's voice. In all honesty, she could throw

318

her arms around him and weep with relief as his face appears, but she suppresses every need and palms away the salt crust on her cheeks, her despair over Marjit that, in a moment of weakness, she could not conquer. But there's no place for that now. The stoic side of Rumi has to dominate everything else inside.

'Everything all right?' Jens says.

'Yes, so far. Pappa and Rubio have gone to get supplies. Hopefully, they'll be back soon. We'll all sleep here the rest of tonight, and leave at first light.'

She notes that he doesn't offer any news of Marjit and she doesn't ask. If she was dead for sure, he would say, wouldn't he? The not knowing is better than facing a grim certainty right now.

He holds up a flask of soup. 'Saviour for body and soul,' he says, and she's forced to smile at the irony.

Rumi opens up the steaming capsule and hands a cup to Anya, shivering despite her layers of wool. They daren't light a fire in the burner for fear of the smoke being spotted.

'You didn't get this from Hilde, did you? That traitorous cow has got us in enough trouble already.' Rumi spits out the accusation like poison, convinced that Hilde had somehow seen or heard Anya next door and run to her friends in the STAPO – doubtless to Bjarne Hansen – and by virtue the Gestapo.

'Calm down,' Jens urges. 'The soup is from a kind soul I know. And don't be so hard on Hilde.'

'What do you mean?' Rumi feels ready to explode. The misery at losing Marjit has turned to pent-up fury at their betrayal – and the betrayer. 'It's either Hilde or her witch of a mother, I'd bet my life on it.'

'I'm fairly sure it wasn't either of them,' Jens says plainly.

'Of course it was her,' she bites back. 'Who else could

it have been, with her mother's views so plain? I should have listened to you and not Pappa. Shouldn't have kept Hilde on in the house.' Rumi is railing, winding herself into a frenzy, recrimination that won't spring Marjit from the dreaded Grini camp, or from the coffin she might already be in. But she can't stop, with nowhere else to channel her utter despair.

Jens catches both her wrists and holds them firm; her face crumples as she recognises the same level of desolation in his. He pulls her into his shoulder, but still she resists, terrified that if she starts to cry, the flow may never stop.

'I'm certain it's not Hilde, because I'm pretty sure who it is,' Jens says into her ear.

She pulls away. 'Who? Who else would do this?'

Aside from too many Quislings in Bergen and across Norway, who feel it's their right to betray fellow Norwegians for Reich favours, she means.

Who else *that we know?*

'Sit down,' Jens says, and his dour tone guides her to the bench.

He nudges in beside her, looking intently at the grubby wooden floor, elbows resting on his knees. 'From what I've gathered, I think it was probably one of your neighbours.'

'Really? But we've know them for years. They would never . . .'

'Unwittingly, perhaps, but that's what the grapevine says.' Jens sighs. 'You know how it is – a stray comment here, someone repeats it. Only this one proved dangerous.'

Rumi feels like a balloon, pricked, bled of air and kicked in the dust for good measure. The damage never seems to end. And yet Marjit's reaction was simply to look out for everyone else – again.

320

'Let's go over the plan,' Jens says defiantly, as if to dispel the cloud of gloom hanging over them.

Rumi shrugs. 'So far, Pappa can take us north to Vikanes, then somehow we'll have to make our way overland towards the coastal inlet at Brekke – we know the Bus pulls in there sometimes and Pappa has a friend who we can look out for.' Rumi gestures towards Anya, now asleep again under her mountain of blankets. 'It's just over forty kilometres. I only hope she can make it.'

'There's things I need to do in Bergen first,' Jens says, 'but I'll meet you at the place Peder leaves you, and go with you both to the Bus.'

'What? No. You have other work here. Important work.'

'*This* is important,' he cries, checking his own voice and glancing at Anya. 'What could be more important than a child? I'm sick of playing off one prospect against another, betting on people's futures, like life is a set of scales.' He runs his hands through his hair. 'I can help and I will, whether the SOE likes it or not. For Christ's sake, *you* are important, Rumi Orlstad.'

The salt on her face cracks as she musters a smile. 'Thank you, Jens Parkes. The feeling is mutual.'

Footsteps interrupt what might have become a second kiss, but each is relieved when the noise outside is clearly Peder, too ungainly to be a covert Gestapo approach.

'Jens!' Pappa is glad to see him intact, though his sadness at Marjit's unknown fate clouds his smile all too soon. They've all been hit by the news, Rubio too.

Feeling the space suddenly crowded, Rumi heads up on deck as Jens prepares to go.

'I'll see you in Vikanes,' he pledges with certainty in his voice. Again, she wants to embrace him tightly – just in case it's the last time, as it was with Magnus. But she holds

321

back once more. She can trust him; unless he's dead in a ditch somewhere, he will be there. Now that every ounce of her faith has been washed away by this war, she has to cling on to something. And Jens Parkes is it. He's Marjit's blood. And he's Norwegian.

62

Calling on a Friend

Bergen, 11th December 1942

Jens

Squatting in the ebony black of an early winter morning, not a chink of light to be seen, Jens tries to shake his exhaustion away. His eyes are bone dry and his mouth clammy, despite an entire pot of coffee that he'd brewed doubly strong and sunk in great gulps. The house he's watching remains dark and silent, and he wonders how long he should leave it before disturbing the occupants. Not too long, as he's already lost contact with his toes. In all honesty, he could close his eyes and just drift off; it might only be the cold that would wake him. Or he might die from exposure in this very spot, like the vagrants he remembers from London's streets before the war, and who are probably still dodging the German air attacks and making their homes in bombed-out buildings.

His mind wanders with fatigue, but Jens forces himself back to the houses lining Tartargaten. There's so much still to do, and no time for sleep, though Jens knows he dropped off at some point on Marjit's sofa, having returned around three a.m. to right the upturned furniture and general chaos the Nazi raid had left behind. He was wholly relieved to find no body or blood, though it doesn't signal any kind of certainty for Marjit's future. Even so, he figured it was the last place they would come back to look for anyone. He'd spent the early hours bent over Marjit's parlour table, purposely blinkered to her pins and needles strewn around, the sewing paraphernalia that was – *is* – worked into her very fabric, lingering for several minutes with his face close into her hastily abandoned knitting, the wool she could have been working when they arrived. He drew in the smell of the yarn she had spun and then weaved with concentration and love, and tried not to let the droplets welling behind his eyes obscure the work he needed to complete, in assembling the smallest and most portable transmitter possible.

'Keep your mind on the job, Jens,' he could hear Marjit echoing in his ear. 'As the British say: "no point crying over spilt milk".'

It was the only thing to keep his despair at bay.

A sliver of light seeps from the ground floor of the house he's watching, and Jens checks his watch: just gone six. He's so mesmerised by the glow that he doesn't detect a sudden presence moving from behind, turns rapidly and is startled by the glint of the silver buttons against the dark, navy uniform of the STAPO.

'Bjarne!'

Bjarne Hansen steps back as Jens stumbles upright with almost dead legs. 'What are you doing here?'

They consider for a second, and each breaks into a smile, followed by a swift embrace, the cold breath of relief rising above them.

'I'll never get used to you in that ruddy jacket,' Jens says.

'Nor me, though I hate to say it's a lot warmer than my own,' Bjarne admits. 'What is it you need, Jens? You're not here at this time of the morning on a social visit.'

'Have you still got that old motorcycle and sidecar of your uncle's?'

Bjarne looks confused. 'You're leaving Bergen? I haven't had word of any mission.'

'It's not SOE,' Jens confesses. 'It's for Rumi, and her friend.'

The STAPO man's stance, along with his features, softens immediately. 'Well of course you can have it, with my blessing.'

'The only thing is, I can't promise you'll get it back,' Jens warns. 'I might have to abandon it.'

'And there's every chance it will abandon you,' Bjarne replies. 'It's been sat in the garage for a good while. I had it going in the summer, but not since.'

Jens sighs. 'I've got no other options, so it looks as if I put my faith in a hunk of metal, or nothing.'

They keep the door to the tiny garage closed – and their fingers crossed – as the engine sputters into life after several attempts. Bjarne fills the tank with a can of fuel he has 'put by', and they shake hands. It feels somehow final.

'You will tell Rumi at some point – about me?' Bjarne says. 'That I'm not some bastard Quisling who's turned his back on Norway? About what I'm doing for the resistance?'

'Yes, of course,' Jens assures. 'In fact, I think she's so angry and upset because you mean a lot to her, how close you were, growing up as kids. With Rumi, it's a strange sort of compliment.'

Bjarne laughs, though his tone soon switches. 'I hope we all survive long enough that I can tell her myself, about

325

why I joined up so swiftly, to embed myself in. For our country. But please tell her, Jens – in case I can't.'

'I will, I promise. Now I should go. But will you do me one last favour – for Rumi?'

The bike slips and slides through the dark, snowy streets as Jens gets used to the throttle and the stiff gears; the last time he rode a motorcycle was in Scotland, and then one without a sidecar to offset the balance. But the extra space is needed for Anya, although he can only hope her growing form is able to squeeze into it. He's in no doubt that Rumi will ride pillion with ease.

The prospect of roadblocks means Jens is forced to take the smaller roads north, those with a fresh, powdery coating of snow, so that the wheels churn up a white wave of spray; his thighs quickly ache with having to grip on to the bike's metal body, but it does give off some warmth. His eyes smart with the snow's glare and the unending exhaustion, taking gulps of freezing air to awaken his lungs and feed his brain, driven by the thought of a heavily pregnant woman having to battle with four-foot drifts if he doesn't keep his promise, and the other alongside fighting her way through this unyielding landscape. The woman that he happens to love. He knows it now, and it's what keeps him pushing forward into a white, flurrying abyss.

63

The New Bergen Bus

Bergen, 11th December 1942

Rumi

They're underway by eight, and although it's still dark there'll be other trawlers out in the fjord waters to help them blend in. Rumi notes how Pappa seems, on the outside, unaffected by his mission in harbouring a runaway from the Reich, whistling to himself in the wheelhouse. Or maybe he's just become very good at hiding his anxiety. Something they've all had to perfect.

She chances some fresh air on deck as they draw away from the mooring, glancing back towards Bergen and hoping it's not too long before she's back home again, while dreading the unavoidable absence in Strangebakken.

'Surely not?' she mutters at the sight of a lone figure, staring at them from the wharf, unmoving. Not a fisherman, in that distinct navy coat with the shiny buttons, topped with a rounded face and an all too familiar blond head of hair.

'Bjarne?' she whispers to herself. For a second, alarm

bells are ringing and she's about to duck into the wheel-house and alert Pappa, but something about the man's statuesque nature makes her stand equally firm. There's no one with him, and he's not casting about for comrades. She could be mistaken, but he looks to be observing – checking, perhaps? And is that a slight lift of his hand, the suggestion of a wave from someone she once called a friend? Rumi is surprised to find her brief, inner panic has totally subsided. She merely nods in his direction and watches as he turns away, soon out of sight.

'Rumi? Rumi!'

Rubio's demanding tone reaches up from the hold, and she hops down to find him bent over Anya, both leaning towards the floor. 'What the . . .?'

'It's all right, I'm fine,' Anya manages, her face pained as she straightens up. 'A mild twinge, that's all. The baby shifts and sets them off – they told us to expect it this late on.' She cups her belly and rubs the pain away, a pink flush working its way up her face.

For one brief minute, Rumi wishes a stern and knowl-edgeable German midwife was standing right there with them, to offer reassurance to Anya and those around her. Instead, she has only Rubio's wildly staring eyes as a barometer.

'That was anything but mild,' Rubio blurts as Rumi follows him back on deck. 'She was bent over for ages.' He palms at his dark beard, this huge, hulking man of the sea clearly panicked. 'Well, it seemed like ages. What if she goes into—'

'She won't,' Rumi cuts him off. She's never lied to Rubio before, but now it seems like a kindness. She doesn't know for sure, only hopes it's true. After the last twenty-four hours, that's all they need. Surely Fate can't be that cruel?

Anya is eager to minimise her discomfort, and doubly keen not to be more of a burden than she already feels. Rumi watches her in the hold, balancing her bump with the roll of the fjord's choppy waters as she makes coffee and sandwiches for everyone, smiling away what she calls 'niggles'.

'This baby's not ready yet, anyway,' she tells Rumi. 'I've had firm words with it. It's destined to be Norwegian by blood and a Shetlander by birth, and that's all there is to it.' Her expression is weak and her face pale, but something in Anya's voice tells Rumi her friend is stronger than she has ever appeared, infused by some inexplicable maternal force field. In turn, the thought prompts painful images of Marjit she's forced to swipe away.

Later, Rumi. You can grieve for your own loss later.

The journey through the narrow Osterfjorden sees only one German patrol boat, with a crew who seem to be arguing fiercely among themselves and so wave them on. Rubio shoots Rumi a knowing look and they all breathe again.

Hugging the coast, there's a handful of other trawlers which toot a cheery greeting and motor on: any one of them could be shielding human cargo or ammunition and it's best not to know. Finally, around midday, they move slowly through an inlet, drawing up to a tiny, wooden dock just outside the village of Vikanes, with Pappa and Rubio hopping off to find shelter in a safe place for the two women. With years working this coast, Peder Orlstad has friends in almost every town or village.

Anya has drifted off to sleep again, and Rumi sits alone for what feels the first time in an age. She should embrace the warmth down below, given what the elements may throw at them in the next few days in reaching the Bus, but the air is clearer up on deck. With her face turned to the open window of the wheelhouse, she fingers the gnarled and chipped wood that has steered her father through thick and thin; she imagines the indent of his thumbs on the wheel itself and it's the nearest she can get to home.

What awaits her back in Bergen? The situation seemed tricky enough even before these last few days, juggling the twin demands of the boathouse, scratching enough food for everyone, Trine, then Anya's fears. Her feelings for Jens forcibly denied, Magnus pushed into the background, and the guilt that went with it. And that was with Marjit by her side. What now?

How can she keep herself from sagging into a great heap on the floor – strong, bossy Rumi Orlstad all but beaten by the plundering monsters of the Reich?

Her maudlin thoughts are interrupted by her father's return.

'*Hei,* my girl,' he says. 'Are you all right?'

It's the first time they've been alone since Marjit was taken, and Rumi senses the hurt radiating from her easy-going father. She burrows into his big chest and he's quick to read her long and hard embrace.

'She'll be okay,' Peder mumbles into his daughter's shoulder. 'I have no doubt she'll be organising wherever they've taken her. And that includes the guards.'

'It's what we have to believe, isn't it?' They need to, because the alternative is unthinkable.

'We've found you a house to stay in tonight,' he reports. 'Rubio and I will dock here until Jens arrives and we can direct him to you.'

'That's good.' She nods.

'You know, my love, I would take you further to meet with the Bus if I—'

'I know you would, Pappa,' Rumi says, palming at his rough, bristly chin and the flecks of his red colouring amid

330

the grey. 'But it's too risky this far out of Bergen – the German patrols are bound to spot you. Your trawler is a lifeline for too many people, for the cause. You need to go back. Jens will get here, and we will be fine.'

'Then, much as with Marjit, I have to believe it, don't I?'

'Yes, you do, Pappa.'

And that means I have to as well.

64

Catching Up

North of Bergen, 11th December 1942

Jens

A single, freezing clod of snow on the back of his neck wakes him with a start.

'Shit!' Jens is instantly alert, hand into his jacket and fingering the butt of his gun. It takes him seconds to come to and realise where he is, and that the offending prod is nature's doing and not the steely barrel of a German Luger in his neck.

The confusion clears gradually, and he remembers how he came to be parked under a roadside tree, slumped over the fuel tank. With lack of sleep and the unending blizzard, Jens had become effectively snow blind, causing the bike to veer wildly across the road and narrowly miss driving headfirst into a gulley. He had to stop, or risk not getting to Rumi at all.

The road being high, he'd nestled under a thick bough and unpacked his radio – contacting the Bus was vital, or the whole journey was pointless. It was risky with his unsophisticated transmitter, and he had no way of telling if the Abwehr – and Selig – could be tuning in. But there was no other option.

Jens tapped out his message, his usual deftness hampered by the numbness in his fingers, pain shooting upwards as he punched out each dot or dash. His delivery was so crude that he thought the enemy might not recognise his own messaging 'fingerprint'. Equally, recipients on the Bus radio might view it as suspicious and ignore his plea entirely. There was plenty resting on faith, chance and someone else's good ear. The radio packed away, Jens had climbed back on the bike as a trade of warmth and insulation and closed his eyes for a minute.

Now, he looks at his watch and regrets his own desperation for sleep – it's already late morning. He, Rumi, and Anya need to use every minute of the sparse daylight in moving towards a final pick-up point. 'Come on, come on, girl,' he mutters into the ignition, thankful as the bike responds with a throaty awakening.

We can do this. Trine got away, and Anya will too. It will happen. The words are inside his head, but it's Charlie's voice he hears, clear as day.

Peder's boat is clearly visible as Jens rides slowly into the valley around Vikanes; the tiny village is deathly quiet under its insulation, and several curtains twitch as the engine cruises by and towards the dock. Peder's relief is instant and vocal as he clambers off the bike to meet them, and even Rubio – sometimes a little reticent around Jens – greets him with a friendly jab to the shoulder. Still, the two sailors are keen to leave and return to Bergen, as if they've merely been on a routine supply run.

'Look after my girl.' Peder pats him on the arm. 'I want her back.'

'Please keep her safe,' Rubio echoes, though his tone is neither challenging nor edgy, only infused with a brother's love. 'We can't lose her, too.'

'I will,' Jens pledges. More reasons to succeed.

Rumi's reaction is not in the least muted. The door to the safe house is opened tentatively by an older woman, and as he speaks, Rumi's face appears from nowhere, she pulling him in by the hand and wrapping her arms around him.

'I have never been so pleased to see you, Jens Parkes,' she whispers into his ear.

He's frozen, hungry and exhausted, but bowled over by her sentiment. 'Same here.'

Jens wolfs down a good stew, realising he hasn't eaten since the day before, and dries out by the fire. The family of the house are hospitable, but wary of too much information coming their way and stay largely in the background.

'Where's Anya?' Jens asks.

'Asleep upstairs. She's exhausted by the cold and the travelling.'

'I've just enough fuel to get us to where I think the Bus can dock and pick her up,' Jens explains. 'It means we will have to make our own way back to Bergen.'

He sees the old Rumi in her then — buoyed by the challenge. 'We'll manage,' she says. 'As long as Anya gets away safely.'

'Let's leave in an hour, but in the meantime, I need to transmit again. I have to make sure the Bus has responded.' Jens spoons up the last of the stew. 'I'll ride a good five kilometres to be sure the signal can't be traced back here.'

'I'm coming with you,' Rumi says.

'You don't need to.'

'I want to,' she asserts. 'I need to practise riding pillion so I don't topple onto Anya.'

They find an abandoned hunter's shack a few kilometres out of the village, and the transmitting is easier with thawed fingers. Jens is aware of Rumi watching his work intently, a continuous crackle emitting from the makeshift mass of wires he's cobbled together. He scribbles the response, nodding positively at Rumi: the Bus has come good. The Shetland base says they'll be in Brekke by tomorrow afternoon.

Then, a second message via the transmitter. 'Damn,' Jens mutters, eyes suddenly narrowed and his brow drawn. He pulls the headphones off roughly and throws them down, standing and pacing the tiny floor space. 'Damn!'

'What? What is it, Jens?'

He rubs his unshaven chin. 'Seems the SOE have got wind of what I'm doing, and they've recalled me. Immediately.'

'Back to Bergen?' Rumi's breath is white in the gloom of the hut.

'No, north. Somewhere near Trondheim.'

He watches her mind spinning, eyes narrowed, reaching for her thick plait and stroking the end. 'Well, I can ride the bike – I've done it before. I'll get Anya there,' she says defiantly.

'I know you can, Rumi. But I'm coming, too. I've been in this area before, and in this weather especially, it's crucial to remember the terrain. We've got until tomorrow, but that's allowing for getting lost. It's not much time.'

'But what about the SOE? Defying orders?' she pushes.

'Fuck the orders!' Jens snaps. 'I've said it before – I've spent too long weighing up one life against another, playing

335

to this so-called "greater good".' He seeps anger, frustration bouncing off the wooden walls of the tiny hut. 'What's the point if you can't help one person? Marjit taught me that. She did it one by one, humanity in small steps. She helped so many people, and look where it got her. And yet I know that if . . . well, she could be sitting in that bloody camp not regretting it for a single minute. Because those people are safe.' He hopes Rumi skates over the hesitancy in his thoughts.

Jens paces, agitated and it's Rumi who grabs him, flicks her plait back over her shoulder, and plants a short but concerted kiss on his lips.

'I hear you, Sergeant Parkes. And I'm glad,' she says. 'I'd much rather you're with us. But . . .'

'But what?'

'Afterwards, you promise to go north and try not to get turfed out of your job, and I will come south on my own. Deal? You'd better say yes, because it's the only one on the table.'

'Deal.'

65

Diversion

Vikanes, 11th December 1942

Rumi

It's already getting dark by the time they leave the safe house, but Jens insists on pushing forward for at least two hours – ground that they won't need to make up the next day. Their hosts reassure them the road to the next stop is straightforward and shouldn't be blocked. At a halfway point towards Brekke, another patriot family will feed, water and warm them until they can set off in the morning light for the Bus on their final leg.

It seems easy enough until they try to install a heavily pregnant woman into the bike's sidecar, where Rumi thinks 'leverage' is perhaps the best word to describe Anya's awkward attempts to manoeuvre her girth into the space, huffing and puffing, all the while insisting that she's: 'Fine. Really, fine.' Jens looks on, clearly concerned that the baby might be less squeezed into being.

'Women and babies are made of sterner stuff,' Rumi assures him as she mounts the bike behind him.

'I hope you're right about that.'

'Though perhaps it's best not to go over too many pot-holes in the road, eh?' she says. His head turns in alarm, and she clutches tightly at his waist in response. 'Come on, Parkes, we've a boat to catch.'

Their hosts in Vikanes have been well informed – the road is under a layer of white but negotiable if Jens takes it slow and his headlights stay on full beam. The chances of meeting a Nazi patrol are something they're forced to leave in the lap of the gods. Rumi's head is swaddled in a thick hat and scarves wound about her face, her eyes just visible, and Anya is virtually mummified, wrapped top to toe in wool. Even so, Rumi is soon frozen solid, with only the small portion of her body in contact with Jens maintaining any kind of feeling. She wonders how he's coping in front of her, having to face into the bitter wind and grip firmly on the handles, four lives entirely dependent on his focus. But he ploughs on for more than an hour, shoulders hunched and head dipped forward, pushing the laboured mechanics that are struggling with snow and the weight of the load. In the unending navy and white landscape, punctuated only by the odd tiny cottage, Rumi fights against her eyes drooping, having to jolt herself awake and grip firmly around Jens's waist to steady herself. *If he has to stay firm, so do you*, she chants to herself, but in all honesty, she would give all of her possessions for the chance to sink into a warm bed, and everything of her soul for the world to be righted when she woke.

The awakening comes all too soon. There's a resounding bang behind her, in the exact second that the bike lurches violently and Jens's body tenses to fight with the wayward handlebars as they swerve across the road. He twists the

338

front wheel sharply away from a lengthy drop to the side and they slide into a bush, the smell of burning obvious.

'What the hell was that?' Rumi cries as Jens dismounts and squats at the bike's rear.

'A blow out.' He sighs.

'A tyre? We can fix it, surely,' Rumi says. 'I've done that before.'

Jens stands, shakes his head and shoots a desperate look at Anya, and then gravely at Rumi. 'Engine,' he mouths.

There's no point in wasting words: the dirty, grey smoke spewing from the metalwork is enough to know this is journey's end for their modern chariot. Jens pushes it further into the bushes, hoping more snowfall will hide the rest.

Anya hasn't said a word; it's hard to tell if she's asleep, wedged in her wool and metal cage, but Rumi imagines the bang and violent swerving must have forced her to come to. Still, she says nothing. The air is dark, still and silent, aside from the creak of nearby branches.

Stranded.

She watches Jens turn a full circle, scanning and sniffing the atmosphere, as she's seen him do before. He's gauging, she thinks, better than any map, drawing the lines inside his head and joining up the dots. *Please let him join the dots.* She's used to the snow and the inky blackness of a Norwegian winter, but the two combined, alongside the responsibility of Anya as a fugitive . . .

Her homeland is different suddenly. Eerie, and yes — Rumi Orlstad is afraid. Who wouldn't be?

'I'm sure I've been on this road before, about six months ago,' Jens says at last.

'So how far do you think we are from the next village?'

'At a guess, a good ten kilometres,' he says, his eyes on Anya, who is trying to worm her way out of the sidecar with difficulty. With help, she's released and stumbles onto the snowy ground, rubbing blood into her limbs and arching her back to relieve the ache.

'How are you feeling?' Rumi asks.

'All right,' Anya says, though it's unconvincing. Her gloved, frozen fingers brace her bump as if it might simply fall away into the snow.

Rumi sidles up to Jens as he's pulling their packs from the sidecar. 'She'll never make it ten kilometres on foot,' she says.

'I don't think any of us will in this weather,' Jens replies. 'Our best bet is to find a cabin and keep as warm as we can, wait for first light.'

'And then? With no transport?'

Jens shrugs, in a manner that sketches out only one sentiment: We hope.

The torch strafes across a virgin white blanket, flakes falling less rapidly now, and they can just about make out the confines of the dirt road. Their footsteps squeak on contact and Rumi cringes at the noise in the stony silence, though it doesn't feel as if there's a soul around for miles. Jens's beam catches something just off the track and down a short ridge, what looks like a man-made wooden edge in among the firs.

He nudges at Rumi. 'I'll take a look and see if it's habit-able. Wait here.'

His form disappears in a small flurry of snow as he descends the bank. Anya holds on to her, tight to Rumi's arm – partly for warmth but mostly to stay upright. It's clear she's flagging and needs to lie down soon. Within minutes, another burst of white spray is kicked up in the blackness and Jens appears, panting from the brief but steep climb.

'It'll do,' he says. 'It's small, but there is a grate inside and some debris we can burn.'

Rumi searches his face in the yellow torch light, poses the question with her knitted brows, the one that says: But will we survive in this?

'It will have to do, Rumi. We've no other choice.'

With one each side of Anya, they skate and slip down to the cabin, wrinkle their noses at the overpowering stench of rotting skins inside, and then give thanks for hunters everywhere that they even think to pepper the landscape with these refuges.

The 'debris' Jens talks of is the offending animal leftovers, and he soon has a pile collected, lighting it with whatever dry material he can find. With Anya lain on her side on the bench, wedged with every bit of spare clothing, Rumi dishes out the bread and cheese they have left. Having eaten, Anya is soon asleep, her lips quivering with cold and possibly a dream, one that Rumi hopes is not a nightmare destined to be reality.

She and Jens sit close on the opposite bench, huddled together through necessity but − she senses − feeling easy with it, the touch of their bodies, albeit through layers of clothes.

Jens stares at the flames, sipping at the weak tea they've brewed. 'I used to love camping when I was a kid, cooking food around the fire.'

'In this weather?'

He laughs. 'No, we don't generally do winter camping in England, though I remember it was often very wet.'

'With your family − your father?'

'Hmm, not my father's type of thing,' Jens says. 'It was mostly with the Boy Scouts, weekends away orienteering and walking. It was where I found my love of maps.'

341

'And thank goodness you did,' she says, leaning her head against his. 'Or where would we be now?'

'Lost in a cabin somewhere in a snowstorm in Norway?'

'You have a point,' she admits. 'But I'm convinced we're not lost. Not with you here.'

They sit in silence for a while, watching the fuel dwindle and knowing they should get some sleep. It's barely six o'clock but they're exhausted and the day ahead is sure to be full of challenges.

'How are you now?' Jens says softly, out of the blue.

Rumi fidgets, feels a shudder somewhere under her layers, the fizzle that sits dormant in her heart, only sparked into life by such questions. She guesses at his meaning by the way he says it. Marjit's loss is still too new for anything other than the pain of an arrow. It's Magnus he's talking of, and the lengthy, grinding ache of grief. Is she drowning or treading water? Or beginning to paddle towards something other than the depths?

Instead, she's startled when the answer comes easily, and with clarity.

'I'm all right,' Rumi says. 'I'll never forget him, of course, but I think I'm working through it all – the guilt, and the anger.'

'I'm glad,' he says. 'For you.'

'You've helped.'

'Have I? How?' He seems genuinely surprised.

'Poking at me, challenging, not letting me wallow in self-pity. It's kept me on my toes.'

'That makes me sound quite harsh,' Jens says.

'No,' Rumi comes back. Moving aside a layer of wool from her face, she turns and looks at him. 'You're exactly what I needed. A friend.'

'Same here,' he says.

'What do you mean?' She knows full well that underneath the SOE layers he is human, but he's always appeared whole and unbroken.

Jens prods at the fire, speaking in a low, slow tone. 'I thought for a long time, since Dunkirk, that I killed my best friend. Charlie. But I've come to realise that he would have reached out to help anyone, in paying the ultimate price. It just happened to be me.'

'I'm thankful,' Rumi says quietly. 'That he did, but also that you've come to terms with it. For years, I was too practical to believe in fate – thought we made our own luck. But now I'm not so sure. Thank goodness for friends, eh?'

'So, now we're almost fixed, I hope that doesn't mean I'm redundant, as a friend?' He says it lightly, but his eyes are narrowed and tinged with sadness.

'No, of course not. Though maybe it's time to have more.' She fidgets, unsure whether to lay herself bare. *If not now, then when?* The words tumble out: 'You could always complete the trio: friend, fishwife and lover?'

She holds her breath for his reaction, feels his arm encircle and tighten, her head moulding into his shoulder, his long fingers creasing into her body.

'You know I have to go away, after this,' he says. 'Can I dare to hope you'll be there, in Bergen, when I come back? Because I will come back, Rumi. I'd move heaven and earth and a thousand damn Nazis for you.'

She's learnt not to rely on it; for her the commitment is his gift. Magnus would have come back if the bloody war hadn't swallowed him whole. Jens, too; he means to return. If he doesn't, it won't be his fault. That has to be enough.

'I will,' she says. 'I'll be there.'

66

A Hound on the Scent

North of Bergen, 12th December 1942

Jens

Jens wakes with a start at a noise, pushes his head up and looks immediately to Anya for signs of her waking, disturbed by the baby, perhaps. He'd heard her once or twice in the night shifting and moaning slightly. Now, though, her eyes are firmly closed and the sound is coming from outside. Above them, towards the road.

Gently untangling himself from Rumi's sleepy hold, Jens ties his bootlaces in seconds, retrieving his gun from his pack and tucking it in his jacket pocket.

Outside, it's semi-light and freezing, but no longer snowing. Thank God. The silence has gone too, with muffled voices — maybe two or more — drifting from above. He cocks his ear: German, if he's hearing right.

Jens scales the incline on a new, silent layer of snow and dares to peek over the top, sees the thick, heavy boots of the Wehrmacht, two pairs collected around the half-concealed motorbike. Their weather-savvy *Kübelwagen* is parked only metres away.

'Do you think it's his?' he hears one saying.

'Better call . . . they will . . .' The voice and his translation is patchy. He's about to turn tail back to the cabin when he hears one word almost sing out into the vast space, crystal clear: 'Selig'. His ears prick and his stomach roils uncomfortably.

'We'll radio it in,' the other says. 'He'll want to know.'

'Rumi, Rumi! Wake up – we have to go.' Jens is hastily packing their things when the women come to. 'We've got company.'

Again, he's thankful that she reads the concern wrapped up in his tone. Instantly, Rumi is alert and urging Anya into her boots, giving her the last swig of the boiled water from the night before, and standing sentry outside as she relieves her overblown bladder.

'How did they know where to find us?' she asks Jens, who's shuffling his feet impatiently.

'I have no idea.' He sighs. 'I spent hours of my last night in Bergen running everywhere, sending signals and laying a false trail for Selig, clues for a route heading south buried in my messages. I thought it was enough to put them off the scent.'

He looks towards the road, and the prowling cat lying in wait for his scurrying mouse. 'Selig's got a bloody good nose, that's all I can say.'

345

67

Forging On

Rumi

They travel in a line below the road and under cover of the feathered trees, Jens in front, and Rumi behind Anya to make sure she doesn't slip. With Anya's 'cargo' and the snow a good ten centimetres deep in places, her sense of balance is compromised. One hand rests permanently on her belly, the other outstretched to steady herself, but there's no complaint. Rumi can only imagine the terrifying thoughts that must be running through her.

Jens halts when he hears the throaty growl of the *Kübelwagen* driving away, then ploughs on again. Being off the road makes it harder and slower but they don't dare venture onto it again, feeling so exposed if there's a concerted search. Whether the target is Anya or Jens, they are all Selig's prey now.

Every quarter of an hour, Anya has to stop a minute to rest, her face flushed despite the cold, blowing out hard into the air. Rumi can't tell if it's her lungs or her belly making her so breathless but Jens clearly has other worries; she sees him check his watch each time they stop, rubbing unconsciously at his thigh as he does so. They're confident the Bus will wait a short while, but it's too risky to dock for too long, in sight of German patrols or Quislings only too happy to report any unusual activity. It means there's no choice but to keep moving.

By ten o'clock they reach a small village, though can't chance knocking on any doors for help. Instead, Jens finds a small barn where they eat the last of their food while resting on hay bales, with one old goat for company, who nuzzles with interest around Anya as she's breathing away another twinge of discomfort. The ones that Rumi notes are coming more frequently and make her friend huff a little more each time.

'*Hei,* let's hope we don't have an early nativity scene here.' She tries to lighten the mood, and Anya attempts a smile in response.

'I promise you that I am *not* planning to have a goat attending my baby's arrival,' Anya manages, though it's clear her humour is equally forced.

Jens steers them on through an unknown landscape, looking down at his watch whenever they stop, and then up at the grey, muddy mass above now sending down more snowflakes to hinder their progress. Like the sky, his expression grows darker each time Rumi catches sight.

'How's she doing?' he whispers as Anya makes another stop to relieve her bladder.

'She won't admit it, but I think she's struggling,' Rumi says. 'Her belly is obviously tightening, and it looks quite painful.'

'Do you think she's . . .?'

347

Irritation rises briefly. 'How would I know, Jens? I'm a fishwife, remember. Not a damned midwife.'

'Fair point. Perhaps we'll just hope and pray then?'

By one p.m., they're at the bottom of an escarpment; the wind is picking up and all three look upwards with dread at the cloaking sky and the crest of the steep, pure white landscape. For a while they were tracking the road at a distance, hearing military vehicles roll up and down. But the only path they could negotiate has veered downwards and away from the road, its sounds further away. Now, the only way is up.

Jens is turning circles again, his nostrils flaring. To Rumi, he looks displaced. Lost. In a seamless snowy blanket, with no shades of green, red or yellow to help in his construction. Just a bleached, treeless, frozen void. Up in the Bergen hills, on a terrain she's known since childhood, she would be the one to lead them to safety. But now she's equally blind in this unknown landscape. Only she doesn't have anything like his talent for mapping. As long as it hasn't deserted him.

She watches Jens squeeze his eyes tightly shut, pulling on those skills and tuning into his own in-built direction finding. Are the signals tampered with by the weather, anxiety, or by a desperate urgency to make his brain work it out?

For endless minutes, he merely stands, nose into the air. Rumi has one eye on him and the other on Anya, who's struggling to stand, her teeth noticeably chattering.

Suddenly, his eyes flip open and a half-smile spreads across his purplish lips. 'We won't make it in time if we don't go up and over,' he says. 'I think Brekke is just beyond the hill, but finding and following the road will add a lot of time.' He looks at Anya, and then at the sheer, white incline in front of them, the equivalent of Mount Everest to a heavily pregnant woman. 'Can you make it?'

Anya swallows and nods, and Rumi can see such determination in the small amount of flesh visible behind her scarf. It's the timely bloom of a mother's strength. Marjit's face comes careering into Rumi's mind again, along with her own mother's, their combined voices crystal clear: '*Get on with it*', they say.

'Let's go,' she says.

They climb in a line again, Jens half pulling and Rumi pushing, with Anya wedged and staggering in between. Towards the top, it's obvious she needs more help. Jens is already carrying a double pack, and Rumi can see he's beginning to limp a little, but still he shoulders most of Anya's weight and they manage to move up and over the crest, the wind whipping fiercely, the snow turned from flakes to tiny, frozen arrows. They linger for less than a minute and take brief cover in a clump of firs on the other side, Rumi and Jens exchanging wry smiles over their last encounter amid trees. It's less than a year but seems so long ago. Life couldn't be more changed, upside down in an entirely different way.

By the time they descend into another small village, it's evident that Anya can't go on; she's clutching at her belly and her legs drag through the drifts.

'Just leave me,' she says, almost delirious with exhaustion. 'You must go on and be safe.'

They ignore her words and find another hut to shelter in, where Anya is instantly asleep.

'I'll scout for a villager who's got transport,' Jens says.

'Can we risk that?' Rumi is beginning to lose hope of reaching Brekke at all.

'Sometimes you just have to,' he says and disappears.

He's back within twenty minutes, an old man in tow, gnarled skin under his thick woollen hat and a toothless smile, but his eyes are bright – and friendly. 'Look who I've found,' Jens says with satisfaction.

'You're Peder's girl, aren't you?' the old man says, pumping Rumi's hand fervently. 'I'm Harald. The word's gone round that you didn't make your next stop and we've been looking out for you. We'd better get you to Brekke.'

They load onto Harald's small flatbed truck, only room for one passenger in the small cab. Rumi insists on travelling in the back of the truck with Anya, wedged between several bales and under a large, grubby tarpaulin. It's out of the cruel wind at least, though they're forced to share the space with the carcass of a lone sheep, long dead by the smell. Much like the cabin, it's unpleasant, but – Rumi reasons – way more inviting than any prison cell.

She peeks out as Jens goes to secure the cover. 'Just ask him to take it easy over the bumps.' Rumi's eyes gesture to Anya, blowing away another pain.

Jens nods. 'Bang on the back of the cab if you need us to stop.'

Anya is sitting upright, bracing her belly with both hands and snoring gently, while Rumi dozes off as they bumble up and down endlessly, terrain that she's certain Anya would never have made it through, even with her in-built strength. Rumi hunkers down into the relative warmth of the bale. Already, she's become used to the pungent odour and allows herself to drift and dream: knitting images of her and Jens strolling along Tyskebryggen, sitting at a bar serving real beer, without a German in sight. Spring is upon them and it feels as if a lucent blue sky of the entire universe is fixed on Bergen.

Maybe, just maybe, it could be like that.
'Halt!'

The word, the tone, and the accent makes Rumi stiff with anxiety in one beat, pushing out a hand towards Anya, who wakes with a start, confused and disorientated. Rumi instantly pulls a finger to her lips to signal silence. Under the tarpaulin, both women order a freeze on their lungs.

Rumi hears Harald do the talking through the open cab window. 'Yes, dreadful weather,' he's saying, 'though the sheep don't seem to mind it, mostly.'

Some mumbling, no sign of Jens's voice. 'This lad? No, he doesn't say a thing,' Harald is lying convincingly, 'stone deaf since he was a boy. You won't get much out of him.'

Good man, Rumi thinks. He's done this before.

Steps crunch, closer and closer, a resounding scrape on the side of the truck. Rumi has an instant memory of Trine lying undercover in Pappa's truck, unseeing, holding on to her baby, body, soul and blind faith. Now she knows that terror for real. And she can read the same in Anya's wild eyes.

They hear more footsteps, alongside Harald's jovial voice. 'Yes, not all the sheep fare so well out here.' His words speed up as a pair of boots rounds the back of the truck. 'I've got one in the back, dead as a flower in winter. You can have a look if you like, though I don't recommend it. She's been gone awhile – you might lose your dinner.'

Pause. Crunch. A scrabbling towards the end of the truck, though too close for Rumi's liking. She braces herself for the point of a bayonet into the tarpaulin, recoiling as far as she can into the stiff bales. In the corner of her eye, she sees Anya staring intently at her bump and, if she's not mistaken, blowing and praying in unison.

351

That's not mere discomfort, Rumi is certain. It's pain, pure and simple.

The voice that is not Harald's grunts. 'You can go, but you know what we're looking out for, don't you? We want information, old man, all right?'

'Yes, I understand,' Harald says, then climbs into the cab and revs hard on the throttle.

A second German voice barks loud enough to breach the tarpaulin: 'Hurry. We've got more roads to check. We're wasting time here.' It's deeper, more commanding, and despite being a world away from the solid buildings of Bergen she recognises it instantly from outside the Hotel Bristol. The bearer had been kind and conciliatory then, but now Rumi reads only an intense irritation. She doesn't need to see the scar to be sure.

The truck lurches away and the women finally pull in a breath, squeeze each other's hands in relief.

Several minutes down the road, the truck stops and Jens's face appears through a gap in the cover. 'Are you both okay?'

'We're fine, though that wasn't pleasant,' she says. 'Did you see Selig?'

'Yes, it's him all right.'

'And he didn't recognise you?'

'I had my hat pulled right down, and the only time he's seen me in the flesh was at the Norge – and then I was dismissed pretty quickly. It's my call sign that he knows intimately.'

'Well, let's hope. How much longer?' Rumi's expression darkens, gestures again at Anya, blowing hard into her lap again.

'Harald says another twenty minutes until Brekke. Can you hang on?'

'We'll have to,' Rumi says, and then thinks of her pledge to a panicked Rubio, that lightning won't strike twice in the form of an unexpected birth. If only she could make herself the same promise.

Hang on in there, baby – it's a cold, hard world out here.

68

Rumi's Challenge

Brekke, 12th December 1942

Jens

Jens peers hard through the windscreen of the truck as they descend at a snail's pace towards Brekke, his vision hampered by a grimy smear of snow spray. He can see the water, a seam of shifting blue against the white rooftops hugging the coastline. There's a small cluster of boats moored, but is one of them the Bus? It's a good thirty minutes beyond the agreed rendezvous time – can the Bus boys afford to wait that long, with Gestapo and Wehrmacht constantly patrolling, and now Abwehr, too?

He looks at Harald for reassurance, but the old man is focused hard on keeping to the road and not sending them all sliding down a steep embankment on one side. As they level out and roll into the village, Harald pulls up in the blanketed, almost deserted streets.

'It's too narrow for the truck to go any further,' he says. 'It's just a ten-minute walk to the dock.'

Fifteen, Jens thinks, with Anya the way she is. Rumi, however, looks rested as he pulls back the tarpaulin and helps the two women down, feeling a distinct heat coming from Anya, even through her swaddling.

'Can you manage?' he asks Rumi. 'I'll run on ahead and check which trawler it is.'

Rumi nods, her eyes seeming to push out a renewed confidence. *We've made it.*

Maybe, he thinks. With luck and the staying power of the Bus.

He runs towards the dock as much as the deep snow allows, and it feels like the newest of his dreams to crowd precious sleep in past days, trudging when he should be sprinting, the mast of an illusory trawler never seeming to get any nearer. He's breathless, exhausted and desperately in need of some good luck, and for reality to be kinder than his nightmares. The ever-present shrapnel, too, is burning like a hot coal inside his thigh, becoming harder to ignore.

The first vessel he comes to is closed up, hatches well and truly battened down, the second looks the same. The third appears to be closed up too, and Jens stops and bends double, hands to his knees and a sense of dread falling on him like the snow that's still drifting. He can just see the faltering forms of Rumi and Anya appear at the far end of the dock. How will he tell them the Bus isn't here? That they'll have to wait, or move on?

A noise to his left, a click, and a voice projects from somewhere on the vessel, a porthole perhaps: 'Good weather if you're a polar bear.'

Jens straightens up, instantly lighter. 'Not without the right kind of fur,' he throws back into the white, swirling air.

The code. Word for word, the right one. The Bus. *Thank you, thank you, thank you.*

A hatch to the wheelhouse opens with a metallic clang and a man emerges, an archetypal blue cap on his head, thick sandy beard and a jumper that could have easily sprouted from Rumi's needles. He doesn't introduce himself, but offers a large, calloused hand in greeting. 'Captain of this good ship,' he says.

'Am I glad to see you,' Jens says, unable to hide his intense relief.

'Where's our passenger? We should be underway soon. There's another storm brewing.'

Jens turns and gestures at the two women, both bent and shuffling towards them, Anya by necessity, he guesses, and Rumi propping up a friend who quite obviously needs the support.

The captain's face turns from jovial to grave. 'Is she sick? We don't have a medical man on board.'

Jens shakes his head. 'Pregnant.'

'We weren't told.' There's irritation in his voice. 'Is she about to . . .?'

'No,' Jens feels himself lying. 'It's weeks away yet. She's just bone-tired from the journey.'

He doesn't look convinced, especially as Anya draws close, her face working to push out gratitude through the discomfort. They move inside, and lead Anya into the captain's cabin, as he offers it up for the journey.

'There's one thing we need from you before we leave,' the captain says, back on deck. 'I assume you've got a radio?'

Jens nods. 'It's risky. There are trackers everywhere.'

'We'll all be long gone soon, but we've not been able to let Shetland know we've arrived. The storm we came through was bad, and the agents dropped on the way are vital. They need to know we got here in one piece.'

Reluctantly, Jens sets up the radio – it's the least he can

do when the Bus crew has risked all to meet them. He transmits quickly, minimising his time on the airwaves.

'Okay, it's done,' he tells the captain. 'Now we all need to get out of here.'

The two men descend to the cabin, where Anya is already dozing.

'The both of you should be all right down here, even with the storm expected,' the captain says to Rumi.

Her concentration swerves from Anya, face awash with panic. 'But I'm not coming,' she tells him firmly. 'I have to get back to Bergen.' Her features are set, rigid. Eyes wide like a cornered animal.

The captain gestures heavily for them to take the conversation up top, away from Anya's ears. In the wheelhouse, he strokes at his beard. 'I'm no doctor, but I am a father twice over,' he starts. 'While that doesn't make me a midwife, I don't believe that woman should be on her own. Not now. I'm sorry, but either someone comes, or I can't take her.'

He looks to Jens, and then to Rumi. Uncompromising.

Jens feels the fear emanating from Rumi, filling the space, seeping out of her. He's certain that just stepping onto the deck would have taken every ounce of her courage; boats she's lived with and loved all of her life, but the Bus is something different. The trawler may look like hundreds up and down the fjords, but the institution – its very name – took away what was hers for life: Magnus, her love and faith in the ocean, part of her being. It's a saviour to some but to her it represents danger and death. And then there's the prospect of a storm.

'I . . . I can't. Jens, I . . .' Her voice cracks. This is not the unrelenting Rumi of past days. This is Rumi in pain, terror swirling in her like the flakes around them.

He pulls her away by the hand, onto the open deck,

dreading the task in front of him. They can't go back as a trio, it's as simple as that. He doesn't care about the wrath of the SOE, but Anya won't make it, and they might not either, with Selig hovering.

Jens faces her, reaches behind and under her hat, pulling out her long plait and offering it up to her. She takes it, rubbing at the bristly ends, and he reaches for her other hand, grasping it tightly.

'I don't want you to go, believe me,' he says. 'But I also know you, Rumi Orlstad, and how much you give. How much you want to see Anya and her baby safe. I'm certain you can conquer this, because I know for sure that you of all people can overcome anything. I've seen it, how strong you are. It's not the sea or the Bus you have to fear, only what these bastard Germans have nurtured in us.'

He stops, wonders how much the speech is for himself as well as Rumi.

'But, Jens, how can I? There's a storm out there, it's exactly what Mag—' Her strength seems cowed.

'This is different,' he asserts, perhaps more firmly than he believes. 'No two people or situations are the same. They can't be. This is *not* fate − it's your journey, and yours alone.'

She breathes and shivers in unison, as if processing and purging the fear.

Seconds tick away, the near soundless flakes landing around them.

'I'll go,' she says at last. 'But I swear to you, Jens, I am coming back on the next boat. For Pappa and Rubio, just in case Marjit . . .' She swallows. 'I said I'd be there for you.'

'I know you will,' he says. 'I have no doubts.'

Her lips are beyond cold − his, too − but their frozen flesh binds easily as they connect. He feels the hardest thing will be to break away, severing the cool touch that fires up his entire body within seconds. Why can't good things last forever? But he does – forces himself to draw away and disconnect. He has to.

'I can't watch you go,' she says as he turns. 'I'll be down below.'

'I will see you soon, Rumi Orlstad. I'll see you very very soon.'

69

The Fury

Brekke, 12th December 1942

Rumi

Rumi makes herself busy in the cabin, while on the deck above there are the familiar sounds of a crew preparing to leave. Anya rouses from her doze and stretches out a hand from under her covers.

'Thank you,' she says. 'I know this can't be easy . . .'

'It's fine,' Rumi reacts quickly. She fears that if Anya gives her the slightest excuse to leave, to relieve her of a moral duty to a friend, she might run towards the dock as fast as her weary legs will carry her.

Instead, she talks herself round. A week ago, it would have been Marjit laying down the common sense in person. 'These boys on the Bus do that journey all the time,' she would have urged. 'Sadly, Magnus fell foul, but many more survive, and find freedom. You have to believe it, Rumi. There are still good things in this cruel world.'

Her wise neighbour might have been pasting over some

360

truths, Rumi knows, but she would have believed Marjit, because she'd been right far more than wrong. Somewhere inside, Rumi only hopes that wisdom remains alive.

It will be fine. Rough, but okay. We'll survive.

More than anything, she thinks: I have to. There's so much more out there.

He's out there.

The reassuring clank above their heads is replaced by a new noise out towards the vessel's side, still tethered to the dock. The sound cuts roughly through the muted, still air; the hurried growl of an engine, wheels spinning on snow in a desperation to hold a straight line and keep going at speed. Her concentration fixes on its urgency: that's not Harald's old truck.

Rumi sprints up on deck, sees first the stricken faces of the sailors, static with shock for an instant and then rushing to cast off as the *Kübelwagen* careers onto the dock and towards the lone figure of Jens. He hasn't walked away, staying instead to watch the trawler's departure. Her departure.

It means he's trapped: closed up buildings behind and the freezing waters to one end. Yet she's certain he won't leap onto the boat and endanger anyone else by drawing a spray of machine gun fire towards the crew. Because she knows him.

The vehicle skids to a halt and two figures leap out, guns immediately trained on Jens: at his head, and his face, which Rumi notes is strangely passive. Jens will go with the Abwehr, she's sure. He will sacrifice himself, and she will have to witness it. She didn't think anything could be worse than losing Magnus into a void, but here it is. And it's Selig that will have the satisfaction of picking off his prey, that scar facing towards her, red and raw against pig-pink skin and the panorama of white.

361

A volley of frantic shouts pins Jens to the spot, facing down his predator. Selig won't see it, but from her angle she does: Jens's hand moving slowly to his back, perhaps to his gun.

No, no, Jens, please no.

One shot to Selig and it's certain death for Jensen Parkes. His life extinguished, their future gone.

The next second happens as if through the lens of a sailor's spyglass, like the ancient one Peder has next to the ship's wheel; she's a few metres away but it seems as if Jens is at the far end of a long jetty, the world a badly cut film reel. A crack comes out of nowhere and splits the air, echoing up through the valley, and the soldier next to Selig slumps to the ground, the body instantly motionless and a river of red seeping into the snow.

The crew freezes and Rumi clutches at the bounding in her chest. The captain alongside her holds his gun close to his thigh, out of sight, his fingers twitching on the trigger, though the fatal shot came not from his barrel but from somewhere in the trees. He will know any move now could be equally dangerous, is calculating the risk to those who still have a chance, and whether to react.

Instead of instant retaliation in planting a bullet into Jens, Selig flashes a look at the fallen soldier, then left and right. Rumi sees the pink of his skin turn purple as he launches himself at Jens, raising the butt of his gun and bringing it down hard in a fierce rage. She hears bone crack and Jens crumples to his knees with the force, both hands clutching at his eye as more red runs onto the pure white below, shielding himself from Selig's ferocity and the violent kicks to his body. The Abwehr hound is screaming wildly, cursing in German, his wrath laid bare. Out of any human control.

Rumi sucks in a large, icy breath and – without thought or reason – snatches the captain's gun and leaps over the boat's side onto the dock. There's nothing but fury driving her forward: red hot frenzied rage. *He will NOT do this.*

Selig only stops his merciless beating as she comes near, her gun trained directly at his head. She watches a spark of recognition wash across his face. 'You,' he says. He's half kneeling and pressing his own gun barrel snug into Jens's temple, watching the fear ripple across her face.

'So he's yours, is he?' Selig scoffs in Norwegian. 'Look at your pathetic Norboy. Can't hide behind his radio now, can he?'

She says nothing. Every ounce of focus is in her fingers, the tip on the trigger pulsing hard. Whose reflexes are faster – his or hers? That's all she can calculate now.

'No, Rumi,' Jens rasps from the ground, red hands clutching at his left eye, the other pupil pleading with her. 'No.'

But her eyes are on Selig. His scar twitches upwards, along with the sides of his mouth – an arrogant sneer that relays with supreme confidence: *you won't. You wouldn't dare.*

It pokes at the molten fire inside her, anger surging through every artery, speeding towards her finger. Magnus, Karl, Marjit, every Norwegian lost. Jens beaten and bleeding on the ground. Trine. Anya's baby. Marjit's parting words: 'Use that anger only when you need it.'

I will.

Her fire spews. The shot rings out, a second echo that seems to cause a shiver in the surrounding trees. His scarred face falls to the ground, ruined this time by the bullet she delivers. She aimed directly to be certain. A clean hit – the way Pappa had taught her as a teenager, insisting that one day it would be useful in a hunt. This hound is dead prey.

She's down towards Jens in the next second, stroking his hair now matted with blood, as the captain and one of the crew arrive quickly beside her, with bandages to hand. Jens can't help a groan of pain as she peels away his hand, and even the unshockable Rumi Orlstad recoils in horror. His beautiful pale blue eye is a mess of contorted flesh, the socket streaked red and white, displaced and unseeing. The eye that had lit up so many times in her company. Maimed.

'Rumi – go, please,' he's saying, hoarse and weak. 'There could be more of them behind. You have to go.'

She turns back to the captain as Harald arrives on the dock, shouldering the rifle that accurately picked off Selig's partner from afar. 'We can take him, surely?' Her voice is cracked, pleading.

The captain shakes his head with regret. 'It's three or more days to Shetland. He needs a doctor in hours, or he might . . .'

She doesn't hear the rest, looks instead to Harald, who nods solemnly. 'We'll get him to a doctor,' he says. 'Do the best we can. I promise.' He grips her shaking hand in a way that injects some hope.

She bends to Jens, close enough to his ear that she can almost taste the metal in his blood.

'Remember what you said, Jens Parkes,' she whispers. 'You will be there, or God help me I'll come looking for you in heaven or hell.'

She feels him nod, squeeze her hand with waning strength. 'I'll be there.'

70

A Bus in the Storm

The North Sea, 13th December 1942

Rumi

It was bound to happen. They've been dodging Nazis and pushing the risk for days, relying on fortune and luck to win through. Now it's time for nature to take the reins.

Rumi hears Anya through her veil of fitful sleep, thinks at first it's the boat straining against the increasing swell of waves on the open water. She takes a minute to focus, to disengage from the images of Jens behind her eyes, those where his limp body is pulled onto a cart by Harald and hauled away. But is the crimson trail in her mind truly genuine – a slice of the scene she forced herself to watch as the trawler cast off from the dock minutes after Jens was beaten down by the man she then killed in cold blood? Or is that vivid red simply woven into her dreams as part of a heavy, constant dread? The fear that says she will never see him again.

The moan from Anya is a new sound, a low pitch of a groan, but more intense; blowing isn't enough now.

'Anya? Anya — what is it?'

Her eyes open, peer into the cabin's gloom. 'Something's different,' she croaks. 'Oh God, Rumi, I think it's coming.' Tears push from her lower lids. 'What shall we do? It can't be born here. Not now.'

It can and it will, if the baby decides. An altogether new dread sets in.

Rumi helps her up between pains, with Anya stiff and slow after a night curled in a foetal position against the cold and discomfort. She's better moving around, though, and the tightenings seem to come in fits and starts; nothing regular, sometimes lasting a few minutes, or just a second's sharp twinge. *Maybe it's a false alarm,* Rumi thinks. Hopes. You hear new mothers talking of them all the time, don't you? She casts back to a conversation with Marjit after Trine's birth; her saying that nature often waits for women to feel safe before labour begins. How secure did Trine feel in the back of Pappa's truck? Though, presumably, Marjit was using that episode as an exception to the rule.

Safe. It's not something that Rumi can contemplate until her feet are on Shetland soil. Any solid land. And safe is not this boat.

Rumi brews tea and makes food for the crew, anything to distract herself from her own thoughts and the lurch of the vessel, which sends Anya back to bed after a bout of vomiting. It must be the sheer force of the waves, Rumi convinces herself; if she weren't a fisherman's daughter herself, she would be feeling as sick as Anya, the boat tossed mercilessly by the North Sea.

Up on deck, the men are lashing down everything they can as the boat lunges forward, and the captain's face is locked, muscles in his neck strained as he grips the wheel tight.

'How bad is it?' Rumi shouts above the sea's roar. What

she means is: will it get much worse? Part of her would much rather not know, but she can't help asking.

'Not too bad – yet,' he says and tries to reassure with a smile, though his eyes don't move from the crest of another breaker, higher and more powerful, its freezing waves crashing onto the deck.

'How is she?' The captain gestures to Anya down below.

'Seasick, but all right,' she lies. Perhaps if they both lie convincingly, it might not get any worse.

It does, in every way.

Anya's been asleep for an hour or so, and Rumi has grabbed the small bag of knitting squashed into her pack, more valuable to her than another change of clothes. She focuses hard on each stitch worked, dropping several when the roll of the vessel takes her unawares. Inside herself, she's drowning at the thought of what's ahead, going under slowly, but – as always – the feel of the soft wool sliding against her fingers helps and the routine of counting stitches stops her flailing. She forces her gasps into a steady breath. *One, two, three – keep going, Rumi.*

Gradually, a calm emerges as she creates something tangible under her hand, levelling the panic in her brain. In this moment of relative peace, she wants to think of Magnus – feels she should – but the memories conjure images of his own terror; his fighting the elements, and losing, knowing he will soon take his last breath. She tries to think of Marjit and Jens, but they feel equally lost. Only Pappa and Rubio stand firm in her vision, and even they will be under suspicion now.

The boat dips violently in the second that Anya's eyes flip open and a piercing cry fills the cabin. The needles are down and Rumi is quickly at her side.

367

'What?' she says stupidly. What else can it be?

Anya blows hard, squeezing her eyes shut, clutching harder at her bump than she's ever done before. As the pain wanes, she sucks in air, levels her own breathing.

'Oh Rumi, that was the worst one yet,' she pants. 'I don't think we can fool ourselves anymore.' She looks hard into her friend's eyes, the same serious gaze as when they'd discussed love or husbands as teenagers, thinking then there was nothing else in the world more important. 'This baby won't wait until Shetland.'

Anya gets up again, the pain clearly more manageable when she's moving. Rumi brews tea, stares at the boiling kettle. Christ. What would Marjit do, and why isn't she here? The momentary calm deserts her again and she wants to crumble, weep on the floor of the cabin in a way that Rumi rarely allows herself to do, succumbing to weakness. What use is strength anyway in the middle of an unforgiving sea, when you don't have a clue, when you're up against nature, war and the evil of Adolf Hitler? Selig is gone, but there are many more like him. Jens may be gone, too, Marjit as well. What else can be robbed from her world?

The shrill whistle of the kettle pierces her self-pity, its climax noisy and sobering: if she doesn't step up now, and face the challenge, then this bloody annihilating war will take them too. It will win. The sea Rumi cannot command – that's up to the captain and some superior Poseidon-like fate now – but what happens in this cabin can be determined in part by her, even with the little she knows. She can try at least.

Magnus died trying to help others, and she owes him that.

Rumi fights her way on deck against the wind, rough spray scouring her cheeks, and opens the wheelhouse door. 'Looks like we're going to have a baby,' she says flatly.

The captain's eyes flick towards her, only briefly surprised. 'I can't spare any men,' he says, 'but what else do you need?'

As a crewman gathers as much dry cloth as he can find, Rumi descends again. In the few minutes she's been away Anya has changed; cheeks flushed red, sweating despite the damp chill of the cabin, fingers wrapped tight around the blanket as she rides another contraction. They must be the real thing by now, Rumi thinks. 'Pain' simply doesn't do them justice.

She wracks her brain to think of Trine and what Marjit said and did in those moments. She recalls her making some kind of nest on the floor, safe and dry. Clean might be a step too far, judging by the grubby sheets the crewman has left outside the door, rapping hard and turning tail rapidly.

Rumi rifles in Anya's small bag, full of everything she and Marjit had made for the baby. Despite a strong desire to stop and draw in every particle of Marjit's scent from the neat stitching, Rumi works fast to lay out everything, recalling that Marjit dried and wrapped Trine's newborn quickly, despite the heat of that day. 'Babies lose their own heat so rapidly,' she'd explained then, and for some reason that knowledge had stuck with Rumi.

Anya is pacing endlessly, like the stray dog that once produced puppies suddenly on Pappa's boat, circling to find comfort, settling for a second before padding about again. Sometimes, they are tossed end to end of the cabin forcefully as the storm howls its rage, spray whipped into a frenzy against the tiny porthole. Always, Anya moves to protect her belly before her own body, falling at times and grazing her own skin, drawing pinpricks of blood and yet never complaining.

Bit by bit, she unravels her wool coverings, hot one minute and freezing the next, Rumi bathing her neck with warm or cool water. The labour and the storm continue in tandem for several hours, with no finale in sight, and yet Rumi somehow knows this cascade will not stop now, not without a baby at journey's end. The storm she has no clue about.

Gradually, there's only a short respite between contractions, Anya's words only half-lucid as she mutters into her belly, bowing her head and moaning into the air. She asks Rumi for very little, only for water to wet her dry lips or pressure on her back, pleading tearfully to some greater being that it 'be over'. The escalation within the cabin is mirrored by the force outside, and yet Rumi's fear of the storm – of dying under the waves – is muted by the focus on Anya, by the watching and waiting she does when Anya needs to be left untouched. It's what Marjit did with Trine, in between the frenetic breath of each contraction. She waited. Now, Rumi has hot water to hand, a freshly sterilised knife, and wool ties ready for severing the physical bond of mother and baby, just as Marjit had done. What else is there to do but wait?

A sudden crash against the portside sends them both reeling, the dim cabin lights flickering, and it feels for a second as if the entire vessel has gone under. Rumi holds her breath as if she were fully submerged already, watches the tiny porthole for signs of the ocean giving way to the sky again. It does, eventually. She scrabbles up top, peers through the hatch window and sees the deck is empty of men, checks they are not in the galley. She spies some movement in the wheelhouse window and prays they are

370

nose to nose in there, all accounted for. Praying themselves. Much like the events down below, there's nothing else to do but wait. For fate and survival. Hope and luck, too; throw them all in the blistering pot that is the sea's fury and trust it will boil itself dry.

Back in the cabin, Rumi recognises another change to Anya's pitch instantly. Low and bass, like the sound of the Kraken described to them as children, by older boys who delighted in scaring the younger ones with fearful fables.

A rumble to behold. To Rumi, it could easily come from the eye of the storm. In reality, it stems from the slight mouth of her gentle friend, whose eyes are ablaze, shocked at her own resonance.

'Rumi, Rumi, what shall I do?' Anya pleads in the next breath. 'Tell me, tell me.'

It's the same words that Trine uttered, and Rumi repeats back what Marjit said then: 'Just follow your body. Don't hold back. Your baby is strong.'

Does she know it? No. Does she want Anya to hold in everything, batten down her bodily hatches and not produce a baby that Rumi will have to keep alive? Yes.

But like the storm, there's no abating. They have to ride it, cope with whatever nature hurls at them.

Anya flops to her knees on the floor, swaying between the pains, in line with the constant roll of the boat. Rumi mimics Marjit and uncovers her buttocks from behind, a mucousy snake of blood visible now. She remembers as much from Trine's birth, and Marjit didn't seem alarmed. All she can do is wipe it away, fixed on the movements of Anya's flesh as she begins urging her baby into the world with deep, long thrusts, working her buttocks up and down, side to side in a brief recovery and then driving down again with an unstoppable force. Anya's hands hover under

371

her belly, barely resisting a touch, muttering between the earthy groans.

To Rumi's eyes, the taut skin around Anya's buttocks takes on the rounded shape of a tiny, human head. There's nothing to see or touch, but she knows it's there, and she's frozen in wonder and disbelief. Fear, too, which she brushes aside irritably. No time for that now.

In two or three contractions, there's something to see: the pink skin pulls back as a balloon of opaque white eases through; Anya's sudden screech is enough to rise above the clamour of the storm. Rumi finds herself saying: 'blow slowly, Anya, blow. Slow now.' Where does that come from? Marjit, probably, somewhere deep in her subconscious. It just seems right.

The skin rounds over the balloon as another wave batters the portside, sending the trawler listing dramatically, Anya falling to the floor with a sudden gush of fluid across the sheets, straw coloured. At least it's not blood.

When Rumi looks again, the baby's head is almost born, slowly breaching its mother's skin, eyes closed, mouth and nose flattened by the journey through.

Anya is on her left side, panting, embracing a lull in the pain. One hand crawls down towards the baby's head and her fingertips make contact with the wet skin. Anya's eyes open, and the sheer breadth of her smile floods the silent space. Is this right, Rumi worries, the delay? Only the baby's response is anything like comfort, one eye and then two open, blinking into a strange new world.

It's pure instinct that leads the mother and her reluctant midwife in the next seconds – Anya's right leg rises like a ballerina in practice, coupled with the moan and thrust of intent, and Rumi watches in awe as the baby's shoulders twist one way and then the other, inching forward. Only when they stop does Rumi reach down and help, not pulling frantically, but grasping lightly and coaxing. She feels a familiar slippery balm so common in sea life, oiling the way through as Anya gives one last almighty effort towards the life of her child, and a slippery fish of a boy child lands on the most solid ground they can provide.

71

That's for You, Magnus

The North Sea, 13th December 1942

Rumi

He sees with staring eyes but doesn't breathe. Trine's baby had kicked its way out with vociferous complaint, and the noise alone ensured a succession of deep breaths which saw his colour turn from blue to pink in under a minute. Any worry had drained from Marjit's face instantly.

Now, Anya's baby is wide-eyed and mute, a mottled whale-blue from head to foot on a body that's yet to lay down much fat. No experience so far has prepared Rumi for this, except for when Rubio fell through the ice on the lake as a boy, his friends scrabbling to pull him out, and Rumi shouting at them to almost bundle on top of him, despite his distress; she simply knew they had to force the life back in him, with their zealous, near cruel chafing.

Now she does the same with Anya's baby, rubbing at his skin firmly, roughly, in her desperation.

Come on, breathe. Breathe! There's no sound inside her head but the thunder of her own demand, the storm outside relegated to what's in front of her now. What would Marjit do? *Please Marjit, tell me.* Again, Rumi plunders the corners of her brain for an old woman's wisdom.

She would let the mother do it.

Oblivious to the panic, Anya is stirring from her efforts as he's lifted onto her depleted belly, Rumi still rubbing at his soft skin.

'*Hei,* my darling,' Anya murmurs into his soft ear. She blows gently onto his face, stroking at his head, cajoling him with her voice into living, to see this odd world he's crashed into. His moan is barely distinguishable at first, so that Rumi has to lean in close, holding her own breath to hear above her thumping pulse. Then a whine, the cough and choke of a stuttering engine – that it sounds like Pappa's old truck makes her laugh at last. Then his wail of complaint, of being out here, plucked from the warmth and safety of inside.

'Oh Rumi, look at him,' Anya coos. 'He's beautiful. Just beautiful.'

Like a little limpet, his hand reaches and claws at his mother's hot skin.

'He is,' Rumi says.

Up above, the fake herring barrels shift and fight their tethers, the storm thrashing against the trawler's battered hull. Inside, it seems to matter less as the minutes of a new life tick by. Despite the lurch of the cabin, Rumi feels unusually calm, her fear of death receding to almost nothing. If the worst happens, it will be destiny and not Hitler who takes them. Life has triumphed in the last hours and she thinks it might just win out.

She looks at the new mother tending a fresh hope in their midst.

That's for you, Magnus.

★ ★ ★

375

Rumi surprises herself by her actions after. Much like her shifts on Pappa's boat, she works logically and efficiently – with a large helping hand from Mother Nature. The placenta is expelled in one push, and the alarming gush of blood that follows ebbs soon after, and Rumi can only suppose that's good; she's heard sad talk in Bergen of women losing their lives to excess bleeding after birth. The cord connecting mother to baby turns from a bumptious, functioning pump to a limp thread, and common sense tells Rumi it's not needed anymore, not when the baby is pink, breathing and licking eagerly at his mother's breast. She ties it tight and severs it with the knife scalded in boiling water.

There's so much to do that she hardly notices the storm waning outside, only that it's suddenly easier to move towards the galley and boil water for tea. Staring into the steam, the full force of the last days catches up: she's seen one life violently extinguished and a new one emerge – both at her own hand. The justice of the former she will wrestle with later, but for now, the latter needs celebrating.

The captain descends, sopping and clearly exhausted. 'How is your friend?' he says eagerly. 'Is she still holding on?'

'*They* are fine,' Rumi says, with a surprising surge of pride. 'You might even have gained a reputation as the captain of a maternity ship.'

He laughs and looks skyward through the porthole, to where the danger appears to be receding. 'Then the gods really were with us, above and below deck. That's the worst storm we've weathered in a while – we nearly lost a man overboard. But I think we're through it now.'

'How long until Shetland?' Rumi feels her confidence and nursing skills might not stretch for much longer.

376

'Forty-eight hours, if the wind's with us.'

Anya's exhaustion has been replaced with a babbling high of motherhood, and she's pushed herself upright on the bed, the baby suckling keenly under a mound of blankets.

'I can't believe we did that,' she sighs. 'In here. Just the two of us.'

'Three – he did a good deal of the work.' Rumi gestures at the baby. 'Somehow, he knew what to do.'

'And you, too!' Anya says. 'I don't know what to say, Rumi. You were so calm. I can't thank you enough.'

'Calm?' she cries. 'That's the least likely description of me.'

'Well you were. You are,' Anya insists. 'You've changed, Rumi.'

Maybe I have, she thinks, sipping her tea. The anger had surfaced and spewed in that moment facing Selig, but it was a flash of fury, a rabid animal let out of its cage, perhaps kept back for a purpose. Only, she feels the cage has vanished, too, her body no longer harbouring some beast that's waiting with vengeance.

There's anxiety, there's a deep dread over Jens and Marjit, and whether Pappa and Rubio will be persecuted back in Bergen, but inside she feels oddly at peace.

She wonders, has the unrelenting rage truly fizzled and died in Rumi Orlstad?

'I know what I'm going to call him,' Anya says.

'Yes?'

'Magnus, of course.'

'Oh, Anya, you don't have to, not for me.'

'But I want to,' Anya goes on. 'It feels right, the life he's been given on this ship, through the storm. It's the perfect name, as long as you don't mind?'

'No, of course not. Magnus would have loved that, and

Pappa will be so proud. I'm just delighted that the *only* baby I will ever be midwife to is named after Magnus.'

Anya strokes at the white-blond nap of her baby's head, kisses him softly. 'Then welcome to this topsy-turvy life, Magnus Lindvig.'

PART THREE

72

A Flame from the Embers

Somewhere in Northern Norway, February 1943

Dear Rumi
I know you will never read this, since I'll toss it into the fire the minute I've signed off, for safety and security. Writing it down helps, though, so that I can convince myself our connection is still there, a fragile one lived through imagination and ink, and that you're somewhere, thinking a little of me and what we had. Have.

If I picture you to be living, possibly in Norway some-where, maybe still in Shetland, I can maintain some hope. Oh, Rumi, I wish I were telling you this in person, but this endless war is a constant wedge and there's no other choice but to keep chipping away at it.

It's a nervous time for us in the cabin we're holed up in. A small force has left to carry out what we believe is the most crucial operation SOE have ever planned, sabotage on the heavy water plant near Telemark. A big, destructive raid, if it all goes to plan. The success of it will be a turning point in the war, a real setback for the Nazis in their plans to build atomic weapons – another one in the eye for Hitler, the boys say. Ha! How ironic that is. I can't be with them on tonight's assault because of my blasted eye – you need good night vision for what they're doing. I have, though, been part of the team laying the groundwork for the mission, observing and mapping the area for weeks now, assessing guard movements and planning routes. That I can still do, at least. It's amazing how the Nazi troops dismiss me as no threat when I'm walking around now, as if my face means I can't possibly be part of a resistant force, throwing me off as redundant and no longer worthy of any threat. It makes me smile inside when they wave me on, more determined that we must keep fighting, for people like Harald and his wife, the lovely woman who nursed me after that horrible day on the dock. Their basement was my whole world for a month, a good doctor visiting and Harald bringing me snippets of news with his wayward, jolly smile. Rumi, I thought of you every single day, as I lay there. It was only my promise to you that stopped me from giving up.

I'm alive. That's the main thing – and it's thanks to you. I may never be more grateful for your fury, your determination and courage on that day. I'd seen it before, in flashes, my first few days in Bergen, and at the time I wanted it to be gone, for you to have peace inside yourself. I hope there's some truth in that now, but in the moment, facing the barrel of Selig's gun that I couldn't see but felt digging into my flesh, I was glad that your anger surfaced, for a purpose. Retribution will never win wars, but I wish for your sake that it's helped in your battle for calm.

I hope, too, that the crucial message reaching my ears made it to you – that it's not safe for you to be back in Bergen yet. Norway, in fact. Selig had lodged his suspicions with the Abwehr before he left Bergen, your family's name among them. He was there when Marjit's house was raided, I saw him for myself.

You need to know, too, that it was Bjarne who helped us get away – your lifelong friend remains a patriot, just a well-hidden one, deeply embedded as our vital ears and eyes in the Quisling hierarchy since the war began. He deserves our thanks, living a lonely double life for Bergen. He talked of you and Rubio often with real fondness, and I know he's been active in steering away suspicion from Peder after our departure as much as he can. Rubio, too, has been largely protected from persecution.

Rumi, I wish I had news of Marjit, but there's none. The SOE have tried to root out information, but there's no trace of her, and little or no information trickling out of Grini camp. For myself, I have to imagine that she is there, even with the hardships inside the camp – we can only hope, together, that the spirit which makes her so special will carry her through. I've ordered plukkfisk for our reunion meal, so she'd better come back!

I have to finish now – the fire is dying, and my frozen hand won't hold out much longer. I know that when I put this among the embers, it will flare and burn brightly, if only for a short time, just as you did for me. I feel sure your flame is somewhere out there in this world. I sense its warmth, even in this freezing cabin.

In case you're wondering, I still plan to be there. Just hold on, Rumi, my beautiful fishwife.

All my love, Jens

73

Listening Out

Scalloway, The Shetland Isles, June 1943

> *Dear Jens*
>
> *Here I am again with my pen, sending out another missive into the world, hoping you might at least read this one. I've no idea if you've received the other five or six letters, as there's been no reply. No word at all, in fact. All they will tell me is that you're alive, but where, I have no idea – Norway, England, Scotland, or some far flung tropical place that never sees a fleck of snow. More and more, infiltration by the Abwehr remains a real fear, and there's a tight rein on information coming in and out. So, I can only send this into the ether, in the pocket of some good sailor bound for Norway, and hope it finds its way, assuming you're still in our home country.*
>
> *'How' you are is another matter for my overworked imagination. I can't get that last vision on the dockside out of my mind – you crushed and bleeding, mutilated by that man out of sheer vengeance.*
>
> *I had never in my life, even throughout this ugly war,*

thought I would — or could — kill another human being. After all, isn't that what we're fighting for? For peace. To oust the murderous Hitler. In the end, it was instinct and survival for the one I love. Selig was about to take one of the most precious things in my life away, forever, and I couldn't let him do that. I'm not proud of myself, Jens, but I don't regret it. Not if it saved you. Not just for me, but for your mother and father, and everyone else — Marjit especially, if she's still with us somewhere. The world is a better place with Jens Parkes in it. I might not have known that on the first day I met you (which makes me laugh every time I think of it), but I do now. Every single day I imagine you in it, and hope that somewhere I'm in your thoughts, too.

Life here in Shetland is fine, and I really can't complain. I'm writing this at three a.m. as I'm on night watch — something about your codes and ciphers must have rubbed off on me, because I'm working as a transmission clerk for the Navy, attached to the Shetland Bus. I'm apparently quite good at it, and very glad to help out after our welcome reception on Shetland — since drawing up on the dockside there hasn't been a day when Anya and I haven't felt the kindness of the people here. But there is also a selfish element in my new posting. I scan the airwaves for any signs of your signature, for when I might hear 'Norboy' tapped out, or a message coming in that could well have your touch. After Selig, you've most likely changed your call sign, but I hope that I would recognise you somehow, the nuance of your language, a tiny part of you pushing through the static. Each shift, I will myself to hear those signs through the headphones. I'm convinced if I listen long enough they will come.

I see Anya and the baby every day, since we both have rooms in the same house here. Magnus is six months old

385

and gorgeous, blond and blue-eyed, bubbling with sound. He smiles endlessly. You'd be very proud of me, Jens, as I'm actually becoming a little maternal, hopelessly in love with the little man.

Among the Shetlanders, he's firmly Norwegian – Anya and I had long discussions, and the re-telling of her tale says she was widowed by a patriot and needed to escape. Later, she might choose to tell her son the truth, but for now it makes his passage in life easier. A baby – an inno-cent – shouldn't have to suffer for the sins of his father. Rightly, or wrongly, that's how it is. And it looks as if he may have two Norwegian parents in reality, since one of the Bus mechanics – Konrad – has taken a definite shine to the both of them. Anya seems very happy with him, and he dotes on the baby as his own. Better still, his job keeps him on dry land in the workshop. I wouldn't be surprised if we hear wedding bells very soon.

Meantime, Anya and I spend our evenings knitting, as there's a real desire for the traditional Nordic sweater, and the servicemen pay well for them. If I'm not tapping out with my hands at work, I'm furiously clicking away with my needles, which brings back its own memories, of course. I try to make them positive ones, of knitting in Marjit's parlour, you stretched across her old battered chair, the sound of the radio in the background with Pappa and Rubio badgering at each other alongside. Everyone I love, safe.

Despite plenty of Norwegians on the islands, I miss Bergen madly – that unique light on the wharf at six a.m. in summer and the bustle of the fish market (and the smell, of course!). Those are the sounds of my beloved city at work. Not the snow, maybe, since Shetland has plenty of its own. I'll head back home as soon as I'm able, when the word says it's safe to do so. Selig's death left a legacy of revenge, and it hasn't faded yet. Pappa is no writer, but Rubio has managed to get a note to me once or twice, in some ridiculous code that talks of fish quotas! Mostly, I'm left to gather gossip from the Bus boys about them both, and how they're still playing their resistance games on the trawlers. I'm desperate to get back and protect them from their own zeal. Or foolishness.

There's little else to tell — one escapee of the camps arrived here a month ago, with word that an older woman is helping to run the hospital at Grini. I quizzed him endlessly, but as much as I wanted it to be true, I couldn't make it sound like our beloved Marjit. The need to know for certain burns each and every day, and I'm certain you'll feel it, too, if you have the same dearth of news. This waiting, for the world to right itself in every way, seems unending.

I need to sign off, now, as there are messages coming in. Who knows, you may be behind one of them. I listen out in constant hope.

Be sure that when I know — when I get the slightest inkling that you are there — I will be too. I have not, and will not, give up on the idea that we should start what I foolishly pushed away. I know now that my grief and guilt over Magnus has mended. He will never leave me, but I feel in my heart that he would want me to be happy.

We have too much of a future for that monster Hitler to get in the way of our plans, and those of our country. I only hope you feel the same.

Hold on, Jens. Just hold on for me to prove myself. I will come.

Always,
your loving fishwife, Rumi

74

Liberation

Jens

Torgallmenningen is buzzing. It's so changed from the last time Jens stood looking into the square, that day when he forced himself to watch the brutal hangings in retaliation for the fire at Hotel Bristol. Then, the mood was sombre and desperate, acidic grey clouds looming above. Now, faces are lit up, smiles from ear to ear, men and women are hugging tightly, some who are friends, others who are working their way through the crowd with abandon, spraying kisses and utter joy, the cheerful rump-tump of a brass band in the background. Children on their parents' shoulders are frantically waving vibrant red Norwegian flags, scarlet hats bobbing amid the throng. Bergen's fallen buildings and bomb damage are testament to a scarred city, but the world has colour again, Jens thinks, the dour grey or green uniforms distinctly absent since the official surrender of German forces at midnight.

It's over. Norway and Europe are no longer at war. Hitler is dead, the Reich crumbling day by day in the wake of his cowardice. It's a ragged, blitzed and ugly peace across nations, but a concord all the same, and Norwegians have their country back.

In place of the occupying forces, a new invasion of Norwegian troops began trickling in several days ago, openly displaying their nation's uniform at last while the Nazis and their collaborators were rounded up. Free from their status as outlaws, resistance forces have sprung from their hideaways, scuttling like mice from a hole now that the cat has given up the chase, and they are celebrating as victors. Wildly and noisily. They are instantly recognisable as fighting forces by the sheer relief they wear across their features, that they can walk down the streets once again without fear for their lives.

With his height, Jens's blond head stands above the crowd, scanning diligently. He's delighted to see so many jubilant faces, but he's peering and searching for just one; a distinct red cap of hair, a bright beacon in a sea of bodies.

'You said that she'd found passage?' Jens asks of Peder, for only the third time in the space of a few hours. 'That the boat is due in today? And she promised to make it?'

'Yes, today, but that letter was a few days ago and they might well have been held up.' Peder rubs his beard, clearly trying not to show his own concern. Jens has no doubt that Rumi's father will have pored over the shipping reports, those which say that the North Sea is unusually calm. There shouldn't be any delay.

Rubio comes in from behind, nudges at Peder, and then taps Jens on the shoulder. 'Any sign yet?' he asks. 'No new vessels arrived in the last hour – I've just been down on the wharf.'

She will come back, Jens knows for sure. She'll return for Peder and Rubio, for the prospect of Marjit, and because it's home. That's a certainty. But will she be coming back for him, too?

Jens has had no direct word; for two and a half long years he's lived as a war nomad, secrecy his currency for survival, moving up and down the country, in and out of Sweden when the Abwehr or the Gestapo got too close, dodging capture and death more times than he can count. Sometimes, he was desperate for any contact with Rumi, and at other times so tired, low and dejected that he wondered if the conflict would ever be over, let alone won. *What use would I be to her anyway?* he often thought, defeat lodged in his own personal war.

But with the peace comes hope – he sees that in front of him, here and now, feels it in his own heart. As the Reich fell and the resistance rose up, Jens had been recalled to Oslo for an SOE debriefing, making spurious excuses to his superiors that he was 'needed' in Bergen. It was partially true – the need was in him, craving to be in the place he thinks of as home now, to where there's a slim chance that Marjit may return as prisoners from Grini trickle back into the city daily. To where Rumi will surely gravitate.

Only since his arrival late the day before has Jens discovered any detail of Rumi, of her long war spent in Shetland, and her expected return, begging a hasty passage home when reports of the imminent surrender came. In the last few hours with Peder and Rubio he's pestered for every morsel of news, though they have little to tell. She's alive, that's the main thing.

He just needs to set eyes on her, read her touch and to judge that famous Rumi tone.

'You think she will come here, to the square?' Jens asks of Peder again. 'You're certain?'

'Wouldn't you?' Peder replies, gesturing to the crowds that move in shoals across the streets, singing and clinging to each other for the certainty that this is real at last.

Of course, she will. It's what she's been waiting for, to see her city and country reclaimed, the crowd's elation snaking like unfettered mercury around the tiny streets and lighting up the city. So where is she?

There's a lengthy pull on a boat horn out towards the wharf; all heads turn to a military vessel drawing in. Jens instantly recognises it as one of the speedy and sleek submarine chasers the Shetland Bus has used since 1943, reluctantly replacing the loyal fishing trawlers – perhaps not so Norwegian, though no man has been lost or tossed overboard since the sturdier ships came into play. No others like Magnus.

'Come on.' Rubio beckons, and he and Jens break into a run towards the dock, Peder left behind in their wake. As they approach, people are already pouring down the gangplank, men and troops mostly, but one or two women, too, hauling their lives in overstuffed suitcases. There are hugs and tears all around them, reunions and relief. But no Rumi.

She said she would be here.

But that was a long time ago, he reminds himself.

'There! There!' Rubio cries, and points to a form moving down the gangway, fighting the weight of several large bags. But the fiery tip of her hair is unmistakable, the way she moves, too, with determination and stealth.

Rubio runs forward, using his hefty build like the prow of a boat to part the sea of bodies. Jens watches her recognition turn to delight at the sight of her near-brother; she throws her arms around him, a hug that lasts an age, then Jens reads her lips for the inevitable questions: 'Where's Pappa?' Then tentatively: 'And Marjit?' She'll be asking if there's any sign on the trains arriving from Grini. He doesn't, however, read 'Jens' on that full, ruby mouth. Rubio hoists the bags over his shoulder, trails her by the hand, sweeping through the crowd.

Jens feels the emotion well and choke in his throat; she looks good from afar, a little thinner, but unmarked. She's whole on the outside, at least. There's fear brewing, too, as she steps ever closer. What will she think of him?

With each second, his anxiety multiplies, heart racing. The crowd thins and she catches sight of him then; Jens sees her trying to control the shock on her face when he's there in her path, no time for her to turn away from how he is now. The damage.

Her hand drops from Rubio's and she steps up to Jens slowly, less than an arm's length away before she speaks. Her eyes are filling. With pity? He hopes not.

Then, that broadening of her lips. The look that has carried him through every freezing night in the snow, every breathless pursuit by Nazis set on killing him – the Rumi smile to signal her humour has fought the anger successfully to win through.

'You came,' she says. It's a whisper, a hush amid the surrounding commotion.

She reaches one hand up to his face, traces a finger pad over the black eye patch settled on his cheek. He can feel her light touch, but underneath it burns.

He swallows. 'And you did, too.'

75

Facing Reality

Bergen, 9th May 1945

Rumi

The sight of him standing there is like manna to her soul, her hope for the past two and a half years, but it's startling nonetheless. The crowds, the noise, everyone around them – even Rubio – shrink into nothingness as Rumi plies a finger under the patch and lifts it. Jens is stock still as she gently explores the scarring on his skin where the butt of Selig's gun ripped into his flesh, healed in stiff folds like cold candlewax. The eye – his beautiful pale blue orb of old – is a misty, white globe, a faint centring of grey where his sooty black pupil once was. Like Jens, it is unmoving.

She swallows back the shock, for his sake, and replaces the patch. 'You'd make a very handsome pirate,' she says, forcing mischief into her voice. 'If only you could stand life on the water.'

'Then it's a good thing I'm still a very good fishwife.' His face darkens, suddenly serious. 'Is it hideous?' he whispers.

The other eye searching her face tells her it's what he fears. What he sees in the mirror's reflection daily.

'No,' she says, measured and with more truth in her quiet words than if her denial had been too eager. She truly believes it. He's still Jens. And he's alive. And looking at him, her feelings haven't changed. She thought they might; time and too much life experience, too many knocks, seeing the raw underside of a world at loggerheads. But the rush inside her is the same, the exhilaration that she can't explain – it all comes hurtling back.

He reaches for her hand. It's warm, not soft, though his flesh gives. 'I . . . I don't know what to say,' he stammers. 'I can't believe . . .'

It's Pappa's turn then to cut a swathe through the surrounding bodies as he catches up with them, flinging his arms around his daughter and thanking every god he can muster for her safe return.

As a foursome, they make their way up to Strangebakken. All of them want to stay and celebrate in town, but the pent-up hope in each has fallen away to relief, adrenalin plummeting, running with fatigue. Rumi is exhausted, by the last half hour, the previous days knowing the Allies were steaming towards victory, and the long five years of war. She's arrived home alone, Anya staying for the time being in Shetland with Magnus, now two, and her new husband, Konrad.

Going home will be hard, without Marjit next door – there's still no sign of her on today's train, Pappa says – but she needs to face those empty rooms, to begin re-building.

They file through the alleyway towards the back entrance noisily, with a dawning realisation that they no longer need to mind their words or draw the blackout curtains, that soon they will be able to switch on the radio at full volume and dance in the parlour with real abandon.

Rumi is about to step through the back door of her house, though she can't stop her reflexes throwing a look towards next door, as she's done a hundred times before.

She gasps, hand to her mouth, doubting her own eyes. Is it real, or just her wishful imagination – the face of an angel peeking through the curtains of the window alongside?

76

Homecoming

A man offers her a lift from the main train station, as the carriages spill their human content and the refugees from Grini stumble onto the platform. Some fall, quite literally, into the arms of relatives with expressions of extreme relief, and she sees the legs of one or two buckle under as they realise the ordeal is over at last. For her, there's no one. It's what she's used to and what she expected. But for the man standing next to her on the platform, his eyes scanning the sea of gaunt, wanton faces and hoping to identify a loved one, there's only disappointment.

'A week,' he mutters into the air. 'I've come here every day for a week, and still nothing. I know she went to Grini, my Ida. So where is she? Where's my wife?'

She says nothing, because there's no comfort to give. Instead, she stands for a minute, as if giving credence to his vigil, and he lifts up his chin in a mark of thanks. In the spirit of Bergen's new-found liberty – the joy of which she can hear beyond the station – he pushes his own dejection aside and offers her transport.

'Where to?' he asks, and it's then Fru Nesse realises she doesn't

actually know. As with millions across Europe, she is displaced. They've won, the country is reclaimed, but there are no real prizes. Except to be alive.

'Hop,' she says at last. She has no money, and only a half empty suitcase since most of her possessions were bartered or donated to those more in need. And she's tired. So weary. The thought of searching for lodgings and having to repay with toil is beyond her right now.

Their silence on the journey is an unspoken pact; the man knows where she's come from, and he doesn't need to be faced with the hardships his beloved wife will have endured: the cruelty, scrabbling and sometimes fighting for sparse rations, alongside the scars she's hiding under her thin clothing.

Each and every day, though, when she thought of Anya, and her baby who — if he's survived into being — will be a toddler by now, she's never regretted her path. Whatever has gone since, it was the right choice. She found something, too, alongside self-respect: her voice — one of dissent, at times. Not enough to welcome the flash of a bullet, or a beating that she might not have survived. But enough to help defend others, enable them to hold their heads high.

And she's alive. Mainly intact. Just so, so tired.

'Shall I leave you here?' the man says, drawing up in Hop, the town still recognisable, which makes her heart twist.

'That will be fine, thank you. Good luck.' She stops short of saying 'I hope you find her,' because he might not. She witnessed plenty leaving under a ragged shroud of death.

Something other than herself takes her automatically to the house, and she's not sure of her purpose. Who on earth will be there? Not the Germans, but who else is left to recognise her beneath the prisoner's pallor and the lingering stench of confinement?

Her legs are like lead as she walks up the drive, noting the flower borders are not quite what they were and concerned that something dreadful has happened to Gunnar. But there is activity; she can sense it, if not see anyone about. The house may have been abandoned by the Reich but not by humanity.

'Fru Nesse?' A voice breaks through the birdsong overhead and a form emerges from the doorway. 'Is that really you?'

It's Arne, the Lauritzens' eldest son, older and maybe a little grey around the temples, but not changed in the way she is. He seems to be alone, perhaps assessing the state of the house in the wake of German abandonment. Without hesitation, he steps towards her, his face alight, and for the first time since he was a lad, he throws his arms around her, squeezing tightly with affection.

'Oh, Fru Nesse,' he whispers into her unwashed hair. 'You're back. You came home.'

'Yes,' she murmurs. 'I came home.'

77

Surprises

Jens

Peder has some explaining to do, after the endless hugs and kisses showered between them all, with a true deluge of salt-crust tears.

'How could you be so cruel, Pappa?' Rumi asks, though it's no real accusation, not when Marjit is standing there in front of them, smaller and perhaps a little greyer, but alive.

Peder excuses himself, saying he felt the 'best surprise of all' was worth the half hour delay in telling Rumi and Jens. Rubio, of course, had been in on the secret, having lived in Marjit's house since her arrest, to protect it from German army squatters. Toiling in the kitchen alongside her was Rubio's new wife, Jenny.

Marjit had only arrived home the day before, Peder tells them, turning up at the boathouse almost as if she'd just been out to buy a few groceries. 'So you see why I waited,' he adds, his wiry, muscled arm clasped around Marjit's tiny

399

shoulder, her bones visible through thin skin and the single layer of her dress.

To Jens, she's shrunken physically, and who knows what she's feeling inside, but he's certain the core of the old Marjit remains. At least a good portion of it. The lengthy hug he gives her is unrestrained, relieved that her skeleton is solid and steely, unbending as always. His eye goes to the deep welts on her wrists, and she looks back silently, gesturing at his eye with her knowing gaze. *None of us are untouched,* she's hinting. Much like Rumi, Marjit is unafraid to explore his wound, caressing it as she did the cuts and scrapes of his boyhood, with her practical but gentle touch.

'And are you all right, really?' she whispers to him in a quiet moment.

'I am. Now that you're here, safe.'

'And her?' Marjit looks towards Rumi, joking with Rubio at the table, the colour high in her cheeks. Captured, imprisoned and perhaps tainted by it, Marjit still doesn't miss a trick.

'Yes. And her.'

'Then, Jens Parkes, don't waste another moment.'

'Yes, aunt.'

Peder pushes his chair back and stands, pats his full stomach and taps at his cup with a knife several times. The repeated chink silences the table, spread with the debris of the *plukkfisk* they'd all dreamed of eating again.

'Even Rubio helped make it,' Jenny had teased, to applause from the table.

'I have something rather important to say,' Peder announces, his rough cheeks flushing under his beard, 'and this remarkable day seems like the perfect time.'

Across the table, Jens watches Rumi's face skew with curiosity, her lower lip pushed out a little.

Marjit is sat next to Peder and he reaches for her hand, suddenly bird-like, which she gives willingly into his broad, fisherman's fingers. He takes a breath.

'This morning, I had the very great honour of proposing marriage to a woman I have admired for many years, come to love and respect, and lately adored from afar. Far too much time has been stolen from us, and I am happy to tell you Marjit Sabo has consented to be my wife.' He shakes and squeezes at her flesh. 'Though, of course, she may live to regret it.'

She won't, not by the look on her face, Jens thinks. It's pure happiness.

Once, he might have felt jealous at someone taking Marjit's attention, but having come to know Peder and his steadfast loyalty, Jens is only delighted. Marjit can be alone, has already proved she's more than capable, and yet Jens feels strongly that she shouldn't be. She deserves to grow old with someone beside her, to look after and take comfort in each other.

And if Peder had worried at Rumi's reaction, he needn't have done. Shock gives way to joy; true, heartfelt pleasure spread across her face, that her surrogate mother for so many years will now be for real. Jens watches her intently – sometimes he thinks that looking out from one good eye makes it easier to hide his own curiosity – and it's as if Rumi's anger has been scrubbed away entirely. The turmoil of the past five years, what she's seen and experienced, has made her softer, instead of hardened by conflict. Maybe it's him that will have to work at being tolerant now, to brush off the tough, mental calluses he's developed over this war.

How she'll love that, he thinks – *massaging my anger. How that will make her laugh.*

78

War is Over

Bergen, 9th May 1945

Rumi

She and Jens sit on the back stoop, looking out to the gardens lately tended by Rubio and Jenny; neither can remember how long ago they sat on the same spot after a meal, musing, with that nervous kiss to follow. The meeting of their lips is better now, less tentative on both sides, making Rumi's head roll with added pleasure to the day. How much better can it get? The people she loves most in the world are safe. There will be some healing to do, but no one seems badly broken. It's almost a miracle, though her pragmatism doesn't allow her to indulge in that kind of thinking. Not after the war, and not after Magnus. Even so, it is incredible, all of them sat around the table earlier, celebrating.

'I can hardly believe it's over,' she muses into the spring air.

His reply is slow and considered. 'Hmm, though it still feels like a dream, these last five years.'

'A bad one?'

'In places,' he admits. 'But the country came through. The people. That's the main thing. And beyond Norway, I think a good portion of mankind has survived. At least I hope it has.'

The best surprise, she thinks, is sat beside her, staring out in the dusky garden, both of them hearing the gulls wane in the distance and a distinct absence of aircraft droning. Jens is here. Not a figment, or a dream, or a wish. Really here, just as she imagined in countless hours spent staring out from the Shetland coastline at the crashing waves. So real now that she can't help pinching lightly at his arm.

'I'm going to knit you a patch,' she says, determined their mood shouldn't be melancholy, not tonight.

He chokes with laughter. 'No offence, but please don't. A ski hat will be more than enough.'

'Plan to stick around long enough to see snow, do you?'

'If they'll let me.'

'They can't make you leave,' Rumi says plainly. 'You're Norwegian.'

He turns to her, more of a shift now that he needs to direct his vision. Even in the gloom, she reads emotion in his features, perhaps for what she's just said. A wetness hovers on the lower lashes of his seeing eye.

'I was thinking I might stay quite a lot longer,' Jens ventures. 'As a Norwegian.'

'Oh yes?' That flip and fizz again. *Will he say it? Is it too fast, or too soon, even for this incredible day?*

'What do you say to a double wedding?' he goes on. 'I'm positive Marjit will see the making of two dresses as a welcome challenge, even from a pair of old curtains.'

'What can you mean, Jens Parkes?' Her voice is high

and flighty, and not at all the Rumi she knows. Knew. *Say it, say it. SAY IT.*

He turns, full face towards her and takes her hand. 'Rumi Orlstad, fishwife extraordinaire of Bergen city, will you marry me?'

She pauses, purses her lips. 'Well, since tradition says that I cannot refuse the request of a fellow fishwife, my answer has to be yes.'

'You just made that up, didn't you?'

'Absolutely. Unashamedly. Everything apart from the yes bit.'

The kiss as betrothed man and woman is longer, deeper and definitely more involved. Rumi feels herself entirely absorbed, insides unravelling like the most silken of yarns.

Finally, he pulls her to standing, kisses her again. 'Shall we go and tell them? Our turn to spring a surprise?'

EPILOGUE

We're Coming

Bergen, June 1946

Rumi

She reaches blindly into the air, grasping with the one hand that's not holding her body somewhere in a fantastical, airless world of unknowns under the blackness of her eyes screwed shut. Right now, she wouldn't care if the hand to clasp hers was the leathery, fish-stinking skin of a seasoned trawlerman, as long as it offered the comfort she so desperately needs.

But Rumi Parkes is luckier than that; the flesh that makes contact is worn but giving, so familiar that she's coaxed into opening her own eyes, staring into the turquoise gaze that is uniquely Marjit.

'You *can* do this,' Marjit whispers into her ropes of sweat-laden hair, hanging loose around her face that's dipped towards the floor. It's said with conviction, as if Marjit possesses true belief. *Can I?* Rumi questions herself. *Can I really?*

I will. But why is it so long, and so intense? Long enough that she can hear the murmurings of Jens next door, returning from the walk that Pappa and Rubio have forced him on, trying to keep him busy. She feels his angst seep through the cracks in the door, his urge to forsake the tradition of expectant fathers and be with her. *I can do it, Jens. I can. Just wait for us.*

The white hot wave comes again and her concentration dips, threatening to scamper away, but she yanks it back with the help of the midwife's calm but confident tone behind her. 'We're nearly there, nearly there. Just trust your body.' It's another voice, but inside her head, it's Marjit's lips moving. In front of her, the short grey crop nods, and the soft features reflect faith and certainty. Her light touch strokes in rhythm with Rumi's out of this world efforts, and in turn she squeezes down so tight on Marjit's hand that she fears the bones might break, and then thinks again: don't be silly, this is Marjit.

We're coming, Jens.

'She's simply amazing,' Jens says, only for the fifth or sixth time, one finger looped into the tiny digit of his daughter and the other stroking at her vibrant red strands of hair.

'Thanks. I can always put her back, you know, and you can take over and have a go if you like.' Rumi's tone is short, sharp, and all too familiar.

Jens starts, and then breaks into a smile to match his wife's teasing look. 'Sorry. It just goes without saying that you are fantastic. But I should, and will, say it: you are amazing, Rumi Parkes. Astonishing.'

'Too right.' Marjit bustles in with tea and the pungent, welcome smell of real coffee. 'She's the hardest working woman in this room. And the strongest. So, any decision on a name yet?'

Jens looks to Rumi, and she nods. 'We thought one particular name appropriate,' he says. 'For us, and the family. For everyone around us, too.'

'So?' Marjit looks to the both of them, firmly in the fold of that family now.

'Hap,' Rumi announces. Whichever way you say it, in either of this girl's two mother tongues, it doesn't matter. It means the same.

Hope.

Acknowledgements

Research underpins so much of a historical fiction work, and this book is no different. In the absence of being able to walk Bergen's streets and visit museums dedicated to the resistance, I am indebted to a whole host of historians and enthusiasts who helped piece together 1940s Bergen in my head: Kjerstin Kragseth and Ole-Jacob Abraham for detail on wartime Norway; Kåre Olsen for his invaluable insight into Norwegian Lebensborn; Ingrid Haugrønning for her material on traditional knitting, and Bård Gram Økland for maritime history. Their patience helped fill what would have been glaring gaps in daily life of the time.

Yet again, I am hugely grateful to my editor at Avon, Molly Walker-Sharp; more than ever, she has been my third eye on this book and helped me see the wood for the trees in bringing out the characters. So too, my agent Broo Doherty at DHH Literary Agency, for keeping me on track and always being there with a speedy email to boost flagging spirits. Thanks goes to all the teams at HarperCollins worldwide, a huge combined effort to keep my words bubbling away out there and on the shelves.

In and around my beloved Stroud, there remains a posse of dog walkers, plus an entire coven of current and former midwives and maternity workers, whose support I couldn't do without: Gez, Sarah, Micki, Jo, Kirsty, Annie, Hayley, Ruth, Marion, Isobel, Kelly and Heidi. Too many to mention who keep me sane, but thank you. In the world of writing, it's my pals Loraine Fergusson (LP Fergusson), Avon stablemate Lorna Cook, Stroudies Sarah Steele and Mel Golding who lift and inspire, as well as the regular gatherings of Gloucestershire writers (and there are a lot of us in this creative county!).

Regular readers will know by now that I don't function without good coffee and cafés, so enduring thanks to the crew at Coffee #1 for making me feel so welcome, Felt Café too; you are my respite and my office and my friends all in one.

A special mention to my mum, Stella – who is a one-woman selling machine all by herself, and never ceases to support – and to my readers: to receive even a short message on social media from across the world – to know that someone likes your musings – is fuel to the fire for any writer. Booksellers and librarians – we love you endlessly too!

Germany, 1944. Anke Hoff is assigned as midwife
to one of Hitler's inner circle. If she refuses,
her family will die.

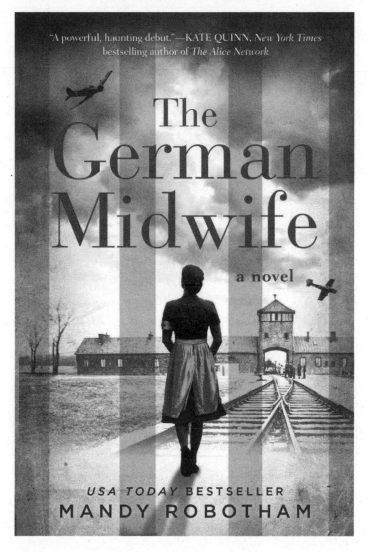

"A powerful, haunting debut."—KATE QUINN, *New York Times*
bestselling author of *The Alice Network*

The
German
Midwife

a novel

USA TODAY BESTSELLER
MANDY ROBOTHAM

A gritty tale of courage, betrayal and love in the most
unlikely of places, for readers of *The Tattooist of Auschwitz*
and *The Alice Network*.

The world is at war, and Stella Jilani
is leading a double life.

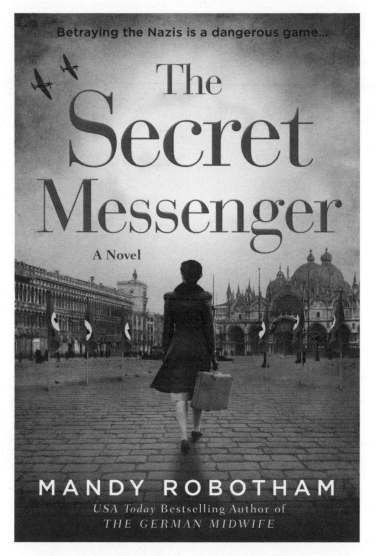

Betraying the Nazis is a dangerous game...

The
Secret
Messenger

A Novel

MANDY ROBOTHAM

USA Today Bestselling Author of
THE GERMAN MIDWIFE

Set between German-occupied 1940s Venice
and modern-day London, this is a fascinating
tale of the bravery of everyday women in the
darkest corners of WWII.

Berlin, 1938
It's the height of summer, and Germany is on the brink of war.

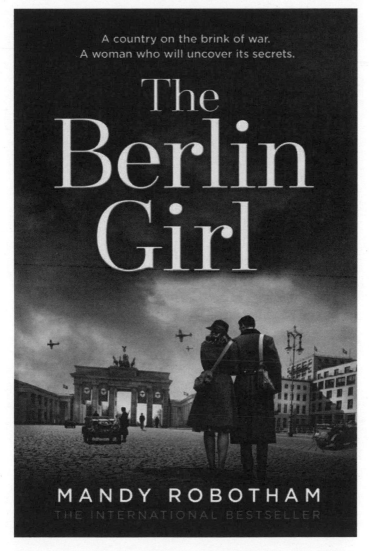

A country on the brink of war.
A woman who will uncover its secrets.

The Berlin Girl

MANDY ROBOTHAM

THE INTERNATIONAL BESTSELLER

From the internationally bestselling author comes the heart–wrenching story of a world about to be forever changed.

A city divided.
Two sisters torn apart.
One impossible choice . . .

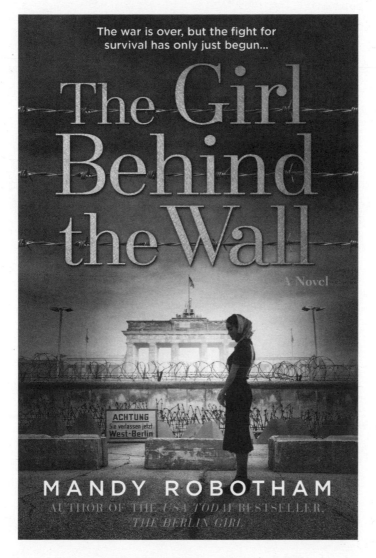

The war is over, but the fight for
survival has only just begun...

The Girl
Behind
the Wall

A Novel

ACHTUNG
Sie verlassen jetzt
West-Berlin

MANDY ROBOTHAM

AUTHOR OF THE *USA TODAY* BESTSELLER,
THE BERLIN GIRL

Set against the dawn of the cold war,
this is a timely reminder that, even in the darkest
of places, love will guide you home.